WILD
HORSES

Another spirited novel by the bestselling Amish author!

LINDA BYLER

WILD HORSES

SADIE'S MONTANA
Book 1

Good Books

Intercourse, PA 17534
800/762-7171
www.GoodBooks.com

Cover design by Koechel Peterson & Associates, Inc.,
Minneapolis, Minnesota

Design by Cliff Snyder

WILD HORSES
Copyright © 2011 by Good Books, Intercourse, PA 17534
International Standard Book Number: 978-1-56148-736-3
Library of Congress Catalog Card Number: 2011032602

Library of Congress Cataloging-in-Publication Data
Byler, Linda.
  Wild horses / Linda Byler.
     p. cm. -- (Sadie's Montana ; bk. 1)
  ISBN 978-1-56148-736-3 (pbk. : alk. paper) 1. Amish--Fiction. 2.
Horses--Fiction. 3. Montana--Fiction. I. Title.
  PS3602.Y53W55 2011
  813'.6--dc23   2011032602

Table of Contents

Chapter 1

IT WAS EASIER TO LOVE A HORSE THAN IT WAS TO love people. Horses understood. Oh, Sadie knew her sisters rolled their eyes about that philosophy, but that was all right. It meant they didn't understand, same as Mam and Dat. Especially Dat.

He was the one who made her finally part with Paris, her old, beloved, palomino riding horse. Paris wasn't really her own horse. Her uncle had kind of loaned her to Sadie to see if she could do anything with the unruly monster who bit, bucked, and even attacked men—especially small men who were assertive in their way of handling her.

Sadie understood Paris. Underneath all that bucking and kicking was a timid spirit—perhaps too timid—and that's why she bucked and kicked. It was hard to explain, but Paris was afraid of being controlled by someone she could not trust completely.

Paris was beautiful, but she hadn't always been that way. When Uncle Emanuel brought her in a silver horse trailer, Sadie was shocked at the sight of the pathetic creature that was coaxed out of the trailer's squeaking door.

The truck driver, a tall, skinny youth with a wad of snuff as large as a walnut stuck in his lower lip, refused to help at all. Paris terrified him, there was no doubt about that.

Sadie crossed her arms tightly across her stomach, watching every move Uncle Emanuel made, urging, talking, threatening, and pulling on the dirty halter. First she heard an awful commotion—dull, thudding clicks against the side of the trailer and yelling from Uncle Emanuel. Then he came skidding down the manure-encrusted ramp, his eyes rolling behind his thick glasses, his straw hat clumped down on his head of riotous red curls.

"Yikes!" he shouted, grinning at Sadie.

Sadie smiled and said nothing. Her stomach hurt so badly, she couldn't utter a word. She was afraid, too. She didn't have much experience with horses, other than with their fat, black, little Shetland pony named Chocolate that they had when she was barely six years old.

She had always wanted a horse of her own—one she could name and brush, a horse whose mane and tail she could braid. She'd give the horse its very own saddle and bridle and pretty saddle blanket with a zebra design on it, and she'd put pretty pink ribbons at the end of the braids.

She was almost 15-years-old when she heard Mam tell her sister Leah about being at sisters' day. Uncle Emanuel's wife, Hannah, had related the story of this palomino horse he bought, saying, "She was a pure danger, that one. Emanuel was scared of her, that was all there was to it." Mam was laughing, thinking of her brother and his quick, funny ways.

Sadie had been standing at the refrigerator, peering inside for a stalk of celery to load up with peanut butter. She was so hungry after having spent the afternoon with her cousin, Eva, who lived down the road.

Slowly, as if in a dream, she closed the refrigerator door, completely forgetting about her hunger, the celery, and the peanut butter.

"What?" she uttered dreamily.

"Oh, my brother Emanuel. Can you imagine him with a horse he can't handle?"

Mam laughed again and plopped another peeled potato into her stainless steel pot.

"What kind of horse? I mean, did he buy her or him? Is it a driving horse for the buggy or a riding horse?"

"I think a rider. He bought her for his son, who I'm sure is not old enough to ride a full-grown horse."

"Mam!"

Mam's knife stopped slicing through the potato as she turned, giving her full attention to Sadie, her oldest daughter.

"What, Sadie? My, you are serious!"

"Mam, listen to me. Could I… Would I be able to… Do you suppose Dat would let me try to…?"

Sadie swiped nervously at the stray brown hair coming loose from behind the *dichly* she wore for everyday work. A *dichly* is a triangle of cotton fabric, usually a men's handkerchief cut in half and hemmed, worn by Amish women and girls when they do yard work or anything strenuous.

Sadie's coverings were always a disaster, Mam said, so she only wore one to go away on Sundays, or to quiltings, or sisters' day, or to go to town.

"Ach, now, Sadie."

That was all Mam said, and the way she said it was not promising in the least.

Her hope of ever having a horse of her own stood

before her again like an insurmountable cliff. There was no getting over it or around it. It was just there, looming high and large, giving her a huge lump in her throat. No one understood. No one knew about this huge, gray and brown cliff ahead of her which had no handholds or any steps or easy ways to climb up and over. And if she told anyone, they would think there was something seriously wrong with her.

She wanted a horse. That was all.

Dat didn't particularly like horses. He was a bit different in this area than other Amish men. He hitched up his big, brown, standard-bred road horse to the freshly washed and sparkling carriage every two weeks to go to church and on the rare occasion they went visiting someone on the *in-between* Sundays. But mostly, Jacob Miller's horse had a life of leisure.

Sadie had knelt by her bed every evening for weeks, folded her hands, bent her head, closed her eyes, and prayed to God to somehow, some way soften her father's heart. As she prayed, she could feel some little crevices in her cliff—just tiny little cracks you could stick one foot in.

The Bible said that if you had faith as small as a grain of mustard seed, you could move a mountain, which, as far as Sadie could tell, no one had ever done. Surely if someone had done it in the past, they would have written about it and stashed it away as very significant history.

But that mustard seed verse is why she decided that it was worth a try. Dat's big, brown horse had no company in the barn except a few rabbits and the cackling hens. He had always said horses do better when there are two or three together in one barn.

Her opening argument came when Dat asked her to help move the rabbit hutch to the other end of the barn beside the chicken coop. She tugged and lifted mightily, pulling her share, glad she had a good, strong back and arms.

"There," Dat said, "that's better. More room for Charlie to get his drink."

Sadie lifted her big, blue eyes to her father's which were a mirror of her own.

"Dat?"

He was already lifting bales of hay, making room for the straw he had ordered.

"Hmm?"

"Dat? Eva got a new white pony. Well, it's a horse, actually. A small one. She can ride well. Bareback, too. She doesn't like saddles."

"Mm-hmm."

"Does Charlie like it here by himself?"

There was no answer. Dat had moved too far away, hanging up the strings that held the bales of hay together.

Sadie waited. She arranged her *dichly*, smoothed her blue-green apron across her stomach, scuffed the hay with the toe of her black sneaker, and wished with all her heart her dat would like horses.

When he returned, she started again.

"Dat? If someone gave me a horse to train, would you allow it?"

Dat looked at her a bit sharply.

"You can't ride. You never had a horse. And I'm not feeding two horses. No."

"I'll pay for the feed."

"No."

Sadie walked away, hot tears stinging her long, dark lashes. Just plain no. Flat out no. He could have at least tried to be kind about it. Every crevice in her cliff disappeared, and the mountain became higher, darker, and more dangerous than ever. There was no getting around it or over it anymore. There was no use. Dat said no.

Sadie knew that a basic Amish rule of child-rearing was being taught to give up your own will at a young age. Even when they prayed, they were taught to say, "Not my will, but Thine be done."

She knew very well that both Mam and Dat thought that was the solid base, the foundation of producing good, productive adults, but why did it always need to be so hard? She wanted a horse. And now Eva had one.

But the good thing about Eva having a horse was that Sadie learned to ride, and ride well. The girls roamed the fields and woods of the rural Ohio countryside, sharing the small white horse named Spirit. They wore their dresses, which were a hassle, but there was no other way. They would never be allowed to ride in English clothes, although they each wore a pair of trousers beneath their dresses. It was just not ladylike to have their skirts flapping about when they galloped across the fields. Even so, their mothers, who were sisters, frowned on these Amish girls doing all that horse-back riding.

Then, when Sadie had given up and the cliff had faded a bit, church services were held at Uncle Emanuel's house. Only Dat and Mam had gone because it was a long way to their house in another district.

Dat and Emanuel had walked to the pasture. Dat looked at this long-haired, diseased, wreck-of-a-horse, and he thought of Sadie. It might be a good thing.

He didn't tell Sadie until the morning before the horse arrived. Sadie was so excited, she couldn't eat a thing all day, except to nibble on the crust of a grilled cheese sandwich at lunch. That's why her stomach hurt so badly when Paris arrived.

She had often told Eva that if she ever owned a horse of her own, she would name it Paris, because Paris was a faraway, fancy city that meant love. Paris was a place of dreams for an Amish girl. She knew she could never go there because Amish people don't fly in big airplanes, and they don't cross the ocean in big ships because they'd have to have their pictures taken. So they were pretty much stuck in the United States. She guessed when they came over from Germany in the 1700s, they didn't need their pictures taken. That, or else cameras had not been invented yet.

So Paris was a place of dreams. And Paris, once Sadie's dream, had now become her horse.

The truck driver grinned around his wad of snuff.

"Havin' problems, are you?"

"Hey, this thing means business!" Emanuel shouted, tucking his shirttail into his denim broadfall pants.

Sadie stepped forward.

"Can I look at her?" she asked timidly.

"You can look, but you better stay out of the trailer."

Sadie moved swiftly up the ramp, only to be met by a bony rear end and a tangled, dirty tail swishing about menacingly.

Uh-oh, she thought.

A tail swishing back and forth without any pesky flies hovering about meant the horse was most definitely unhappy. It was the same signal as ears flattened against a head, or teeth bared, so Sadie stood quietly and said, "Hello, Paris."

The bony hips sidled against the trailer's side, and the tangled tail swished back and forth furiously.

Sadie peeked around the steel side of the trailer. Paris looked back, glaring at her through a long, unkempt forelock stuck with burrs, bits of twigs, and dirt.

"Poor baby," Sadie murmured.

Their eyes met then, Sadie declared to her sister Anna, and Paris sort of stood aside and her tail stopped swishing. A trust was born between Sadie and Paris, a very small one, of course, but it was born nevertheless.

Sadie didn't try to ride Paris for three weeks. She brushed her and bathed her with a bucket of warm, soapy water. She bought equine shampoo at the local harness shop, a new halter, a rope, and brushes.

When she wasn't with Paris, Sadie mowed grass, raked the leaves, watered flowers, worked in the neighbors' yard—anything to earn five dollars. Then she was finally able to buy a nice brown saddle, secondhand, of course, but a saddle was a wonderful thing to own, no matter how used. She put the new green saddle blanket on Paris, whose coat was now sleek and pretty. Her ribs were still quite prominent, though, but they would take time to fill out.

When the day finally arrived when she could put the real saddle on Paris' back, Sadie's heart pounded so loudly, her ears thudded with a dull, spongy, bonging sound.

She didn't tell anyone she was riding Paris. Not Mam or Dat, and especially not her pesky little brother Reuben, or any of her sisters. It was better to be alone, unhurried, quiet, able to talk to Paris in her own language which everyone else would probably think was silly.

She would never forget the thrill of trusting Paris. Oh, the horse danced sideways awhile, even tried to scrape her off, but Sadie sat firmly, talking, telling Paris all the things she'd like to hear.

It seemed that Paris loved it when Sadie told her she was beautiful and her best friend. Her eyes turned soft and liquidy, and Sadie knew she lowered her lashes, those gorgeous, silky, dark brushes surrounding her eyes.

Sadie and Eva spent many days galloping across the rolling farmlands of Ohio. Eva never used a saddle, so Sadie learned to ride without one as well. They walked their horses, they talked, they rode to the creek on hot summer days with a container of shampoo, swam with their horses, washed them—and their own hair—with the soapy liquid. This was their favorite activity when the August heat flattened the leaves against the trees, the sky grew brassy yellow-blue with heat, and crickets, grasshoppers, and ants found cool leaves to creep under. Sometimes storms would come up in the northeast and drive them home, dripping wet and clean and filled with the joy of their youth, their girlhoods, their innocence.

They raced their horses in freshly-mowed alfalfa fields. Sometimes they became competitive—and a bit miffed—when one thought the other got an unfair start to a race. They asked Reuben to call "Go!" then, but he was too busy playing with his Matchbox cars in the dirt under the silver maple tree where the grass didn't grow well. He pushed the dirt with his tiny bulldozer and backhoe for hours on end. The girls and their horses bored him completely, and he told them so, glaring up at them under his strubbly bangs, his shirt collar rimmed with dust, his hands black from the fertile soil around the base of the tree.

It was a wonderful summer for two 15-year-old girls.

Then, one night, when the whole house was settling down with a creaky sort of sigh, the way houses do when darkness falls and the air cools and the old siding expands and contracts, Sadie heard her parents' voices rising and falling, rising and falling. Their sounds kept her awake far into the night. She plumped her pillow, tossed the covers, turned to a more comfortable position, and finally put the pillow over her head to shut out her parents' voices.

The next day, they made the announcement.

Dat and Mam asked Sadie, Leah, Rebekah, and Anna to come sit in the living room with them. They looked extremely sober. Reuben was still out under the maple tree with his Matchbox toys, but they let him there undisturbed.

Sadie remembered hearing his faint "Brrr-rrrm, Brr-rm," as Dat cleared his throat and dropped the bomb, as she thought of it ever after.

They were moving. To Montana. Sadie felt like she was being pulled along by a huge, sticky, rubber band made of voices, and she had no scissors to cut it and get out from under its relentless power.

Montana. An Amish settlement. Too many people. The youth misbehaving. Sadie soon 16.

Mam looked happy, even excited. How could she? How could she be swept along, happily putting her hand in Dat's and agreeing?

The rubber band's power increased as Anna clapped her hands, Leah's blue eyes shone, Rebekah squealed, and Dat grinned broadly.

David Troyers would be going, too. And Dan Detweilers. Sadie sat back on the sofa, creasing the ruffle on the homemade pillow top over and over. The noise around her made no sense, especially when Leah shrieked with pure excitement about a train ride.

What train?

"You mean, we're traveling to Montana on a train?"

Sadie managed to croak, her mouth dry with fear. "What about Paris?"

It was all a blur after that. Sadie couldn't remember anything clearly except the pain behind her eyes that carried her out of the living room and up the stairs and onto her bed. Sadie dissolved into great gulping sobs, trying to release the pain near her heart.

She could not part with Paris.

But she would have to. Dat said she had to. That was that. There was no livestock being moved all those miles.

"Livestock?" Where in the world did he find a word like that to describe two horses, eight rabbits, and a bunch of silly hens? Paris was no "livestock."

The only consolation Sadie had was that Uncle Emanuel found a home for Paris on the local veterinarian's farm. The vet's daughter, Megan, an English girl who loved horses as much as Sadie, was ecstatic, Sadie could clearly tell.

Sadie spent the last evening with Eva and Paris, crying nearly the whole time. Sometimes—between tears—she and Eva became hysterical, laughing and crying at the same time. But even when laughing, Sadie cried inside.

At the end of the evening, Sadie and Paris clattered into the barn and Sadie slid off her beloved horse's back, that golden, rounded, beautiful back. She threw her arms around Paris' neck, and held on. She hugged her horse for every time they played in the creek, for every time Sadie braided her mane, for every ribbon she tied in it, for every apple Paris had ever crunched out of her hand, for every nuzzle Sadie had received on her shoulder, and for every aching hour she would never have with Paris ever again.

Sadie did not watch them take Paris away in the big, fancy trailer. She set her shoulders squarely and went for a walk all by herself, knowing that it would be a long time until she would ever love another horse.

But Paris would live on in her heart. That's why she was named Paris—she was a dream. And love.

Chapter 2

THE FIRST SNOW CAME EARLY THAT YEAR, BLOW-
ing fine and white across the undulating landscape. It
brought the dry cold that was so much a part of Montana—the state Sadie had now grown to love. Oh, it had
taken a while, that was one thing sure. But since she had
reached her 20th birthday, and after five years of growing
in faith and womanhood, she knew she had drawn on a
strength that was God-given. It was a great comfort to
know that your spirit could triumph over fear, loneliness,
or whatever life handed to you.

The Miller family lived high on a ridge overlooking
the Aspendale Valley, where a mixture of sturdy pines,
aspen, and hearty oak trees protected them from much
of the frigid winter winds. Dat had remodeled parts of
the old log house, built a barn large enough to accommodate the horse and cattle they owned, and surrounded
the pasture with a split-rail fence.

It was an idyllic setting overlooking the valley dotted with homesteads, ranches, and dwellings where the
Amish community had settled and thrived.

Dat was no farmer or rancher. His love was not in

horses or cattle, although he owned both—enough to keep the pasture clipped and to transport his family to church on Sunday.

Instead, he built log homes and established a good reputation as an honest, hardworking carpenter. He left his customers happy with their sturdy houses made from the finest quality material and precise workmanship.

Their life in Montana was blessed, Mam said. She was very happy most of the time, although Sadie sometimes found her wiping a stray tear directly related to her homesickness. It was a constant thing, this missing dearly beloved family and friends who were so many hundreds of miles away.

Mam wrote letters and went to the phone out by the barn to talk to her mother and sisters. Sometimes she was laughing when she came back to the house and sometimes crying. It was all a part of Sadie's life now but more manageable than it had been that first year.

The surrounding valley, and on into the hills beyond, held 33 Amish families. It was a good-sized community, which meant it was soon time to divide the church into two districts. Church services were held in the homes. When the house became too crowded, dividing the church became a necessity.

There was a group of 20 or 30 youth, which Sadie had always been grateful for. They had been her friends for quite a few years, good friends with whom she could share her feelings and also Sunday afternoons and evenings playing volleyball and having supper together, often with a hymn-singing afterward. Sometimes the youth went camping or riding or shopping in a faraway location, which was something Sadie always anticipated.

The winters were long here in Montana. Months of

cold wind swept down from the distant mountain ranges, which were always covered with snow. The snow on the tips of the mountains never ceased to amaze her, especially when the sun warmed her back or she felt a gentle summer breeze in her face. But in winter, everything was white and cold, and the whole world felt like the tops of the mountains.

Sadie sat at the table in the dining room watching the snow swirling across the wooden patio floor. Little eddies of it tried to accumulate in the corners of the panes in the French doors but were swept away by the howling wind.

"It's always windy here, Mam."

Mam looked up from the cookbook she was leafing through, took a sip of coffee from the brown stoneware mug, and nodded her head.

"It's Montana."

Sadie sliced half a banana into her dish of thick, honeyed oatmeal, adding a handful of dark, sticky raisins, and nodded.

"I know."

Mam glanced at the clock.

"Jim's late."

"Probably because of the snow."

She finished pouring the rich, creamy milk onto the raisins, stirred, and spooned a large amount into her mouth. She closed her eyes.

"Mmmm. Oatmeal with honey."

Mam smiled.

"What do we want for Christmas dinner this year?"

Sadie looked at Mam, surprised

"Christmas is two months away."

"I can still plan ahead."

Sadie nodded, grimacing as the battered truck pulled

up to the French doors—a dark intruder into the lovely, pristine whiteness outside.

"Oh, here I go."

"You haven't finished your breakfast."

"It's all right."

She put her arms into the sleeves of her black, wool coat, threw a white scarf around her head, and was out the door to the tune of Mam's usual, "Have a good day!"

The whirling bits of snow made her bend her head to avoid the worst of the sharp little stings against her bare face. She pulled quickly on the door handle, bounced up into the torn vinyl of the pickup seat, and flashed a warm smile at the occupant behind the steering wheel.

"How you, Missy?"

"Good. Good, Jim."

Jim put the truck in reverse, a smile of pleasure lighting his pale blue eyes, the dark weathered lines of his face all changing direction. His long, graying mustache spread and widened with the lines, and he touched the brim of his stained Stetson more out of habit than anything else.

Jim Sevarr was of the old western line of hard-working, hard-driving range riders who lived with horses and cattle, dogs and sheep, and were more comfortable on the back of a horse than behind the wheel of a truck. His jeans were perpetually soiled, his boots half worn out, and his plaid shirttail was hanging out of his belt on one side, with the other side tucked securely beneath it.

He ground the gears of the pickup, frowned, and uttered an annoyance under his breath.

"These gears are never where they're supposed to be."

Sadie smiled to herself, knowing the gears were right where they needed to be. It was the hand that was more adept with a horse's bridle that was the problem.

"Twelve inches," he said, shifting the toothpick to the other side of his mustache.

"What?"

"Of snow."

"Really?"

"Yep."

Sadie knew the cold and snow meant more work for her down in the valley at Aspen East Ranch. She was one of the girls who helped prepare vast amounts of food each day for the 20 ranch hands, give or take a few. There were always newcomers, or someone moving on, but the number of men never varied much.

Sadie kept the lovely old ranch house clean as well. There was always something that needed to be cleaned after the food was prepared.

The furniture was rustic, the seating made of genuine leather. Valuable sculptures were placed carefully to complement the costly artwork on the wall behind them. The lighting was muted, casting a warm, yellow glow from the expensive lamps. Candles flickered and glowed in little alcoves built into the rooms. Sadie especially loved to clean the rooms filled with art, expensive objects bought from foreign countries, and the fine rugs on the wide plank floors which were all aged and worn to smooth perfection.

Aspen East Ranch was owned by a man named Richard Caldwell who came from a long line of wealthy cattlemen from the west. He was a man of great height and massive build. His stentorian voice rolled across the rooms like a freight train. Once, Sadie almost knocked an expensive item off a shelf while dusting with a chamois cloth and a can of Pledge Furniture Polish, her body automatically recoiling at his first booming yell.

Everyone snapped to attention when Richard Cald-well's voice was heard rolling and bouncing through the house, and they tried to produce exactly the response he demanded. Patience was not one of his virtues. If the poor, hapless creature he needed was out of earshot at the moment he opened his mouth, woe to that unlucky person. It felt, as Jim once said, like being "dragged across coals."

Richard Caldwell frightened Sadie, but only at first. After the can of Pledge almost went flying out of her nerveless fingers, her initial shock was over. Sadie's eyes stopped bulging and returned to their normal size, and her heartbeat stopped pounding and slowed considerably when that enormous man entered the room. Now she could face him with some semblance of composure.

But she still always felt as if her covering was unbalanced, that her breakfast was clinging to the corner of her mouth, or that there was something seriously wrong with her dress whenever Richard Caldwell appeared. His piercing gaze shot straight through her, and she felt as though she never quite passed his intimidating inspection.

Sadie had been helping at the ranch for almost three years and he could still unnerve her, although she had glimpsed a kindly heart on more then one occasion.

He teased her sometimes, mostly humorous jabs at the Amish ways. Then he would watch her like an eagle, observing her struggle to keep her composure yet answer in the way she knew was right.

"That thing on your head," he would say, "What's it for?"

Sadie blushed furiously at first, appalled as the heat rose in her cheeks, knowing her face was showing her discomfort. After stumbling clumsily and muttering a few words about her mother wearing one too, she asked Mam what she should say if he kept up his relentless questioning.

One day, when almost nothing had gone right and she was completely sick of all the menial tasks, Richard Caldwell's booming questions irritated her. When he pulled on the strings of her covering and asked again why she wore that white thing on her head, she swiped at an annoying lock of brown hair, breathed out, straightened up, and looked Richard Caldwell straight in the eye.

"Because we are committed to the ways in which the Bible says we should live. God has an order. God is the head, then man, and after that his wife is subject to her husband. This covering is an outward sign of submission."

Richard's eyes turned into narrow slits of thought. "Hmmm."

That was all he said, and it was the last time he mentioned "that thing on her head." Sadie had been a bit shaky after that outburst of self-defense, but he always treated her a bit more respectfully than he had previously. Her fear shifted to confidence, making her job less nervewracking.

Richard Caldwell's wife, Barbara, on the other hand, was a formidable figure in Sadie's life—a person to be feared. It wasn't her voice as much as the sheer disapproval that emanated from her cold presence.

Her clothes were impeccable; the drape of the expensive fabric hiding the well-endowed figure, making her appear regal. Scary to Sadie.

She did not accept Sadie, so she knew it was Richard Caldwell who hired her, not Barbara. She was only tolerating Sadie for her husband's sake.

It was always a humbling experience to be with the Lady of the House. Whether she was cleaning, dusting, or running the vacuum, it was always the same. Sadie felt violated, silly even, knowing Barbara held only derision for the Amish and their strange ways.

Sadie always thought that if there was a true version of a woman of the world, Barbara was it: no children, no interest in cooking or cleaning, no need to care for anyone but herself.

Much of her time she spent either buying clothes or arranging them in her enormous walk-in closet. Shoes, hats, jewelry, it was all at her fingertips to be tried on, shown off to her friends, given away, or sent back if things weren't quite up to her taste.

But Sadie knew it was not up to her to judge Barbara or condemn her. She was just being Barbara, the wife of a wealthy ranch owner. Sadie simply did her best to stay out of the way.

She loved her job, she really did. She always felt fortunate to have the beautiful old ranch house to clean and admire, and she liked being a part of the atmosphere—the hubbub and constantly-changing, colorful world that was Aspen East Ranch.

Amish children were not educated beyond eighth grade, spending their eight years in a one-room parochial school, learning the basics of arithmetic, spelling, reading, and English. They also learned German. Their first language was Pennsylvania Dutch, a dialect related to German with a sprinkling of English that kept changing through the years.

So for the short time between age 15 and marriage, most girls took jobs, normally cleaning, cooking, babysitting, quilting, or sewing. They handed the money they earned over to their parents, except for a small allowance.

When a young woman married, her parents provided most of the young couple's housekeeping necessities—furniture, bedding, towels, dishes, and almost everything else. The gifts from the wedding completed their household needs.

Sadie often wondered how it would be to put her entire check in the bank and then have money of her own to do anything she wanted. She understood, having this knowledge instilled in her at a young age, that money, and the earthly possessions it could buy, was not what brought true happiness to any person. Rather, money was the root of all evil if you let it control your life.

No, she did not want a lot of money, just enough to buy another horse like Paris. But she had to admit to herself that she had never connected with another horse in the same way, not even close. She could never figure out why.

Horses were everywhere here in Montana; on the hills, in trailers, in barns, being ridden. Everywhere Sadie looked, there were horses of all colors, shapes, and sizes, but not one of them interested her.

Dat bought a riding horse for the girls, but in Sadie's heart, he was just the same as a driving horse. She treated him well, fed him, patted his coarse forelock, and stroked the smooth, velvety skin beneath his mane, but she never wanted to bathe him or braid his tail and put silky, pink ribbons in it.

She still harbored that longing for just the right horse. Once, she had watched a black and white paint being led from a trailer. He bounced and lifted his beautiful head and something—she didn't know what—stirred in her heart but only for a moment. It wasn't Paris, and it wasn't

Ohio with Eva and the creek and the alfalfa fields.

Mam said it was because Paris was a part of her youth, and she'd never be able to recapture that youthful emotion that bound her to the palomino. It was time for Sadie to grow up and stop being dreamy-eyed about a horse named Paris. Whoever heard of a horse named Paris anyway, she said. But that was how Mam was, and Sadie still knew, at the age of 20, that Mam just didn't understand.

Mam and Dat didn't understand about breaking up with Ezra, either.

Ezra was a fixture in the Montana community. He was 26 years old, a member of the church, and concerned about keeping the Amish *Ordnung* and not being swept up into the worldly drift. A too-small covering, a fancy house, pride in the amount of money one made—those kinds of things seriously worried him.

Worried him and those around him until Sadie felt her head beginning to bow and her eyebrows elevating with these exact same worries. Her life stretched before her in one long, tedious blend of worries, concerns, cannots, and do nots, until she felt like screaming and jumping up and down and rebelling. She wanted to tell Ezra that there was *not* a black cloud hanging over every little thing—that God made roses bright red and daisies white and yellow instead of gray and black.

She did not mean to be irreverent, she really didn't. She just hated the feeling of having a wet blanket thrown over her head and suffocating her freedom and her breathing whenever she spent time in his company.

Being Amish was not hard, and certainly it was no burden. It was a way of life that was secure and happy. When Richard Caldwell asked her if she'd like to take his new Jeep out for a spin in that semi-mocking manner of his, she could truthfully say no. If you don't know any better and are taught to be content, nothing is a hardship—nothing within reason—and Sadie didn't feel that her life was squashed down, flat, heavy, or drained of happiness.

The teachings of her parents were a precious heritage handed down for generations and a firm foundation that allowed for happy freedom of spirit. Honoring her parents and respecting their wishes brought peace and a secure, cuddly feeling like a warm, fuzzy shawl you wrapped up with in the wintertime.

Sadie often thought about this. What if she would have rebelled and refused to accompany her parents to Montana? It would have been unthinkable, but still... So far, no husband and no horse. She wasn't sure which one she longed for more. Probably a horse.

Every husband was apparently a little like Ezra. Sadie sometimes caught Mam compressing her lips into a thin, straight line when Dat said something was too fancy. Like French doors. Mam had her heart set on them so she could look at the awesome, gently rolling, wooded hillside while she ate at the dining-room table. Dat had snorted, saying he didn't know what kind of fancy notion she got herself into now. French doors were too English. But in the end, Dat smiled and agreed, saying Amish houses could have French doors, he guessed. Mam had laughed and her eyes shone and Sadie could tell she was very happy.

So husbands could be a bit intimidating, especially if they were too weird about a lot of different subjects. Horses were easier. If only she could find one.

Jim gripped the steering wheel and slammed on the brakes, hard, drawing Sadie back to the present. She grabbed at the dash, nearly slamming against it, a scream rising in her throat.

"What the...?" Jim yelled.

Sadie struggled to regain her seat, her eyes wide with fear. Through the swirling whiteness outside, a dim, shadowy form leapt in front of the truck, slid, and went down—way down—as Jim struggled to keep control of the careening vehicle. Sadie screamed again as the tires hit the form on the road and bumped to a stop.

Her hands crossed her heart as if to contain the beating, and her eyes searched Jim's, wild with questions.

"I'll be danged if it ain't a cow," he muttered, jerking on the door handle.

"Sh...should I..." Sadie asked, her voice hoarse.

"Come on out. We'll see what we got."

Chapter 3

SADIE GRABBED FOR THE DOOR HANDLE, THEN
hesitated. A cold blast of air from the opposite side of
the truck caught her head scarf, and she was shaken to
reality.

What had they done?

Struggling to stay on her feet in the ice and snow, Sadie
held on to the side of the truck, straining to see what had
gone down, what had been so big, so unexpected, what
had so suddenly disappeared in front of the truck.

She heard Jim's low whistle. In the same instant, she
saw the thick, heavy hairs of...

"Well, it ain't a cow."

Sadie stood and stared. She had never seen a horse
as thin and gaunt as this. In fact, she had never seen *any*
animal as thin as this—a skeleton covered with hide and
a shaggy black and white coat.

"Skinniest horse I ever laid eyes on."

"Is he...hurt?" Sadie ventured.

"Dunno."

"He's... just lying there. Do you think he's dead?"

"Well, no. We didn't hit him very hard. He sort of slid

and went down before we hit him."

"He's likely starving. He could be dying right here."

"Dunno."

Jim knelt in the swirling snow, bent low, and laid a hand on the horse's cheekbone. Sadie stood, holding her arms tightly against her waist, and wondered how a horse's face could be thinner than normal.

Horses don't have a lot of flesh on their faces. The softest part is the smooth, velvety nose, always whooshing warm, sweet breath into your face. Horses don't have bad breath like humans. That's because they eat clean hay, oats, corn, and fresh, sweet grass in pastures. They don't eat greasy bacon and aged cheese and Twinkies and whoopie pies and potato chips that leave their stomachs sour and make gas rise to the top, and then cause them to belch the way people do.

This horse's face was thinner than most, its large eyes sunk into huge cavities. He looked like a skeleton with a head much too large for the scrawny, protruding neck, almost like the drawings prehistoric men etched on cave walls.

The snow kept coming from the sky, a whirling, grayish-white filled with icy little pings which stung Sadie's face. She watched as Jim felt along the horse's painfully thin neck, then down to its shoulder, before touching its pitiful ripples of bone and hide that was its side.

"He's breathin'."

"He is?"

Sadie knelt in the snow by the horse's head, watching for a flicker—any sign of life—from this poor, starved creature. Slowly she reached out to touch the unkempt forelock, still very thick and heavy in spite of his weakened state. She lifted it, letting the heavy hair run through her fingers, and murmured, "Poor, poor baby. Whatever happened to you?"

Jim rose a bit stiffly, then reached in his coat pocket for his cell phone. Sadie stayed by the horse's head, speaking soft endearments, willing this emaciated creature to life.

Jim was muttering to himself, clumsily pressing buttons too small for his large, calloused finger, repeatedly pushing the wrong one, growling over and over before finally stoping, his eys narrowing.

"Hey. Yeah, Jim here. I'm bringin' the Amish girl to the ranch. A half-dead horse jumped out in front of us. He's down. Ain't responding."

There was a pause.

"Huh-uh. No. Dunno. Just… No! Somebody bring a trailer. What? Up on Butte Road. Where? So there's no trailer?"

Jim paced, went to the truck for a pair of gloves, still talking, listening, talking.

"Listen. I ain't stayin' here all day. Either Jeff brings a trailer or I'm callin' the boss."

Jim hung up angrily. Sadie hesitated, then stood up and faced Jim.

"You go get the trailer. I'll stay here."

"No you ain't."

"Yes, I'm not afraid of this horse. I'll stay here. Just go. Hurry."

"Listen, little girl. You ain't stayin' here by yerself."

"Yes, I am. I will. No one will go by here that's dangerous. We can't let this poor, sick horse lying in the middle of the road. Someone else will hit him. I'll be fine. Just go."

Jim stared at Sadie, then shook his head.

"All right. I'll go fast. Be back soon. But…"

"No, Jim. Just hurry."

The truck roared to life, eased carefully onto the road, and disappeared around an outcropping of overhanging rock. The snow kept falling around Sadie and the horse. Little swirls piled up in the strangest places, as if the snow was trying to wake up the inert form on the cold ground. It settled into crevices in the animal's ears, which were so soft and lifeless, and formed tiny drifts in the soft, black hairs. The long, sweeping eyelashes even held tiny clumps of cold particles, making the horse appear to have no spark of life. It looked completely dead.

Sadie shivered, then knelt again.

"Come on, come, boy. Wake up. Don't die now."

She kept talking, more to instill confidence in herself than to elicit a response from this bony, wasted form. Even if he was still breathing, he was indeed a very sick horse—probably too sick for anyone to try and revive.

She straightened as she heard the unmistakable sound of a vehicle, though muffled, the way vehicles sound in the snow. Probably someone I know, Sadie assured herself in spite of her thudding heart.

A large, red cattle truck came plowing around the bend, much too fast on road conditions like this.

Irritation replaced fear, and Sadie stayed in the exact same spot, knowing the truck's occupants would see her much better than one thin horse half covered with snow.

Suddenly it registered in her brain that the road was icy, and she might very easily be hit. She began flailing her arms, screaming without being aware that she was, jumping, and shouting. She was in danger of being swallowed by this monstrous red cattle truck.

Suddenly, the driver saw her but applied the brakes too hard. The truck slowed, skidded, zigzagged, righted

itself, and came to a lopsided halt with its two left tires
in a ditch by the side of the road.

Everything went quiet except for the jays screaming in
the treetops and the sighing of the cold wind in the alders.
The truck door slammed and a very irate person plodded
in front of it, his beefy, red face supporting his battered
Stetson, which he pushed back before yanking it forward
over his face again.

"And just what do you think you're doing, young
lady? Don't you know this is a very good way to get
killed?"

Sadie met his angry gaze, then lowered her eyes.

"I'm sorry. I…well… Look."

She waved her arms helplessly, gesturing toward the
still form on the road, now almost covered with snow.

"What the…"

He smashed his Stetson down harder until Sadie
thought his hat would hide his whole head completely
and just sit on his shoulders. But somehow she guessed
he could see because he said the same thing again.

"What the…?"

He bent lower and asked, "What's wrong with him?
He ain't dead, is he?"

"I think he's dying."

"How are you going to get him off the road?"

"I don't know."

She explained what happened, about Jim leaving, and
assured him he'd soon be back for her and the horse. The
beefy man whistled, then motioned to the truck, moving
his arm to indicate that he wanted the rest of the occupants out.

"Mark, get over here."

Sadie watched a tall person jump down from the

truck. Not really jump, more like bounce, or pounce like a cat. He was huge—tall and wide with denims and very dark skin. His steps were long and lively, and he reminded Sadie of a horse one of her uncles owned in Ohio. He seemed to be on springs and hardly ever held still long enough to... well, hold still.

She thought he was Mexican, except Latinos generally were not this tall. She wondered if he was Italian with that dark skin. Or Indian. Or maybe white but just spent a lot of time in the sun.

He didn't smile or say hello or even notice her. He just stood there beside the beefy man and said nothing. He was wearing a navy blue stocking hat. Everyone wore Stetsons or leather, wide-brimmed hats of some sort here in Montana. The English did, anyway. English is what the Amish people called other people who were non-Amish. This was because they spoke English.

His clothes were neat and very clean—too clean to be an ordinary cowpuncher. But why was he wearing a stocking hat?

"What do you think, Mark?"

Mark still said nothing but lowered his huge frame easily and felt along the horse's neck, flanks, and ribs. He lifted the soft muzzle and checked his teeth, then rubbed his ears.

"Did you call a vet?"

He straightened as he said this, then turned to look down at Sadie with eyes so brown they were almost black and fringed with the thickest, blackest lashes she had ever seen. His cheekbones were high, his nose perfect, and his mouth made her knees turn to jello, so that she lost her voice completely.

Oh, it was sinful. It was awful. She felt deeply ashamed.

She also felt as incapable of changing one thing about her emotions as a seagull feather trying to change direction as it hovered on the restless waves of the ocean. Then to her horror, she felt the color rise in her face. She was sure it was noticeable to both men.

Sadie adjusted her head scarf, lowered her eyes, then raised them to his, summoning all her courage to keep his gaze.

"I..."

She was so flustered she couldn't speak, so she brushed miserably at a stray lock of hair before lifting her eyes again.

Then he smiled.

Oh, he smiled the most wonderful smile. His white teeth turned her knees straight back into the shakiest sort of jello—the kind you got out of the refrigerator before it was fully set, and which Dat laughingly dubbed "nervous pudding."

"I guess you don't have a cell phone, seeing you're Amish and all."

Sadie shook her head.

There was a whooshing, snorting sort of sound. Mark whirled, the heavy-set man exclaimed, and a soft cry escaped Sadie's lips. They all turned, but Sadie was the first one to reach the horse's head. She knelt in the snow murmuring, running her hands along the smooth planes of his face. There was another whooshing sound, and he tried to raise his head before letting it fall back weakly.

"Let's get him up."

Sadie looked up, questioningly.

"How?"

Mark didn't answer. He just kept looking at Sadie with the strangest expression in his eyes, almost as if he was about to cry. Sort of. Not really, though. More like his eyes softened, and he caught his breath before she asked the same question.

"How?"

"Just… Okay, Fred. You help lift his hind end. You…," His eyes questioned her.

"Sadie."

"Okay, Sadie. You stay at his head. Keep talking. Are you used to horses?"

"I live here. Yes."

"Here we go."

The horse was black and white with black lashes circling deep blue eyes, now filled with a strange sort of despair and terror. His eyes opened wider, and he lifted his head again, making soft grunting sounds as he reached forward, trying to get his hooves beneath him.

"Come on, sweetie pie. Come on, you can do it."

Sadie was completely unaware of the fact that she was speaking in her accustomed Pennsylvania Dutch dialect.

"*Doo kannsht. Komm on. Komm. Vidda. Vidda.*"

Mark lifted at the shoulders, urging, pushing. Fred lifted, strained, and fussed as his face grew more and more red. Sadie watched as the horse lay back down, completely at the end of his strength. She shuddered as he laid his head down in the snow and closed his beautiful eyes.

Sadie forgot her shyness, her thoughts focused only on this horse and the fact that she wanted him to live. She had always wanted a paint. Maybe, just maybe, she could have this one if she could get him to survive.

"If we just let him lie down, he's going to die!"

"Whose horse is he?" Fred asked.

"I have no clue."

"I don't know if he's gonna make it," Fred announced.

"Well, we can't just stand here and let him die," Sadie said, her voice conveying her desperation.

"We need a vet."

Mark said this bluntly but quite meaningfully. It was just a fact and had to be carried out.

Fred got out his cell phone and, with nimble fingers for a man his size, called one of the local veterinarians. Then he snapped his phone shut and, grumbling, returned to the truck.

Mark put his hands in his pockets, turned to Sadie, and was about to speak, when a vehicle came rattling from the opposite direction. It was Jim, pushing the old truck to the limit.

He slowed, rolled down the window, and yelled to Sadie.

"Get in."

Sadie's eyes opened wide.

"The boss is all up in the air. Bunch o' extra men and not enough help in the kitchen. Said I'm supposed to get you down there straightaway and let this bag of bones die. Probably some diseased old mustang from out on the range."

He swung his grizzled head.

"Get in."

A lump rose in Sadie's throat. She wanted to stay so badly, just like when she was a little girl and had to leave the playground because the bell rang just when it was her turn to go down the slide.

"Jim, please. I can't go and leave this horse."

"You better if you want your job."

Her shoulders slumped dejectedly, her upbringing stirring her conscience. She knew her family needed the weekly paycheck she brought home from Aspen East, but she couldn't walk away from this horse either. Indecision made her feet falter, until she turned back to the horse without thinking. Quickly, anything, please, please, please let's do something for this horse.

"I...I don't know who you are and I may be asking too much, but if this horse survives, would you let me know? We're Amish, so you'll have to leave a message on our phone, but... Oh, I'm sorry, do you have a pen and paper?"

"I do."

Mark produced his wallet, extracted a business card and a pen, and she said, breathlessly, "761-4969."

He wrote down the number and looked up.

"Just...if it's not too much bother, let me know."

"All right."

With one last glance at the broken form on the ground, Sadie hurried to Jim's old truck, got in, and slammed the door. She didn't look back.

"Who's that?"

"I don't know."

"City slicker, that one. Beanie. Humph."

Jim had no use for anyone covering their ears in cold weather, Sadie knew. She didn't care who wore a beanie and who wore a Stetson or Amish straw hat or whatever, she was sick in her heart about that horse.

Why was it always the same? If she felt any connection at all with a horse, it was taken away. She would never see or hear from that Mark person, and like Paris, this sick animal would disappear and that would be that. It was just the way life was.

Oh, my, but that Mark.

Just wait 'til I tell Leah.

It was a secret the girls shared, knowing Dat would snort and Mam would rebuke them. They talked about who was good-looking, who was available for marriage, who they would accept, and who they wouldn't. Amish or not, all girls talked and giggled about this subject. Sadie and Leah endlessly tried to figure out what Mam meant when she said, "You don't go by looks."

Of course you went by looks. They never told Mam this, but it was a universal truth. The way a courtship began was with physical attraction. Even birds chose just the right one by the beautifully-colored plumage or the best song or the most intricate dance. It was the same way with katydids and bats and frogs and squirrels and every living thing on God's earth.

That was the way it was.

But Sadie wasn't sure if she would tell Leah about Mark after all. She wanted to laugh and giggle and talk and dream, but, somehow, this was not like the other times. This seemed to be something more dangerous. Also more embarrassing. And more hopeless. It was truly horrible. Whoever heard of one's knees becoming weak from looking at another person?

Oh, it was awful.

She glanced over at Jim, almost sure he could tell what she was thinking. Instead, he was frowning, shifting his wad of chewing tobacco from one cheek to another, which always made Sadie swallow hard.

So she looked out the window to her right and watched the snow swirling and the trees and the hillside being converted from dull browns and earthy sage-green to a pristine winter wonderland.

Sadie truly loved Montana. The scenery was absolutely breathtaking almost the whole year-round. Her favorite season was the long winter because of the skiing, sledding, and snowboarding. Another favorite pastime for the youth in Montana was piling on a huge inner tube from a tractor and being pulled with a sturdy rope attached to the saddle of a horse. A good horse lunged through deep snow, easily pulling a person on an inner tube until they were completely covered with snow, like a peanut butter cracker dipped in chocolate—only it was white. And there was nothing that quite matched the exhilaration of riding a horse on an endless sweep of sparkling snow, especially if the horse had been bored from standing in his box stall and was aching to run.

Sadie's thoughts returned to the day as they approached the magnificent entrance to Aspen East.

Elaborate brick pillars rose on both sides of the wide driveway with scrolls of beautiful ironwork across the top. Bronze statues of cattle were cemented into the brick-work—truly a testimony to a local artist's talents. Heavy trees bordered the driveway, bent with the weight of the snow, and the long, low ranch house came into view.

It was built with the finest logs and the shingles resembled old, gray Shaker ones, although they were only replicas. Huge windows and doors completed the look of the house, and the wonderful scenery enhanced the matching barns, stables, and sheds. There were also fences, gates, paddocks, bunkhouses, and garages. Everything was kept in fine form by the many employees that worked around the clock to keep this vast enterprise running efficiently.

The truck stopped, Jim grinned, and Sadie hopped down.

"Try and have a good day."

"Jim, if you find out one thing about the horse, would you let me know?"

"Sure thing, little girl."

Sadie was comforted by his words. Jim was such a good man. He surely deserved to be treated well in return.

The resounding voice of Jim's wife greeted her before she pulled on the door latch.

"...where she got to! Ain't never seed nothin' like it. You get ten extra hands for breakfast, and that Sadie don't show up. Them Amish havin' no phones in their houses is the dumbest rule of 'em all."

Sadie walked in amidst this tirade and grinned cheekily at the tiny buxom woman.

"Here I am!"

"Sadie! Now you heard me yellin' about ya!"

"It's okay. You love me."

"I do sometimes."

"I'm hungry."

"Go get your apron on. How come you're late?"

"If I told you, you wouldn't believe me."

"Try."

"Huh-uh. We don't have time, Dottie."

"Don't Dottie me."

Sadie slid an arm across Dottie's shoulders and whispered, "Good Morning, Dottie."

"Hmmpfhh."

Chapter 4

Sadie immediately felt the pressures of her job, which were unusually demanding today. Dorothy had not arrived at her usual early morning hour because of the snow, which meant there were no potatoes cooked for hash browns, no sausage gravy, and no biscuits made for a count of 44 men.

Sadie grabbed a few tissues from the gold box by the food warmer, blew her nose because of the cold, windy morning, and turned to wash her hands with antibacterial soap from the dispenser mounted on the wall. Then she rolled up the sleeves of her green dress and compressed her lips, ready to start in.

She was starving, having skipped supper the evening before. Mam had made fresh shoofly pie yesterday morning, and when Sadie came home from work a bit early, ravenous as usual, she had eaten two slices. She doused them in fresh, creamy milk from the doe-eyed Guernsey in the barn—completely spoiling her supper.

Shoofly drowned in milk was simply the best, most comforting taste in all the world no matter whether you lived in Montana or Ohio. Mam made huge, heavy pies piled high with rich, moist cake, then covered with sweet, crumbly topping. The brown sugar, molasses, and egg mixture on the bottom complemented the top. Eaten in one perfect bite, all three layers combined to give you the most...well...perfect taste. It was wonderful.

Mam's pie crusts were so good you could eat them without the filling. She always made some *schecka hauslin* when she made pies, and Sadie thought they were better than the pies themselves.

Schecka hauslin were "snail houses"—little bits of pie dough rolled around brown sugar and butter, then popped in a hot oven for a few minutes. Sadie always burned the tips of her fingers and her tongue tasting them, but it was all worth it.

"What do you want me to do first, Dottie?"

"I'm Dorothy. Now don't you go Dottie'n me all morning."

That voice came from the interior of the vast, stainless steel refrigerator, and Sadie turned to see Dorothy's backside protruding from it.

Sadie never ceased to be amazed by the size of this little person and her stamina. She practically ran around the huge kitchen on short, heavy legs clad in the "good expensive" shoes she knew Dorothy had purchased at the Dollar General in town.

"They only cost $29.99!" she had told Sadie proudly. "Them shoes is expensive but they're worth it. Good arch support."

She had them worn down on one side in a few months but still bustled about the kitchen, never tiring, saying it was all because she wore "them good shoes."

Dorothy turned, her face red from bending down.

"Go ahead and make that sausage gravy. I'll tend to

the biscuits."

Sadie smiled to herself, knowing Dorothy would never allow anyone else to make the biscuits. She never measured the ingredients—just threw flour, shortening, and other ingredients into a huge, stainless steel bowl, her short, heavy arms flapping, working the dough as if her life depended on the texture of it. She talked to herself, whistled, sang bits of a song, and pounded away ferociously at the biscuit dough as if each new batch she made had to be the best.

And it always was! Dorothy's biscuits were light, yet textured with a velvety solidity. They were unlike anything Sadie had ever tasted. They were good with butter and jam or honey or loaded with gravy or, like Jim did, eaten cold with two thick slices of roast beef and spicy mustard.

Sadie reached up to the rack suspended from the log beam above, grabbed the 12-quart stockpot and set it on the front burner of the commercial stove. Reaching into the refrigerator, she unwrapped a stick of butter, deposited it into the pot, and turned on the burner beneath it. After it had browned nicely, she scattered an ample amount of fresh, loose sausage into the pot. The handle of the long wooden spoon went round and round, keeping the sausage from sticking to the flour and butter. Her thoughts kept time.

Surely the horse was someone's pet. Why was it out there in the deserted forests and vast empty acreage if it couldn't feed itself? Was there simply nothing there for it to feed on, or was it too sick to search for food? Was it neglected at the home it had come from? Why was it loose and alone?

Wild horses were not uncommon in the west, though

they were centered mostly in Wyoming. Bands of them roamed free, but the government kept them from becoming a threat or nuisance to the ranchers and farmers in the area. Helicopters would herd them into man-made ravines and corrals, always met with outrage by the animal-rights activists. But to Sadie's way of thinking, it was a necessary evil. You couldn't let wild horse herds grow too large. They could do lots of damage or graze areas meant for cattle, which was almost everyone's livelihood here.

But, oh, horses were so beautiful! There was no other animal on earth that Sadie could relate to quite as well. She could lay her cheek against a horse's, kiss its nose, smooth that velvety skin beneath the heavy waterfall of mane, and never grow tired of any of it. They smelled good, were intelligent, and came in all different shapes and colors. There were cute, cuddly ponies and tall, big-boned road horses, as the Amish referred to them.

The steady, brown or black, Standardbred driving horses were the backbone of the Amish community. They obediently stood in forebays of barns while heavy, leather harnesses were flung across their backs and then attached to thick, heavy collars around their muscular necks and shoulders. A horse allowed itself to be led to a carriage, backed into the shafts, and attached to the buggy. They waited patiently while family members clambered into the buggy, then trotted off faithfully, pulling them uphill and downhill in all sorts of weather.

The most amazing part of hitching up a horse was the fact that these docile creatures allowed that hideous steel bit to be placed in their mouths. This is the part that goes between their teeth and attaches to the bridle that goes up over their ears. Good, responsible horses never seemed to mind, lowering their heads so the bit could easily slide into their mouths.

There were some horses, of course, who were cranky and disobedient, but Sadie always felt sorry for them. Very likely, at some point in their lives, these horses had been whipped or kicked or jerked around simply because they were born with a stubborn nature and made their owners' tempers flare like sticks of dynamite. This destroyed the trust and any thread of confidence they had once acquired.

Usually, a calm, obedient horse had a calm, quiet owner and vice versa. Horses didn't require much of their owners: a quiet stall and a bit of pasture, decent feed and hay, water, and enough attention to know they were cared for and appreciated.

Sadie browned the sausage until it was coated all over with the butter and flour mixture. Then she went to the refrigerator for a gallon of milk, which she poured slowly into the sizzling sausage, stirring and stirring after this addition. She added the usual salt and pepper, then reached up to the rack again for the huge cast-iron skillet.

"Watcha getting' that for?" Dorothy asked.

That woman has eyes in the back of her head. Seriously, Sadie thought.

"Hash browns."

"Them potatoes ain't even cooked. How you gonna make hash browns? That's what happens when young girls moon about boys and stuff."

Sadie suppressed a giggle. She knew Dorothy always got a tiny bit miffed when the pressure was on. She never failed to let Sadie know when she did something wrong, implying that Sadie's misstep was the reason for the pressure to begin with.

After working with Dorothy for almost three years, Sadie knew she had the best heart and kindest demeanor of anyone she had ever met. Her scoldings were sort of soft and harmless beneath all that fuss, and Sadie often suppressed her laughter when Dorothy was bustling and talking and scolding.

"Oh, I forgot."

"You forgot. Moonin' around, that's what."

Dorothy went to the pantry, which contained 50-pound bags of potatoes, lugged one out to the sink, and proceeded to throw the potatoes in by the handfuls. Grabbing a sharp paring knife, she set to work, the peels falling into the sink in rapid succession. Sadie joined her.

"I'm hungry," Sadie announced for the second time that morning.

"Make some toast. Didn't you have breakfast? You need to get up earlier. Set your alarm 15 minutes earlier."

"No, thanks."

"Hmmpfhh. Then be hungry."

She slid a pan of perfectly-rounded, precisely-cut biscuits into the oven, and Sadie hid another grin.

The kitchen door banged open, and Jim hurried in, a box under his arm. Snow clung to his greasy Stetson, and he took it off, clapping it against his legs. Snow sprayed in every direction.

"Jim Sevarr! You borned in a sawmill? Whatsa matter with you? Gettin' my kitchen soakin' wet. I'll fall on them puddles. Now, git! Git!"

She waved both arms, then her apron, as if her husband was a huge cat that needed to be chased away from her work area.

"Don't you want a doughnut?"

Immediately Dorothy's expression changed, like the

sun breaking through clouds, spreading warmth through the kitchen.

"Now, Jim, you know if there's any one thing I can't resist, it's them doughnuts. You got 'em at the Sunoco station?"

"Sure did. Coffee on?"

"Sadie, come on. Take two minutes to eat a doughnut. There's only one way to eat 'em—big bites with the cream filling squishing out the side."

Sadie laid down her knife, wiped her hands on her apron, and smiled as she selected a powdered, cream-filled doughnut from the box Jim held out to her.

"Mmmmm," she said, rolling her eyes as the first soft sweetness of the confectioners sugar met the taste buds on her tongue.

"No news of the horse?" she asked, wiping the corners of her mouth. Jim's mouth was full of doughnut, so he shook his head.

"May as well have the vet put 'im down. Sorriest bag of bones I ever laid eyes on," he said after chewing and swallowing.

Sadie said nothing.

"What horse?" Dorothy asked, slurping a mouthful of coffee, then grimacing and shaking her head at the heat.

Jim related the morning's events, his heavy mustache wagging like a squirrel's tail across his upper lip. His lower face was a dark brownish-red, etched with lines from the sun and wind, but it never failed to amuse Sadie the way his complexion lightened as it met his hat or the shade from the brim. The top of his balding head was creamy white with thatches of graying hair sticking out the way a hat causes hair to stick.

He'd look a lot better if he took off that Stetson

sometimes, Sadie thought. At least long enough to tan that pearly, white head.

Jim slouched on a chair, and Dorothy moved over to pat the top of his head.

"Thanks, hon. That was so nice of you."

Sadie felt quick tears spring to her eyes. The sight of those work-roughened, cracked hands so tenderly touching the bald head of her husband was a sight she wished she could portray on paper. They had been married at least 40 years, and Sadie had seen them at their best. She smiled as she watched the slow, easy grin spread across Jim's creviced face.

"You better get that breakfast on. There's a bunch of hungry men out there."

"Jim, do you... do you think they'll all agree to put him down?" Sadie broke in.

"What? Who?"

"The horse."

"Ain't none of their business."

"Well, whose business is it? Who's going to say what gets done with him?"

"I dunno, missy. Likely the boss."

Sadie turned back to peeling potatoes, her shoulders sagging a bit. She stiffened as she felt Jim's hand on her shoulder.

"Listen. That there horse is gonna die, okay? He's on his last breath. Don't even think about him 'cause he ain't gonna live."

"He wants to live, Jim. I saw it in his eyes."

Jim shrugged. Dorothy caught his eye and shook her head, and the conversation was over.

Sadie put the potatoes on to cook, then began breaking dozens of eggs into a large glass bowl. She added milk, salt, and pepper, then set the mixer on low, preparing the huge amount of scrambled eggs. Great loaves of home-made wheat bread were sliced and put into the toasters, slabs of butter spread thickly across the bread, melting into the crusty slices. The grill was loaded with bacon sizzling into curled, darkened, salty goodness. Dorothy kept forking finished pieces onto a serving platter and replenishing the grill with more long, limp slices of raw bacon.

They worked quietly now, both concentrating on finishing all the food at approximately the right time. This was all routine work. Today there was just a larger amount.

The dining room was majestic. At least Sadie always thought of it as majestic. There was simply no other word to describe it. The ceilings were vaulted and the beams exposed with great chandeliers hanging from the lofty height on long, thick chains. The windows were huge, allowing a view that was one of the most beautiful Sadie had ever seen.

She never tired of cleaning up after the hungry cow-hands had eaten. Just being in that room made her happy. But she hardly ever ventured in while the men were there eating, being strictly warned by her mother not to be gallivanting about while that room was filled with those cowboy "wannabes."

Sometimes when Mam spoke in that derisive tone, Sadie could tell that she thoroughly disliked some aspects of the West, but her pride and her upbringing would not allow her to say it directly. When Sadie mentioned it to Leah, she was met with stony opposition.

Of course Mam loved the West. She loved her house and Dat, and why in the world would Sadie come up with something like that? Sometimes she was just disappointed in Mam, that was what.

Sadie carried the square, stainless steel pans filled with scrambled eggs, biscuits, sausage gravy, and all the food they had prepared that morning. She dropped them expertly between the grids of the ornate steam table, an oak table with lights above it and hot water beneath the shining, stainless steel pans to keep the food piping hot.

She checked the number of heavy, white stoneware plates, the utensils wrapped in cloth napkins, and the mugs turned upside down beside the huge amount of coffee in shining urns.

The long pine tables were cleaned and polished to perfection with long benches on either side. The floor was wide with heavy planks, worn smooth and glistening from the many coats of polyurethane varnish that had been applied years ago.

Two massive glass doors stood at the end of the dining room, and Sadie's heart skipped, stumbled, and kept going as she spotted a white pickup pulling a large gray trailer through the blowing snow.

Could it be? Would Mark... No, they were in a red cattle truck. It would be months before she heard anything, if ever. Jim was probably right.

She retreated when she heard the voice of Richard Caldwell in even louder tones than was normal, leading his men to breakfast.

"Never heard anything like it!"

Someone answered in quieter tones. Then, "But a whole herd? How are you ever going to make off with a whole herd at one time? I mean, yeah, years ago when the range was wide open, but now people are going to notice a bunch of horses together. Come on!"

Sadie couldn't go back to the kitchen. Not now. She

had to hear this. She turned her back, which was much the same as not being in the room at all. A herd of horses stolen? She agreed with Richard Caldwell. Not in this day and age.

She cringed inwardly as the huge doors opened and the men began to file in. She busied herself folding napkin and replenishing the ice bin, being quiet and straining her ears to hear what the men were saying. She hardly breathed when she realized the conversation was very serious. The men never stood around like this when there was breakfast to be eaten, especially at this late hour.

"Did you watch it?"

"Nah. Don't watch TV."

"Well you should watch the news."

"Bah!"

"Yeah, but listen," Richard Caldwell's voice was heard above the din. "This guy in Hill County is wealthy. His horses are worth thousands of dollars. Thousands and thousands. I mean, he has a very distinguished bloodline going on there. He's been breeding horses for years and years. All of a sudden, this guy goes out to the stables, and 'Poof!' his horses are no longer there. It's unheard of."

"The work of some extremely smart men."

"Terrorists."

"Arabs."

"Oh, stop it. Those people wouldn't bother with our ordinary horses."

"I can't think of one single person in a thousand-mile radius that would be brilliant enough to carry this off. Not a one."

The conversation became more animated, each acquaintance contributing his voice, until it was hard to comprehend what they were really discussing. And they thought women at a quilting were bad! They couldn't be much more talkative than this.

Now she heard Jim's voice.

"Yeah, it's weird. But hardly much weirder than a starved and dyin' horse jumping down a bank out of the woods smack in front of my truck bringin' the Amish girl this morning. That thing appeared outta nowhere. Hit the brakes and skidded 'fore we hit 'im."

"Did you kill 'im?"

"No. I got 'er stopped in time. But don't think the horse'll make it. Skinniest thing I ever seed. Ever."

There was a murmur among the men, nods of agreement as each contemplated the scene in his own imagination.

Sadie knew Jim was well-liked and highly esteemed among the men. The few times he gave his opinion, the men considered, talked about, and respected it.

"Easy for a horse to git pretty skinny in this weather."

"He weren't just skinny. He was pretty bad."

"What happened to him?"

"That Fred Skinner came along in his cattle truck. City guy with him was gonna call the vet."

The snorts were unanimous.

"Spend a couple hundred for the vet when the poor miserable creature'll go the way of nature anyhow."

"Yep."

"Them city people."

"Looks as if breakfast is ready."

Sadie slipped through the swinging doors into the kitchen, unnoticed.

Now that bit of news was something to think about. And...well, she may as well give it all up. Maybe that horse lying on the road was really just like a mirage to a person dying of thirst and walking in a desert. You thought what you wanted was there, but it never really was, despite the fact that you were absolutely convinced of its existence. Maybe instead of a look in a horse's beautiful eyes, it was only her own emotions—all a fleeting mirage, her imagination run wild.

It was probably the same with Mark. Whoever he was. Of course, any girl would react to someone as good-looking as him. What did Mam say? Don't go by looks. So there you go. It wasn't real attraction.

Sadie tackled the pans, scraping their residue into tall garbage cans lined with heavyweight garbage bags, getting them ready for the commercial dishwasher. Thankfully, today she would not encounter "Her Royal Highness, the lofty Barbara Caldwell," as Sadie was prone to thinking of her.

Sadie had long decided some people were wealthy and you would never know by their attitude. Only their clothes, the cars they drove, or their homes revealed their monetary value. And some people... Well, Barbara was a piece of work. If she could, she would clean the floor with a Lysol disinfectant wipe after Sadie walked on it. She had no use for those pious, bearded people, even refusing to speak the name "Amish." Sadie had found it extremely hard at first, cringing whenever Barbara approached, but, after three years, Barbara actually addressed Sadie, though only on rare occasions.

One of her favorite put-downs was asking Sadie to pick up the dry cleaning in town. Then she would wave her long, jeweled fingers and say, "Oh yes, I keep forgetting. You don't have your license."

Each time, Sadie ground her teeth in an effort not to tell Barbara that if she did have her license, she wouldn't pick up her dry cleaning anyway. In fact, she wanted to say to Barbara that she could just heave herself and all her excess poundage off to the dry cleaners and pick it up herself. But her upbringing, of course, denied her that wonderful luxury.

Jim said Barbara wasn't like that when he was around. But Dorothy heartily disagreed and told him so.

"You can't be peaches and cream at one person's table, then turn around and be sauerkraut at the next."

Sadie never said much, if anything at all. She was taught at home not to speak ill of anyone, and Sadie knew without a doubt that was one of the hardest things for human nature to overcome. How could you respect someone who so obviously viewed you with only contempt?

Chapter 5

SADIE WAS ALWAYS HAPPY TO RETURN TO HER home in the evening. She just wished Jim would push that old truck a bit faster and never failed to be amazed at how slowly he navigated the winding, uphill drive to the house. Tonight, though, the snow made the hill treacherous, so she was glad he didn't accelerate around the bend.

The warm, golden square windows of home were welcoming beacons through the grayish-white evening light, and Sadie could almost smell the good supper Mam had already prepared.

"See ya!" Sadie said, hopping lightly out of the old pickup.

"Mm-hm," Jim grunted.

Sadie swung open the door to the kitchen, which was awash in the bright glow of the propane gas lamps set into the ornate wooden cabinet next to the kitchen cupboards.

"I'm home!" she sang out.

There was no answer, no supper on the stove, no table set by the French doors.

"Hey! I'm home!"

Leah came quietly into the kitchen, making no sound at all, her face pale, but smiling a welcome in the way sisters grin at one another after an absence.

Sisters were like that. A grin, a look, a soul connection, a mutual knowing that one was just as glad to see the other, an understanding of "Oh, goody, you're home!" but with no words.

Leah was only two years younger than Sadie, and, at 18, one of the prettiest of the sisters. Blonde-haired, with the same blue eyes as Sadie, Leah was always light-hearted, happy, and upbeat about any situation. Mam said Leah was the sunshine of the family.

But today there was a soft, gray cloud over her sister's blue eyes, and Sadie raised an eyebrow.

"What?"

"It's Mam."

"What?"

"I don't know. She's…" Leah shrugged her shoulders.

"She's what?" Sadie asked, feeling a sickness rise in her stomach like the feeling she used to have in school before the Christmas program.

Leah shrugged again.

"I don't know."

Sadie faced her sister squarely, the sick feeling in her stomach launching an angry panic. She wanted to hit Leah to make her tell her what was wrong with Mam.

"Is she sick? Why do you act so dumb about this?"

Sadie fought to keep her voice level, to keep a rein on her sick panic so it wouldn't make her cry or scream. She would do anything to stop Leah from looking like that.

"Sadie, stop."

Leah turned her back, holding her shoulders stiffly erect as if to ward off Sadie's obvious fear.

"Leah, is something wrong? Seriously. With our Mam?"

Leah stayed in that stiff position, and Sadie's heart sank so low, she fought for breath. The lower your heart went, the harder it was to breathe, and breathing was definitely essential. It wasn't that your heart literally sank. It was more like the sensation you had whenever something really, really scared you.

Sadie sat down hard, weak now, struggling to push back the looming fear. Sadie put her head in her hands, her thoughts flooding out any ability to speak rationally to her sister.

Nothing was wrong. Not really. Leah, can't you see? Mam is okay. I haven't noticed anything out of the ordinary. You haven't either. She's just tired. She's weary of working. She loves us. She loves Dat. She has to. She loves Montana. She has to do that, too. Dat loves our mother, too. He has to. There is nothing wrong in this family. Turn around, Leah. Turn around and say it with me: There is nothing wrong in our family.

Leah turned quietly, as if any swift or sudden movement would enable the fear to grip them both.

"Sadie."

Sadie lifted her head, meeting Leah's eyes, and in that instant recognized with a heart-stopping knowledge that Leah knew, too.

Leah knew Mam had been...well...weird. She had been acting strangely, but not so strange that any of her daughters dared bring up the subject, ever.

They all loved Mam, and if she changed in some obvious ways, well, it was just Mam—just how some people became older. Mam had always been meticulous. Her housekeeping was her pride and joy. Her garden was tended lovingly.

Mam was always hoeing, mulching, or spraying, and her vegetable garden produced accordingly, which kept them busy canning and freezing all summer long.

One of Mam's secrets to gardening was how she kept the weeds at bay. She attacked them with vengeance, using old, moldy mulch hay. She brought it in and spread it until the weeds had no chance of maturing or taking over everything.

Sadie could still feel the slimy hay in her arms, the outer layer scratching her legs as they lugged the gruesome stuff from the wagon to the corn rows. The cucumbers and zucchini squash grew in long, velvety spirals over thick chunks of "old hay," as Mam called it. The old hay kept the plants moist. So they produced abundantly, as did all Mam's vegetables even though the growing season was short in Montana.

Lime was absolutely necessary, Mam said. Pulverized lime was like talcum powder in a bag, and so smooth and cool, it was fun to bury your hands deep into the middle of it.

The strawberry patch was weeded, mulched with clean, yellow straw, and sprayed so it produced great, red succulent berries every year. There was nothing in the whole world better than sitting in the straw beside a plant loaded down with heavy, red berries and pinching off the green top before popping the berry into your mouth.

They grew their peas on great lengths of chicken wire, held up by wooden stakes that Dat pounded into the thawed soil in the spring when the stalks were still tiny. As the rain and sunshine urged them to grow, the peas climbed the chicken wire, and little white flowers bloomed with vigor. Later they would turn into long, green pods, heavy with little green peas.

Picking peas was not the girls' favorite job, but sitting beneath the spreading maple trees on lawn chairs with bowls and buckets of peas to shell definitely was. They would spend all afternoon shelling them—pressing on one side with their thumbs and raking out all the little, green peas from inside the pods.

They talked and laughed and got silly, Mam being one of the silliest of all. And they would make great big sausage sandwiches with fresh new onions and radishes from the garden along with a gallon of grape Kool-Aid that was all purple and sugary and artificial and not one bit good for you, Mam said.

After the pea crop was over, they all had to help with the most hateful job in the garden. Taking down the pea wire and stripping off all those tangled vines was the slowest, most maddening task, and every one of the sisters thoroughly disliked it.

They always fought at one time or another. Often the sun got too hot, and no one was particularly happy, so they argued and sat down and refused to work and tattled accordingly.

Mam was always busy and…well…so very normal. Canning cucumbers, making strawberry jam, canning those little red beets that smelled like the wet earth when she cooked them soft in stainless steel stockpots. She would cook them, cool them, cut them into bite-sized pieces, and cover them with a pickling brew. Oh, they were so good in the wintertime with thick, cheesy, oniony, potato chowder.

All this went through Sadie's mind as her eyes met Leah's. Then Sadie turned her head to look away, out over the valley.

"We didn't have red beets for a long time," she whispered.

Leah nodded.

"It's the little things: dust under the hutch in the dining room, unfinished quilts, the pills, the endless row of different homeopathic remedies…"

"But Sadie, she's still all right, isn't she?"

"Yes. She's just changing. Getting older."

"Hey! Why is there no supper?"

"Well…" Leah began.

Then she looked down, bending her head as great, tearing sobs tore at her throat. Sadie's horror rose, a giant dragon waiting to consume her, maybe even slay her.

How could she? How could Mam be like this?

Hot tears pricked her own eyes, and she sat quietly, waiting until Leah's tears subsided.

"Sadie, I think it's pretty bad. For a few months now, I've watched Mam when she thinks she's alone. She hoards things and…and…oh, I mean it, Sadie, it's too painful to talk about. She keeps certain things like combs and dollar bills and…and hairpins in a certain drawer, and as long as that drawer is undisturbed, she appears… well…she is fairly normal. She works, she talks, and no one notices anything different."

"I do."

"You do?" Leah lifted her head, wiping at her eyes with the back of her hand.

"Well, she's…I don't know. Like this morning, she was leafing through a cookbook asking what we want for our Christmas menu. Christmas is over a month away. Almost two months. It's as if…almost as if she isn't really here. Here in this house. With us and Dat."

Leah sat up, bringing her fist down on the table, startling Sadie.

"She *isn't* here. Her heart and soul are still in Ohio."

"But Leah, by all outward appearances, she wanted to come. She held Dat's hand, her eyes sparkled, she was so excited. I can still see her sitting in the living room with Dat. Oh, I remember. I felt as if she was deserting me. I was so heartbroken about Paris. I felt as if she didn't care about me or Paris, she was so completely with Dat."

"She's not with Dat anymore. Sadie, there's a lot going on that can easily escape us. Dat and Mam are just keeping on for pride's sake. It's...not the way it should be."

"Like...how?"

"Oh, just different ways. When did we last have Dat's favorite supper? Huh?"

There was silence as the conversation fizzled. Was it all in their imaginations? Were they imagining the worst? Maybe it was normal for mothers to change after they turned 46.

"Where are Dat and Mam now?"

"They... argued, fought."

"About what?"

"I don't want to tell you. They didn't know I overheard. I'd feel like a traitor if I spread it around."

Suddenly anger consumed Sadie, sending its fiery tentacles around her body until she thought she would suffocate.

"All right, be that way—all your lofty pride intact, walking around with a serene expression when you know something is wrong—way wrong—with our mother. We have to face it. We can't just sweep it under the carpet and then go around acting as if we are one perfect, happy family, when we know it isn't true because it's not."

Leah sighed.

"Sit down and stop that. All right, Mam told Dat she wasn't feeling good, but she refused to go get help. They...well, it wasn't pretty. She finally agreed to go to the chiropractor in town."

"As if a chiropractor is going to help."

"Well, it's something."

"Pffff!"

Rebekah appeared, straight pins stuck in the front of her dress, thread stuck to her sleeve, an anxious expression in her eyes.

"What's for supper? Where's Mam and Dat?"

Reuben and Anna followed Rebekah into the room, laughing about something. Sadie could tell they had been in the basement playing their endlessly competitive games of ping-pong. Reuben was 10 years old now, old enough to let Anna know that his ping-pong game was worth worrying about.

Sadie groaned inwardly. Oh, they were so precious. So innocent and sweet and dear and good. Why couldn't things just remain the way they used to be?

Sadie walked over to Reuben, wrapped her arms around him, and pulled him close, kissing the top of his thick, blonde hair. She got as far as "How are you...?" before he pulled away from her, straining at her arms, pounding them with his fists, twisting his head, shouting, "Get away from me!" His eyes squinted to a mocking glare, but his mouth was smiling, although he tried desperately to hide that fact.

Ten-year-old brothers had a serious aversion to hugs.

Leah sat up then, bolstering a new-found courage, and said brightly, "Who's hungry?"

"We all are," Anna said.

"Everybody vote. Grilled cheese and tomato soup?"

"Ewww!"

"Hamburgers?"

"Had that last night!"

"Hot dogs?"

"No way. Not for supper."

Sadie watched Leah summoning more strength, a wide smile appearing, as she said, "Eggs-in-a-nest? With home-made ketchup?"

"Pancakes!" Reuben yelled.

"Pancakes!" Anna echoed.

"All right, pancakes and eggs-in-a-nest it shall be."

Leah marched resolutely to the kitchen cupboard, Rebekah at her heels, and Sadie slipped away, gratefully unnoticed.

Bless Leah's heart. I don't know if I could do that right now. I'm tired, I'm worried, and I'm going to my room.

Wearily, Sadie slowly climbed the stairs, supporting herself with the handrail. She entered the bathroom, lit the kerosene lamp suspended from the wall on a heavy hanger, and braced herself against the vanity top with her hands. Her hair looked horrible, her covering crooked, and there was a greasy sheen on her forehead. Her eyes were puffy and frightened, her whole face a mess.

Well, it's been quite a day, she thought, turning away from the mirror and going to her bedroom.

She felt a strong sense of homecoming, rest, and peace as she entered the cool, beige room with its two large windows facing the west. Heavy, white curtains were parted on each side, held back with sand-colored tiebacks to match the bedspread. Her furniture was fairly new; a matching oak bedroom suite made by her Uncle John from the Ohio district where they had once lived. She had collected some pottery that was handmade in Brentwood, which was her pride and joy. White and beige candles and pictures in subdued hues completed the room.

There was a beige-colored sofa by the windows piled with darker beige pillows, and she sank gratefully into one corner, letting her head fall back as she closed her eyes.

Dear God, if you can hear me in my rattled, frightened way, please, please, look down on us and help us all. What should I do? Should I confront Mam? Talk to Dat?

Suddenly she realized that was her first priority—talking to Dat. He was good and steady and sensible. He would explain the situation, they would find some plausible solution, and this would all be over.

It had to be over. She couldn't bear to think of Mam spiraling out of control, or worse. There had been so much strange behavior lately, but always Mam's good behavior was dominant and erased the questionable times for Sadie and, evidently, for Leah, too. She wondered how much 16-year-old Rebekah knew? Or Anna and Reuben?

Oh, dear God, keep them innocent and safe from worry.

The time Mam insisted there were ladybugs in the pepper shaker was the first Sadie had ever noticed anything amiss, other than her usual lack of energy. Usual is what it had finally come to be. Mam was not the same and hadn't been for a few years now. This became increasingly obvious to Sadie after she and Leah had finally confronted the truth.

First, Mam no longer wanted a garden. Mam not have a garden? It was unthinkable. How could you live without a garden? The growing season was too short, she said, and then the soil was too thin, her back bothered her, and

it was easier to just buy frozen or canned vegetables at
the supermarket in Brentwood.

Dat's irritation flickered in his eyes, but he appeased
his wife, saying if she no longer had an interest in gardening, then he supposed they could survive without one.
Smiles then, but a bit like a clown's, painted on.

After Mam stopped gardening, her fear of bugs began,
but only jokingly. If you laughed about it and said Montana didn't have very many bugs, she laughed with you
and dropped the subject.

Ach, Mam. My Mam. My rock in my youth. In Ohio
she was the best, most supportive, most nurturing mother
anyone could possible ask for. Sadie had always felt lucky
to have one of the best. And that first year in Montana
had been so good, building the barn and remodeling the
house.

Sadie sighed. It was all downhill from there.

She needed to think of something else—something less
burdensome. Oh, she should check messages. Perhaps
Mark remembered to leave one to let her know how the
horse was doing. Or how dead he was.

She ran downstairs, grabbed a coat, swung the door
open, and stepped into the clean, cold, whirling snow. No
one had bothered to shovel the driveway or path to the
barn, that was sure. She wondered who Mam and Dat's
driver was. He'd have to be pretty brave to be out on a
night like this.

She yanked on the door to the phone shanty, clicked
her flashlight on, picked up the telephone receiver, and
punched numbers to check messages.

There were three.

The first one from the blacksmith who would be there
on the 14th. The second from Mommy Yoder, who said

her cat died the night before and her chimney caught fire, but the Lord had been with her. The cat was buried and the fire put out without the fire company having to come. She had tried to tell Ammon the wood was too green, but Ammon was still the same as he always was and didn't dry his wood properly and if their house didn't burn down someday she'd be surprised...

Dear, dear fussy Mommy Yoder. She ate tomato sauce with dippy eggs for breakfast, and called oatmeal "oohts," and was round and soft and cuddly. She was a treasure, talking nonstop in her eccentricity. She always had a story to tell, like the first time she went into the drive-thru at the bank and that round canister went flying up the pipe. She just knew the end of the world was near.

As the third message came on, headlights wound their way slowly up the drive.

Her heart took a nose dive and fear enveloped her. She hung onto the phone shelf, lowered her head, and prayed for help. She knew she must confront her father.

"Hey," a deep voice said, "this is Mark Peight."

She bit down hard on her lip, holding the receiver against her ear as tightly as possible.

"The horse was seen by a vet. He has a chance. He's at Richard Caldwell's stables. I'll be by to check up on him."

That was it. No good-bye, no wishing anyone a good day, still no information on whose horse he was or why he was there or anything—just a few clipped sentences. Definitely Mark.

But the horse had a chance!

A chance!

Oh, praise God!

Tomorrow morning could not come soon enough. But first, she needed to talk to her father. Things didn't seem quite as hopeless as they had before her heart was filled with joy about the message. Surely if there was hope for the dying horse, there was hope for all kinds of situations—Mam's included.

As Sadie walked out into the snow, Dat was paying the driver and Mam was stepping carefully onto the sidewalk. Sadie hesitated until Mam closed the kitchen door before calling to Dat. She had startled him, she could tell, but he found his way through the snow to Sadie's side.

"Sadie."

"Dat. I was checking messages, but…I really need to talk to you about Mam."

"Why?"

Instantly Dat was alert, defensive.

"She's…she's…there's something wrong with her, right?"

"What do you mean?"

"She's…she's acting strangely, Dat."

There was a slight pause before he stepped close, thrusting his face into hers, only the thin, swirling snow between them.

"Sadie, if I ever catch you saying anything like that to anyone in this community…I…I…don't know what I'm going to do. Never, ever, mention Mam to anyone, do you hear me? There's nothing wrong with her. She's just tired."

"But…but Leah heard you arguing."

"Leah didn't hear anything. Do you hear me?"

His large hand clamped like a vice on her forearm, and he shook her slightly.

"You do hear me, don't you?"

Sadie nodded dumbly, her feet like dead weights in the snow, her body shivering as a chill swept through her. As Dat turned on his heel and walked away, Sadie leaned against the rough boards of the barn and thought her heart would break in two.

Chapter 6

Mam was in the kitchen at six o'clock the following morning, frying bacon in her good Lifetime pan, her hair neatly in place beneath her covering, a fresh white apron tied around her waist. Dat sat at his desk in the adjoining room, his gray head bent over a few papers spread before him.

So normal. A fresh start. Last night was all a bad dream which would soon evaporate like a mist, Sadie thought.

"Good morning!" she said.

Dat returned the greeting, avoiding her eyes, and Mam turned, the spatula dripping bacon grease, and smiled.

"Good morning, Sadie."

Sadie sliced the heavy loaf of whole wheat bread, then spread the thick slices in the broiler part of the gas oven to make toast as Mam broke eggs into another pan.

The ordinary silence was deafening this morning, taut with undiagnosed worries and fears. Sadie desperately wanted to chatter needlessly, the way families do, comfortably knowing their words are accepted, considered worth something of importance. Not until now had she ever thought of the pure luxury of such simple things.

But they had the snow, the heat from the great wood-stove, the smell of bacon—the usual parts of their lives that bound them together.

She cleared her throat.

"I...guess you heard about the horse, huh?"

"What horse?" Mam asked without turning.

Sadie told them of the previous day's excitement, but her words banged against the wall, slid down, faded into the hardwood floor, and became nothing at all.

Dat was still poring over his papers, and Mam made a sort of clucking sound with her tongue, which could mean a series of warnings or wonderment or amazement. Or she may have done it completely out of habit from listening to four daughters and their views of life in general.

Sadie tried again to part the curtain of indifference.

"Did the chiropractor help you, Mam?"

"Yes."

"Good."

Sadie poured the rich, purple grape juice into short, heavy glasses and then sat down. She pulled her chair up to the table, and Dat, Mam, and Sadie bowed their heads, their hands folded in their laps, for a silent prayer before they began eating their breakfast.

Dat lifted his head, looked questioningly at Sadie, and lifted one eyebrow.

"Where's Leah?"

"Asleep, I guess. She has off today."

"The reason I ask, I saw someone walking down the driveway at one o'clock last night. Was it you? Do you know anything about it? Definitely a dark coat, scarf, and a skirt. The snow had stopped before then, but I still couldn't see clearly enough to tell who it was."

"It wasn't me," said Sadie. "And why would Leah be walking in the snow at that hour? That's creepy. Are you sure?"

"Sure I'm sure." His tone was brusque, his manner brushing off her question like bothersome dust.

Mam bowed her head, shoveling bacon onto her plate with studied movements. Suddenly she raised her head. Sadie noticed the grayish pallor, the dark circles, the shadows beneath her eyes that made her appear so sad, so... almost pitiful.

"It was me. I... sometimes when I wake at night, my thoughts seem like real voices, and they all cram into a tiny space, and I can't quite sort them out the way I should. So I thought perhaps my head would clear if I walked in the snow for awhile, Jacob."

"But I thought you were there in the bed beside me."

"Oh, I just propped up a few pillows so it looked like I was there so you wouldn't worry."

Dat frowned. Mam turned to Sadie.

"You'll probably think there's something wrong with me, but, Sadie, I saw something in the faint light of the half-moon and the stars. The snow wasn't blowing anymore, and over on Atkin's Ridge, just about at the tree line, there were animals sort of milling about in and out of the trees. At first I thought they were elk, then longhorned cattle, then... I'm not sure if they were horses or not, but it was something."

Sadie looked into her mother's eyes. There was an earnestness and sincerity—no reason for her to doubt what Mam saw.

"Wow, Mam! Weren't you afraid?"

"I turned back," she said with a soft laugh.

Sadie hesitated, then dove headfirst into the unknown

waters, realizing the danger but hurtling in nevertheless.

"Mam, why are your thoughts so crammed together? Is there anything anyone could do to help sort them out? Would you like to talk about it?"

"No."

"But, Mam, we... Leah and I...

There she was, diving deeper, lungs straining, desperately needing strength to accomplish this tiny, if not insignificant, step toward finding out how Mam felt.

"Leah and I are worried."

"I'm fine."

"She's fine. You and Leah keep to yourselves. Mam is fine."

Sadie bowed her head, rose to the surface, gulped air, and came up with absolutely nothing. She nodded. Mission not accomplished.

"Well," she said, falsely cheerful, "Jim will soon be here."

Mam got up and went to the corner cabinet to begin taking down her countless bottles of ginseng, St. John's Wort, brewer's yeast, Lifespan supplements, and liquid Body Balance—her usual morning ritual of bolstering her faith with those hopeful little bottles.

Sadie turned away, wanting to flee.

Hurry up, Jim.

✾ ✪ ✾

Down at the ranch, things were normal. Dorothy bustled about, shaking her head at the pools of water gathered on her spotless kitchen floor. Why couldn't the men have enough common sense to dry their feet when they came barreling inside?

Sadie had barely hung her coat on the hook before the kitchen door swung open and Richard Caldwell entered, thumping his hat against his legs.

"Sadie!" he thundered.

Please help me, God.

She finished hanging her scarf over her coat collar, fought to calm herself properly, then smoothed her apron over her hips and turned to face him.

"Yes?"

"Somebody told me you want that horse they brought in yesterday."

"The...the dying one?"

"They didn't bring in any other one."

"Is he still breathing?" Sadie clasped her hands, her eyes shining, her feet refusing to stay on the floor as she stood on her tiptoes.

"I really don't know. But if you want him, you'll have to take him out of here."

"But...I don't know if my father will allow it. I'm sure there will be medical, I mean, veterinary bills to pay, and my...father doesn't like horses much."

Why did Richard Caldwell always do this to her? Why did she stumble over words and flounder about like a half-dead fish and say stupid things that made no sense at all when he was around?

"Well, if you want that horse, it's yours. I don't want him. I have no idea where he came from, and I sure don't want to become involved. That old Fred Skinner has a way with words, or he wouldn't have dumped that horse off in my stables."

Sadie bounced a bit, her eyes still shining bright blue.

"That's very nice of you, Mr. Caldwell. And I do thank you. I just need to get permission from my father."

"Come with me and we'll go see the horse."

Sadie fairly danced over to the hook to get her coat, trying to conceal the excitement that kept bubbling over.

Dorothy confronted her then, like a ruffled, banty hen, her eyes flashing, hands on hips.

"And just where do you think you're prancing off to with all this breakfast to be done, young lady?"

Richard Caldwell's booming laugh rolled across the kitchen, bringing a giggle to Sadie's throat, which she suppressed just in time when she saw how upset Dorothy became. Her eyes popped some serious sparks as she turned and wagged a short finger beneath Richard Caldwell's face.

"Now don't you laugh, Richard Caldwell. It's not funny. I ain't young anymore. I got all these hands to feed and yer gonna go gallivanting all over creation with my best help. I ain't puttin' up with it!"

Sadie knew no one ever spoke to Richard Caldwell like that, except feisty little Dorothy. Sadie hid a wide grin, then ducked her head as she unsuccessfully tried to hold back a joyous bubble of laughter.

"Now, Dorothy. Now, now. We're just going to the barn to see this horse. We'll be back in two shakes."

Dorothy harrumphed disdainfully, turning away to mutter to herself as Richard Caldwell held the door for Sadie.

The fresh, cold air smacked Sadie's face, and the wide, blue sky with its white, brassy sunshine filled her heart with its sheer beauty. She flung out her arms and skipped like a small child.

Snow was like that. It was so cold and so white that even the sun and the blue sky blended together to make everything more cold and white and awesome. She wanted to fling herself on her back and make snow angels the way she used to back home in Ohio, but she knew better. She couldn't do that—she was walking to the stables with her boss, Richard Caldwell.

She stiffened when she felt his big hand touch her shoulder and stay there.

"Sadie, you're a good girl. I appreciate your work here at Aspen East. This horse is a gift, and I hope you have many happy days together."

Sadie was speechless. She could not have spoken one word to save her life, so she stopped walking and turned to face him, hoping to convey her thanks somehow.

Richard Caldwell was not a man given to flowery compliments or words of praise. It just wasn't his way. But there was something about this girl's dutiful demeanor, her faithfulness, that touched a chord in his heart.

☆ ✡ ☆

With hairbrush stopped in mid-air, Barbara Caldwell parted the curtains for a better view. Her breathing grew rapid, and her steely, gray eyes flattened into lines of hatred. Then she flung the gilded hairbrush against the wall, creating a slight dent in the scrolled wallpaper before the brush hit the carpeted floor.

Barbara watched her husband open the stable door for Sadie and disappear inside. She threw the matching, gilded hand mirror against the same wall, creating a larger dent than the first.

So that's what Richard Caldwell is up to, she thought bitterly.

She remembered the sleepless night she had recently alone in the huge, canopied brass bed, wondering what had happened to her husband. Did marriages deteriorate on their own?

That sweet-faced, serene-looking little hypocrite! How could she? Weren't these odd people who drove around in their horses and buggies supposed to be different? Better?

Barbara snorted, a sound of frustration and aggravation, followed by a feeling of helplessness and fear.

She never knew Richard Caldwell to be so cold and distant. He never wanted to go out with her anymore or share an intimate conversation. She wouldn't think of trying to hug her husband—or touch him in any way—as many women did naturally throughout the day. There was an unseen barrier, a frightening, cold, barbed wire fence surrounding him, leaving her completely unsure of herself. So she hid behind an armor of dignity, of cruelty. Or she thought she did.

Sliding the stool over to the vanity, Barbara turned up the lights. She leaned forward, turning her face this way, then that.

She needed more Botox. Her wrinkles were becoming too prominent around her eyes.

As she lifted her thick, blonde hair, a plan formed in her mind, turning her eyes into a narrow line, a calculating thinness.

She would talk to Richard. She had her ways. Sadie would pay for this.

✿ ✪ ✿

The dim interior of the stables was a contrast to the brightness outside, but the warm, wonderful smells enveloped Sadie. She breathed in, savoring the smell of the hay and oats, the saddle soap and leather, the straw and disinfectant—all odors pertaining to the creature she adored most on earth, the horse.

The stable was not an ordinary barn like the place where Amish people kept their horses. This stable was luxurious, housing fine horses with good bloodlines that cost thousands of dollars.

There was a long, wide walkway down the center of the barn with large box stalls on either side. The stalls were built of wood and finished to a glossy sheen. Throughout the barn, black and shiny iron grids were built into the wood. Large airy windows, ceiling fans, and regulated temperatures kept the place comfortable, no matter the weather.

Sadie had been in these stables before, but she had never actually walked along the center walkway. Her eyes roamed the walls, the ceiling, the texture of the floor, marveling at the unbelievable amount of time and expense that went into something as simple as a horse barn. Richard Caldwell must have more money than she could even imagine.

"Over here," he said suddenly in his loud voice, and Sadie instantly clutched at the lapels of her coat, compressing her lips to hide her nervousness.

He slid back a bolt and swung open a heavy gate.

Sadie blinked.

He was standing up! On his own four feet!

She didn't realize that a soft sound escaped her compressed lips. She didn't know she had lovingly reached out to touch the horse. She just knew she had never felt such aching pity for any other creature.

He was bigger than Sadie thought, remembering his still form lying in the snow. He didn't seem that big then. His two front legs were splayed, as if placing them farther apart would enable him to stay upright longer. His breathing was shallow and much too fast. His tender nostrils changed their shape with every breath as he struggled to stay on his feet, to stay alive. But his neck! Oh, it was so horribly thin! His head was much too big!

How could a horse stay alive looking like this? How could he keep from dying? Sadie looked questioningly at Richard Caldwell, who nodded his head knowingly, though she didn't say a word.

Slowly Sadie advanced, not even breathing. Her hand slid under the long, black forelock and stayed there. Up came his head then, the long, black eyelashes sweeping over his blue eyes. And he looked, really looked, at Sadie.

He whinnied. But not really a whinny. More like a soft nicker or a long, shaky breath. But Sadie felt it, she heard it, and she put her hands on each side of this poor broken horse's head and gathered it against her coat. She squeezed her eyes shut, bit so hard on her lower lip that she tasted blood, and still a sob rose up from the depth of her being.

Poor, poor thing. Who did this to you? Where do you come from?

She turned her back to Richard Caldwell, not wanting him to know how emotional she was. She bent her head and murmured, telling the horse how much she loved him, how much she wanted him to be strong, to be better, get well, and be healthy, and did he know that she might be allowed to keep him? She still had to ask Dat, though.

Richard Caldwell blinked his eyes, looked away, cleared his throat, tapped his toes, then yanked angrily at his collar. He never cried. He was never touched by any old, sick horse, and he sure wasn't planning on starting now. But when the horse tried to nicker, and out came only a rumpled breath, he had to swallow hard, fighting back feelings of tenderness and pity. And when Sadie bent her head and murmured to the horse, he was horrified to feel the hot sting of genuine tears, an emotion he had not experienced for so long, he hardly knew he was capable of it.

The sun's morning rays found their way through the glass, highlighting Sadie's shining brown hair, the circle of her dark lashes on her perfect cheek, and the glistening mane and forelock of this black and white horse. The picture rooted Richard Caldwell to the floor of the stall.

Suddenly he could smell earth, dripping leaves, a sort of fishy, wormy wet coolness where he had found the dying dog. It was a stray dog—a matted, dirty, thin dog down by the wet mud of the creek.

He could still feel the holes in the knees of his jeans and the way the frayed denim stretched across them, almost hurting if he bent too far. He had used his old t-shirt to lift the dog. He strained and slid but whispered the whole time to the frightened animal.

You poor, poor thing. Come on. I'll take you home. What happened to you? Poor baby.

Now he felt his father's wrath. He felt the words he said, the finger he pointed.

"Get that flea-infested mongrel away from me, and don't even think of keeping him. The only thing good enough for that dog is a shot of lead. Get away. Get away!"

Oh, he got away, both ears stopped with muddy, shaking fingers. But it was not soon enough or far enough to erase the single, mind-shattering slam of his father's shotgun.

He ran then, blindly, through grass almost as tall as he was—the tops of it raking his wet cheeks, slapping his moist forehead as he fell to the ground. He lay there for hours, shaking and crying.

His revenge had been burying the dog. When the alarm clock on his tattered nightstand showed 1:26 a.m., he crept down from his bedroom with a pink towel from the bathroom. He remembered the touch of the soft towel, how sacred it seemed, and how clean.

He was amazed at how loose a dead dog felt. There were a lot of bones and skin and not much to hold him together. His cheeks were wet as he tenderly folded the jumbled limbs, then covered the dog neatly, making sure the towel was straight.

He crept to the shed for a shovel, then dug a hole behind the lumber pile where the ground was low and soft. He carried the dog, laid him carefully into the shallow grave, and wondered what a preacher would say. Shouldn't God be involved somehow?

"God, I need you to look after this dog. If you care about dogs, I named him Sparky. So there you go, God. Be good to him. He has a pink towel."

Richard Caldwell blinked again, then cleared his throat. He had believed in God that night. He had. If he had ever felt the presence of God in the times in between that childhood memory and now, it had never been as real as this. Sadie looked like an angel administering her magic to this lovely creature.

"Look!" Sadie whispered.

Richard Caldwell came closer and bent to look.

"It's a hammer!"

He could see it, too. Beneath the black mane, the shape of the black hair was much like a hammer, depending which way you viewed it.

Sadie stroked and stroked, beaming, her face illuminated by the morning sun.

At that moment, Richard Caldwell promised to himself that this horse would receive the best medical attention from his trusted veterinarian, and Sadie would never know. He would never tell her. He could not bear to think of this horse dying and that angelic face bearing the disappointment.

"Can I...I mean...do you think he'll live? Do you want him moved? Is he a bother? In your way? I don't know what my father will say..."

Sadie broke off, miserable. Richard Caldwell was a hard man. How many times had she heard Dorothy say, "If the boss don't see no profit in it, out it goes."

Richard Caldwell knew he could not put a price tag on this feeling. It was a kind of redemption, a chance to prove himself a better man, a moment to show he was not his father.

"Dad, can I keep him? He won't eat much."

The blast of the shotgun.

He cleared his throat to relieve his tightening emotions.

"Let's give him a couple of days. He'll be in no one's way here. If you want, you can come out and talk to him on your dinner break. Probably be best if you came to see him often, but you know Dorothy."

Richard Caldwell smiled, almost warmly, and Sadie could hardly believe the softness it created in his eyes.

"Thank you!" she said quietly.

"You think your Dad will let you have him?"

"I don't know." Sadie shrugged her shoulders.

"Strict, is he?"

"No. Not really. He's just not much of a horse person."

"And he's Amish?"

Sadie grinned, "I know, strange, isn't it?"

"He drives his horse and buggy though?"

"Yes. But, he calls horses 'livestock.'"

Richard Caldwell laughed genuinely. "They're not livestock?"

"No."

She didn't know why she did it, but as she stroked the horse's neck, she began talking to Richard Caldwell—of all people—about Paris. She never mentioned Paris to anyone, not even her sisters. But Richard Caldwell listened as Sadie's story unfolded. When she finished, a bit hesitantly, he looked out over the snowy landscape for a long time, then bent his head to look at her.

"Sadie, I know how it feels. We'll get this horse better. What will you name him?"

Sadie's intake of breath was all the reward he needed.

"Nevaeh."

"Nevaeh?"

"It's 'heaven,' backwards."

"Sounds like a girl's name."

"Maybe... but this horse is just so... perfect... and... well... the name just seems to fit."

Richard Caldwell turned away, opened the box stall door, and said, "Nevaeh it is."

It was too gruff, but a man couldn't get emotional now, could he?

✡ ✡ ✡

A few evenings later, Richard and Barbara Caldwell sat in their private dining room, the oak table seeming incongruous as it stretched out far past the two large people seated at one end.

Barbara was dressed in red, her husband's favorite color, her hair and make-up perfect. She had spent hours in town at the hair salon as she hatched the perfect plan for revenge.

Sadie Miller would have to go.

Richard Caldwell's favorite dishes were served: crusty baked potato and filet mignon with horseradish and dill. The wine was perfect. Her husband was in a jovial mood.

"So, what was going on at the barn today that the Kitchen Help needed your assistance there?" she asked, heavily emphasizing "Kitchen Help."

Richard stopped chewing and slowly laid down his fork. He picked up the monogrammed napkin and wiped his mouth before he cleared his throat.

Their eyes met. Clashed.

"Jim Sevarr almost hit a horse. Sadie was with him. The horse is in our barn and Sadie wants to keep him, but her father won't let her."

Barbara stabbed at her meat as her lips compressed.

"I thought Amish daughters are expected to obey their fathers. Why wouldn't you respect that?"

"I am. That's why the horse is here."

"I see."

The words were cold, hard pellets stinging Richard Caldwell's mind. She was making him as uncomfortable as only cunning Barbara could. When she looked up, Richard Caldwell checked a mental urge to shake his wife. Malice glittered in the hard eyes he once thought beautiful. He shuddered and stopped himself, thinking of the look in Sadie's eyes as she knelt by the failing horse—eyes so unlike his wife's eyes.

"So does that mean she needs you to escort her to the barn?"

"Barbara. Stop. Of course not."

"Well, I'm letting her go. She isn't capable in the kitchen. We need a better helper for Dorothy Sevarr."

"You will do no such thing. I hired Sadie Miller, and I say whether she stays or goes."

"She's been stealing food."

Barbara's breath was coming fast, her agitation rising, as she sensed her husband's unwillingness to cooperate and his loyalty to Sadie Miller. Fear goaded her now, her words making very little sense as they hammered her husband.

"She…she took two biscuits. And ground beef. And…and tomato sauce. She…picked up the dry cleaning and kept $20. She…oh, I know now what she did. She broke my mother's heirloom watch. She also broke her vase. On purpose."

Richard Caldwell's head went from side to side, like an angry bull pawing the ground.

"Barbara, you have no idea. I could never even imagine anything—any wrong notion—with her. She's too good with that horse. She's too pure. Firing her is out of the question. Sadie Miller and her horse are staying. I… need to see this, to see what happens."

Barbara's mouth fell open in astonishment as she watched the change in her husband's eyes, his voice. He kept his voice low and even, but there was no doubt in his wife's mind that he did not believe her. He never would. And if she wanted to feed her own sick jealousy, she could go right ahead.

Defeat wilted Barbara. She faded before her husband's quiet anger in disbelief.

They ate dessert in silence, the edge of the room in darkness.

Chapter 7

DAT WAS IN A JOVIAL, IF NOT DOWNRIGHT SILLY, mood. He was singing snatches of "Old Dan Sevarr" when he washed his hands at the small sink in the laundry room, which made Sadie wince. Why did that make her cringe, she wondered? Maybe because she was still smarting from his rough words the evening before. Now she wished he'd just stop that silly tune.

The Miller family sat together for the evening meal as usual. The ordinary, everyday, white Correlle plates with the mismatched silverware and clear plastic tumblers sat a bit haphazardly on the old, serviceable knit tablecloth. The tan and beige-colored Melmac serving dishes holding the steaming food were homey and comforting, bolstering Sadie's courage.

Dat reached for the bowl of mashed potatoes, piled high with the usual little stream of browned butter coming from the small well on top. As a child, Sadie loved the taste of the dark browned butter, but now she knew that if she wanted to stay thin, she needed to work the serving spoon around it.

The chunks of seared beef, which had simmered in rich gravy as the potatoes cooked, were passed around the table followed by green beans liberally dotted with little bits of bacon and onion cooked just long enough to soften them.

"I was going to toss a salad," Mam said, "but the price of tomatoes was just too high at the IGA in town."

She looked apologetically in Dat's direction, but Dat never looked at Mam or gave any indication that he heard. He just bent his head over his plate and ate fast and methodically. He was no longer being silly.

"It's okay Mam. We don't always need a salad," said Sadie hurriedly to ease the uncomfortable moment.

"I hate salads," Reuben said loudly, with no pretense. "They're not good."

"Tomatoes aren't," Anna agreed, always a staunch supporter of Reuben and his views.

"I love tomatoes," Rebekah said smiling.

"Mmm. So do I," agreed Leah.

"Not when they're $4.99 a pound," Mam said shaking her head. "I never heard of prices like that 'til we moved here."

Dat looked up and sighed.

"Pass the potatoes," he said brusquely.

Plates were scraped, dishes passed, forks lifted to mouths, everyone chewing and swallowing silently. Mam got up to refill water glasses, and a soft fog descended over the supper table, a fog that you didn't see unless you knew Mam and noticed the change in her. The change was subtle, but it was there, just like fog that swirled and hovered.

Sadie pushed back her plate and said too quickly and loudly, "I'm full."

"Don't you want dessert?" Mam asked, her eyes blinking rapidly.

"What do we have?"

"Well, I guess just canned peaches from the IGA. I was going to bake a chocolate cake but sort of...got side-tracked. I...couldn't find the recipe."

Sadie looked at Mam, her mouth hanging open, stupidly.

"But, Mam...," she began.

Mam's eyes stopped Sadie. They were brimming with terror. Mam was afraid—frightened of her own inability to bake a chocolate cake without a recipe. Mam never used a recipe. Never. Not for chocolate cakes or chocolate chip cookies or even for pie crusts. It was all written in her mind, emerging the minute the big Tupperware bowl of flour hit the countertop.

"It's all right, Mam."

"I want ice cream!"

"We don't have any."

"We do. I saw it in the freezer."

Reuben got up, walked to the freezer, and yanked the door open dramatically.

"See? There it is!"

Anna swung her legs across the top of the bench in one little-girl movement and dashed over to peer around the freezer door.

"You're right, Reuben."

Reuben bounced back to the table, the ice cream clutched firmly in his hands.

"Chocolate marshmallow!"

Dat leaned back in his chair, grinned at Reuben, and said, "Guess who bought it?"

"You did!"

"I did. That's my favorite and Mam forgets to buy it."

Sadie winced. Come on, Dat. Did you have to say that?

As Dat helped himself to a large portion of chocolate marshmallow ice cream, Sadie's mind drifted to something more pleasant. Her horse. She knew she had to ask Dat, and now was a good a time as ever. She had to do it. Dat was kind and good to them all. He was. Surely he would allow it this time. He had said no to Paris and then relented later. So he wanted her to have a horse, right? Surely.

She cleared her throat.

"Dat?"

He lifted his head, swallowed, and acknowledged her question.

"You know the horse? The one...that one I told you about? The one that was dying?"

"Mm-hmm."

Firmly pleating the knit tablecloth beneath the table, she plunged in.

"I...he's down at Richard Caldwell's stable. He's alive. Breathing on his own. He's standing up. Can you imagine? He's barely able to, but he's standing. He's so skinny. His neck is pitiful. Richard Caldwell doesn't want him, and he said I can...can have him. Keep him."

Reuben stopped eating ice cream, watching Sadie with calculating eyes.

"Whose horse is he?" asked Dat.

Sadie relaxed, then launched into recounting the whole story to the family.

"Wow!" Anna said slowly, her mouth forming a perfect "O" around the word.

"It has to be someone's horse. What if you keep him and the owner shows up? It happens all the time. People rescue dogs, fall in love with them, name them, and one day the owner appears at their door."

"Yeah. What are you gonna do then?" Reuben asked, returning to his pile of ice cream, which was entirely too much for one 10-year-old to consume by himself.

Anna looked at him, her eyes narrowing before helping herself to a large spoonful from his bowl.

"Hey!"

"You don't need all that ice cream. It's already melting."

"Children!" Dat's voice was firm, his frown a significant indicator of their less-than-perfect behavior.

They both bent to their own bowls, but Reuben's elbow found Anna's side, fast and smooth, bringing smiles to both of their faces beneath their demure, downcast eyes.

"So?" Sadie began.

"What? You're telling me you want this stray horse kept in our barn?"

"Well..." Sadie lifted her hands and shoulders, then lowered them, along with her expectations.

"Where else would we keep him?" she asked respectfully.

Dat breathed through his nose, hard, the way he often did when he felt strongly about something. It wasn't a snort. It was more of a whoosh of air, but it meant the same as a snort.

"For starters, I think the whole deal is odd. We don't want a stray horse. How can we prove we didn't steal him when the owner comes looking for him? He wouldn't believe our story."

"Dat! You know there are acres and acres of government land without a single soul around for miles!" Sadie burst out. "The horse could have wandered from there."

"Why didn't this horse seek shelter in someone's barn? Or on someone's ranch? Something's fishy."

"But, Dat, the horse is sick! He's not just starved, he's sick!"

"Well, then, we don't want him for sure. Charlie will catch whatever this horse has.

"Please, Dat. Just let me have a box stall. Just one. You won't have to do a thing with him. Not feed him, not water him. Nothing."

"I've heard that before."

Sadie's shoulders slumped, defeat settling in. She wasn't going to beg or whine or grovel at Dat's feet. If he said no, then no it was. She had expected it all along, in a way, like an underlying riptide in the ocean that you suspected was there but didn't know for sure until it carried you out to sea. And here she was being flung about, pulled steadily along.

But she had to try one more time.

"But I'll never have another horse. Not like this one. He's so much like Paris."

"We don't have room," Dat said firmly.

Afterward, Sadie didn't know what had possessed her to give vent to her despair. Leah told her, quite seriously, it was because she was stubborn and would never give up. That thought scared her.

She had leapt up, talked loudly and forcefully, and told her father he was being selfish. Why couldn't she have a horse of her own? She had given up Paris for him and now this one, too. Why? Why?

She remembered Mam's white face, Dat's disbelief, Leah's shock, but she had been beyond caring. She had gripped the table's edge until her fingers were white and told Dat exactly what she thought. Then she turned and fled to the refuge of her room.

She had tried to pray, she really had. But her prayers hit the ceiling and bounced back down, not appearing to reach heaven at all. So she lay across her bed, too angry and upset to cry. She knew she should be remorseful, at least a little bit sorry, but she wasn't. She was glad she had told Dat all that stuff. She was.

He had no right. He had no right to keep that horse from her. There were two empty box stalls in the barn, but his excuse was always the same: If every stall was full, then where would visitors tie their horses?

How often did they have visitors? And if company did show up, they could always tie their horses in the forebay. They could even tie Charlie and put the company's horse in the same stall. There were options

Dat was cruel. He had no sympathy for horses or any-one who loved horses. He said horses didn't have stable manners, kicking against a good, strong wall for no rea-son at all, and they were always looking for a chance to run away. Well, maybe his horses did, and no small wonder. She would run away, too, if she was Dat's horse. He didn't like horses, just sort of put up with them, and the horses knew it. Why didn't he just go Mennonite and get a car? Or a bike?

Angry thoughts swirled around and around inside Sadie's head, bringing only a weariness of body and mind and no peace. She felt old and tired, her future uncertain. With no horse, what did she have to look forward to? Just work at the ranch and give Dat her paycheck, on and on and on. Go with the youth on the weekends, same old supper crowd and hymn-singings. On and on and on.

There weren't even any interesting boys. Not one Amish guy in all of Montana caught her eye. Not one. They were all too young—not old enough to date—or too old—too set in their ways, too much like a bachelor. It was all so annoying, She bet, too, that behind Dat's refusal was his own unspoken feelings about Sadie and his expectations of her. He thought she was being childish and that young Amish women shouldn't ride horses anymore. Why couldn't she grow up and get married the way other Amish girls did at her age?

Sadie guaranteed that Mam thought the same thing. She just didn't say it quite as readily as Dat. Well, what was she supposed to do? Marry someone English? They'd have a fit about that.

There had been Ezra. They had been on a few dates—dated quite awhile, actually. But it didn't last. Ezra was too … too … well … strict. He lived by the law—acting prideful and judgmental of others—and he expected as much from her. It was suffocating. So they broke up, much to the chagrin of Dat, Mam, and what seemed like the rest of the Amish community.

Sadie sat up, kicked off her shoes, then flung herself back on the pillows. She was hungry now, especially since her supper remained mostly uneaten, but she wasn't about to go down there now.

"Sadie! Phone!"

The voice calling for her sounded urgent—that same rushed tone that occurred whenever someone was on the line. The telephone was out in the phone shanty by the shop, and the person who had called was fortunate if someone heard the phone and could answer its insistent ringing. Otherwise, they would need to leave a message and wait for a return call.

Sadie leapt up, stuck her feet into her shoes, and without bothering to tie them, raced down the stairs. She grabbed her coat and went out into the starry night.

"Hello?" she said, lifting the receiver.

There was no answer.

Bewildered, she repeated, "Hello?"

Silence.

Annoyed now, she fitted the receiver back on its base and pushed the door open to leave. So much for that interesting caller.

Back in the kitchen, Sadie hung up her coat, then went to the refrigerator in search of something to eat. The kitchen was dimly lit, the gas light in the living room the only source of light. Usually, after dishes, the light in the kitchen was turned off, the one in the living room was turned on, and everyone gathered there to read or write.

She found some lunch meat, which seemed less than fresh, and a pack of Swiss cheese. Montana Swiss cheese was so tasteless, not at all like the Swiss cheese in Ohio. Mam was right; this cheese tasted a lot like the packet it came in.

She yawned, then pulled out the produce drawer. There were two green peppers and a big sweet onion. Mmm. She would make a sandwich.

Finding a soft sandwich roll, she spread it liberally with home-churned butter, and then put sliced peppers and onions on top. She sprinkled it well with salt and pepper and closed the lid.

She was just about to enjoy a big bite when the kitchen door was flung open and Dat stuck his head in.

"Phone!"

"For who?"

"You."

Grabbing her coat, the sandwich forgotten, Sadie dashed back to the phone shanty. What was going on?

Lifting the receiver, she said, "Hello?"

"How are you, Sadie?"

Sadie's heart sank. Ezra!

"I'm doing well, thank you. And you?"

"Fine, fine. I'm fine."

There was a long, awkward pause.

"Sadie, there is a practice hymn-singing at Owen Miller's tomorrow evening. You haven't been attending them, and I called to inquire why."

Sadie swallowed her annoyance.

"I...I've been busy."

"Doing what?"

None of your business, she thought, instantly on guard.

"I work full-time at the ranch now. I guess that's most of it."

There was a long pause.

"Well, tell me if I'm being impertinent, but I'm surprised your parents continue to allow you to work there."

"Oh. Why is that?"

"It's a worldly place. The way I understand it, quite a few men work for that Caldwell."

"Yes."

"Are you... Do you meet up with any of them? Do you work with them?"

"No. No, I work in the kitchen with Dorothy, an older English lady. Her husband, Jim, takes me to and from work."

"I see. Is that all you do?"

"No. I clean. I keep the big house in order—or most of it."

"I see. Do the ranch hands come in while you clean?"

"Oh, no. Never. They're working outside."

"Uh-huh."

Sadie doodled on a Post-it note with a pen.

"Do you speak to Richard Caldwell or his wife?"

"Sometimes."

"Is he trustworthy?"

"Who? Richard Caldwell?"

"Yes."

"Certainly. He's very kind to me now."

"The right sort of kindness, I would hope."

"Ezra, I..."

"Sadie, I worry about you working there. No good can come of it. You are not well-versed in the Bible, and you always did have an inclination toward rebellion."

Anger swelled up in Sadie. How dare he speak so boldly to her. He had a few faults of his own, too. She wanted to scream at him—tell him to mind his own business—but that would never do. It would be disrespectful, and she would only have to apologize later.

Sadie took a deep breath, "I appreciate your concern, Ezra. That's kind of you."

"May I pick you up tomorrow evening to take you along to the practice singing?"

Sadie's heart sank. No, no, no, she whispered silently.

"Leah, too?" she ventured, looking for a way to avoid another one-on-one date with him.

"If she wants. But it would be more appropriate if you and I went alone."

"Why would it be more appropriate?"

"I have a question to ask you."

Oh, help! Just say no. Say it. She did not want to ride all the way to Owen Miller's with Ezra. It was just unthinkable.

Then she almost pitied him. He was so good and he tried so hard to do what was right—even if he didn't always have much tact. She couldn't bring herself to say no, imagining his pleasant, open, sincere face. Why couldn't she go with Ezra?

"All right."

A pleased sigh.

"Good. Oh, Sadie, we'll have a lovely time. All the memories we share. Thank you, Sadie. Are your parents well?"

"Yes, they are."

"Give them a hello from me."

"I will."

"Good-night, Sadie."

"Good-night."

Slowly, she replaced the receiver, then sagged against the wall.

No, Ezra, we're not all well. Mam is going crazy and Dat is a stubborn mule. I don't like him much. I don't like you either. I don't want to live the way I do—working at the ranch with no hope of a future. I want a horse I'm not allowed to have.

So I'm inclined toward rebellion, am I? Am I? Is that what's wrong with me? Give up the horse the way good, obedient girls do and marry Ezra instead? Maybe if I learned to give up, I could learn to love Ezra.

She touched her eyebrows. She knew they were already elevated into that "holier-than-thou" Ezra attitude.

Sadie began walking toward the house. What should she do? Mam probably did not want to hear all this, and she wasn't going to tell Dat. He'd start planning her wedding that same hour.

"Who was that?" Mam asked the minute she entered the living room. Thankfully Dat wasn't around.

"No one."

"Now, Sadie!" Mam chided.

"Ezra Troyer."

"What did he want?"

"There's a practice singing at Owen Miller's tomorrow evening. He wants to take me."

"Are you going with him?"

"Yes."

"I'm surprised."

Reuben looked up from his drawing pad. He brushed the hair out of his eyes, then said bluntly, "I thought you didn't like Ezra?"

"You need a haircut, Reuben."

"Mam won't give me one."

"Mam, don't you think Reuben needs a haircut?"

"Yes, he does. But I'm afraid I can't cut his hair straight. It's hard for me to do that job right—the way it should be done, I mean. His hair is so straight, and... well, Dat said I should do it better."

To Sadie's horror, Mam began to cry. Not soft crying, not wiping a stray tear here or there, but huge, gulping, little-girl sobs. Sadie instantly tried to stop them by rushing over and holding her mother's shoulders firmly, murmuring, "Don't, Mam. *Do net*."

Still her mother cried on.

"*Do net heila, Mam.*"

Anna and Reuben looked up. Rebekah laid down her book, coming to Mam's side in one long, fluid movement.

"I just...feel so dumb. Things I used to enjoy are like a big mountain now. Jacob—Dat—is so terribly unhappy with me. I just don't seem to be able to do some things I used to."

Sadie sat on the sofa beside her mother, holding her hands.

"Mam, I think you are depressed. I think you need to see a medical doctor and let him diagnose you. They can give you something to help you cope with the worst of this."

Mam sat up, her eyes alert, cunning even.

"You mean drugs?"

"Yes."

"No. I won't take medical drugs. They're poison to my system. You know that. Dat feels very strongly about that. So do I. I am taking natural pills—building up my body—to cope with these new and strange wanderings. Sadie...my mind will be fine, won't it?"

Sadie sighed.

"No, Mam. I don't think it will."

"Here comes Dat!" Mam hissed, returning to her book, the afghan thrown hastily across her lap.

Sadie turned to look as Dat hung his hat on the hook. He washed his hands, then came into the living room, surveyed it, and said, "Bedtime, Reuben."

"I'm not done drawing this."

"What is it?"

"Sadie's horse."

Dat bent to look, then he straightened, laughing uproariously.

"I doubt if Sadie's horse looks like a giraffe!"

Reuben swallowed, attempting to keep his face a mask of indifference. Slowly he closed the drawing pad, put his pencil and eraser in the coiled springs on the side, and got to his feet.

Dat was still chuckling as Sadie rose, pulled Reuben close with one arm, and together, went up the stairs to bed.

Chapter 8

SADIE WINCED AS SHE DRAGGED THE BRUSH through her thick, heavy mass of brown hair. Her thoughts were tumbling through her head, so the uncomfortable chore of brushing her hair was a welcome diversion.

Why had she promised Ezra she'd go? She seriously did not know. Maybe life was like that. You didn't know why you said or did certain things, but it was all a part of God's great and wonderful plan for your life. Maybe God's will just happened no matter what.

Dat and Mam thought Ezra was truly a special young man who would make a terrific husband for her. But why do parents think they know better than you do? They just didn't understand. There was not one other person in this community of Amish families for whom she could even try and summon some kind of love.

She often wished she could express her true feelings to Mam. And she wanted to ask questions, too, especially, how deep should the feelings of love be before you know you are fully committed and ready to marry? How could you know if you were ready to spend the rest of your days here on earth with this one other person?

The Amish were expected to date for a few years before getting married. They were also expected to not touch each other while dating. Not hold hands, not hug, not kiss, not have any other physical contact. The couple would be blessed by God if they entered into a sacred union in purity.

Sadie always thought that this was all well and good. But if she was really, really honest, she wondered how you could tell if you wanted to marry someone if you never touched him. What if you were pronounced man and wife and then discovered that his touch repulsed you? Wouldn't that be a fine kettle of fish, as Daddy Keim used to say. She didn't believe every couple stuck to that hands-off policy anyway.

Sadie clasped her hair into a barrette and firmly gathered the heavy mass on the back of her head, fastening it securely with hair pins. Her new covering followed, and she turned her head first one way and then the other, adjusting the covering more securely as she did so.

Some girls spent close to an hour arranging and rearranging their hair and coverings, which always drove Sadie to distraction. If you didn't get it right that first or second time, you sure weren't going to get it any better the seventh or eighth round, that was one thing sure.

She was glad she had a new dress and that it was a soft shade of light pink. She supposed it was a bit daring, but Mam had allowed it, though grudgingly. Grudgingly or gladly, it was pretty. The fabric hung in soft folds, the sleeves falling delicately to her wrists. It made her feel very feminine and, if she admitted it to herself, more attractive than usual.

She wondered vaguely how the person who was driving the buggy to take her away to the hymn-singing would feel about the dress. When she thought about it, she was glad she would wear the black coat, as Ezra would never approve of the soft, pink shade she was wearing.

Why did she wear it? She wanted to, that was why—and not for Ezra either. Maybe that was the whole reason after all. She wanted to be who she was—not who Ezra wanted her to be.

Nothing like real old-fashioned honesty with oneself, she thought wryly.

Sadie parted the white curtains in her room. Darkness had already enveloped the Montana mountainside. But the night sky was so brilliant, it seemed only a dimmer version of daylight. The starlight blended with the moon and snow to create a stark, contrasting portrait of the landscape, as if painted black, white, and gray.

Sadie watched for the lights she knew would come slowly up the driveway. Ezra was very kind to his horse. Wasn't there an old saying—The way a man treats his horse is the way he will treat his wife.

The moon was full. It made the stars seem tiny and insignificant, like afterthoughts. Each one twinkled bravely in spite of being outdone by the moon.

The pines on the ridge seemed so dark, they were black and ominous-looking. Sadie thought they were beautiful in the sunlight, each dark bough harboring glints of light woven with deeper shadows. She loved the smell of pines, the sticky, pungent sap that seeped from their rough trunks, and the soft carpet of needles that covered the ground beneath them.

The lulling sound of the wind through pine branches was like a low, musical wonder—like a song. There was no other sound on earth quite like it. It was haunting and inspiring and filled Sadie with a deep, quiet longing for something, but she never understood what. Perhaps the song was God—his spirit sighing in the pine branches, his love for what he had created crying out and touching a chord in Sadie's heart.

From earth we are created, and to earth we return, she thought. She supposed it was a melancholy kind of thought, but it felt comforting and protective. But the sound of wind in the pines reminded her that life is also full of unseen and unknown forces.

> *Down in the valley, valley so low,*
> *Hang your head over, hear the wind blow.*
> *Hear the wind blow, dear, hear the wind blow,*
> *Hang your head over, hear the wind blow.*

It was an old folk song that Sadie often heard Mam humming to herself as she went about her daily chores. It was a kind of spiritual for Mam. She always said she felt the same passion her "foremothers" felt in that song. Women were like that. They heard many beautiful songs in the wind that no one else could comprehend. Subject to their husbands, women often hung their heads low. Many of them—Mam included—had to. It was just the way of it.

So, that's what's wrong with me. I go off wearing a light pink dress, yearning for a horse of my own, not submitting to kind, conservative Ezra because I can't hang my head low.

Sadie caught her breath. She pushed the curtain back farther with unsteady fingers, then leaned into the windowpane. It seemed as if the pines became alive and did a kind of undulating dance, but only the lower branches.

What was that? What was running, no, merely appearing and disappearing on the opposite ridge?

Sadie strained her eyes, her nerves as taut as a guitar string.

Wolves! There were wolves in the pines. But wait. Wolves were not as big as … as whatever … that was.

Sadie gasped audibly and her hand came to her mouth to stifle a scream as the dark shadows emerged.

Horses! Dark, flowing horses!

Like one body, the horses broke free of the pines that held them back, and in one fluid movement, streamed across the snowy field, disappearing again in a matter of seconds.

Whose horses were loose? Who owned so many? It was like a band of wild horses. And yet… Had she really seen them? Or was it a mirage of wishful thinking?

As if to bring her back to earth, the yellow glow of two headlights came slowly around the bend in the driveway, making steady progress up the hill.

Ezra.

I cannot imagine what possessed me to try this again, she thought, suddenly face-to-face with reality.

Her eyes turned back to the black and white serenity of the moonlit ridge. There wasn't a trail or dent, not even a shadow, in the snowy hillside to show her if what she had seen was actually real. Tomorrow! Tomorrow she would climb the ridge and see if she could find anything.

Tonight, however, belonged to Ezra.

Sighing, she shrugged her shoulders into her black, wool coat, grabbed a pair of warm gloves and her purse, and went slowly down the stairs.

"Ooooo!" sighed Rebekah, clasping her hands.

"Pink!" Anna yelled.

Reuben looked up from his book and grinned toothily. "Pink! For Ezra!"

Sadie wrapped a cream-colored scarf around her neck, adjusting it just so.

"It's not a date!" Sadie hissed at Reuben.

"What else is it?" Reuben called from his perch on the brown recliner.

"I'm going to clip your ears!" Sadie shouted.

Reuben howled with glee, slapping his knee, and Sadie ground her teeth in frustration. Little brothers were the most bothersome things anyone had ever endured, like lice or cold sores, and worth about as much, too.

She didn't say good-bye to anyone, just let herself out the sturdy, oak door into the glare of Ezra's buggy lights.

"Hello, Sadie."

"How are you, Ezra?"

"I'm good, I'm doing well. And you?"

"I'm fine."

He came over to the buggy steps, immediately holding out his hand to assist her. She had forgotten how tall he was.

"Thank you."

Sadie settled herself on the buggy seat, sliding over against the side as far as she could, hoping his leg and the side of his coat would not touch her at all.

She blinked rapidly when he stepped into the buggy and his large frame filled three-fourths of the seat, his upper arm secure against her shrinking shoulder, his thigh firmly against her coat. His gloved hand reached down and pulled on the buggy robe, tucking her securely against him, protecting her from the cold. Sweet Ezra—kind and thoughtful as always.

"All right then. Here we go. Comfortable?"

"Y—yes, yes, I am."

She was suddenly aware of how really close one person sat to another in a buggy. It was so…so intimate, especially in winter with both people covered by the same lap robe. She wondered, fleetingly, how you could keep a good and proper courtship for two years while tucked cozily together under a buggy robe like this.

"We've got quite a few miles to go, so I thought I'd be on time."

"I was ready."

"Yes. I remember that about you, Sadie. You never made me wait very long."

"Mmm-hmm."

Sadie shrank against the side of the buggy, the close proximity strangling her or suffocating her or maybe just making it hard to breathe. She wanted to yank open the window, gulp great, deep draughts of cold, winter air so she could survive.

Calm down, Sadie, she told herself. It's just Ezra. He can bring up all the "remembers" he wants, but you still have a choice.

They talked then, easily and as comfortably as possible, but only after Sadie calmed herself and prepared for his reminiscing of the time they dated.

Ezra actually seemed more relaxed and jovial than Sadie remembered. He was not so black and white, not as strict and overbearing as he once was. She actually found herself enjoying the conversation. He and Sadie talked about horses and, yes, he had heard about the theft of the horses in another county. They talked about that being a coincidence, but agreed that it was highly improbable that there could be a connection.

Sadie kept the subject of Nevaeh to herself. It just

seemed too emotional, too intimate to think of sharing the whole story with Ezra. Besides, it might open the subject of Richard Caldwell and her job, both of which he disapproved of so strongly. Better to let that one lie, she thought. No use saying anything.

As if on cue, Ezra blurted out, "So, how's work down at the fancy ranch?"

Sadie cringed.

"Good."

"I heard you had quite a scare with that horse jumping out in front of the truck."

Sadie jerked her head in his direction.

"How ... how do you know about that?"

"What does it matter?"

"Oh, nothing. It's all right, of course."

Ezra's eyes narrowed.

"You ain't hiding anything are you?"

"No, no. Of course not."

"Guess the horse didn't make it, huh?"

"Yes, he did."

"He did? Found the owner yet?"

"No."

"Where is he?"

"At ... at the Caldwell ranch."

"Really?"

Oh, just hush up now. Let it go, she pleaded silently. But Ezra was tenacious, hanging onto a subject like a bulldog with his teeth sunk into his prey.

"Bet old Richard Caldwell wasn't happy."

"No."

"Can't believe he kept him."

"Yes."

"You don't really want to talk about this, do you?"

"No."

"Why not?"

"I don't know."

"You always wanted a horse, so here's your chance."

"Yes."

Ezra laughed. "Yes. No. Yes. No."

Sadie laughed with him.

"Not exactly an exciting person, am I?"

To her complete horror, Ezra stopped the horse, making sure he came to a complete stop before dropping the reins and turning to face her squarely.

"Sadie, nothing could be farther from the truth. You are on my mind, in my thoughts, constantly. I still love you with all my heart."

Sadie went numb with disbelief as his large, gloved hands wrapped themselves tenderly around the wool fabric of her shoulders.

"If I was not an Amish person who takes his vows seriously I would crush you to my heart, Sadie, and kiss you senseless. I would. Just like in romance books. But I want to serve God first, deny myself, and pray about us and His perfect will for my life. I feel I owe that to God and to Jesus Christ who has died for me. It is the only thing that keeps me going. The Christian life, the narrow path."

Sadie had never been so shocked in all her life. Ezra! To think he was capable of such speech, of such emotions, of such...such tenderness and...love and of shameful thought...of desire.

"Now I've said too much, right?"

His hands fell away and reached for the reins while a thousand words and feelings crashed through Sadie's senses. Was this Ezra? Was Ezra able to voice these kinds of feelings?

"I've ruined it now, the little thread we were hanging onto. Or I was. You probably let go a long time ago."

Sadie was still speechless, although she managed to put a hand on his arm. For what? For reassurance? For conveying regret? She didn't know.

"Ezra, it's quite all right. It really is. I just...didn't know."

"I've had a lot of spiritual struggles. When we dated, I was obsessed with perfection according to the *Ordnung*, to our walk in life. I can see so clearly why you broke up with me."

But you're still like that.

Sadie couldn't keep the thought back, although she said nothing. She was more than happy to ride the remaining miles in silence. It was not entirely uncomfortable. She felt as if they had reached a truce. For now.

When they turned in the Owen Miller drive, Ezra began again.

"I'm sorry, Sadie, for that bit of..."

He laughed nervously, ashamedly.

"I guess I'm sorry for what happened between us. But a lot has happened since we broke up, and I've let go of my iron resolve to be the perfect Christian man. You know there is no such thing. I am a weak person and you are my weakness—my undoing. And that is the truth. I used to imagine that the more I walked perfectly with God, the more he would bless me for that and give you to me. You are all I wanted in life."

He shook his head ruefully.

"Selfish, aren't I? Do you know how stupid that is? I'll be good if you give me what I want. But don't we all sort of bargain with God in a way?"

Sadie was in disbelief again.

Ezra! Talking this way! It was mind-boggling.

"Well, here we are. I'll be ready to take you home after the singing."

He smiled down at her. From the light of the head-lights, Emma could see his genuine, broad smile containing more honesty than she could have ever imagined from him. Tenderly, he laid the back of his hand on her cheek, then let her go. She thought she heard him say, "So perfect." But perhaps it was only her imagination.

Her mind reeling, Sadie made her way dizzily into the *kessle-haus*, or laundry room, the part of the house most families used as a catch-all for coats, boots, umbrellas, and laundry, for mixing calf starter, warming baby chicks, canning garden vegetables, or like now, for containing a gaggle of fussing girls. They were dispensing coats and scarves, giggling, leaning into mirrors to adjust coverings, swiping at stray hair, sharing secrets, and squealing with glee at the sight of a close friend too long unseen.

"Sadie! Oh, it's been too long! Missed you terribly!"

Lydiann grasped Sadie's gloved hands.

"What's wrong with you? You look as if you've seen a ghost!"

Sadie laughed nervously, waving it off with one hand.

"No! You're overworked imagination is seeing things as usual, Lydiann!"

"Come with me to the bathroom! Come on!"

Lydiann pulled her along, and Sadie was profoundly grateful to be in the small bathroom with only one person until she could gain a semblance of normalcy. Her hands were shaking so that she could barely fix her hair or adjust her covering. Lydiann prattled on about Johnny, her current crush, while Sadie nodded, smiled, said yes or no at the right times, and, in plain words, acted like a zombie.

"What in the world is up with you?"

Lydiann stopped prattling, stood squarely in front of her friend, put her hands on her hips, and eyed Sadie shrewdly.

"Who brought you?"

Sadie said nothing, just looked down at the toe of her shoe, rearranging the brown shag of the carpet.

"Who?"

"The man in the moon, that's who!" Sadie said finally, laughing.

"Oh, he did, did he? I bet he's a real nice guy!"

They burst out laughing together.

"Seriously, Sadie, who brought you?"

"I told you."

"Stop it, Sadie. It's not funny."

"How did you get here?"

"All right. Ezra."

"Ezra?"

"Yes. Ezra. So what's wrong with that? Huh? Can you tell me? What's wrong with Ezra bringing me to the singing? We used to date, you know."

Lydiann's mouth hung open, her eyes wide.

"You can close your mouth any time now," Sadie said as she flung open the bathroom door and walked out, Lydiann on her heels.

The girls filed into the Miller living room, greeting the parents that were seated on folding chairs along the wall. Furniture had been pushed back to accommodate the long table in the middle of the room. The gleaming, varnished church benches sat on each side of the table. The brown hymn books were placed along the table in neat piles, waiting for the youth to open them and begin the singing.

At a hymn sing, the youth sang the old songs of their forefathers in German, although they sang some classic English tunes and choruses as well. The singing was a fine blend of youthful voices, and the evening was meant for fellowship in each other's company, while practicing new songs to replenish the old.

The girls sat on one side of the table, the boys on the other. When the boys slid into place on the smooth bench opposite the girls, Sadie looked up and straight into brown eyes that seemed strangely familiar.

Mark!

His look of recognition mirrored her own. Cheeks blazing, she looked at the only safe place—down at her hands in her lap. Her first thought was, what is an English person doing here at our hymn-singing? I wonder what the parents will think?

"Sadie? *Vee bisht doo?*"

Bravely, she looked up and calmly said, "*Gut.*"

He smiled then, relaxed and at ease. Opening the hymn book, he talked to Nathan Keim beside him and acted like a total veteran of hymn singings—as if he'd been attending them all his life.

How did he get here—and him not being Amish? He had nerve. He probably picked up that "*Vee bisht doo*" thing tonight. Imagine. He would not get away with this, that was one thing sure.

Her head lowered, Sadie stole glances, watching Mark when he was not looking.

The singing began in earnest then, leaving Sadie completely nonplussed again. Mark joined in the singing! He knew the verses. He knew the words. He knew German perfectly. But how could he? He was not Amish! His hair wasn't even Amish. It was cut close to his head.

She bet the Miller parents were silently having a fit. This would be the talk for months—that brazen, English person who came to the singing.

And he knew the German.

Likely, he came from Germany. With a name like Peight.

Chapter 9

A FEW WEEKS LATER, SADIE OPENED THE STABLE door, catching her breath after her fast sprint from the ranch kitchen. Warm smells swirled around her, sharp pungent hay and sticky, sweet molasses mixed with the nutty odor of oats and shelled corn.

Gomez, one of the stable hands, nodded, averting his eyes shyly and ducking his head beneath the bill of his cap as he pushed the wide broom back and forth across the aisle between the stables.

"Good morning!"

Sadie jumped.

"Oh, it's you! Good morning to you, too!"

Richard Caldwell was standing at the door of Nevaeh's stall, shaking his head back and forth. As he turned to look at her, Sadie saw a soft gleam in his eyes, a sort of excitement, a different light than she had ever seen in him.

"Sadie Miller, I think we have us a winner here!"

Sadie stood, surveying the dim interior of Nevaeh's stall. He lifted his head, his nostrils quivering with soft, little breaths. It was a movement of recognition and of gladness the moment he spied Sadie. Immediately, the horse made his way through the sawdust and straw to stand before Sadie. She slipped past Richard Caldwell and slid her arms around Nevaeh's neck, bending her head, murmuring her greeting in Dutch.

It was a sight that never failed to bring a tightening to Richard Caldwell's throat. The connection between the girl and this horse was amazing. That horse knew Sadie as sure as shooting, and he would do anything Sadie asked of him.

"Yep! We got us a winner!" he said, in his normal, much-too-loud kind of voice.

"You mean…?" Sadie asked.

"This horse is no ordinary one. You can tell by the lines of his shoulders, the way he holds his head, the deep chest. The more he's gaining, the easier I can tell. He's no wild mustang, this one. He's someone's horse with out-standing bloodlines running in them veins of his."

Sadie's heart sank at his words.

"Then, he's someone's horse?"

"He has to be."

"So why are we bothering to spend all this money? All these veterinary bills? The feed?"

Richard Caldwell looked out the window of Nevaeh's stall.

"It doesn't mean the owner will be here to reclaim him," he said flatly.

"But…it's not our…your horse," she insisted.

"Sadie, I told you, this horse is yours. I give him to you. I gave him to you a few weeks ago. He's getting bet-ter—improving much faster then I thought possible. Your visits, the grooming, the apples and carrots and sugar cubes you take from the kitchen…"

"I'm sorry."

Sadie was deeply ashamed. She hadn't meant to steal, just figured Richard Caldwell wouldn't mind the few treats from the kitchen.

"Don't worry about it. You can feed this horse a bushel of my apples if you choose. You're doing something right."

"How long until I can try to ride him?" Sadie asked, bolder now by his words of praise.

"You want to try this afternoon?"

Sadie clasped her hands, sighing, before she said, "Thank you! Oh I'm so glad! I think he'll do just fine. I won't gallop him—just walk him. He's still not very strong. Do you have a saddle and bridle I could use? I still have Paris' tack, but it's stored away and likely all cracked and dusty. Did you know I could ride Paris without a sadle? I never told you that, did I? Eva and I both did. Her horse's name was Spirit, but he listened to anything we wanted him to do. Spirit was a unique horse; small, but very muscular. Paris was the beauty, though. Her color was exactly the shade of honey—you know, the good kind that is done right, not that darker, brownish stuff in the grocery store."

Suddenly, realizing she was rambling and allowing her stern boss to see her with her guard down, she stopped. She was just being herself, but she felt embarrassed about her open display of emotions. She looked down and kicked gently at Nevaeh's hoof with the toe of her boot.

Richard Caldwell's eyes crinkled at the corners, and he smiled from the heart.

"You really loved that Paris, didn't you?"

Sadie nodded.

"And that dad of yours still won't allow you to have a horse?"

"I guess not. I tried."

Sadie shrugged her shoulders helplessly.

"Well, if that's how he feels, we'll just keep him here. You can ride in the afternoon or stay an hour later—whatever you decide. If that fearsome Dottie allows it."

"Don't call her Dottie," Sadie said grinning.

☆ ☆ ☆

Dorothy fussed up a storm when Sadie told her she was allowed to ride for an hour each afternoon. Forgetting the ham and beans on the stove, Dorothy waved the wooden spoon she was using in irritation. Her eyes sparked and her hair bounced around for emphasis.

"And who, young lady, is going to help me out? Who? Barbara Caldwell? Gomez? Harry? I can't cook these gigantic meals myself! At my age? It's too much! If I didn't have this good pair of shoes on my feet, there's no way I'd be here now. No way."

She returned to the pot of beans, stirring, muttering, shaking her head about the young generation, while Sadie hastily began loading the dishwasher. Guilt swirled around her heart. Maybe riding Nevaeh and caring for him here at the ranch was not a good idea. Dat didn't approve of the horse, and now Dottie was upset. Perhaps she should just tell Richard Caldwell to allow the horse to finish his journey back to good health and then sell him, or better yet, search for his owner.

Isn't that what computers were for? Couldn't Richard Caldwell go on-line or post something about a lost horse, perhaps a stolen horse, and the owner would see it? She'd have to ask him.

Another thing—it would probably be best if she never rode him at all. Once the bond between horse and rider

started, there was no turning back. Not for her, anyway.
She'd just become attached to this horse, and like Paris,
would have to give him up in the end.

But she had to try, just once, just this afternoon.

✿　✪　✿

Sadie glanced at the clock then back to Dorothy. It
was two o'clock, and Dorothy was having her afternoon
rest, which was a nice way of saying she sat down in the
soft rocking chair in the corner of the huge kitchen and
fell asleep so soundly, her glasses slid down her nose, her
mouth gave way to gravity, and loud snores erupted at
regular intervals from her dilating nostrils. But it was not
a nap. "No, siree, I never take a nap," she'd say, "Just
rest my eyes, just rest my eyes. Need to go to the optical
place and get my lenses changed."

What a dear person! Sadie wanted to be exactly like
Dorothy when she grew old. Like Dorothy and Jim, a love
and commitment eternal.

But for now, it was out to the barn.

The everyday coat Sadie wore to work was perfect—
warm and loose-fitting, leaving room for her shoulders
and arms to move. She wore an extra pair of socks, riding
boots, her well-worn pair of jeans beneath her dress, and
a warm, white scarf on her head.

Her breath came in little gasps, short puffs of nervous energy. She fully admitted to herself that she was
afraid—only a little—but scared nevertheless. Who could
know what might happen when she swung herself up on
Nevaeh's back? Horses could be the most docile creatures
until the minute someone sat on their back, and then,
WHAM!

Sadie went to the tack room, which held all the saddles, bridles, harnesses, brushes, combs, polishes, waxes, and anything else a person—or horse, for that matter—could need or want. She stood hesitantly beside the door, not entirely sure what she should do. There was a dizzying array of saddles in all colors, sizes, and shapes. She wasn't sure which were to use and which were for display.

Maybe she should have asked Richard Caldwell to accompany her this first time to the tack room. She had wondered if Richard Caldwell would be here to help her, but she knew his business, the many hands he managed on the ranch, and numerous other ventures kept him extremely busy. She supposed Nevaeh was only a small blip on the screen of his life.

What to do? She looked past the cabinets to the row of gleaming, leather bridles, then walked over quietly, her hand reaching out for the one closest to her. It looked like an average size, and it had buckles along the side so she could adjust it. Well, she had to start somewhere.

The opposite end of the room sprang to life when the door burst open, and a small man charged through it. He had a huge, black mustache, a greasy, filthy coat, and a slouched leather hat.

"Hey, girl, whatcha doin' in here?"

Sadie put her hands behind her back, the color seeping from her face.

"Ain't you s'posed to be in that there kitchen helpin' the old lady?"

"N-not now. I have an hour to ride Nevaeh, the black and white paint."

"Richard Caldwell, the boss, know this?"

"Yes. He…he is the one who wants me to ride him."

"Yer gonna need a saddle then."

Sadie's eyes narrowed as she picked up courage.

"And a bridle. And a blanket."

The black mustache lifted from its long, droopy shape to a higher, friendlier look, and a massive brown hand went out.

"Lothario Bean! Master of the Tack Room."

Large white teeth flashed below the mustache, looking for all the world like a giant Oreo cookie. His skin was the color of a Brach's Milk Maid caramel that Mam used when she made a turtle cake.

Sadie shook hands, wincing as her sturdy, white one was crushed in the huge hand of Lothario Bean.

"Ain't you the prettiest thing? You remind me of m' daughters, only whiter. Got five daughters. 'Fore every one was borned, thought sure God give me a son. Never was. All daughters. All five of 'em. Felida, Rosita, Carmelita, Frances, and Jean Elizabeth."

He ticked them off on thick brown fingers, his beady, brown eyes polished with love and pride.

"All girls. Love of my life."

Sadie smiled warmly, instantly liking this individual with his thick Latino accent.

"Jean Elizabeth, you know? She named that to break up Jean Bean!"

He laughed uproariously, slapping his leather chaps so hard, Sadie felt sure his hand stung afterward.

She laughed genuinely. Poor Jean Bean.

Lothario squinted at Sadie, cocking his head to one side like a large, overgrown bird.

"You know Christmas is coming? You celebrate Christmas? Your religion believe in Jesus' birth?"

"Of course."

"Good. Good. So do we, so do we."

"You know Christmas is coming. Me and my darling Lita, we is planning a huge surprise—a huge one! No presents this year, none. A trip! We gon' take a long trip back to the ol' country!"

He spread his arms, joy crossing his face, and the Oreo cookie became bigger and wider as he told Sadie the wonders of returning to South America.

Sadie finally glanced apprehensively at the large clock on the wall of the tack room. Twenty minutes had already gone by, and she hadn't even seen Nevaeh yet.

"I must go, please. I have only one hour."

"Oh, oh, oh, I am please to be excused. Forgive me fer keeping ya here. Here. Here. This is your bridle, and this? No, this? This one? This is your saddle."

Moving as swiftly as he talked, he pulled off a saddle, snatched a bridle, and collected a blanket. Keeping up a constant chatter pertaining to his mother's corn tortillas, Lothario swept through the door and into the stable, released the latch of Nevaeh's stall, then stepped back. He bowed deeply, one arm across his back, in a manner so genteel, it warmed Sadie's heart.

"Thank you, Mr. Bean. Thank you so much!" she said smiling.

"No, no Mr. Bean. Lothario. Lothario. Just like the romantic hero in the book!"

Sadie laughed, then went into Nevaeh's stall as Lothario Bean hurried off to do what masters of tack rooms did.

She was still smiling as she led Nevaeh out and began brushing his coat—which was still not as glossy and smooth as Sadie hoped it would be by this time.

Nevaeh was a perfect gentleman for grooming. He stood quietly, allowing Sadie to brush every inch of him, down to his grayish-brown hooves. He never pranced away or refused to budge, the way Paris had always done.

Sadie slid the horse blanket gently over Nevaeh's back, lifting and settling it down a few times to let him get used to the feel of it. His head lifted, ears flickered back, then forward, and Sadie knew he would readily accept the saddle if that was all he had to say about the blanket. Standing on tiptoe, she threw the beautiful brown saddle up and over his back. Nevaeh still stood quietly, ears flickering.

"Good boy. What a *braufa gaul*. Good boy."

Sadie kept up the soft speech while she stroked and patted, adjusted straps, and tightened the cinch strap beneath his stomach. Sliding her hand between the strap and the stomach, she checked to see if it was too loose or too tight.

Nevaeh seemed comfortable, keeping a good-natured stance. He lowered, then raised his head, but in a calm manner so that Sadie felt more relaxed, her erratic heartbeat becoming more normal.

When she introduced the bit, he clamped his teeth and lifted his head to avoid it, but Sadie gently coaxed him to cooperate. She had to remove the bit to adjust the leather straps on the side of his head, but the second introduction to the bit didn't seem to bother him too much.

Taking a deep breath, Sadie took the reins and spoke to her horse.

"*Bisht* all right, Nevaeh? *Doo gehn myeh*."

She lifted the reins, tugged, and Nevaeh followed. She rolled open the door. Nevaeh stood quietly, then followed her outside into the brilliant, white world.

They stood together, surveying the ranch before them. Nevaeh's head came up and his ears pricked forward as he stood at attention, waiting to see what Sadie would do.

Sadie cupped his nose in her gloved hand, murmured, stroked his silky neck beneath the heavy mane, and told him what a wonderful, big, handsome horse he was. Then she swung into the saddle, as light and gentle as ever.

"Good, good boy, Nevaeh."

✿ ✡ ✿

In the garage where the black Hummer and the cream-colored Mercedes were kept, Richard Caldwell stood, feeling more foolish than he had ever felt in his life—at least since he was in sixth grade and had thrown up in math class.

He wanted to see how Sadie would handle a horse, yet knew it was probably best not to let her know this. He knew she'd do better on her own. He was also curious about what this modestly dressed young woman would do with her skirt, and he did not want to embarrass her by asking silly questions.

What was it about Sadie that brought on these emotions, these feelings he had long forgotten? He was in awe of her—if any such thing was possible for the great Richard Caldwell. Could it be that this is how fathers felt when they had grown-up daughters? How would he know? He and Barbara never had children. She never wanted them.

Shortly after they were married, he knew. She had no time for babies. They cried, took up all your time, and in this day and age, who knew if they would even turn out all right?

Parenting was hard. Barbara thought it would hardly be worth the effort, even with one child.

He didn't know how he felt about having children. He guessed he always figured there would be an heir to his ranch, an acquisition he had obtained in his 30s. And now, almost 20 years later, he was old. His wife was much younger, but just not the type to have children.

He shrugged, passed a hand across the sleek surface of the Mercedes, and thought about having a son. He would teach him to ride and buy him a miniature horse.

Richard Caldwell laughed, covering his weariness with humor. What else could he do?

Surely he was not in love with Sadie. Falling in love? No. Flat out no. Sadie was too pure, too good, almost angelic. Besides, how could he defile something that reminded him of home? Somehow she gave him that same cozy feeling he had from a snowy, white tablecloth set on a cheap, wooden table that held his mother's breakfast of homemade pancakes—a stack of three, dribbling melted butter and sweet, sticky home-cooked syrup. No, Sadie was not the type of girl that brought the wrong kind of emotions to his head. Not at all.

He just wanted to see if she could handle this Nevaeh. He was afraid he would come to regret letting her try to ride. He doubted the whole situation—and the outcome.

Sliding his huge frame over a bit, he peered through the glass. Well, she was up. Looked as if she had a bit of a problem now, though. Didn't that Nevaeh just stand there now? Refused to budge. Typical horse with no brains. Should have let him die.

He slid back from the window when Sadie's gaze swept the house and garage. Still she sat, relaxed, looking around. The horse pawed the snowy ground with one forefoot.

Richard gasped.

Now he was going to throw her! She had better get off.

He had to restrain himself from leaving the garage, walking out and grabbing that stubborn horse's bridle. The beast was going to hurt Sadie.

The forefoot pawed again. The head lowered, then flung up. Sadie leaned forward, loosening the reins when he lowered his head, gently gathering them when he raised it.

Still she sat.

Now she leaned forward again, patting, stroking, playing with the coarse hair of the mane, talking. On and on, until the tension in Richard Caldwell's back caused him to swing one shoulder forward painfully.

Now Nevaeh was prancing—a sideways dance that could have easily unseated a lesser rider. He saw the leg of the jeans. The boots. The skirt adjusted in a modest manner. So that was how she rode.

Nevaeh's two forefeet came up in a light buck. Sadie leaned forward, still talking, still relaxed.

Now he was definitely going to throw her. She'd be hurt.

Richard Caldwell sagged against the silver bumper on the Hummer and clenched his fists. Why didn't she get that stubborn piece of horseflesh moving?

Now they stood quietly again.

Nevaeh shook his head back and forth. He snorted. He dug the snow with one foot, sending a fine spray back against the stable wall. He shook his head and snorted again.

Oh, great. Just great. He was a balker, culled from the herd for his stubborn behavior...running loose. No one could handle his obstinate conduct.

Just when Richard Caldwell thought he would pop a vein in his head, the horse stepped out. He was cautious, but he stepped out, the beginning of a walk.

And so they walked. They moved around the circular driveway twice. Nevaeh was still prancing sideways, still snorting, but moving along.

Now Sadie was turning the reins against the side of Nevaeh's neck, first one way and then the other, testing her beloved horse's response to the rein.

Perfect.

Richard breathed again.

Sadie's head came up, her back straightened, and she nudged Nevaeh ever so slightly. Then she leaned back into the saddle, relaxed, prepared. Nevaeh broke into a slow trot, followed immediately by a slow canter, a sure-footed, springy, graceful motion that took Richard Caldwell's breath away.

What a horse! Unbelievable! Still too thin, the hair still coarse in spots, but, like an unfinished painting, emerging beauty.

The horse and rider disappeared behind the barn, and Richard Caldwell slowly made his way out of the garage and into the kitchen, looking for his wife, Barbara. He didn't typically share with others—often keeping feelings to himself—but this time he just had to talk to someone about this remarkable Sadie and her horse.

He encountered Dorothy waving a soiled apron and yelling for her poor, hapless husband, Jim, while black smoke poured from the broiler pan of the huge commercial oven. Carefully, Richard Caldwell backed out, knowing it was up to Jim to quench that volcanic outburst. He backed into his wife and expertly steered her away from Dorothy's angry screeches and into the safety of the living room.

They sat together on the leather sofa and he told her, with eyes shining, about Sadie and Nevaeh.

He stopped when he saw the icy, cold glint in her eyes.

"You have no business monkeying around out in the stables with that pious little Amish do-gooder. On the outside, that's what she looks like, but on the inside, she is no different from any other 20-year-old looking for a husband with money," she told her husband.

On and on her voice grated, hurling selfish words, hurting, imagining the worst.

The powerful emotions that welled up in Richard while watching Sadie with that horse contrasted greatly with Barbara's sordid accusation. They were vile, worldly, dirty, and horrible—words that were as untrue as they possibly could be.

Springing up, Richard Caldwell restrained his wife.

"Stop!" he thundered.

She stopped. She cowered. She had never heard her husband speak to her in that tone, ever.

Then, he softened and opened up. He told her many things he should have spoken before, how both of them had no idea what goodness was, or purity or selflessness.

"She's like a daughter. I think I believe in some sort of God when I watch her with Nevaeh."

Barbara's mouth hung open in a ghastly way as she listened to her big, rough husband. She didn't know he was capable of talking like this. What had gotten into him?

"And, Barbara, why did we choose not to have children?" he finished, his eyes soft, the crows-feet at the corners smoothing out the way they sometimes did.

"You chose," Barbara whispered.

"I thought it was you," Richard Caldwell said, quietly, calmly.

"It wasn't."

The sun slipped below the barn, casting shadows across the opulent living room, and still they talked. They rang for coffee, for a light dinner. They turned on lamps and continued talking.

Later, when Dorothy came to the living room to remove the dishes, she saw a most unusual sight—Barbara's hand resting on her husband's shoulder, his arm around hers.

"Well, I'll be dinged. Lord have mercy. A miracle has occurred," she whispered, stepping back lightly in her Dollar General shoes.

Chapter 10

SADIE TUCKED THE LAP ROBE SECURELY AROUND her knees, shivering in the buggy, her breath visible in small puffs of steam.

Glancing sideways, she checked Ezra's profile. Hmm. Not bad.

He had asked to take her to the hymn-singing again on Wednesday evening, which was a source of some discomfort—like a cut on your finger. It annoyed you if you bumped it or got salt in it or put it under hot water.

The thing was, she liked Ezra—especially the new and improved version of Ezra. He was a good friend, and she was comfortable with him. She had absolutely no reason at all not to go back to him, date him regularly, and succumb to the love she felt sure God was already supplying.

Love was a strange thing. It could be elusive, like the wildflowers in spring that grew in great clumps on the ridges, turning into purple, yellow, and white splendor. All you wanted to do was be there among the flowers, spreading your arms and running to them through the soft, spring winds. Then you would fling yourself down on the soft hillside, your senses soaked with the smell of those beautiful flowers.

But often when Sadie climbed the ridge to pick great armfuls of wildflowers, the earth was still slick and wet with patches of snow hidden among sharp thistles. The black flies, mosquitoes, and a thousand other flying creatures either bit or sat or buzzed or zoomed toward her, causing her to flail her arms wildly between grabbing handfuls of columbine. The flowers were never nearly as beautiful as they were from a distance.

The thought of Ezra was better than Ezra himself, which was awful to admit even if it was true. He was so pleasant, attractive, a good Christian, and had oh, so many other good qualities. Her parents silently pleaded with her to accept him, marry him, and be a good wife, fitting of their culture.

Aah, why? What kept her from doing just that?

"Sure is getting colder."

The sound of Ezra's voice jerked Sadie back to reality.

"Yes, it is. It'll be snowing again soon."

"That's one nice thing about Montana—we always have a white Christmas."

"Always!" Sadie agreed joyously.

Christmas was a special time in Amish homes and had always been as long as Sadie could remember. It was filled with gifts, shopping, and wrapping packages. Christmas-dinner tables were loaded with all sorts of good food from old recipes, handed down from generation to generation.

There were hymn-singings, too, where voices blended in a crescendo of praise to their Heavenly Father for the gift of his Son born in the lowly manger. The songs of old, printed hundreds of years ago in the old land and in the German dialect, were still sung together with thankful hearts.

When Sadie turned 16 and was allowed to go to the youth's singings, the songs were never as meaningful as they were now. Youthful hearts were like that. They were more interested in who sat opposite, which boy was most handsome, who started the songs, and whether the snack served at the close of the singing was tasty or just some stale pretzels and leftover pies from church that day.

Sadie suddenly realized that Ezra was having a hard time holding his horse to a trot. His arms were held out in front of him, rigid, a muscle playing on the side of his face. The buggy was lurching and swaying a tiny bit, the way it did when the horse is running faster than normal.

Sadie watched Ezra, aware of his arms pulling back, his gloved hands holding the reins more firmly.

"Don't know what's getting into Captain. He better conserve his energy. We've got a long way to go."

Captain's head was up, his ears forward. He was not just running for the joy of it. He was wary. Scared.

"Ezra, I think Captain senses something."

Ezra's jaw was clenched now. With a quick flick of his wrist, he wrapped the reins around his hands to be able to exert more pressure on them without clenching his fists.

"Nah, he's just frisky."

Sadie said nothing, but watched Captain's ears and the way he held his head in the white-blue light from the buggy. Captain's ears flickered back, and the muscles on his haunches rippled, flattened, as he leaned into the collar.

Ezra shook his head.

"Guess he's getting too many minerals. There's a hill up ahead, that'll slow him down some."

"Are we... Are we on Sloam's Ridge?"

"Starting up."

Now Sadie watched the roadside. The pines and the bare branches of the aspen and oak were laden with snow—picture-perfect. Shadow and light played across them in the moonlight and highlighted the steep embankments on either side.

Captain was slowing his gait, the long pull up the ridge winding him. Ezra unwrapped the reins from around his hands, shook one and then the other, took off the glove, flexed his fingers, and laughed.

"He sure wants to run!"

Then she saw them. She swallowed her fear, said nothing, and leaned forward. Was it her imagination? Straining her eyes, she searched the pines. There! There was a dark, moving shadow.

There. Another!

"Ezra!"

"Hmmm?"

"I think...we're... We might be followed."

"What?"

"There!"

Sadie pointed a gloved finger, her mouth drying out with the certain realization of what had caused Captain to run.

"In the woods. Up that bank. Horses are there."

Her heart pounded, her breath came in gasps.

"Captain knows it."

"I don't see anything," Ezra said quite calmly.

"I think it would be safer for us to stop the buggy, get out, and try to hold Captain. We think...my mother saw...and I think I did, too...a herd of horses here on the ridge two weeks ago. Well, not this one—on the one they call Atkin's Ridge. It's the one closer to our home."

"There are no wild horses in this area. Here among the Amish? Someone would capture them."

Sadie opened her mouth to reply but had no chance to utter a word. Captain lunged and her body flew back as the seat tipped, then settled forward again. Sadie grabbed the lap robe, stifled a scream, and opened the buggy door on her side to see better.

Here was a figure! A crashing sound! There, oh my!

"Ezra!" she screamed. "We must stop Captain! We're almost at the top of the ridge. These horses are following us. He'll break! He'll panic! Ezra, please stop."

Ezra was holding onto the reins, staying calm.

"He won't run away. He has more sense than that."

"The top of the ridge is just ahead. There's a wide bend, then straight down. The embankment to the left is hundreds of feet down. Please Ezra!"

She had to physically restrain herself from reaching over, grabbing those reins, and making him listen. If those horses emerged from the woods, if there was a stallion among them…

Sadie felt the hot bile in her throat. Her eyes watered and her nose burned, but she had no sensation of crying. It was raw fear.

The top of the ridge! Oh, dear God.

Despair as Sadie had never known sliced down her spine, like the ice water with which Reuben loved to attack his sisters. Now she was crying, begging, pleading with Ezra, but they kept traveling around that long bend, straight toward the dreaded embankment.

A horse! The clear, dark form of a large, black horse appeared beside the buggy. Two! They were on each side of them, streaming down from the woods with hooves clattering, manes whipping in the moonlight. Horses everywhere—black species of danger. Light in color to deep black—a whirl of hooves, wild eyes, lifted heads. They pounded on.

Now they surrounded the buggy.

Ezra yelled out as he lost control. Captain broke into a frenzy, lunging, rearing, coming down, and galloping on. The buggy was swaying, bouncing, careening left, then right.

The black horse in the lead was so close, Sadie could have touched him.

"Ezra!" she gasped. "Just try to stay…"

Her words were torn from her mouth as she felt the buggy whipping to the right. Captain was running neck and neck with the huge black horse, downhill now, completely out of control.

Sadie felt a certain pity for Captain, but inside she felt terror and a horrible fear as the black horse came closer, his mane whipping, his long forelock flying, his mouth open, reaching, reaching.

It wasn't fair. Captain didn't stand a chance. He was at a severe disadvantage with the blinders on each side of his head and with being hitched to the cumbersome buggy. He strained into the collar and gave everything he had, every ounce of sense and power he owned, but it was not enough. He was so loyal, and it made Sadie sad, this knowledge of how far a good horse would go to protect his beloved master.

The black horse reached out, his long, yellow teeth extended. His jaws reached the top of Captain's mane and he bit.

Sadie's world exploded as Captain went down. There was a sickening, ripping sound as the shafts broke, parting with the buggy, and they were thrown to the left.

She remembered Ezra's yell of disbelief, her own hoarse screams, the buggy beginning to fall, and then she was hurled into a cold, white world filled with jagged pain.

Glass was sharp; rocks cruelly insensitive to human forms thrown against them. There was a roaring in Sadie's ears, and she felt as if her head was severed from her shoulders. She screamed and screamed and screamed. The pain was excruciating, but she remained conscious.

The buggy! Oh, Lord have mercy! It rolled and crashed and tumbled.

Ezra!

Mercifully, then, everything went gray. A white, hot explosion inside her head turned her knowing into a blessed nothingness. She guessed she was dying now. So peaceful.

Something hurt. It was annoying. Why didn't it stop?

Then she slipped into that softness again. It was so peaceful there, reminding her of the memory foam pillows her mother loved so much and told everyone about. If you laid your head on Mam's pillow, it was firm and soft and supportive all at the same time. It seemed impossible, but wasn't. Sadie's whole body was made of memory foam. That was nice.

Ouch.

Shoot! It hurts. Stop that, Reuben. That ice is cold.

Reuben wasn't made of memory foam. Just her. At least, her legs were made of memory foam. That was nice. Nothing hurt there.

Oh, it was so cold. She needed to stop Reuben from pouring that ice on her neck. Why was her voice so quiet? She was suffocating now. Great swells of horrible, dark ink enveloped her, wrapping her in murky, stinking arms.

Get away from me. I can't breathe! Get away.

Fight, Sadie. You have to fight this.

She was stuck on the bottom, held tight by the inky, black mud. She was clawing, clawing, gasping, using all her strength. Memory foam was better.

Just let go. Let it go. You don't have to breathe. Just lay back.

A great and terrible nausea gripped her. She clawed, swam, up, up, her lungs like a balloon with too much air. They would surely pop.

Someone smacked an icy rag against her face.

Stop smacking me, please. I have to throw up. Don't smack me like that.

She burst to the top, retching, her face hitting the side of the cold gray rock. She tried gasping for great, deep, breaths of pure air to banish the black ink forever, but the horrible retching completely overwhelmed her.

Blood!

She tried sitting up, raising herself a bit. Where was all that blood coming from? If she could only stop heaving, throwing up, but her body wanted to rid itself of all its stomach's contents.

All right. Think now.

She regained consciousness, of this she was certain. She just couldn't see anything but blood. The ink was still there.

Raising one hand, she slowly brought up her arm. One arm. Okay. She touched her face, then recoiled in horror. The ink was everywhere. No, it wasn't ink. She wiped weakly at her eyes now. Over and over, tiredly, back and forth, back and forth.

Clear the ink.

Grayish light was her reward.

Keep working.

Painfully blinking.

Why was a blink so excruciating?

Aah, now she could see white. And black. Stones. Rocks. Snow. Snow everywhere.

She reached to the top of her head with a shaking hand. It was still sticky from the ink that had stayed on her head when she burst through it. She brought her fingers down.

Red! Blood. It was coming from her head, falling into her eyes. She had a gash in her head. Oh, it was so cold.

Where were her legs? She better check.

Reaching down, she found one. The other. Was that her foot? Way out here? Turned like that? She better fix it.

Willing her foot to move, she felt a stab of pain unlike anything she had ever known. A scream escaped her, only it wasn't really a scream, more like a hoarse moan, as she laid her head against the gray, cold stone and fought to stay out of that horrible hole—that place she had been and clawed her way out.

Breathe now. Slowly. You can do this. Count. Just count and bear the pain.

Women were created to bear children, so pain was not unfamiliar or unbearable. It was certainly not going to put her back into the ink. She was afraid if she went there, she would never be able to claw her way to the top again. It had taken every ounce of life and energy she could muster to get out, so she had better focus on staying conscious.

That was important.

All right. Leg broken, yes. Gash in head, yes. Nausea, yes. Might have a smashed stomach.

It was very cold. She might die.

How long did people live in the cold? And survive? She tried to think of books she had read. No clue. She guessed as long as one breath followed another, she would live.

She thought of Mam, Dat, Leah, Rebekah, Anna, and Reuben, all at home, all happy and secure in the knowledge that she was being taken to the singing by the beloved Ezra.

Where was he?

Where was Captain?

A shiver of fear.

The horses? Where were they? Oh, that black stallion—as dark and sinister as the devil himself. But still, he was a stallion. Protecting his mares. Keeping his turf.

Dear God in heaven, my leg hurts so terribly. Please help me. Send someone to find me. I'll die out here. Wolves will smell my blood. Or mountain lions. I heard they introduced the wolves back into the wilds of Montana to manage the elk herds. Smart. Unlucky for ranchers.

Her thoughts wandered away from her prayer.

Where was the buggy? Was she at the bottom of the embankment? Or halfway down?

Leaning away from the gray rock, she tried to assess her surroundings.

Oh, that blood in my eyes. I have to stop it somehow.

Her breathing stopped completely, but her heart beat on as the howl of a wolf split the air in two with that mournful, undulating wail of the wild. One clear howl brought chills and fear of the awesome creatures into Sadie's world of pain.

Momentarily, she surrendered.

Okay, this is it. Tumbled down a cliff, half dead, and wolves will finish me. No one will ever know what happened. Posters tacked on telephone poles in town—at the post office, the IGA. Missing. No picture. She was Amish. Just information.

No, they would find her. They would!

Another howl hit a high note, joined by more voices now and more long, drawn-out calls of the wolves.

I must get out of here. I have to try.

She leaned forward, her hands clawing the snow, searching for a handhold, anything to propel herself forward. Blood spurted, a fresh, warm stream flowed down her forehead and into her eyes.

I must stop this bleeding first. With what?

Reaching up, she touched her covering, still dangling on the back of her head. Gratefully, she pulled it off and rolled it into a type of tourniquet. Her hands shook. They were too stiff.

I can't do this.

Slumping against the gray rock, she bowed her head as hot tears ran down her face. Tears and seeping blood mixed together and dripped into the snow.

It was hopeless. Maybe it would be easier to just let go now. She could go to the memory foam.

I would just let go—but I'm afraid of the ink or whatever that horrible stuff was. Why was it like that?

She looked up.

Where was the road?

She couldn't have fallen very far off the road. She heard a car but saw no lights.

Oh, yes. The buggy fell. Ezra must have fallen along with it. Captain ran away, attached to the shafts. So no one on the road at night would have any idea of the accident.

Oh, Mam.

Dat.

Somebody come find me.

She could feel her strength ebbing, going out like the tide. They had been at the beach once, along the bay, and she watched the tide come and go. Piers that were almost submerged at one point in the day stuck way out of the water later that same day. Reuben said—he always knew these things—that it was because the world tilted on an angle and spun as fast as it could go, and the water tilted back and forth with the moon's force. Amazing.

Well, the tide was slipping out for her, and she didn't know if it would come back.

So tired.

She closed her eyes.

Just for a minute, I'll rest.

The wolves aren't close yet.

No ink this time. That was a relief.

Just a white light. So white. So bright.

Stop yelling at me.

No. I said, no.

Mark Peight. Go away.

But wait, Mark was a small boy. That was odd. His hair was not cut close to his head like the English. So innocent. So ... so pathetic?

She reached out her arms.

Come, Mark Peight.

But wait.

Behind Mark Peight—a large, rotund man. He was smiling, talking, persuading. He had a whip. A real whip. Not a quirt.

Come, Mark.

That bright light was so annoying.

"Sadie! Sadie! Can you hear me? Wiggle your toes. Lift your finger."

Well, forget that. Duh, people. I can't do that.

"I think she's hearing us, but she doesn't seem to be able to do what we're asking."

"Sadie! Sadie!"

What in the world was Mam doing here on Sloam's Ridge by the gray rock? She had better get up to the road. She'd fall and hurt herself. And now she was crying, rocking herself back and forth, back and forth, moaning, mumbling.

"*Schtup sell*, Mam. *Do net.*"

"We're going to inject a solution into her veins. If she is close to being conscious, this will completely revive her within 30 seconds. If it doesn't work, she will sleep much longer."

Who was that?

The lights were too bright. She couldn't open her eyes. She wanted to leave them closed. The lights reminded her of summer daisies when the sun hit them just so in the morning when the dew was still on them.

So beautiful, daisies. You are so beautiful.

Chapter 11

THE FIRST THING SADIE REMEMBERED SEEING WAS the brilliance of the green and red in the large Christmas wreath on the wall—the shining, white wall. The Christmas wreath was much too bright. It made her eyes hurt.

Was it Christmas?

"Sadie! Sadie!"

Dat was crying. Dat never cried. Why was he crying?

She rested her eyes again, closing them gently, succumbing to the all-consuming sense of total exhaustion. Nothing had ever felt better than closing her eyelids and letting her body sink into the soft, soft mattress, the soft, soft pillow.

"Sadie, can you hear me?"

Whoa, better answer. Someone's at the door.

She willed herself to go to the door but was much too tired.

"Sadie, lift your hand if you hear me."

Of course I can lift my hand. I'm coming to answer the door. I'm walking to the door. Can't you see?

She lifted her hand. Then she opened her eyes, looked

around, and saw the Christmas wreath again, the window with the blinds pulled, the flowers on the wide sill.

She saw Mam, Dat, a doctor, two more doctors, a very large nurse, and another person with a chart. There were hums and beeps and clicks and whirs and a clear plastic bag hanging from a clean, silver pole.

"Hello, Sadie."

She tried to smile and say "Hello," but her eyelids wanted to fall down again, completely on their own.

"Hi," Sadie croaked, then fell into a deep, peaceful sleep.

✡ ✡ ✡

Sadie woke on her own, no one calling her. It was nighttime and the room was dark. There were still clicks and buzzes, whirs and hums, but except for these machines, it was all very quiet.

She tried turning her head to the right to see what was beside her. That worked okay. There was a night stand and a pitcher—a plastic one, covered with Styrofoam.

Hmm.

She turned her head to the left and closed her eyes as great spasms of pain shot through her temple. She sucked in her breath, squeezed her eyes shut to bear the pain, and cautiously opened them again.

Wow! That hurt.

Gingerly then, her hands traveled across her body. Shoulders intact, face weird, bandage on head, hand wrapped in bandage, waist and hips hurting but tolerable.

Whoops. That leg.

Opening her eyes wide, she saw her right leg held upward at an angle, encased in a heavy cast, wrapped with that white stuff where people could sign their names.

Oh, boy. She was really banged up.

She pieced together the remnants of what happened as best she could, although there was very little she actually remembered.

Snow.

Cold.

And that was about it.

Sighing, she lay back. She was in the hospital being taken care of by competent people—competent, trained personnel who knew how to operate the machines that clicked and hummed around her, she thought wryly.

She wondered vaguely whether Mam and Dat had gone home and she was here alone, or if someone from her family was here sleeping at the hospital.

She thanked God for the fact that she was alive. Her heart was beating, battered, but alive.

Himmlichser Vater, Ich danke dich.

"You awake, Honey?"

Sadie started, smiled, then nodded slowly.

"You are! Welcome aboard, Sweetie! Good to see you awake."

The nurse wore a flowered top. Her round arms turned machines, released the rail on the side of the bed, and checked the IV drip in swift, fluid motions, confident and sure.

"You in pain?"

Sadie winced.

"My back."

The nurse clucked.

"Let me tell you, Honey. We've got you as comfortable as possible, but you'll be experiencing some discomfort, 'til it's all said and done. You are one fortunate cookie, you are."

"Am I?" Sadie asked, her voice hoarse.

"Indeedy. If it's all true what they say."

"Is … my family here?"

"No. They went home to get some sleep. You'll be fine. How badly are you hurting, Sweetie? From 1 to 10?

Sadie grimaced.

"Eleven."

The nurse laughed.

"You're awake, Sadie."

She pushed a few buttons, wrote on a chart, asked if she needed another blanket, pulled up the sheet, patted her shoulder, and was barely out of the room before Sadie drifted into a wonderful, cushioned sleep.

✡ ✡ ✡

The heavy blinds were yanked open, the sun streamed through the window, the nurse trilled a good morning, and Sadie turned her head away, moaning.

Everything hurt. Everything. Even her fingers and toes. She groaned.

"We're getting you out of bed this moring!" the nurse chirped.

There was no way. Absolutely not. They can't. I can't, she thought.

"My leg is … uh … sort of attached!" Sadie said.

"Oh, we'll get you a pair of crutches. See how you'll do."

"I'll pass out."

"Oh, no! No, you won't."

And she didn't.

They sat her up, and she thought her head would explode. They held her, prodded her, stuck crutches under her arms, held the heavy cast, and watched her wobble down the hallway. The nurses talked and encouraged her, and Sadie gritted her teeth in determination. Her forehead seeped perspiration, but the heroic effort she made was evident to the hospital staff.

When they finally reached the bed, Sadie sank onto the edge of it. She felt as if she had run a marathon, which they assured her she had.

After a bath, clean sheets, and a clean gown, she was exhausted. Hungry, too, although she was too shy to ask about breakfast. Maybe they allowed only juice or ice water.

A rumbling in the hallway and a jolly voice calling out made Sadie listen eagerly. She hoped it was some sort of food. Even a package of saltines would take that dull ache away from her stomach. She wondered if this was how the poor, starving children in Africa felt. Innocent victims of civil war, suffering and dying, so hungry.

Sadie grimaced, then turned her head to watch eagerly as a small, stout woman bustled into the room. Her head was covered with an aqua-colored cap that closely resembled what Mommy Yoder wore to take a shower if she didn't want to wash her hair. The woman balanced a dish covered with a plastic lid.

"Breakfast!" she called out gaily.

Sweeter words I have never heard, Sadie thought, smiling to herself.

The woman hurried to Sadie's bedside, pulled up the tray on wheels, and plunked down the dish.

"There you go. Piping hot. Have a wonderful day!" She bustled back out, the aqua shower cap bobbing with each step.

Sadie lifted her right hand quickly, eager to lift the lid and peek underneath. Stopping, she looked at the bandage in dismay. But then she shrugged. Food could be conveyed to your mouth with your left hand if that was what needed to be done.

Removing the plastic lid was relatively easy, but unwrapping the utensils from the napkin was not.

The food looked all right—scrambled eggs, a few pieces of bacon, and an orange slice arranged on dark, curly lettuce—a bit wilted, but still inviting. Buttered wedges of whole wheat toast, juice, and milk completed the meal.

She lifted a slice of toast, eating half of it in one big bite.

Mmmm. Delicious.

She remembered to bow her head and thank God for the buttered toast in a silent prayer of gratitude. The fact that she was alive and able to eat brought tears of gratefulness—and completely renewed thanks.

The toast was a bit squishy and thin. Sort of flat. It was not the thick, heavy, whole wheat toast her mother made in the broiler in the gas oven at home

Reuben told her once that the cheap, whole wheat bread they bought in the store in town wasn't one bit whole wheat. It had artificial coloring so it looked like whole wheat. It was the same as white bread, but because it was the color of whole wheat, people felt they made a healthy choice.

He probably learned that around the same time he learned about the earth being tilted and spinning as fast as it could go, causing the tide to go in and out.

Sadie realized that she had not known these things before he told her, but she would never, ever tell him—that little know-it-all.

Quite suddenly, then, she was overcome with love for Reuben, for that sweet little troublemaker. Oh, she hoped he would be allowed into the hospital to see her.

She was filled with light, a joyous light of love for her family. She could hardly wait to see all of them! Mam, Dat, her dear sisters—everyone—even annoying Anna who always stuck up for Reuben.

Quite a bit of the scrambled eggs landed on the tray or in her lap, but she could eat enough to feel comfortable. The orange juice created a certain nausea—like a summer virus when you knew it was not going to be a good day for your stomach—so she pushed the tray away and lay back on the pillow, turning her head and closing her eyes.

Her head felt as if it was twice its normal size, but she supposed that was because of the bandage around it. I hope I'll be normal again soon, she thought.

And then the room was filled with her family. All of them.

Dat was there, and Mam. They cried, hugged her carefully, held her hand, exclaimed quietly, talked in their Dutch dialect, and asked questions. Tears streamed down Sadie's face as she nodded or shook her head. She smiled in between the tears and was grateful.

Reuben hung back, clearly not wanting to be there. Sadie called out his name. The rest of the family stood aside, Mam prodded his shoulder, and he came reluctantly to stand by her bed—self-conscious and obviously uncomfortable.

"Reuben!"

"Hey, Sadie."

"What do you have in your hand?"

Instantly, a wrapped package was thrust into her lap.
"Here."

"A package! Thank you, Reuben!"

She struggled with her left hand, trying to undo the Scotch tape, until he stepped forward saying, "I'll do it."

Sadie peered into the cardboard box, then gasped.

"Nevaeh! My... The horse! Reuben, where in the world did you get a picture of Nevaeh?"

"Jim."

"Jim? He gave this to you?"

Reuben nodded.

"I made the frame."

"It's gorgeous, Reuben!"

Anna stepped up proudly.

"I sanded and varnished it. Three coats. Dat said to do it that way."

Sadie looked questioningly at her father and was rewarded with a look of such tenderness, so much love, it took her breath away. Dat never expressed his feelings in such a way. He shuffled uncomfortably.

"You... I just thought you may as well bring the horse home if he's yours."

"Oh, Dat!"

That was all Sadie could say, but it was enough.

Rebekah cried, grabbed a few tissues, and hid her face in the white softness she held to her nose. Leah smiled a crooked smile, then gave in and cried with Rebekah.

"We cleaned the box stall and put down three wheelbarrow loads of sawdust," Anna chirped proudly.

"I'm so glad. Did you really? Someone had to work hard to clean that box stall."

"We did!" Reuben announced triumphantly. "Me and Anna!"

Sadie laughed, her throat swelling with emotion. Her dear, dear family.

Mam stepped up then, took Sadie's hand, and asked her how much of the accident she remembered. Sadie shook her head and lowered her eyes from Mam's gaze. Her hand grabbed the sheet, pleating it over and over.

"Do you remember being picked up at our house? With Ezra?" she asked, very gently.

Sadie was puzzled.

"Well, he…took me to a singing once."

"Yes. But do you remember this time—the second time?"

Sadie shook her head, her brow furrowed as she tried to remember. Then she shook her head again.

"Well, we need to tell you if you feel strong enough to hear everything. Do you?"

Sadie nodded.

With Dat leading, her family pieced the story together, like sewing scraps of fabric for a quilt. They told her about the ride, the unexplained slide down the side of the steep embankment, the long wait when she did not come home, the hours of agony for her parents. They knew she had gone to the singing with Ezra, but she never returned that night. When daylight arrived, they hired a driver and went to Amish homes asking questions. No, they had not been to the hymn-singing. No, Ezra's horse and buggy were not at home.

They found Ezra's parents in the same state of anxiety. They searched the roads between homes. Word spread fast and more men came to help. The local police were contacted—English people coming to help.

Then, they found Captain. He was hurt and bleeding, and his harness was partially torn. There were parts of the shafts, too. It was worse then, in those hours when they knew there had been an accident, but they still hadn't found the buggy.

Jesse Troyer found it first. The buggy was in pieces, smashed on the overhanging rocks. Ezra was nearby.

"Life had fled," Dat said quietly.

"What do you mean, 'life had fled'?" Sadie asked, bewildered.

"Ezra is gone. He was killed. The autopsy showed his neck was snapped. They think he died instantly and didn't suffer."

"But ... but ... how could he die? It wasn't that far down the cliff, was it?"

"Oh, it was, Sadie! We've been back to the site, and it was only the hand of God that kept you alive. You were in that snow for almost 20 hours. You were, Sadie," Mam said, the fear and agony of those hours threading through her words.

Ezra gone. He died. But how could he?

She would have dated him. Married him. She and Ezra and Captain and Nevaeh would have lived together in a new log home, the home of Ezra's dreams. He already owned a large tract of timber on Timmon's Ridge, and he had spoken of his dreams to her. He may have told her in an off-hand manner, but still, he couldn't have made solid plans that included her without knowing how she felt in her heart. Towards him. About being his wife.

Great walls of black guilt washed over Sadie. She lifted agonized eyes to Mam.

"I would have married him, Mam! I would have. I was planning on dating him. That night. I would have. And now he is dead, and he never knew that. I would have come to love him. God would have provided that love for me," she said, sobs shaking Sadie's battered body.

Then Dat spoke, his roughened carpenter's hands gently, clumsily, stroking her hair.

"But, Sadie, you must come to understand. The love you would have had with Ezra is only a drop compared to the love of our *Himmlischer Vater im Himmel*. We mortals will never fully grasp a love that great, joyous, and all-consuming. Ezra will be much, much, better off in his heavenly home than he could ever hope to be here, even if it meant having the love of his life.

"Marriage here on earth is good, and every mortal longs for that certain person to share his life, but it is only peanuts compared to the love of God. Remember that, Sadie. Ezra is in a much better place now, and you can be thankful he enjoyed those last few buggy rides with you. I'm sure he passed on a happy person because of it."

Sadie nodded, silent.

"Don't carry any guilt, please. God's ways are not our ways, and his thoughts so high above ours that we can't figure these things out. You still have a purpose here on earth."

"Yes, Dat. I do understand that. I do."

Rebekah stepped forward.

"You've been sleeping a long time, Sadie."

"How long?"

"Four days."

"What?"

Rebekah nodded.

Sadie slowly shook her head.

"Then… Ezra… the funeral…"

"Yes, he is buried in the new cemetery beneath the trees. It was a large funeral. There were many vans and buses from out of state. It's very sad. His family is struggling to accept this. They want to say 'Thy will be done,' but it's very hard to do that for one who died at such a young age."

"It had to be sad."

"It was, Sadie. I'm almost glad you weren't there."

The remainder of the visit went by as a blur, Sadie only half-listening, struggling to remember.

Why? Why had they gone down over that embankment?

Nurses came and went, but they continued talking about that night. Leah told her part of the story, her eyes still wide with the horror of it.

The doctor arrived and asked the family to step outside. He removed the bandage on her head, and Sadie lay back as he redressed the cut. Then she asked how severely she had been wounded.

"You have a very deep cut with 22 stitches. I suppose the cold saved your life, and the fact that your blood clotted easily."

"My hair?" she asked.

"Lets just say a significant amount was removed," the doctor said smiling.

Sadie wrinkled her nose.

"Bald?"

"Just on one side. Don't worry. It'll grow back."

Sadie touched the new bandage tentatively, then turned her head and closed her eyes. She wondered how long this all-consuming weariness would stay in her bones. She heard Mam's favorite expression ring in her ears. After a day of back-breaking labor, she would say, "I feel as if a dump truck rolled over me." It was a gross exaggeration, but fitting.

If anyone feels like she was flattened, it's me, she mused. That accident must have been severe.

The doctor finished jotting on a chart, spoke tersely to the nurses, then probed Sadie's stomach to check for more internal injuries. He asked questions, patted her abdomen, spoke to the nurses again, and was gone before Sadie thought to ask how long she would need to stay.

Her family streamed in to say good-bye and that they'd all be back that evening. Reuben gave her a bag of M&M's, a Reese's Peanut Butter Cup, and a small package of salted peanuts.

"You can eat these while you watch TV," he announced importantly.

Sadie laughed, then gasped, grabbing her stomach as pain rolled across it.

"Oh, I just hurt everywhere," she breathed.

Anna patted her arm.

"You'll be okay, Sadie. Hey, you know why Reuben got you all those snacks? Because he loves putting quarters in vending machines and pushing the buttons. He has a whole stash of candy, and not one of us has any quarters left in our wallets."

Reuben punched her arm, Mam herded them out, and Dat winked at her as the door closed softly behind them.

Sighing, she snuggled against the pillows and closed her eyes.

Ezra. Dear, dear Ezra.

She was suddenly very, very glad she had consented to go with him to the hymn-singing. It was a consolation— a sort of closure—pathetic as it seemed. Dat was right. Ezra had been a fine young man—a devout Christian, baptized, trying to do what was right, listening to his conscience.

Sadie fell asleep, peaceful.

Chapter 12

THE BUGGIES STREAMED TO THE JACOB MILLER home. There were brown horses, black ones, beautiful sorrels, and saddlebreds hitched to the surreys and smaller buggies. Some of them plodded up the curving drive beside the group of trees, others trotted fast, their shining coats dark with sweat, turning into lather where the harness bounced and chafed on their bodies.

The buggies were filled with smiling occupants, friendly members of the Montana Old Order Amish coming to visit the Miller family to see how Sadie was doing. They brought casseroles, pies, home-baked raisin bread, cupcakes, and heavy stoneware pots of baked beans wrapped in clean towels to keep the warmth inside.

They grasped Sadie's hand and asked questions. Kindly faces smiled shakily, eyes filled with tears of compassion. Rotund grandmothers clucked and shook their heads, saying surely the end of the world was near; God was calling loudly, wasn't he?

Shy children peeped from behind their mothers' skirts, their eyes round with wonder. This was that Sadie—Jacob Miller's Sadie—who almost died on that snowy hill. They had heard it all—around oil-clothed kitchen tables and as they played in the snow and dirt outside the phone shanties, listening while their mams were busy talking.

Most of them had been taken to the viewing of Ezra Troyer at his parents' home. Viewing the deceased was part of life, death, birth, a heaven, and a hell. The children were not kept from life's tragedies and sometimes brutal truths; it was all instilled in them at a young age.

Parents explained gently about death and what happens after someone dies. There was very little mystery. They made it all simple, uncomplicated, a concept any child could grasp. It was enough to soothe them, comfort them when they questioned with serious eyes while mulling things over in their childish minds. Then they ran out to play, forgetting, as children do.

Jacob watched his wife as her face became troubled, her countenance high with anxiety. He was afraid this whole incident would prove to be too much for her, although he didn't speak of it to anyone. Sometimes, he believed, if you hid your feelings and fears and worries, they all disappeared and no one ever knew. This left your pride and sense of well-being intact.

But still he watched her.

He was drawn into conversation when it turned to gossip at the local feed store in town. Simon Gregory, the feed-truck driver saw it on the news, but everyone knew that Simon stretched "news" to the limit. There was real news and "Simon news" at the feed mill, and everyone grinned and raised their eyebrows when Simon related another new item.

This time it was "them wild horses roamin' them ridges and pastures. They's there. I seen 'em. They said on th' news, they's stealin' horses all over th' place. No one's safe. You Amish better padlock yer barns. They don't care if you wear suspenders and a straw hat, or a Stetson and a belt, all's they want is yer horse."

"No one's horse was actually stolen," Levi Hershberger stated, sipping his coffee and grimacing at the heat. He stroked his beard. Heads shook back and forth.

"No one had any horses taken in this community," Alvin Wenger agreed.

Men nodded, drank coffee.

"How about that Simon down at the feed mill? Isn't he the character?"

There were chuckles all around.

"But you couldn't find a guy with a bigger heart. He'd do anything for anyone. Remember the first winter we were here? How many driveways did he open that year? Not a penny would he take," Alvin said, reaching for a cookie.

"Elsie baked him many a pie that winter."

Calvin Yutzy, a young man with a louder than normal voice, chimed in. "Yeah, you know what he says now? He says those wild horses could have caused that accident. He claims they're running loose up there on Sloam's Ridge."

"Nah!"

"Sounds just like him."

"I know, but if there's a stallion, and he's territorial, a buggy at night…"

Sadie was listening half-heartedly, laying her head against the cushioned back of the recliner, willing herself to keep the weariness at bay.

If there's a stallion…

He was black! He was so large.

Why did she know this?

She sat up, her mouth dry, her breath coming in short jerks. Somewhere, she had seen that black horse. She knew he was powerful. He was dangerous. How did she know?

She remembered Captain, that faithful, dutiful creature. She remembered his loyalty that night.

It would have been too bold to break in on the men's conversation, so Sadie sat up and listened, her face pale, her heart hammering, every nerve aware of what the men were saying.

"I dunno."

"Sounds a bit far-out."

Calvin leaned forward, his excitement lending more power to his voice, "A stallion will kill another horse if he's protecting his mares."

"Ah, I wouldn't say that," Levi shook his head.

"In books, maybe," old Eli Miller said, smiling, his eyes twinkling.

"All I'm saying is, it could have happened the way Simon said. What else caused that buggy to go down over?"

Sadie put down the footrest of the brown recliner. Instantly Mam was on her feet, going to her, reaching out like a nervous little hen always expecting the worst. Frankly, this drove Sadie's endurance and patience to the limit.

"I'm all right, Mam. Just go sit down."

The men's conversation slowed, then stopped as heads turned to look.

No doubt about it, Jacob's Sadie was a beautiful girl. Almost too beautiful—if there was such a thing. No one meant to stare, but they did just for a moment, perhaps. Beauty was appreciated among them.

It was God-given, this thing called beauty. A face in perfect symmetry with large, blue eyes, a small, straight nose, clear complexion, and a smile that dazzled was appreciated and admired. Who could help it?

But the women knew that beauty could be a curse as well. The girl may become completely self-absorbed, loving only herself. She may turn down many suitors, because she could marry anyone she wished. Plain girls, on the other hand, knew they were fortunate to be "asked," and they made good wives—thankful, obedient, loving to their husbands, glad to be married.

This mostly held out, but not always.

Most admitted that Sadie Miller was a mystery. She was soon of age—nearly at that 21st birthday when she would be allowed to keep her money and everything she earned. She could open a savings account at the local bank and be on her own financially, although still living with her parents.

When a girl like Sadie turned 21, eyebrows rose. Knowing she was past the age when girls dated and were betrothed, everyone wondered why she was not.

She must be too picky, they thought.

Independent, that one, they said.

She has it too nice with that good job down at the ranch. I wouldn't let my girls work there. Mark my words, she'll fall for an "English one."

No, not her, they said.

And now Ezra was gone, so what would Sadie do?

Sadie reached out to the arm of the recliner to steady herself. She lifted blue eyes to the men and addressed them quietly.

"I…was listening to your conversation. And…," she hesitated and then shook her head.

Everyone waited, the room hushed.

"You know I don't remember much, if anything, about the night the … the … buggy … you know. Well, you mentioned the wild horses."

Suddenly she sat up straight and began to talk.

"That night, there was a huge, black horse. I don't know why I remember this. I don't really. All I know is that a really big, black horse was running beside the buggy. I coud have reached out and touched him. He was so powerful, so wild-eyed, and angry. Like the devil. He reminded me of an evil force in the Bible story book when I was a child.

"And I remember, or I think so… I remember Captain, Ezra's horse, trying so hard. He was so loyal. Oh, he was running—running so desperately."

The men leaned forward. Coffee cups were set on the table, forgotten. Sadie fought her emotions, her chest heaving. Mam came to her side, her hands fluttering like a helpless bird.

"I wanted Ezra to stop. I… we would have been safer out of the buggy."

Dat sat up, then got to his feet.

"Sadie, you don't have to put yourself through this."

"I'm all right, Dat. Really."

Calvin Yutzy was on his feet.

"Hey, if this stuff is true, we have got to do something. Simon may be on to something."

"Sit down," Dat said smiling.

Calvin's wife, Rachel, holding her newborn son, smiled with Dat.

"Sounds like some real western excitement to Calvin," she said.

Old Eli Miller shook his head.

"Sounds a bit mysterious to me."

He turned to Sadie.

"Not that I'm doubting your word—I think you do remember some of what happened—but if there are horses out there, whose are they?"

"Where do they come from?" Calvin asked, almost yelping with excitement.

Everyone laughed. It was the easy laughter of a close-knit community, a comfortable kinship. It was the kind of laughter where you know everyone else will chuckle along with you, savoring the little moments of knowing each other well.

"Mam and I both saw them a few weeks ago."

"Seriously?" Calvin asked, his voice breaking.

Laughter rippled across the room. Men winked, women cast knowing glances as comfortable and good as warm apple pie.

"Sadie, tell them about the...your horse."

"Go ahead, Dat. You tell them."

Immediately Dat launched into a colorful account of her ride to work with Jim Sevarr, the snow and cold and the black and white paint. He described how Richard Caldwell kept him at the stable and what an unbelievable horse he would be, if he regained his health.

Calvin sat on the edge of his chair, chewing his lip.

"I bet you anything this horse of Sadie's is connected."

"Huh-uh."

"Aw, no."

Sadie sat back then, the room whirling as a wave of nausea gripped her. It was time to return to her bedroom, although she didn't want to. The weakness she felt was a constant bother, and she still faced weeks of recovery.

Rebekah and Leah helped her to her bath and finally

to bed as the buggies slowly returned down the drive. Anna and Reuben would be helping their mother clean and wash dishes while Dat went outside to sweep the forebay where the horses had been tied.

Lights blinked through the trees, good-nights echoing across the moonlit landscape accompanied by the dull "think-thunk" of horse's hooves on snow.

And now Christmas was a week away.

✿ ✡ ✿

Sadie sat at the breakfast table, her foot and cumbersome cast propped on a folding chair. The bandage was gone from her head, leaving a bald spot showing beneath the kerchief she wore, although, if you looked close enough, new growth of brown hair was already evident. Her eyes were no longer black and blue, but the discoloration remained and cast shadows around them.

It was Saturday, and Rebekah and Leah were both at home, a list spread between them on the table top.

"Where's Mam?" Sadie asked.

"Still in bed."

Leah rolled her eyes.

Rebekah sighed.

"Are we just going to go on this way? Just putting up with Mam?" Sadie asked. "I could spank her. She acts like a spoiled child at times."

"Sadie!"

"Seriously. She's been driving me nuts since the accident. She's not even close to being the mother we remember back in Ohio. She does almost nothing in a day. Just talks to herself. She irritates me. I just want to slap her — wake her up."

"It's Dat's fault."

"Her own, too."

"Why won't they get help? Sadie, it wasn't even funny the way she caused a scene at the hospital when you got hurt."

"Someone should have admitted her then."

"How?"

"I know. The rules are so frustrating. As long as Dat and Mam insist there's nothing wrong, and she doesn't hurt anyone or herself, we can't do anything."

"In the meantime, we have Christmas coming," Leah said, helping herself to another slice of buttered toast and spreading it liberally with peanut butter and grape jelly.

"I hate store-bought grape jelly."

Leah nodded. "Remember the strawberry freezer jam Mam used to make! Mmm."

"I have a notion to get married and make my own jelly if Mam's going to be like this," Rebekah said slowly.

Sadie howled with laughter until tears ran down her cheeks. Her face became discolored and she gasped for breath.

"And, who, may I ask, will you marry?" she asked finally, still giggling.

Leah and Rebekah laughed, knowing the choice was a bit narrow.

It was a Saturday morning made for sisters. Snow swirled outside, Dat and Reuben were gone, Anna was working on her scrapbooks in her room, the kitchen smelled of coffee and bacon and eggs, the cleaning was done, and laundry could wait until Monday.

They were still in their pajamas and robes, their hair in cheerful disarray, all of them feeling well rested after sleeping late. Rebekah was trying to think of things they could buy for Reuben and Anna and the person she got in the name exchange at school.

"Gifts, gifts, gifts. How in the world are we ever going to get ready for Christmas if Mam isn't in working order?" Rebekah groaned.

"Well, she needs to shape up," Leah snorted.

"And, then, here I am, leg in cast...," Sadie began.

"You're going to get fat."

"Another slice of toast! Did you guys eat all that bacon?"

"Well, you're not getting more."

"I'm not fat!" Sadie finally said, quite forcefully.

"You will be. You don't do a thing."

Sadie threw a spoon, Leah ducked, and Rebekah squealed.

"Watch it!"

They were all laughing when Mam emerged from the bedroom down the hallway. Her mouth was twitching as she talked to herself in hurried tones, her voice rising and falling. Her hair was unwashed, greasy even, and she had lost enough weight to make her face appear sallow and a bit sunken. She walked into the kitchen as if in a dream, her eyes glazed and unseeing as she continued the serious conversation.

Sadie felt a stab of impatience, then guilt. Poor Mam. After the initial shock of accepting their Mam as less than perfect—realizing she was unwell, depressed, whatever a doctor would call it—the girls had all decided to do their best, especially if Dat was too stubborn to do anything.

"Mind bother" was not something anyone wanted in their family. It was whispered about, secretly talked of in low tones. It was discussed in close circles, a never-ceasing debate. Was it always chemical? An imbalance?

Or had the person done it to herself by refusing to bend her will, living in frustration all her days? Who knew? In any case, it was looked on as a shameful thing. It was a despised subject.

Sadie had spent a few sleepless nights mulling over the subject. She read everything she could get her hands on. She even asked a friend, Marta Clancy, the owner of the small drugstore in town, to print information from her computer at home.

Old myths about "mind bother," suicide, and other unexplainable troubles were like a wedge in Sadie's mind. Prescription drugs probably wouldn't make a difference if it was a spiritual problem, so it had to be a chemical imbalance. So what unbalanced the chemicals? And round and round went Sadie's troubled thoughts and her frustrations.

She could never fully settle the matter within herself, so she decided it was not something she could figure out on her own. She would have to let all that up to the Almighty God who created human beings and knew everything, right up to each tiny molecule and cell and atom.

But why must we live this way?

Mam could be so normal. When Sadie was hurt and Mam forgot herself, thinking only of Sadie, she almost seemed like the Mam of old. But now that Sadie was recuperating, Mam was worse than ever, and this morning it was annoying.

Sadie ricocheted off walls of impatience, battling to keep her voice low and well-modulated. She felt like shaking some sense into Mam, then quickly realized how hard and uncaring she was being. Mental illness, depression, whatever you called it, was like a leech. It just sucked the vitality out of your life.

It was almost Christmas, and Sadie was determined to make it as normal as possible, especially for Reuben. But always, always, Mam and her condition were in the background.

Ignoring Mam, Sadie turned to Leah.

"Okay, Miss Leah. 'Christmas is coming, the goose is getting fat...'"

Rebekah chimed in, and they sang together.

"'Please put a penny in the old man's hat.'"

Sadie glanced at Mam, who was smiling.

"It is Christmas, isn't it?" she said, her voice like gravel.

"What's wrong with your voice, Mam? Does your throat hurt?" Sadie asked, concerned about the roughness, the rawness in her mother's words.

"A bit, yes. I should have dressed warmer last night. I was out walking." She shook her head from side to side. "I just wish I could get a good night's sleep. Maybe the voices in my head would stop."

Rebekah turned, stood by her mother, and said gently, "Mam, won't you go to a doctor if we take you? Dat doesn't need to know. The doctor could give you a correct diagnosis, give you the proper medication, and soon you would feel so much better."

"No! Drugs are bad for us!"

She turned her back, opened the cupboard door, and proceeded to take down the many bottles of vitamins and minerals she so urgently depended on. She insisted they were what sustained her.

A determination, a sort of desperation, expanded in Sadie's chest.

All right. If this was how it was going to be, then they would rise above it. Like a hot air balloon in a cloudless sky, they would soar. They would have Christmas, and they would have a good Christmas in spite of the many obstacles set in their way. There was the accident, the thousands of dollars in hospital and medical bills that needed to be paid, and Mam's ever-worsening condition, but no matter, they would figure out a way to have a happy Christmas.

"Rebekah, let's make a list of gifts we want to buy. Then we can talk to Dat and arrange to go shopping today. We'll see how much money we can have, then shop accordingly, okay?

"Sure thing," Rebekah chirped, sliding down the bench toward her.

"First, Reuben and Anna."

Immediately, they were faced with a huge decision. Reuben was 10 years old. He was too old for most toys and too young for serious guns and hunting things. He had a bike, two BB guns, and a pellet gun, but no hunting knives.

"Not a knife," Sadie said. "It's too dangerous."

Anna was mixing Nesquik into scalding hot milk, adding a teaspoon of sugar and a handful of miniature marshmallows. She stirred, sipped, and lifted her shoulders, a smile of pleasure lighting her young face.

"Taste this, Rebekah!"

"Is it good?"

"It's so good I'm going to make a cup for each of you after mine is all gone," she said, grinning cheekily.

"Anna, what can we get Reuben for Christmas?" Sadie asked, toying with the crust of her toast.

"A puppy."

"We can't. Mam and Dat will never let us get another dog."

"He wants a puppy."

Sadie wrote "puppy" on the list, dutifully.

"What else?"

"A football and a new baseball bat."

Sadie bent her head and wrote it down.

Leah helped, and with Rebekah's common sense, they had a list that was actually attainable. After checking the money they could use, which was, in fact, a decent amount, the idea of Christmas settled over them like a warm, fuzzy blanket, comforting and joyous, the way Christmas had always been.

"Hot chocolate's ready!" Anna called.

"You better let up on the hot chocolate-making, Anna. We're going shopping at the mall!"

Anna squealed and jumped up and down, rattling the cups on the counter.

"The mall? The real mall?"

"Yes! Let's all wear the same color... Something Christmasy!"

"We have to push Gramma Sadie on her wheelchair!"

"Let's rent a wagon—make her sit on the wagon!"

"Let's do!"

Mam watched the girls' joy, then turned her head, sighing. She couldn't remember the last time she felt that way.

Chapter 13

Rebekah stomped in from the phone shanty after calling a driver, her eyes sparkling. Leah washed dishes and Sadie watched. She longed to go to the barn to see Nevaeh and talk to him, but she knew it was best to remain in the house. The upcoming trip to the mall would be about all she could handle.

There was a general hubbub of activity as each one returned upstairs to shower, dress, and comb her hair. The ironing board was set up in front of the gas stove, a sad iron heating on the round, blue flame. Last minute ironing of coverings was always a necessary part of the routine.

After she was ready, Sadie sat on her chair and watched her mother. She was lying on the recliner, hair uncombed, no covering, her face turned to the wall. Mam's breathing was even and regular—she was so relaxed, she seemed to be asleep. Sadie decided to try again, just one more time.

"Mam?"

"Hmmm?"

"You sure you don't want to come with us? You know how much you enjoy Christmas shopping."

"We don't have any money."

"Now, Mam, you know that's not true."

Mam sat up very suddenly, her face a mask of anger and despair.

"It is true. Can you even imagine how much your hospital bill was? And there you go, traipsing off to the mall to spend money on Christmas gifts that should be used to pay that bill. And then there's that useless horse standing idle in the barn, eating up our hay and feed—but no, you don't think about things like that. You're all wrapped up in yourself and your own broken foot, and everyone pities you because poor Ezra died."

Sadie was stunned, speechless. Never had she heard her mother speak with such anger.

"Mam, won't you please see a doctor? You are not well. You would never have spoken like this before. We'll even put off the shopping trip to take you."

But Mam had turned her face to the wall and would not respond no matter how Sadie pleaded. It was like rolling a large rock uphill. You couldn't do it. You budged it an inch, and it always rolled back.

Mam had become so much worse since the accident. Her rapid decline was especially evident to Sadie, who spent most of her time in the house with Mam. She no longer did her small duties, like washing the dishes, dusting, even reading her Bible in the morning. The largest part of her days was spent lying on the recliner, her face turned to the wall.

Even her thought patterns had changed. She became obsessed with one subject at a time. The amount of money they owed the hospital weighed heavily on her, as did the cost of feeding Nevaeh. She seemed to resent the black and white horse, of this Sadie was quite certain.

She sighed and looked out across the snowy landscape as the other girls came rushing down the stairs.

Clattering! Sadie thought. What a bunch of noisemakers!

"Driver's here! He's coming up the lane!" Anna yelled.

"Where's my coat?"

"Did someone see my big leather purse with the two handles?"

"I can hardly keep track of my own purse in this house, let alone yours," Sadie said laughing.

"'Bye, Mam!"

"'Bye!"

And they were out the door, Sadie hobbling along on her crutches, the girls helping her into the 15-passenger van.

Most people who drove the Amish owned a large van so a group of them could travel together. They divided the cost among themselves, which made for cheaper fare, even if they needed to exercise patience while making stops for the other passengers. The cost of traveling was roughly a dollar per mile, so they usually planned to go to town together.

Today, however, was Christmas shopping, a special treat that required no other passengers. They knew the driver, John Arnold, a retired farmer, well and were at ease in his presence.

"Good morning, my ladies!" he boomed. "How's Sadie coming along?"

"I'm doing much better, thank you!" Sadie answered, although she already felt a bit lightheaded after swinging between the crutches.

"So where we going?"

"To the mall in Critchfield!" they echoed as one.

John Arnold grinned, put the van in gear, and said, "Waiting time is $20 an hour!"

And they were off, down the winding drive and along country roads until they came to the state road leading to the populated town of Critchfield. Traffic was heavy this close to the holidays. The occupants of cars looked a bit harassed as they waited at red lights, made U-turns, and tried passing just to arrive a minute before anyone else on the road.

At the mall, a huge low-lying structure made of steel and bricks, the vast parking lot was filled with vehicles of every shape and size imaginable. Christmas music already filled their ears as the girls hopped out of the van.

"How long?" John Arnold asked. "All day till ten tonight?"

"No-o!" the girls chorused.

"'Til four or five?" Rebekah asked.

"Sounds good. I'll be back around four."

"Thank you!"

"Take care of your cripple here," he called.

The girls waved, the van moved slowly out of the parking lot, and they were on their own. What a wonderful feeling to be free and able to browse the stores completely at ease, spending all these hours Christmas shopping!

"Listen to that song!"

"Oh, it's so beautiful it gives me goose bumps!"

"I love, love, love to go Christmas shopping!"

"One love would have been enough! We get the point!"

Laughing, they entered the huge glass doors of the mall. Immediately, they were surrounded by sights and sounds that took their breaths away—bright electric lights, Christmas decorations, beautiful music wafting in the air, real Christmas trees lit with brilliant, multi-colored lights. The wonder of the season, coupled with the achingly beautiful music in the air, brought unexpected tears to Sadie's eyes.

Christmas music did that to you, especially the instrumental music the Amish were not accustomed to. It elicited emotions of pure joy, lifted your spirits, and elevated you in almost every way. It was enough to bring forth thanks, a gratitude as beautiful as new-fallen snow, for the wondrous gift of the baby Jesus. He was born so humble and poor, wrapped only in swaddling cloths, which Mam told them was a type of long diaper that served as clothing as well.

God was, indeed, very good.

Ezra's death was still painful, but it was accepted now, unquestioningly, in the way of the Amish. There was a reason for his death, and they bowed to God's will. So be it. Heartaches were borne stoically without complaint, as was the heartache of Mam's illness.

Dear, dear Mam, Sadie thought. Her heart filled with love as she listened to the swelling strains of the Christmas songs.

I wish you could be here with us and have your poor, battered spirits revived again.

With Reuben in mind, they entered a sports store and had too much fun dashing here to this gigantic display of skateboards, then there to the tower of footballs, then back again to the baseball section. Their red and green dresses swirled, faces flushed, voices chattered—brilliant birds with white coverings.

They chose an expensive football for Reuben. They discussed at length the merits of a skateboard, but decided against it, opting for a new set of ping-pong paddles to go with the football. Reuben had acquired a mean serve, Anna informed them, shaking her head with wisdom beyond her years.

Next stop was JC Penney where the girls oohed and aahed, fussing in Pennsylvania Dutch—the Ohio version, where they rolled their "r's" into a soft "burr." Giggling, they loaded up with a new sheet set in beautiful blue for Mam and good, heavy Egyptian cotton towels for their bathroom in blue and navy. They were sure this would please their mother.

They found a package of good, warm socks for Dat and two soft chamois shirts, one in dark brown and another one in forest green.

"Who's going to volunteer?" Rebekah asked slyly.

"Volunteer for what?"

"You know, remove these pockets."

Sadie groaned from her perch on the rented wheelchair.

"Probably me, since I sit here all the time."

"Why don't Amish men wear pockets on their shirts?" Anna asked.

"Dunno!"

"Some people just sew them shut."

"Not at Dat's age. The older men should be an example to the younger ones, so we need to take off these flaps over the pockets for sure."

"'We?' You mean, me!" Sadie said.

"Why do we have an *Ordnung*?" Rebekah asked. "The English people dress any way they want, and we have to sit with a razor blade and remove a stupid old pocket from a perfectly nice shirt."

"Rebekah! That is so disrespectful," Leah scolded, crossing off Dat's name on their list.

"The *Ordnung* is like anyone else's rules. The world has rules, too, and police officers enforce them. Our rules are according to Biblical principles—about dressing modestly and being old-fashioned in thoughts and attitudes. I would never want to be anywhere else but right here in the Amish church in Montana. I love our way of life," Sadie said.

"I know. I was just having a fleeting 'rebel moment,'" Rebekah said.

"We all have them, especially at a mall," Leah assured her, draping an arm across Rebekah's shoulders.

"Wonder what we'd look like in jeans and t-shirts, our hair done, makeup, the whole works!" Anna piped up.

"No!" Leah gasped.

"Want to?" Rebekah asked, laughing.

They all laughed together, knowing it was not a priority. It was a subject to wonder about but certainly not one that brought any amount of genuine longing. It was simply not their way.

They paid for their purchases and, with shopping bags in hand, began the long walk through the rest of the mall.

Sadie announced that she needed to go to the ladies' room, assuring everyone she would be fine on her own and that she'd find them later. Leah voiced her concern, but Sadie told her no, she was perfectly capable, and besides, she wanted to buy a few things for them, too.

As she wheeled herself down the wide center of the mall, her heart beat rapidly, and she slowed down.

What a weakling, she thought. I am just not worth two cents since this accident. I suppose it will take many more days of being patient, but it drives me crazy.

On the way back from the restroom, Sadie spied an Orange Julius booth. The frothy orange drink would definitely give her a shot of much needed energy. Besides, it was a drink she loved, having sampled it only a few times before.

She wheeled over, then hoisted herself up to order her drink, carefully settling her weight on one foot. When she had her drink, she turned to sit down again, but her wheelchair was gone!

Her eyes grew large with anxiety. She gripped her drink, then turned carefully, hopping on one foot, wincing as pain shot through her calf.

Where was her wheelchair? Who would take it? Maybe her sisters had found her and grabbed it to tease her.

Looking around, she saw a young boy pushing it around and around a display of calendars in the middle of the hall.

Where in the world is his mother? He could use a few lessons in proper behavior.

Perhaps if she yelled. But no, that would cause too much attention.

People streamed past her, no one really noticing her dilemma. They were all too intent on their own destination. An elderly lady, bent at the waist, smiled sweetly but went on her slow way. She thought of asking the server at the Orange Julius booth to dial the mall office when she heard someone say, "In trouble again?"

Irritated, she looked up and into the deep, brown eyes of Mark Peight.

He was watching her, eyes shining, causing her immediate discomfort.

She shook her head.

"No."

He pointed his chin toward her foot.

"No?"

"Well, I...was in a rented wheelchair. This kid took off with it!"

"No crutches?"

She shook her head, and as she did so, the floor tilted at a crazy angle, and she gasped, reaching out with one hand toward Mark—toward anything or anyone to hold on to.

Instantly, he grabbed her arm.

"Are you...?"

She shook her head, swaying. Instantly, his strong arm moved around her waist, supporting her.

"Can you lean on me enough to walk?"

She shook her head and whispered, "I...have to hop."

Mark looked around, then down at Sadie's face turning ghastly pale. The drink slowly turned in her hand.

"Give me the drink."

She shook her head again, and the mall swam in all sorts of crazy directions. She heard the orange drink slam against the tile and Mark say, "Hang on!" in his deep voice. With his other arm on the back of her knees, he lifted her, swung her helplessly up, up, against the rough, woolen fabric of his coat.

She wanted to say, "Put me down," but if she said anything, she'd be sick. She could not protest. She could not even speak. Great waves of nausea terrified her. She could certainly not be sick.

She heard his breathing. She heard him say, "She'll be okay."

People must be watching. Oh my! What would Mam say?

Then she was deposited gently on a wooden bench, his arm supporting her. She smelled Christmas smells—pine and some sort of spice that actually helped keep her awake.

"Are you all right, Sadie?" he asked.

She wanted to nod, but the nausea still threatened to make her lose her breakfast. She lay her head against his shoulder and could feel the perspiration pop out on her face as she struggled to overcome the embarrassing weakness.

A clean white handkerchief appeared, and Mark began gently wiping above her eyes and around her face with his large, brown hand.

"There. Feel any better?" he asked.

"I think so," she whispered.

A crowd had gathered, so she kept her head lowered. She heard Mark assuring them that she would be okay, saying emphatically that if someone spied a kid with a wheelchair, they'd appreciate having it back.

Tears formed in Sadie's eyes. Another sign of this all-consuming weakness, she thought, irritated at feeling humiliated.

She sat up, swayed a bit, then steadied herself as Mark's arm dropped away.

"Thank you," she said quietly and looked up at him.

She was unprepared for the look of tenderness in those deep brown eyes, or the length of time he kept looking at her.

"Sadie, believe me, it was my pleasure. I would gladly rescue you from awkward situations every day of my life."

"You shouldn't talk like that, seeing…that…I mean, Amish girls don't go out with English boys. You shouldn't come to our singings, either. It's going to cause a fuss," she finished breathlessly.

She was deeply embarrassed when he threw back his head and laughed, a sound of genuine happiness.

"I'm not English."

"Yes, you are."

"I am?"

She sat back, grabbing the arm of the wooden bench to steady herself.

"Your…your hair is cut English. You wear English clothes."

They stopped and turned as a harried, very overweight man appeared with Sadie's wheelchair. The small boy was in tow, his hair sticking up in many directions, a grin as wide as his face making him appear far friendlier than his father.

"I apologize," the man said breathlessly, his chins wobbling, making him appear a bit vulnerable. Sadie felt only sympathy for the overwhelmed parent and his energetic offspring and assured him it was quite all right. His relief at being forgiven was so endearing—the way he thanked her politely, but profusely.

"Eric is six years old and a bit of an adventuresome kid. I lost him at the food court!"

"I have a little brother at home," Sadie said, "and I know the stunts little boys can pull off at the drop of a hat."

They smiled, exchanged "Merry Christmas," and the overweight man shuffled back to the food court, his son firmly in hand.

"Would you like to get something to eat?" Mark asked.

Oh, my!

She wanted to go with this man. In fact, she wanted to stay with him always. That truth slammed into her with the force of a tidal wave. She knew her sisters would look for her, might worry about her, but oh! She wanted to go with Mark.

"Yes. I would," she announced firmly.

Mark pushed the wheelchair up to her, then extended his hand to help her sit in it. She placed her small hand into his firm, brown one and felt a touch of wonder, of complete and honest truth, of homecoming. How could a touch convey this message?

Mark pushed the wheelchair, and Sadie sat back, her eyes shining, her strength returning.

At the food court, they were fortunate to find a table. Mark pushed the wheelchair against it hurriedly, before some frantic, last-minute shopper grabbed it away from them.

"Just bring me whatever you're having," Sadie said, looking up at him.

"Okay."

He shouldered his way through the crowd, and Sadie relaxed. She smoothed her hair and straightened her covering, hoping she looked all right.

When she spied him carrying a tray, she marveled again at his height. He had to be over six feet tall.

Why did he claim to be Amish? He sure didn't look like an Amish person. Perhaps she shouldn't be here.

He set the tray carefully between them.

"Cheese steak for me, and one for you," he said grinning.

Sadie eyed the huge sandwich and laughed.

"I'll never eat that whole thing!"

They ate big bites of the fragrant, cheesy sandwiches as onions, peppers, and tomato sauce slid down their fingers and onto their plates. Mark brought more napkins. They laughed and talked about everyday things. Mark ate his whole sandwich and what remained of hers. Then he sat back and looked at her quite seriously.

"I am from the Amish, you know. I really am. My parents still live where I was born and raised—in Buffalo Valley, Pennsylvania."

Sadie looked up, questioningly.

"Why do you look English?"

He shrugged his shoulders, then a cloak of anger settled over his features. He looked away, out over the sea of people, his eyes completely empty of any feeling or emotion.

Finally, he turned back to her.

"I am Amish, Sadie. I was raised Amish. The strictest sect. I suppose I lost faith in any plain person, not just the Amish. In anyone who dresses in a pious manner and is…" He stopped, his fingers crumpling napkins restlessly.

"Ah well. I have no business being here with you. I know what I am. You are…like a beautiful flower, and for you to be with me…It just wouldn't be right."

He pushed back the tray, then gripped the table as if to leave.

"You know that time I went to the hymn-singing? I went just to find you. Seriously. I know I can't have you, but I…guess I get a kick out of tormenting myself by spending time with you."

"Why do you put yourself down like that? Why do you say such things?" Sadie lifted troubled eyes to him.

"Let's change the subject. Tell me about the horse."

Sadie knew she had lost him. That certain trust, as delicate as a drop of dew, was gone. So she told him about Nevaeh, and his eyes turned soft when she explained why she named him that.

"You must really like horses," Mark said.

"Oh, I do. Just certain ones, though. Like Paris."

"Who?"

"Paris. She was my other horse, back home in Ohio."

"Why 'Paris?'"

Sadie blushed, shrugged her shoulders, then surprised herself by telling him every detail of her days with Eva and Paris. He listened, his eyes watching her face. He took in her emotion, her perfect eyes, her exquisite features, filing the images away in his heart for future examination.

When she stopped, he said, "You still didn't tell me the reason for naming your horse Paris."

"Maybe someday I will, but you'll think I'm silly and sentimental."

His eyebrow arched.

"Someday?"

"I mean ... What?"

She was flustered now, embarrassed, floundering for something to say.

Why had she said that? Maybe because she wanted to see him again. Maybe because she wanted to be with him. And she wanted to tell him that. Oh, how she wanted to!

And then they were surrounded by three very worried and very excited sisters. There were shopping bags, ice cream cones, soft pretzels, and tacos. All talked and ate and admonished.

Mark stood up, smiled, acknowledged the introductions, and was gone through the crowd.

Sadie finished her Christmas shopping in a daze — exhausted, but so happy that she thought she might just float off the wheelchair.

He was not like other young Amish men. When would she ever see him again? And how?

Chapter 14

Early Christmas morning, the moon slid down below the tree line, making the silver-white and darkly shadowed landscape seem like night. In winter, there were very few night sounds at the Miller home—perhaps a falling icicle or the creak of the log house, wood falling a bit lower in the great wood stove or one of the horses stamping his feet or snorting.

The Miller family was sound asleep, even Reuben, who seemed to have endless energy on Christmas Eve. He had helped the girls wrap gifts, prepared food, ran in needless circles, bounced on the sofa, slammed the handle on the side of the recliner until he almost upset it, lost the Scotch tape, spilled the whole box of name tags, and was finally sent to bed long before he deemed it necessary.

At a very early hour, however, Reuben sat up. He sat straight up—his mouth dry, his heart pounding. He had heard a sound. It was not a usual night sound of little clunks or squeaks. It was a larger sound, a harder sound. Not a distant gunshot. Not snow sliding off the roof. It was the kind of sound that woke you right up and instantly made you afraid, although you hardly ever found out what it was.

He turned the little plastic Coleman lantern that was his alarm clock and peered at the illuminated numbers. Four-thirty. It was Christmas!

He wanted to get up but knew he'd be in big trouble with the girls. That was the whole thing about having only sisters. They were bossy and sometimes downright mean. Like that Sadie last night. Whoever heard of someone getting so mad about the Scotch tape?

Reuben lay back, listening and thinking. There were some seriously big packages on the drop-leaf table in the living room, and that thought kept him awake after hearing the rumble in the dark.

Whoa! There it was again!

Reuben rolled over, pulled the flannel patchwork quilt way up over his head, and burrowed deeply into his pillow. Maybe there was a cougar in the barn. Or a wolf. Or a coyote. Likely all three.

That was the end of Reuben's night. The nighttime sounds, along with the thoughts of the brightly wrapped and beribboned packages, kept him awake.

Finally, there was the sound of Dat lighting the gas lamp downstairs and filling the teakettle for the boiling, hot water he poured over his Taster's Choice coffee.

Reuben sat up, swung his legs across the bed, and without further hesitation, dashed out of his room. Slamming the door unnecessarily and pounding noisily down the stairs, Reuben slid into the kitchen and grinned up at Dat.

"Hey!"

"Is it Christmas yet?" Reuben asked, his hair tousled and bearing that famous bunched-up look in the back. If he'd only rinse his hair properly and not sleep on it wet.

Amish boys don't have their hair cut close to their heads the way English boys do. Their hair is longer and cut straight across the forehead, then bowl-shaped and a bit lower in the back. That is the *Ordnung*, and no one ever thought to cut their little boy's hair any different. It is just the way of it.

Reuben's hair, and that messed up bunch of it in the back, was the source of many battles between him and his sisters. Rebekah, the worst of them all, told him if he didn't start using conditioner and rinse his hair better, she was going to march right into the bathroom and rinse it for him. Reuben told her if she ever dared set foot in that bathroom while he was in it, he would pour bucket after bucket of hot, soapy water all over her. And he meant it. He knew she wouldn't think about the fact that there was no bucket in the bathroom.

Dat grinned down at Reuben.

"Yes, Reuben, it's Christmas, that is, if you can persuade your mother and sisters."

"Do we have to have breakfast and the Bible story before presents this year?"

"Oh, very likely. We always do."

"May I wake the girls?"

"At your own risk," Dat said, chuckling.

Reuben weighed his options. He could sit on the couch and think about the packages while watching the hands of the clock—which was torture—or he could go to his room again—which was worse than watching the clock or thinking about packages. Or, if he was really brave, he could knock on the girls' bedroom doors, but that would bring some serious consequences, now wouldn't it?

He sat back against the couch, rubbed the unruly hair on the back of his head, and sighed. Christmas shouldn't be this way. English kids woke up and opened their packages without breakfast and a Bible story. It wasn't fair.

Dat slurped his coffee in the kitchen, and Reuben sat on the couch watching the clock, estimating the size of the oblong package and listening for any sign of activity upstairs. Finally, when the suspense was no longer bearable—like a burn in his pant's leg—Rebuen simply marched right up the stairs and knocked loudly on each sister's door.

There were muffled "Reuben!" sounds, but nothing very seriously angry, so he knew they were aware of Christmas morning as well as he was. They were just trying to act mature and not get too excited about it.

Eventually, they all straggled into the kitchen with their robes clutched around themselves and their hair looking a lot worse than his. Anna was the only happy one. Leah bent over the wood stove, shivering, and asked Dat why he didn't get this thing going. Rebekah yawned and stretched. Sadie just sat there. She didn't say anything at all. What a bunch of lazy girls!

After breakfast was eaten, everyone dressed faster than normal. Dat read the Bible story about the birth of Jesus, choking up the way he always did. Reuben knew the story of the angels, Joseph and Mary, the shepherds, and Baby Jesus. It was a good story and one he was taught to be very reverent about. This was a serious miracle, this *Chrisht Kindly* who grew up to be Jesus, the Savior of all mankind.

Reuben knew there was no Santa Claus. They weren't allowed to have pictures of Santa Claus in school, and no one thought Santa delivered their packages. Reuben knew Mam bought them and the girls wrapped them, and likely Dat paid for them. The reason they received gifts on Christmas day was to keep the tradition of the Wise Men who brought gifts to Baby Jesus.

Finally, the story was over. Dat wiped his nose, and Mam smiled as Reuben asked, "Now?" He said *"Denke"* to Mam as nicely as he could, hoping it conveyed all the love he felt at this moment. And then, he was allowed to open his packages—that wondrous moment he had been waiting on for much too long.

He tore off the wrapping paper of the first package and sighed with the wonder of it. Here was a full-sized, very expensive, grown-up-looking football that would impress all his friends at school. The ping-pong set was an added bonus he had not expected. He squealed, pounded the arm of the couch, and yelled to Anna to come here and look right this minute. Anna screeched, and they bent their heads to examine the new, heavy paddles very closely. Then, Mam handed him another package—the biggest one of all.

Reuben looked up, questioningly.

"Are you sure this is mine, Mam?"

"Yes, Reuben. It's for you. It was under my bed!"

Reuben's mouth fell open.

"But...I already have a football. And a ping-pong set."

"Open it!" Mam urged.

He couldn't remember ever having been speechless before. He simply couldn't think of anything to say, so he didn't say anything at all.

It was a skateboard.

A real one.

For bigger boys.

It had a heavy, gritty top and flames painted on the bottom. Bright orange wheels finished it off. The wheels were absolutely unreal. They spun like mad. It was twice as big as anything he had ever owned.

And then Anna got one just like it, except hers was fluorescent teal—a girl color.

The whole thing was unbelievable. Reuben felt so spoiled, so completely greedy with three big items for Christmas. It almost wasn't right.

"*Denke*, Mam!" he said, over and over, his voice thick with the emotion he felt. Anna echoed his thanks. Then they set their skateboards on the hardwood floor and tried them out through the ribbons and wrapping paper. Dat wiped his eyes again.

The girls started opening packages, but, to Reuben, it just seemed like girl things—fabric for new dresses, ice skates, dumb-looking candleholders, framed pictures that weren't a bit pretty. They giggled and fussed and yelled their high-pitched, silly girl sounds, but Reuben wasn't interested in all that useless stuff.

Sadie received a really nice saddle blanket, though. It was black and white, sort of like a zebra—the exact one she had always dreamed of for Paris. It would look sharp on Nevaeh.

Dat gave Mam a beautiful battery lamp for the bathroom, which made her smile a lot. Reuben wished Mam would smile the way she used to, but he figured when you got as old as Mam, you had to take a lot of pills to keep going. He guessed you were often tired and didn't feel like smiling.

✢　✳　✢

Later that morning, Sadie sat at the kitchen table chopping celery and onions, her leg propped up on a folding chair. Mam was peeling potatoes, Rebekah was putting together the date pudding, and Leah was mixing ginger ale and pineapple juice.

"Mmm! That ham smells heavenly!" Sadie sighed.

"Lets eat at eleven, instead of twelve!"

"Uncle Samuel's coming this afternoon?" Rebekah asked.

"Oh, yes. And Levi's."

"Oh, goody! I'm so glad. I love to sing with Samuel," Rebekah said.

Sadie smiled to herself, settling contentedly into the Christmas atmosphere. Thank God, Mam appeared so normal—making dinner and enthusiastic as always. For Reuben and Anna, it meant so much for this special day.

"When I get married, I want date pudding on my *eck* in a trifle bowl just like this one," Rebekah announced, putting the final layer of whipped cream on top. Standing back, she admired her date pudding.

"That bowl was on my *eck*," Mam said, putting down her paring knife to go to Rebekah's side.

"Really, Mam?"

"Yes, it was. It's beautiful, isn't it? And I was so in love," she sighed.

Date pudding was the best thing ever. Once you started eating it, you couldn't stop until you were quite miserable. That was true. First you baked a rich, moist cake filled with dates and walnuts. Then you cooked a sauce with butter and brown sugar and chilled it in the refrigerator overnight. The next day you assembled this sticky, sweet cake in layers with the sauce and whipped cream.

Next, you crumbled the cake in the bottom of the clear, glass trifle bowl. Then you carefully spooned the rich, brown sauce over it, spreading it evenly. This was followed by a generous layer of sweet whipped cream. Then the layers were repeated.

Some people used Cool Whip, which was all right, but Mam insisted on the real thing. Whipped cream was just better.

Sadie thought about her own *eck*—that highly-honored corner table where the bride and groom sat after they were married in the three-hour service beforehand. It was a wondrous thing, that *eck*.

The designated corner was the place where long tables, set hastily against two walls, met. The bride and groom sat on folding chairs with the two couples who were members of the bridal party. The bride's best table linens were used on the *eck*, as were her china, stemware, and silverware. These were gifts from the groom while they were dating. It was all color-coordinated, and each bride dreamed of her own *eck* as her teenage years went by.

Sadie was no different than any other young Amish girl. She thought about marriage, her wedding day, the guests, and the food, much the same as everyone else. There simply was no one for her to marry.

A career was out of the question. Being raised in an Amish home, she had only one choice, really. Well, no, two: to marry or not to marry. But being a wife and mother was the highest honor and the one goal in every young girl's life. If you didn't marry, you could teach school or get a job cooking or cleaning or working in a store or maybe caring for someone who was sick or disabled.

Sadie sighed as she dropped the small bits of celery and onion into a bowl.

"Here, Mam. This is ready for the stuffing," she said.

With the girls' help, the stuffing was made and put in the oven, and the potatoes were peeled and put on the gas burner to boil. Rebekah bent over to retrieve a head of cabbage from the crisper drawer in the refrigerator while Sadie sat tapping her fingers on the wooden table top, absentmindedly humming the same Christmas tune over and over.

"Stop that, Sadie. You're driving me nuts!" Leah warned.

"Testy, testy," Rebekah said.

"Hey, what am I supposed to do? I have to sit here or get around on crutches, which isn't real easy in a kitchen filled with three other people."

"You could get your wheelchair and set the table," Mam said.

So Sadie did. That wasn't easy either.

Someone had to get the plates from the hutch cupboard. Then she had to balance them on her lap as she wheeled into the dining area. She opened the oak chest containing the silverware that Dat had given Mam before they were married. She laid each piece carefully side by side on the tablecloth beside the china plates. The whole task took about twice as long as normal, leaving Sadie in no mood to seriously pitch in and help with the rest of Christmas dinner.

By eleven, the table was set with Mam's best tablecloth and her Christmas china, which had an outline of gold along the plates' rims with a circle of holly berries surrounding the center. They used the green stemware Mam had purchased at the Dollar General. It was exactly one dollar for one pretty glass tumbler. It was all very pretty and so grand and Christmasy, with the red and green napkins completing the picture.

The whole house smelled of the salty ham cooking in its own juices in the agate roaster in the oven of the gas stove. They mashed the potatoes with the hand-masher. Rebekah and Leah added lots of butter and salt, and then took turns pouring in hot milk until the potatoes reached the proper consistency.

Mam made the rich gravy with broth from the ham, adding a mixture of flour, cornstarch, and water. She whisked in the white liquid carefully until the gravy was thick and bubbly.

They took the pan of stuffing out of the oven and spooned it into a serving dish. The edges were brown, crisp, and salty with bits of onion and celery clinging to the sides. There was a dish of corn, yellow and succulent, with a square of butter melting so fast that no one was really sure it was there in the first place. They had grated the cabbage on a hand-held grater and mixed it with Miracle Whip, salt, sugar, and vinegar. They placed bits of red and green peppers on top for Christmas. A Tupperware container of fruit salad held maraschino cherries and kiwis, mixed in just for their colors.

The layered jello, called Christmas Salad, was made with lime green jello on the bottom, a mixture of cream cheese, milk, and Knox gelatin in the middle, and red jello on the top. It was the most perfect thing on the table—all red, green, and white and cut in shimmering squares. It looked so festive sitting on a small dish beside the green glasses.

Rebekah had baked a Christmas cake made of apples, nuts, raisins, and dates. The heavy cake, so rich and moist with a thick layer of cream cheese frosting, stood on Mam's cake stand with the heavy glass cover.

Mam had not baked the usual pecan pies, which no one seemed to notice, and certainly no one commented on if they did. She was doing as well as she could. Sadie knew she was using up all her reserve energy and determination to keep going, joining the Christmas spirit for Reuben's and Anna's sakes.

After everything was put on the table, they all gathered around, slid into their chairs, and bowed their heads for a silent prayer of thanksgiving for all the food and the gift of the Baby Jesus.

They ate with enormous appetites, enjoying the rich home-cooked food unreservedly. After all, Christmas came just once a year.

Dat proclaimed the meal the best ever. He said the ham was similar to the kind he ate as a child when they butchered their own hogs and cured their own meat. He couldn't believe this was from IGA. Mam beamed with satisfaction, her cheeks flushed with pleasure.

Reuben just grinned and grinned, eating so much it was alarming. Sadie asked him where all the food was going, and he shrugged his shoulders and grinned some more.

Reaching for his second whole wheat dinner roll, he spread it liberally with butter. Then he turned the plastic honey bear upside down and squeezed with both hands until a river of honey spread its golden stickiness across the snow-white tablecloth. That was no problem for Reuben who lowered his head to lick it off the tablecloth before being firmly reminded about good table manners. Dat's gray eyebrows lowered in that certain way that drew instant respect.

Sadie ate two squares of Christmas Salad, ran a finger inside the belt of her dress, then eyed the date pudding.

"Go ahead," Leah laughed, her blue eyes sparkling.

Sadie caught her eye, knowing Leah had seen that exploratory search for a measurement of her waistline.

They threw back their heads and had a good old, little-girl belly laugh, one that floated up through the region of their stomachs and felt as delicious as all the good food. It was truly Christmas, a time of celebration and joy, a special time of happiness when families remembered Christ's birth and were made glad, as in times of old.

They lingered around the table and made plans for the New Year festivities. That was the evening they had reserved for Richard Caldwell and his wife, Barbara. The Caldwells had asked for an invitation, never having visited an Amish home before. So the Miller family talked and planned ahead, knowing they would try and do their best in cooking and baking the old-fashioned way.

Reuben said Richard Caldwell was only a human being, same as everybody else, so why would you have to go to all that trouble?

Sadie wanted to invite Jim and Dorothy, too, but it was a bit questionable whether Dorothy would be comfortable with Richard Caldwell, him being the boss and all.

Finally, the dishes were done, leftovers were put away, and snacks were set out on the counter top for all the families coming to spend the afternoon singing the German Christmas hymns. There was Chex Mix, Rice Krispie Treats, chocolate-covered peanut butter crackers, homemade chocolate fudge, peanut butter fudge, and all kinds of fruit. Vegetables and dip were arranged in a colorful display.

They had just finished when the first buggy came up the driveway, the spirited horse spraying chunks of snow with his hooves. Smiling faces entered and were greeted warmly. Soon the German hymnbooks were brought out, and Uncle Samuel's beautiful, rich baritone filled the room with song. They sang *"Shtille Nacht, Heilige Nacht,"* the women's alto voices blending perfectly. They followed that with *"Freue Dich Velt."* When the volume increased, chills went up Sadie's arms.

What a wonderful old song! The words were a clear message of joy; the assurance the Lord had come and all heaven and earth were to rejoice. It was so real and so uplifting, Sadie rose above the worry about Mam, the sadness of Ezra's sudden death, the horror of the accident...just everything. God was in his heaven. Yes, he was! He loved all mankind enough to send the Christ Child, and for all lowly sinners, it was enough.

Sadie was ashamed of the tears that sprang to her eyes, so she got her crutches and left the room, her face turned away. They would think she was crying about Ezra, perhaps, or that she had "nerve trouble" since the accident, so it was best to keep the tears hidden.

The kitchen door banged open, depositing Reuben and three of his cousins in a wet, breathless, fast-moving, fast-talking bundle on the long, rectangular carpet inside.

"Sadie!"

She stopped, leaned on her crutches, and raised one eyebrow.

"Do you absolutely have to be so noisy?"

"Hey, Sadie! Did someone borrow Nevaeh? He's not in his stall! He's not in the pasture! Where is he? Did Richard Caldwell come to get him?"

Sadie leaned forward, looking sharply at Reuben.

"Reuben, stop it! It's not funny. Of course Nevaeh's out there somewhere. You know he is."

"He's not! Uncle Levi's and Samuel's horses are tied in his stall. Charlie is in his own. No horses were left in the pasture."

"Was his gate broken down? Does it look as if he got out?" Sadie asked, her voice rising to a shrill squeak.

Reuben shook his head, snow spraying from his dark blue beanie.

"No! He isn't around anywhere."

"Go ask Samuel and Levi if he was there when they arrived."

The singing soon stopped, and Sadie listened as she heard the boys relate their news. She heard Dat exclaim, "He was there this morning. I know he was!"

"Well, he's not now."

The men all trooped out to the kitchen, grabbed their coats and hats, pulled on heavy gloves and boots, and went to the barn. Sadie hobbled over to the kitchen door, her heart banging against her ribs, waiting, watching anxiously for the men's return.

They were gone for a very long time, an eternity it seemed. Then they appeared, talking and waving their arms toward the phone shanty.

Now what?

Dat came out, spoke a few words, then hurried to the house. Sadie stepped aside as the door was flung open.

"Get your coat on. There's a phone call for you. Think you can make it? It's a guy."

"What?"

"Hurry, Sadie. It's going to take you awhile. Reuben, you go with her, make sure she's okay"

Sadie looked up, "Nevaeh?"

"He's not around. We're going to search the pasture."

Rebekah and Leah looked on worriedly as they helped Sadie into her heavy, wool coat. They watched from the dining room window as she swung herself between the crutches through the ice and snow. They didn't relax until the door to the phone shanty was closed.

Sadie picked up the black receiver, "Hello?"

"Merry Christmas, Sadie."

All the air left her lungs when she heard the unmistakably masculine voice of Mark Peight.

Chapter 15

"I..." WHOOSH, HER BREATH LEFT HER COMPLETELY on its own accord.

"Are you there?" the deep voice queried.

"Yes, yes, I'm here. Just...catching my breath."

"Oh, that's right, you would have to go to the phone on your crutches."

"Yes."

Just "yes." Why couldn't she say something wittier, something a bit more knowledgeable, something smarter than just "yes"?

"I'm calling to see how you are doing. You sort of scared me there at the mall. Do you feel better?"

"Yes."

There I go again. Yes. Why can't I say something more?

Her heart was beating so hard and fast that there was the sound of the ocean in her ears.

"Did you know there's a skating party at Dan Detweilers? On Friday evening?"

"Leah told me, but I can't go with crutches."

"When does your cast come off?"

"At least another two weeks."

"I … what if I came to pick you up? You could stay in the buggy and watch for awhile. Your sisters could join us."

"Mark, seriously, do you even have a horse and buggy? Where do you live? And are you Amish? For real? I mean, I don't wish to sound ignorant, but suddenly you appear out of nowhere, not looking Amish like the rest of the young men in this area, and … well…"

She was floundering now, but she needed to know.

He laughed a deep, comfortable, rolling laugh.

Oh, she could imagine his face. She remembered every line, even the way little pleats appeared beside his brown, brown eyes when he smiled. And his teeth were so white and perfect. She could look at his face for a hundred years and never tire of it.

That thought struck her, slammed into her knowing, and she clutched the receiver tightly to steady herself. These thoughts were absolutely ridiculous.

He was talking again. She needed to hear what he was saying.

"Sadie, my life is a long story. I suppose to you, I'm a bit of a mystery."

He paused.

She pulled her coat down over her lap, shivered.

"All right, I'll tell you what I really want to say. I would love to sit somewhere with you and talk for a very long time. Sadie, I'm almost 30 years old. And to think of … well, I went to the hymn-singing just to see you."

Sadie watched the afternoon light on an icicle through the phone shanty window. She straightened her covering and cleared her throat.

"I mean, I don't really want to join the youth group.

I'm too old. I've been through too much to...I don't know." His voice fell away.

And now she could not think of a word to say. Not one word.

"I guess I'm sort of messing up this conversation, Sadie."

She loved the way he said "Sadie," sort of dragging out the "e." Her name became something fabulous when he said it, not just plain old Sadie.

"No, no, not at all. Are you really 30 years old?"

"Twenty-nine. I'll be 30 in May."

"Wow! That's old. A lot of young men have four or five children by that time."

He laughed again, that rolling, comfortable sound.

"Yeah. Well, not me."

"I guess not."

"How old are you?

"Twenty."

"That's good. At least you're not 16."

"Yes."

"So...if I come by with my horse and buggy, which I happen to have, will you go with me to the skating party?"

Sadie searched frantically for the proper answer. Of course she would go! But what would people say? Who was he really? She hardly knew one thing about him, other than his astounding face. Well, not just that, everything about him was astounding. From the moment he had stepped out of Fred's truck, she had been speechless and dumb around him. How could she sit in a buggy with him? She'd prattle away like a child, or else have nothing to say. Just yes.

"I better not go."

"Why?"

"Well, I'm...not well, really."

"Okay"

Don't hang up. Don't. She lurched into desperation.

"Mark, Nevaeh is missing. We...our uncles are here and they put their horses in the barn, and now Nevaeh is not in his stall. We have no idea where he is. And Mark, have you heard of the wild horses—the ones that presumably are running the ridges? The state game lands? I'm just afraid, I mean, what could possibly have happened to Nevaeh? He was in his stall this morning. Dat said he was. There is no gate broken down, no sign of a scuffle, nothing. I'm so terribly worried."

"Do you want me to come over?"

"Well, where are you? What would Dat say? I mean..."

"I'll be over."

Click.

Sadie held the receiver away from her ear, panic rising in her throat.

Mark! No! You can't come here. Nobody knows you. You're English, sort of.

Sadie sat and stared out the window at the day's disappearing light. Her hair was a mess, her nose a shiny red, no doubt, and she had stuffed herself with all that food! Groaning inwardly she got up, swung herself through the snow, and wondered how long before he got there.

Yanking open the door to the house, she hobbled through, banged her crutches against the wall, and shrugged out of her coat without bothering to hang it up. Now if she could just get upstairs without anyone noticing, she'd be all right.

"Sadie! Who was on the phone?" This from Dat.

She kept going, hoping he wouldn't ask again.

"Sadie! Come here. Who was on the phone?"

Resignedly, her shoulders slumped, she turned obediently into the living room.

"It was Mark Peight."

"Who?"

Her uncles stopped drinking their coffee, a chocolate-covered Ritz cracker held in midair.

"Just someone I know. He's coming over to help look for Nevaeh."

"He doesn't need to. We'll find him. We're going to head out soon."

"Well, he says he's coming over."

The men resumed their talking and she turned, grinding her teeth in frustration.

Parents! Nosey old things. Why did Dat have to act so *grosfeelich* in front of Samuel and Levi?

Panting, she reached the top of the stairs. Rebekah and Leah were in their rooms unpacking Christmas gifts. Sadie decided not to say anything—just go to her room and fix her hair.

Which dress?

Oh, my.

Just leave this one on? No, she spilled gravy on the front. Red? No, she had worn it at the mall. Blue? She had a gazillion blue dresses. Green? She looked ugly in green. Well, not the deep, deep forest green with nice sleeves. Anna said that color made her eyes look blue for sure and her skin a beautiful olive color. Anna was a bit dramatic. Whoever heard of olive skin? Well, forest green it was.

Her back ached and her arms slumped wearily as she put the final hairpin into her wrecked hair. She felt as if her strength would never return, sometimes being impatient with her lack of energy.

She had experienced trauma, she knew. Ezra was gone, and sometimes, at the oddest moments, she missed his kind face. Always she was glad she had planned on dating and marrying him. She would have. But in all things there is a reason. This is what she was taught.

God knew what he was doing from his throne on high. The ministers assured everyone in the congregation about this. God had a plan for each individual life and cared about each one. When things like the accident happened, you had to bow your head in true submission, saying, "Thy will be done." It afforded a certain peace in the end, if you could mean it.

Sadie had gone through moments of self-blame. She wondered if she was false-hearted and if she should not have gone with Ezra that fateful evening. Her sisters assured her those thoughts were the devil trying to destroy her, and she needed to be watchful. What would you do without sisters? They were, indeed, the most precious thing God had ever thought about creating.

When two heads appeared at her door and two more nosey questions were thrown into the room, Sadie grinned.

"Oh, someone's coming to help look for Nevaeh."

Rebekah came in and plunked herself on Sadie's bed.

"Let me guess. Mark Peight or Mark Peight or Mark Peight?"

Sadie whirled, throwing her hairbrush.

"Smarty!"

He showed up then, and in a horse and buggy, too. Sadie could tell it was not his team. It was an "old people's" horse and buggy. The difference was plain to see. The youth had sparkling, clean, new buggies with lots of reflectors and pretty things hung inside the windows.

There was brightly-colored upholstery on the walls and seats and matching carpet on the floor. The horse's harness was usually gaily decorated as well, with shining collar hames, a colorful collar pad, and a bridle studded with silver.

This horse and buggy looked exactly like the one her parents' had. It was clean but dull, with a black, traditional harness without silver or color—a very Amish team.

Just as English youth enjoy a nice car, so it was with the Amish buggies. Sadie often thought about that. Youth were youth, each one trying to be someone—nature's way of calling for a mate. Wasn't that true? She had never said that. It sounded too ... well, sort of primitive or a bit vulgar perhaps, depending who heard you say it.

English people liked to think Amish people were elevated a bit or in a highly esteemed place, and so just a bit better than they were. Hopefully the Amish were good, although Sadie knew they were certainly also human. Sadie guessed, that some areas, their heritage was a God-given thing, a gift they had acquired at birth. She wondered if Mark truly had been born and raised in an Amish home.

Who knew?

He definitely was a mystery.

And then, he saw her standing hesitantly at the door. He waved and said he'd put his horse in the barn and be right back.

Sadie swung to the kitchen table and sat down a bit weakly, trying to appear calm and nonchalant—if that was even a possibility.

Oh, my!

Dat, Uncle Levi, and Uncle Samuel had the worst

timing in the world. How could they? The exact minute Mark appeared in the kitchen hallway, they all crowded in, all talking at once, trying to come up with a feasible plan to find the missing horse.

"What I cannot understand is how that horse got out in the first place," Dat was saying.

"Someone had to let him out," Uncle Levi said, setting down his coffee cup and reaching for a handful of Chex Mix. He chomped down on the salty mixture, scattering half of it across the clean linoleum floor.

Sadie sighed. Mark stood in the hallway. Then Samuel turned and caught sight of him.

"Hi, there!"

Too loudly. Too boisterously. Sadie despaired.

"Come on in. Make yourself at home, whoever you are. One of these bachelors that feel the pull of the West?"

Oh, no! Sadie wanted to disappear through the floor, down into the basement, and through that floor, too.

Mark grinned, and said quietly, "Yeah, I guess so."

"Dat? This is Mark Peight. Mark, my father and his brothers, Samuel and Levi.

"You all live around here?"

"Oh, yes. We do. Been here for five years, almost six."

Dat's eyes narrowed.

"How do you know Sadie?"

Sadie tried to salvage her pride by telling them Mark was the one who came upon her on the road with Nevaeh before Richard Caldwell had the veterinarian nurse him back to health.

"Mmmm," Uncle Samuel said, nodding his head in that certain way, his eyes twinkling.

Levi grinned outright. Sadie willed him to be quiet.

They talked loudly now about other horses who had

gotten away, the size of the pasture, if anyone believed there were actual horse thieves in this day and age, and whether there was a band of wild horses. The conversation turned to the night of the accident.

Sadie caught a movement behind the bathroom door. Mam!

What was she doing pressed between the door and the shower curtain? Listening? Why wouldn't she come to the kitchen?

"I know that horse was there this morning. I know it," Dat insisted.

"But if he was, someone had to let him out. Do you think there could be a horse thief in broad daylight?" Levi asked around his Chex Mix.

"Hey, they do anything these days."

"Let's go search the pasture."

They got into their coats, smashed their wool hats on their heads, stuck their feet into boots, pulled on gloves, and were gone.

Mark turned back, searching Sadie's eyes.

"We'll find him," he assured her.

"Oh, I hope," she whispered.

She held his gaze. Too long. The kitchen was filled with nothing at all. It all went away, except for the look in Mark's eyes. It was a look so consuming, she heard singing, sort of a tune in her mind, a speck of happiness in song she had never heard before in her life.

Was love a song? Sort of, she figured.

Boy, she was in dangerous territory now, letting that happen. But she could have no more looked away than she could have stopped breathing. It was so natural.

Oh, my.

She sat at the kitchen table, her head in her hands, turmoil in her heart.

An hour passed with Aunt Lydia and Aunt Rachel sitting in the kitchen with her. They drank coffee, sampled desserts, and talked of things women talk about—having babies, which laundry soap works best, how to secure towels to the wash line without the ceaseless wind tearing them off and away, whose teacher was strict, whose was incompetent, and so on.

Sadie was becoming very worried and uneasy. She tapped her nails on the tabletop. How long could it take to find a horse in a pasture? It wasn't that big.

Finally she heard voices and stamping feet.

Mark came in first, his face grim, followed by Dat, Levi, and Samuel. Their noses were red, eyes serious.

Sadie rose, standing on one leg. A hand went to her throat.

"What? Did you find him?"

Mark looked at Dat. Dat shook his head, saying nothing. Mark cleared his throat and looked away. Sadie knew, then, that something was wrong.

"What? Did you find him? Someone tell me."

They told her.

They got to the very lower end of the pasture where the alders and brush almost hid the fence. The fence was torn, even the post pulled out. Brush everywhere. Snow mixed with the dirt and brown winter grasses. Signs of a terrible struggle. Blood. Lots of blood.

The blood left a trail that was easy to follow. They found Nevaeh. He was down, a great gash torn in the tender part of his stomach. There was a pool of blood and he was holding his hind leg at a grotesque angle.

Mark's head was bent, one shoe pushing against the baseboard.

"But..." Sadie stammered.

It was not exactly clear what happened, what caused Nevaeh to become so frightened he became impaled on the fence post. Perhaps there was a cougar.

"But...how could he bleed to death?" Sadie whispered.

"He didn't...completely. His leg was broken, almost off. We...we had to put him down."

Sadie lifted agonized eyes to Dat, Levi, Samuel, and finally to Mark.

"Why?"

It was all she could think to say. Paris, then Ezra, and now Nevaeh. Would she be able to bow her head in submission one more time? What purpose was there in letting that beautiful horse die? There was no reason that made any sense. God was not cruel this way, was he?

Dat came over with Rebekah and Leah. They all touched her, trying to convey some sort of hope, sympathy, caring, but Sadie was past feeling anything. She was numb, completely numb.

"We'll get you another horse, Sadie," Dat said, so kindly.

"We have a hospital bill," Mam said sharply.

Everyone turned to stare at her, most of them in disbelief.

Dat straightened, said grimly, "I know we have a hospital bill. God will provide a way for us to pay it."

Rachel and Lydia exchanged glances as Mam turned, her eyes black with hatred, and...what else?

Sadie was afraid, shaken.

Dear God, help us all.

They had company now. She must brace up for Dat's sake.

Sadie squared her shoulders, took a deep breath, and willed the pool of tears to be contained for now.

"Well," she said, quietly. "He didn't suffer long."

Dat shook his head.

Mark said, "He was brave. That horse was…"

He stopped.

Sadie nodded, then said, "Well, it's Christmas. Why don't we make another pot of coffee?"

Everyone smiled in agreement, relieved at Sadie's strength. Lydia gave her shoulder a squeeze of reassurance, and Rachel smiled a shaky smile in her direction.

Reuben, Anna, and the gaggle of towheaded cousins clattered up from the basement. Dashing into the kitchen, they slid to a stop when they saw all the serious faces.

"Did you find Nevaeh?" Anna asked innocently, helping herself to a large dish of date pudding.

"Yes, we did," Dat answered.

"Good!"

Reuben grabbed three large squares of peanut butter fudge, was told to return two of them to the platter, and then he dashed out the door. The cousins followed, clumping back down the stairs to the basement.

"There's some serious ping-pong going on down there," Levi grinned.

Mark came over, stood by Sadie, and asked if she wanted to see Nevaeh.

"How would I?" she asked, gesturing to her cast.

"Do you have an express wagon?" he asked, looking around.

Dat brought the express wagon and Mark spread his buggy robe on it. Her sisters bundled Sadie up and deposited her unceremoniously on the wooden wagon. Then she and Mark were off.

They didn't talk. Mark focused on using his strength to pull the express wagon through the trampled snow, and Sadie had nothing to say. The whole afternoon had a sense of unreality and, now that the sun was casting a reddish glow behind Atkin's Ridge and creating the color of lavender on the snow, it all seemed like a fairy tale.

Sadie shivered, then smiled up at Mark when he looked back to ask how she was doing.

They came to the place where the fence was torn. The post hung by one strand of barbed wire. Its top was rough and not cut evenly, the way some western fences were built. Snow was mixed with dirt, grass flung about, bits of frozen ground clinging to the post as if reluctant to let go.

Mark showed her where Nevaeh had started bleeding, then began pulling her through the thick brush. She held up an arm to shield her face as snow showered her from the branches. She used the other arm to hold onto the wagon. She bent her head to avoid the whipping brush. Then the wagon stopped.

"Here he is."

That's all Mark said.

Sadie looked and saw the beautiful black and white coat—saw Nevaeh. It's strange how a horse's head looks so small and flat and vulnerable when it lies on its side. Its neck, too. Its body seems much too large for that small head. Dat told her once that horses don't lie flat like that for a long period of time; they have difficulty breathing.

Yes, Dat, I know. But Nevaeh is not having difficulty breathing. She's not even breathing. She's dead.

Sadie gathered her thoughts and remembered Mark.

She was not going to cry, not when she was with Mark.

She was always in some kind of stupid trouble when he was around, so no crying. Certainly not this time. Nevaeh was only a horse.

And then she lowered her face in her hands and cried hard. She sniffled and sobbed and needed a handkerchief. Her eyes became red and swollen, and so did her nose. Tears poured through her fingers, and she shook all over with the force of her sobs.

Mark made one swift, fluid movement, and he was on his knees at her side. His arms came around her, heavy and powerful, and he held her head to his shoulder the way a small child is comforted. He just held her until her sobs weakened and slowed, the way a thunderstorm fades away on a summer day. Tears, like rain, still fell, but the power of her grief was relieved.

"I'm sorry," she said finally, hiccuping.

"Sadie, Sadie."

That's all he said.

She didn't know how long they were there, Sadie seated on the wagon, Mark on his knees. She just knew she never, ever wanted him to go away. She wanted those strong, sure arms around her forever. Of this she was certain.

Besides, nothing else made any sense.

Finally he released her, leaned back, searched her eyes. "You okay?"

Meeting his eyes, Sadie nodded.

That was a mistake, was her first coherent thought, before his arms came around her again, crushing her to him. He held her so tightly, her ribs actually hurt a bit. Then he released her quite suddenly, stood up, cleared his throat, and went to pick up the wagon tongue. He trudged back to the house, not saying a word.

Sadie was stung, mortified. What had she done wrong? Had she offended him?

At the house, he declined her invitation to come in for coffee. Instead he hurriedly hitched his horse to the carriage and flew down the drive at a dangerous speed. It seemed he couldn't get out of there fast enough.

Sadie knew she had lost him again.

Chapter 16

AFTER THE CUMBERSOME CAST WAS REMOVED, Sadie returned to the ranch.

It was wonderful to be back. Richard Caldwell welcomed her with his powerful voice bouncing off the cathedral ceilings. Jim told her, in his drawly, shy manner, that the place was not the same without her.

"Yer sorta like one o' them sunbeams that comes down out o' the gray skies, Sadie," he said, sliding the ever-present toothpick to the opposite side of his teeth.

"Why, thank you, Jim. That's a very nice compliment," Sadie told him.

Dorothy held nothing back. She wept, she hugged Sadie close, she stood back to look deep into Sadie's eyes, wiped her own eyes with a paper towel, honked her nose into it, then shook her head.

"In all my days, Sadie honey, I never seen nothin' like it. When I walked into that there hospital and seen you layin' there, I thought the hand o' God was hovering right above your head. God brought you through. Only God. Praise his Almighty Name, an' I mean it."

Dorothy paused for breath, plunked her ample little body onto a kitchen chair, reached for her half-empty coffee cup. She set it down, pulled at her skirt, and began rubbing her knee.

"You know there's a new store in town called Dollar Tree? Well, that's where I got you that china cross. The artificial flowers around that cross looked so real, I swear I coulda pulled 'em out o' my own flower patch. You liked that, didn't you?"

Sadie nodded enthusiastically.

"Oh, yes, I put it away with the rest of the things in my hope chest," she said carefully.

Dorothy's eyes brightened.

"You did? See? I knew you'd like that! Too pretty for your room, wasn't it? You had to put it away for your own house once you get married! Well, I always had good taste when it comes to gift-giving. Just have a knack there. I'll tell you what, on your weddin' day, I'll get you another one, an' you can have one on each side of your hutch cupboard." Dorothy slapped her knee with enthusiasm, watching Sadie's face like a small bird.

"Well you can, can't ya?"

"Of course, Dorothy. I will."

"Now that Dollar Tree, it's not quite like my Dollar General. They don't have them good shoes, mind you. Their Rice Krispies is two dollars a box, though. That ain't so dear."

Sadie nodded.

"Well, here I am runnin' my mouth about the price o' cereal and you didn't tell me how you're doin'."

Sadie took a deep breath, then poured herself a large mug of coffee.

"My leg and foot are still swollen and sore. I have to be careful how I walk on it. My hair…"

She reached up to brush back the unruly, short strands on one side of her head.

"Be glad you're alive. Just be glad!" Dorothy said, nodding her head for emphasis.

"Oh, I am, I am. I don't mind my hair so much, but it's hard not having the strength to be able to work the way I used to."

"Well, today yer gonna do the light dusting and run the vacuum. Then you can sit right here at this table and chop vegetables. I'm havin' vegetable soup with lots of ground beef and tomatoes, the way the boss likes it."

There was a knock on the kitchen door, a small tapping sound.

"Now, who'd be knockin'? No need to do that!" Dorothy said, her eyebrows lowered.

She lifted her head and yelled, "You don't need to knock!"

Sadie cringed when she saw Barbara Caldwell enter the kitchen, her long, white robe clutched around her middle. Her hair was disheveled, and without makeup she looked young and vulnerable. Her face was a ghastly color, so pale Sadie was afraid she'd fall over right there in the kitchen. Her voice trembled as she told them she'd been sick all morning, and was there anything Dorothy knew of that could help her digestive system?

Sadie held her breath, knowing Barbara was not Dorothy's favorite person on the ranch, but Dorothy was cordial. She clucked and stewed, fussing on and on about the merits of gingerroot tea and how she would put in plenty of sugar for strength.

Barbara Caldwell sank gratefully into a kitchen chair, then looked at Sadie and smiled.

"How are you, Sadie?"

Sadie could not believe the smile or the question, especially since she had refused to come to their house on New Year's Eve. Richard Caldwell had canceled at the last minute, apologizing profusely, and the whole family had eaten the delicious food all by themselves, shrugging their shoulders in resignation. Barbara was probably just too high-class to eat in an Amish home, they thought.

"I'm doing much better, thank you," Sadie said politely, ducking her head to hide her embarrassment.

"You've come through a lot. Richard tells me your horse was killed."

"He was put down, yes. His leg was broken."

"Must be hard."

"It is."

Dorothy bustled over with the tea, setting it daintily on the table at Barbara's elbow.

"There now. Try it."

Barbara sipped appreciatively, then grimaced at the heat.

"Taste good?" Dorothy asked hopefully.

Barbara nodded.

Sadie got up, went to the closet, and got down the Pledge furniture polish and a clean cloth. It would be good to dust the beloved house again. She'd do the upstairs first, working her way down. She left the kitchen then, letting Dorothy care for Barbara.

Humming, Sadie started in the den—the great oak-paneled room that housed all of Richard Caldwell's treasures. It was a massive room with great windows reaching to the height of the cathedral ceiling where fans moved quietly to ease the stuffiness of the baseboard heat.

She was whistling low under her breath, the way she always did when she dusted, enjoying the smell of the lemon furniture polish and the luster of the well made furniture under her hand.

"Hey! Sadie!"

Sadie jumped at Richard Caldwell's booming voice.

Calm. I will be calm, Sadie told herself, giving one last swipe to the tabletop and turning slowly to face him.

"It's real good to see you back, Sadie!"

"Thank you. It's good to be here."

"Sit down."

Sadie obeyed, pressing her knees together nervously, smoothing her gray skirt over them.

He came straight to the point.

"What happened to…to your horse?"

Sadie thought of the fact that he always called Nevaeh "your horse." Perhaps he wasn't comfortable pronouncing her name. Either that, or he thought it was a foolish name for a horse.

"He tried to jump the fence. He…suffered a lot."

Sadie stopped, the dreaded emotion rising in her throat.

"But why would he have the urge to try and jump the fence?"

Sadie shook her head, bit her lip.

Richard Caldwell got up, and in his abrupt way, grabbed the remote off the coffee table and pressed a button.

"I kept this for you."

The huge flat-screen TV flashed to life on the opposite wall. Sadie saw the newscaster finish the story of a local murder in Billings, then look straight into the camera before beginning the news item Richard Caldwell wanted her to hear.

"There is increasing concern in the Aspendale Valley east of Billings as ranchers and landowners report seeing wild horses. The fact that it is a fairly large group is reason for concern. Stories of an enormous black stallion are circulating."

The picture changed to a weather-beaten old rancher wearing a sweat-stained John Deere bill cap. He was in desperate need of a shave and a toothbrush.

"Yes, sir! They're runnin'! I seen 'em. Big black devil's the leader. They're dangerous to other horses. Keep yer's corralled or in the barn."

They interviewed another rancher, and then the camera returned to the spokesperson.

"The Amish buggy accident may have been caused by this band of horses running loose. In the meantime, Harold Ardwin of Hill Country is offering a $20,000 reward to the person who can find his missing herd of blue-blooded horses. Could there be a connection between these horse stories? Local ranchers say it's highly unlikely."

There was music, the picture changed to a map of the weather forecast, and Richard Caldwell pressed the button of the remote control device.

He turned to look down at her.

"What do you think?"

Sadie shook her head, her eyes wide.

"Do you think there was a herd of wild horses that night—the night the buggy went down over the ridge?"

Without hesitation, she said, "Yes, I do. As time goes on, I remember bits of ... well, more. Captain was scared. He was running scared... He..."

"Who's Captain?"

"Our ... Ezra's horse—the horse that was hitched to the buggy. His ears were flicking back and forth, his head was up, his pace much too fast."

"Did you see the wild horses?" Richard Caldwell asked intently.

"Yes, I did. Well, at first I felt them. Do you know what I mean? I knew some animal or some person, just something, I guess, was running behind us."

She stopped.

"I'm not wording that very well, am I?"

"That's fine."

"A horse hitched to a buggy does not normally run uphill at breakneck speed, but Captain was doing exactly that."

She shuddered, remembering, then continued.

"He was there, beside us. He was."

"Who was?" Richard Caldwell sank back against his desk, crossed his arms over his chest, and watched her from beneath his shaggy eyebrows.

"The big, black one. The one the..."

She pointed to the television on the wall.

"You're sure about that?"

Sadie nodded.

The door opened quietly and Barbara Caldwell entered, still clutching her white robe against her body. Richard Caldwell instantly moved to go to her, putting his big hands on her shoulders. His voice lowered as he asked her how she felt, and she looked up into his face with an expression Sadie had never seen before.

What had happened between these two? It was amazing.

"I'm feeling much better. Dorothy fixed a cup of gingerroot tea for me and some dry toast."

He smiled down at her, and she held his gaze, returning his smile. They didn't notice Sadie at all, these two middle-aged people suddenly so happy in each other's presence.

Richard Caldwell turned, keeping his arm around his wife's shoulders.

"We were discussing what happened the night of Sadie's accident. On the news last evening, they talked about the band of wild horses. More and more ranchers are seeing them."

Barbara nodded, listening intently, watching Richard Caldwell's face.

Sadie got up, picked up the dust cloth, and was ready to finish her work when Richard Caldwell told her to sit down again.

Sadie sat.

"Your horse—the one you had to put down. Do you think there's a possibility of him becoming frightened by this same band of horses? Is your pasture very big? Is it isolated?" Richard Caldwell was very serious, his voice only a little less than booming.

What? Oh, it couldn't be. Poor Nevaeh. Was he terrified by that huge, black stallion? Was that why he tried to leap the fence? Had he felt threatened?

It was too much for Sadie to comprehend. Pity for her beloved horse welled up inside her until it became an object so painful, she felt physically sick.

What had that poor horse encountered in his life? First alone, sick, and starving. How had that all come about? Then his life ended much too soon by some foolhardy act of his own?

All these thoughts swirled in Sadie's mind until she

remembered that Richard Caldwell was waiting for an answer.

"Uh, yes. Yes, our pasture is at least 20, maybe 30, acres. And, yes, it is very isolated. The lower part anyway."

Richard Caldwell nodded.

"But," Sadie continued, "The biggest mystery about Nevaeh's death is why he was in that snowy pasture to begin with. Who left him out? Or how did he get out of his stall? We had visitors that day—on Christmas Day—and my uncles put their horses in Nevaeh's stall without knowing he belonged there. Dat…I mean, my father never lets him out in winter."

She stopped, wringing her hands on the gray fabric of her dress. Richard Caldwell held up his hand and said he didn't mean to upset her. She assured him she was fine. It was just hard sometimes to accept the fact that Nevaeh had to die in such a mysterious manner.

As she went about her work, Sadie kept thinking of a terrified Nevaeh all alone in the snow, and it was more than her heart could stand. She had to put that thought behind her and focus on other things, but that just led her into deeper, murkier water where she floundered helplessly.

She forgot the Tilex bathroom cleaner, lost the furniture polish, and couldn't find the crevice attachment for the sweeper. She was tired, her leg hurt, and it was high time to go to the kitchen and chop vegetables for Dorothy.

Then there was Mark.

If she really wanted to get off track and get all mixed up mentally, emotionally, and in her heart, or whichever term was used to describe feeling in your heart... See? She couldn't even think straight.

She was happy about one thing. He had held her in his arms. Twice. Well, the time at the mall had been a very necessary thing, of course. But would he really have had to carry her that short distance? It brought the color to her cheeks to think how his wool coat felt against her face. Mam would have a fit. Well, what Mam didn't know didn't hurt her.

Oh, my! Now she was a real rebel.

Could it be God's will for her life to love someone as good-looking as Mark? Could good looks—no, not just good looks—could downright the most handsome man she had ever seen fall into the same category as God's will?

If it was as depressing as Mam put it, every beautiful girl would be paired off with some homely little person. This was God's will, and the only form of true love, according to Mam. But that little homely man who got the good-looking wife didn't have to give up his own will at all. How could you figure that one out?

Truthfully, more than anything else, Sadie wanted God's guidance in finding the companion he wanted her to have. Ezra would have been the perfect one, according to Mam and Dat. But wasn't she always taught to believe death, too, was the will of our Lord? He giveth and he taketh away, and that was that. So, according to God's will, Ezra wasn't meant to be her husband.

Mark was so handsome, but he was hard to explain. His past, for one thing.

Sadie stopped, sniffed, held the bottle in her hand up to her face, and was horrified to discover she was dusting with the bathroom cleaner! Quickly, she hurried to the bathroom, procured a clean cloth, and washed the top of the dresser she was supposed to have been dusting with Pledge. Her heart pounding, she checked to see the results.

Whew! Looked all right. Hurriedly she sprayed a liberal amount of furniture polish onto the dresser and rubbed furiously with the cloth.

This had to stop.

Perhaps her brain had been injured in the accident and she couldn't think normally. No. More than likely she was falling in love, if there was such a thing.

Dusting finished, she hurried back to the kitchen, where a cloud of steam enveloped her. Dorothy was in a fine tizzy.

"Now what do y' know? Here comes Miss High-and-Mighty, telling me she's having her family tonight for a 'pahty.'"

She straightened, blinked her eyes, and fluttered her fingers beside them to accentuate the way Barbara Caldwell talked.

"Tonight!"

"What time?"

"Seven."

"Oh, well, that's plenty of time. What does she want to serve?"

"Pasta!" Dorothy fairly spat the word.

Sadie hid a smile. How well she knew the disdain Dorothy held for any food that was not plain, home-cooked, and old-fashioned.

Dorothy flopped a tea towel in the direction of the steam coming from the just-opened commercial dishwasher. Sadie went to the wall and flipped a switch. The great ceiling fans were activated, pulling up the steam and clearing the air as Dorothy hustled about, fussing and complaining as she fried ground beef.

"Never saw a woman put on so many airs. Now you know her family ain't that highfalutin. Pasta! Likely them kids don't even know what that olive oil coated stuff is. Fresh green peppers. That means Jim has to drive his truck to town, and fuel ain't cheap. I'll tell you what, it's goin' on my paper when I hand in my hours. I ain't payin' the gas outta my own pocket to get her green peppers for that smelly, slippery pasta dish. No way!"

She gave the ground beef a final stir, banged the wooden spoon on the edge of the frying pan, and slid the whole panful of sizzling meat into the large container of vegetable soup.

Sadie held her breath, hoping none of it would fall on Dorothy's dress front. She was so short and her arms were so heavy, it looked as if the pan was actually higher than her head.

"You better get started, Sadie," she snapped.

It was bad. When Dorothy talked to her in that tone of voice, Sadie knew she'd better buckle down, keep her head lowered, and work swiftly.

She had just reached for the great wooden cutting board when the door burst open so hard, it banged against the counter top. Jim came barging through, a hand going to his hat, clumping it down harder on his head as he sat down.

"Dorothy!"

"James Sevarr, you slow down this instant! If you don't pop a blood vessel in your head, I'll be surprised. What in the world is up with you?"

"I can't slow down now. You know them wild horses?" He reached up and grabbed his hat off his head, his head white in comparison to the rest of his face.

"Them horses, mind you! Hey, Sadie! You know the bend in the road where that horse of yours come charging across and fell that time?"

Sadie hurried over to the table, her hands gripping the edge. She felt the color drain from her face.

"Yes?"

"I was drivin' down through—almost exactly the same place—and here they come! They was scared, every last one. Skinny lookin' bunch. Long hair on 'em. There's definitely a big, black one in the lead. Looks wilder than a bunch of mustangs. I ain't never seen nothing like it in all my days."

He clasped his hat back on his head, shook his hands free of his gloves, and walked over to the stove to warm them, sniffing the pot of vegetable soup.

Dorothy rested her fists on her hips, her feet encased firmly in the shoes she bought at Dollar General in town.

"Jim, first off, decide if you're gonna wear that hat or if you're gonna take it off. Same thing with the gloves. And get away from my vegetable soup this instant. Yer breathin' down into it."

He brushed her off like a fly.

"And, Sadie, I'm havin' a meetin' with the men at the lunch table. We're getting' together with the fire company an' somethin's gonna be done. We're gonna round 'em up. At least go after 'em. They're here, ain't no doubt about it, an' they've racked up enough of mischief, 'n I mean it. You know that feller down by Hollingworth? Somethin' ripped into his fence—barb wire strung out all over the place. It's them horses."

Sadie was breathless with excitement.

"Oh, Jim! I wish I could go!"

"You can!"

Sadie laughed, her cheeks flushing.

"If I had Nevaeh, I would."

"Jim Sevarr, don't you take this here young girl out gallivantin' after some wild horses. Don't even think about it!"

The soup was bubbling over and a whole pile of vegetables needed to be chopped, but Sadie didn't even notice.

Oh, to have Nevaeh, Sadie thought. She knew her mother would never let her go with the men, but to ride Nevaeh like that was all she had dreamed about for weeks. Nevaeh had been like Paris—except in color. But now she would never know how beautiful Nevaeh could become—especially in the summer when he lost all his winter coat, leaving his soft, silky new coat shining in the spring sunshine.

The part of his death that was hardest to bear was the thought of all the rides they could never have. They would have traveled for miles and miles, enjoying the beauty of the Montana landscape which was breathtaking in the spring.

And now he was gone. The truck had bounced back through the snow, and they had winched his large, dead body onto it while the vultures circled overhead in the winter sunshine. Now everything seemed gray and dead and sad, even the sun.

She had ridden along with Dat. He hadn't wanted her to, but she did. She wanted to make sure that Nevaeh's leg really was broken as badly as they said. It was, and that gave her a measure of peace. Nothing is quite as final as a grotesquely bent limb on an animal as awesome-looking as Nevaeh. But it was severely broken, no matter if she wanted to see it or not, and he never could have lived a normal life with it.

They had looked for tracks, but the brush was too thick and the cows had trampled everything.

So there was no use thinking about riding with Jim and the men. Nevaeh was gone.

Chapter 17

THE MEN MADE THEIR PLANS AND RODE OUT, BUT they did not find a single horse. It was as if the horses were phantoms, dark winds, specters in the night. Maybe they were contrived only by people's imaginations.

"A *schpence*," Dat said.

"What's a *schpence*?" Reuben asked, looking up at his father as he lay on the rug in front of the wood stove. He was on his back, one leg propped on an upended knee, balancing a book precariously on top.

"A ghost," Dat replied.

Reuben grunted and returned to his book.

Sadie was curled up on the recliner, a warm throw over her shoulders. She still tired easily, and home was a welcome haven when she returned from the ranch.

Always the dutiful one, Rebekah was finishing the supper dishes. Leah was in the phone shanty, and Anna was doing the crossword puzzle in the *Daily Times*.

The clock on the wall ticked loudly, the pendulum swinging back and forth. A log fell in the wood stove, the propane gas lamp hissed comfortably, and Sadie's eyelids dropped as she felt herself falling into that state of bliss just before sleep overtook her.

She was rudely awakened by a clattering sound. The front door banged open, and she heard a resounding, "Sadie!"

Sadie tossed the cotton throw, sat up, and tried to remember where she was.

"There's a sledding party at Dan Detweilers! Want to go?"

Sadie groaned inwardly.

Hard as it was to admit to herself, she was no longer 16, and Sadie knew it was true, especially in moments like these. She no longer got excited by the same things as she did at 16—that time in your life when sledding parties, suppers, singings, and every event where a group of the youth had gathered, was a great deal.

Now at 20, she seriously had to weigh her options— the warm, cozy living room with the crackling fire versus the cold, snowy hillside where the wind penetrated your back no matter how many coats and sweaters you wore. There was always a bonfire, but that thoroughly roasted your face and your back was still cold.

Her hesitation brought a snort from Leah.

"What a spinster! You act like you're not even thrilled to hear about it!"

"I'm tired, Leah."

"Come on. This will likely be the last one of the season."

"How are you going?"

Leah glanced at Dat.

"Our horse and buggy?"

Dat frowned, then shook his head.

"Battery's dead."

"Our buggy battery is always dead. You never put it on the charger."

"I don't like you girls out on the dark roads with the horses. It's not safe."

Leah sputtered, and Sadie knew she was holding back a quick retort. She managed to ask Dat quite civilly if he had money for a driver since they weren't allowed to have the team.

Dat shifted his weight, searched his pockets for his wallet, and mumbled something about money melting away with a houseful of teenage daughters.

Leah took the money he handed over, thanked him, and said sweetly, "You know you could keep this if you let us have Charlie and the buggy."

"It might cost me a whole lot more than that if you had an accident."

It was Dat's favorite comeback, and Sadie giggled as Leah dashed upstairs, taking the steps two at a time.

Should she go? The only reason she would was for Leah's and Rebekah's sakes. It would be entirely different if she had any hope that Mark Peight would be there, but she had not seen or heard anything from him since that Christmas night. She had thoroughly messed up whatever friendship they might have had at one time. But what had she done? She didn't know. She guessed Mark was like that. He was like that band of wild horses—you could never quite figure him out.

Slowly, Sadie rose. She looked around and asked where Mam was. Dat looked up with pain, shame, indignation. What was it? It flickered in his eyes before he told Sadie Mam had gone to bed. She wasn't feeling well.

Mam had taken to her bed quite frequently of late, but it seemed as if she could do nothing else but sit on the recliner or lie on the sofa if she was awake. Her condition was deteriorating before their eyes, little by little. The girls were learning to live with it as best they could. Mam kept up the appearance of normalcy—going to church every two weeks and doing whatever duty was asked of her, but the girls knew Mam was suffering.

Sadie pushed thoughts of Mam from her mind. Maybe she should go sledding and clear her mind.

That Leah. Dashing up the stairs with the money clutched in her hand, she hadn't even bothered calling a driver.

When the driver finally pulled up to the door, the girls were eagerly waiting—except for Sadie, who was stifling huge yawns, trying to stay awake for the evening.

✿ ✡ ✿

Dan Detweiler's homestead was filled with buggies in the driveway and around the outbuildings. Boys milled about, putting their steaming horses in the barn.

The air was crisp and cold, but heavy. Every noise seemed magnified by the atmosphere which always seemed to amplify sound just before snow or rain. The stars hung low, twinkling as sharp and bright as ever, but Sadie figured storm clouds would likely cover them by morning.

The girls' breaths came in quick gasps as they climbed to the top of the long, sloping hill on the ridge in back of Dan's barn. There was nowhere else in the Amish settlement more suited for sledding.

You can't really call this a pasture, Sadie thought. It's too big. This whole place is more like Richard Caldwell's ranch than our home.

Aidan and Johnny were riding horses below them, pulling a tractor inner tube on a long rope attached to the saddle horn. The only bad thing about a ride in the tube was the snow kicked into your face by the flying hooves of the horse. You had to keep your head lowered or your eyes, nose, and mouth were soon packed with snow.

In spite of herself, Sadie grew more and more excited. She had had some thrilling rides on an inner tube in the snow before, so perhaps if the boys asked the girls, she would try it again.

Leah and Rebekah were already filling a toboggan with shrieking girls. A huge bonfire roaring at the bottom of the slope clearly showed the girls which way to steer the giant sled.

Of course they'd steer close enough to the boys to have their yells of alarm noticed, Sadie thought wryly.

Then she felt very old and very wise and suddenly wished she wasn't there. Her feet were already tingling with the cold, she was sleepy, the wind was definitely picking up, and she knew if she wanted to stay warm, she'd either have to start sledding or go sit by the fire. Neither option sounded overly appealing.

Her best friend, Lydiann, was already flying down the hill, shrieking in a high-pitched tone, which irritated Sadie.

Johnny will see you without that war whoop, she thought, then felt bad. Maybe she actually was turning into a "sour old singleton," as Rebekah put it.

Well, she had reason to be sour. Her leg ached as it did most every day and especially before a storm. She did her best to hide the discomfort from everyone in her family. She had to work. They needed the money to help with living expenses and to make payments on the large hospital bill.

Sadie shrugged, looked around her, and started downhill, dragging her feet to keep from sliding uncontrollably.

The group of girls on the toboggan was starting back up the hill, their noise punctuated by laughter and frequent looks in the direction of the boys who were by the bonfire. They were changing riders of the horses, both with inner tubes attached.

Another horse and rider came from the opposite direction. The horse was large, as was the rider, but Sadie could not distinguish the color of the horse or recognize the rider.

Cautiously, Sadie made her way down the slick slope. She heard someone call her name and turned to find Lydiann slipping haphazardly toward her.

"You need me to help you get down, Sadie?" she yelled panting.

Her hair was a mess, her scarf hanging completely off her head in a snowy loop about her neck. Sadie shivered as she thought of the trapped snow melting down Lydiann's back.

Sadie waved her hand in dismissal and said, "I'm all right."

"You sure?"

"Yes."

Without further ado, Lydiann charged back up the hill, her arms waving as she struggled to keep her balance.

How old is she? Three? Sadie muttered to herself.

Wasn't that just how life was? If you were tired and grouchy, people that were overly enthused and much too happy about everything only made you grouchier.

Especially Lydiann. If she wasn't so excited about the prospect of Johnny Schlabach talking to her, maybe she could calm down and act normal.

When she reached the bonfire, Sadie plopped down on a bale of straw and held her hands out toward its warmth. She felt someone standing close by, and she turned to find tall, quiet Mark Peight beside her.

She blinked, then bent her head. A spray of sparks erupted from the largest log falling inward, fanning the flames higher.

"Hello, Sadie."

Oh, his voice! The way he said her name with the drawn out "e." Her knees felt weak, but she managed a polite, soft-spoken, "Hello, Mark."

She still didn't look at him. He asked if there was room on the bale of straw and she said there was. The whole bale filled with him when he sat down. Her heart hammered against the many layers of clothes she wore. He turned his head.

"How are you?"

She gazed steadily into the fire, then nodded her head. He said nothing.

Then, "So, does that up and down movement mean, yes or you're okay or what?"

Sadie smiled.

"It means I'm okay."

"Back to work?"

She nodded again.

"Can I... May I talk to you?"

Sadie shifted away from him.

"You are talking to me, so why would you ask?"

"Can I talk to you alone, I mean? Away from all of this?"

"What for?"

"Just…ask you some questions."

"Everybody will see us walk away. Then they'll talk."

"Do you care?"

"Not really."

He stood up, waiting.

She didn't want to go with him. There would only be more disappointment. He would just tell her he was going back east or wherever it was he came from. She had no reason to hope he wanted anything more than to explain his sudden departure and tell her good-bye.

"You need help?"

"Let's go back to the farm. We can talk on the way, and then you can leave me at the house. I'll wait there until the girls are ready to leave. My leg is bothering me this evening," she said curtly.

"All right. Do you want up on Chester since your leg is hurting?" he asked politely.

"Chester?"

"My horse."

It would be nice, she considered. She was wearing fleece-lined pants beneath her skirt so modesty would not be a problem. Yes, she would ride. It had been so long since she had been up on Nevaeh.

"Okay."

He walked off, said a few words to some of the boys who were taking turns riding and flying along on the inner tube, then grabbed Chester's reins and brought him back to Sadie.

Chester was a huge boy—built solidly and in top shape. His mane and tail glistened in the light of the fire, and his ears pricked forward intelligently as he approached her. Sadie watched his soft, brown eyes and the way he lowered his head. She forgot Mark, the youth's calls, the bonfire—everything—as her hands went out to cradle the soft, velvety nose.

"Hi there, big boy," she whispered.

Chester nuzzled his mouth into her mittened hands, and she stroked the side of his head over and over, murmuring softly as she did so. She told him how big and beautiful he was in a horse language all her own. The lengthy absence of Nevaeh brought a lump to her throat, and she lowered her head so Mark would not see the emotion she was feeling.

Mark stood aside, watching Sadie. He knew she missed her horse, so he stood quietly, letting her have a few moments with Chester. He listened to every whisper, marveling at her way with a horse. It was uncanny, this sincere rapport she had with these huge creatures. There was no fear, no hesitation, just this loving trust, this connection she had so naturally with each and every horse.

Finally, Mark said, "He likes you."

"He does!"

Sadie looked up at him, completely transformed. She was laughing happily, her somber mood dispelled.

"You ready to get in the saddle?"

"I can get up by myself."

"I know."

He stood back, watching as Sadie gathered up the reins and slid her gloved hand along Chester's neck beneath the mane, talking as she did so. Chester acted as meek as a lamb, which was not his usual way. He was always sidestepping and prancing and doing everything to make Mark's leap into the saddle challenging.

Sadie stopped.

"Oh," she said in a small voice.

Mark stepped forward, listening.

"I forgot. My foot probably won't hold me. It's the one I would put in the stirrup."

"Well..." Mark began.

"I'll walk him," she said quickly, gathering the reins and starting off at a brisk pace.

There was nothing for Mark to do but follow.

They walked through the snow in silence except for the soft, swishing sound of snow crunching beneath their feet. The snow was silver in the starlight, though the stars were slowly being blotted out, as if an eraser was sweeping across the night sky. The air was still heavy with the approaching storm so every night sound was clear. The tree line along the ridge was almost black, the tops of the trees swaying softly as if they sighed at night when the world rested. The young people's noise slowly faded as they walked, the light of the fire gone.

"Sadie," Mark said, then reached for her arm to stop her.

She stopped, and Chester came to a halt behind her, his ears pricked forward.

"I said I wanted to talk to you," he began in his low vice, the sound she loved.

"I want to apologize about Christmas evening. I'm sorry."

"It's okay," Sadie began, but he lifted a hand.

"No, it's not okay. I need to be a man and tell you about my life. I would like to come see you next Saturday evening, if I may. We'll not plan anything. I just need to have a quiet place to tell you things about me, and then you can decide whether it's worth it for you to try ... well, to get to know me better. After you hear the truth, you may not want to. Then I'll go back to Pennsylvania."

"But...why would you go back home to Pennsylvania?"

"Because I don't want to live in Montana if I can't have you."

The music in her heart began then. It was as full and soaring as the music Barbara Caldwell listened to, taking her along to the heights of joy. It was an emotion that lifted her above the snow, the hills, the trees, and the cold. She could not speak, because if she did the music would stop. And she couldn't bear to part with that sound.

"Sadie..."

She blinked, lifted her head, faced him.

"Yes, Mark. We'll sit in the living room after my parents are in bed. I would be glad to hear what you..." She broke off, watching Chester.

His head went up, his ears forward and turned slightly toward the tree line. Mark stiffened, watching. An icy chill went up Sadie's spine, and she turned her eyes, straining. Chester stood stock still. Sadie's hand went to his neck.

"Mark?" Sadie whispered.

"Shhh."

She felt them before she saw them. The wind picked up, there was a sense of rushing, and the ground vibrated beneath her boots with a shuffling of snow.

"Mark!"

She stifled a scream as a line of dark shadows moved along the tree line. It was as if the trees were swaying along the ground in an up and down movement in a mixture of colors and shadows, and yet there was not one horse, or even a band of horses, in sight.

"Mark! Mark! It's them! It's... It's... They're in there!" she screamed in a hoarse, terrified cry.

"Get up! Now! Sadie, you have to listen to me. Let me put you up. Whoa, Chester! Good boy! Hang on!"

She was picked up firmly and dumped unceremoniously on the leather saddle. Chester was prancing frantically beneath her and she hung on, grateful for all the skills she remembered. In a flash, Mark was behind her, turning Chester, goading him back the way they had come.

Sadie leaned forward, the wind nipping her scarf, her hair. The air was frigid. She felt Mark's solid form behind her, felt his breath.

The line of horses was moving with them. They weren't visible except as undulating shadows among the trees. Chester was galloping steadily, his powerful strides covering the slopes easily. Sadie turned her head and screamed as she saw the dark forms emerging from the tree line. Mark saw them at the same moment and called to Chester.

"C'mon, boy! C'mon!"

Chester responded with a gathering of great, powerful leaps. Sadie's mind turned to the night with Ezra. She fought off the panic and fear from the accident.

The black leader called his terrible stallion challenge, a scream of territorial rights. It lent wings to Chester's feet, goading him across the snow. Speed was their only chance, and Mark urged his horse on.

The bonfire!

Brightly it blazed, like a beacon of rest, of safety. Sadie could see the two horses, the youth seated around the blazing light. Sadie felt Chester relax, loosen his gait. She saw the youth scatter, calling in alarm as they slid up to the fire.

Mark was down before Chester stopped, and he lifted Sadie off in a blink.

"Get the horses and stay by the fire!" Mark yelled in an awful voice.

The girls screamed, their hands going to their mouths, their eyes wide with fear. Aidan and Johnny grabbed the reigns of the horses, and they all huddled around the blazing fire. They watched in disbelief as the band of horses streamed past. Chester stood between the youth and the horses, his nostrils flaring as his sides heaved with exertion.

The great black leader shook his head, reared, and pawed the air as if to warn them. They were in plain sight, the firelight identifying the colors, the heads, whipping manes, streaming tails. The snow obscured the feet and legs, but as one body they galloped in perfect rhythm.

Sadie watched in wonder.

The horses were not any old, scraggly, wild mustangs. They were not the usual stock that were a nuisance to all the ranchers in the area. These horses were different. Sadie had caught the wild-eyed look on a small mare. She was afraid. These horses were running scared and they were very thin.

Something was not right.

And, oh, that black stallion! His cry! She would always remember the sound in her worst dreams and nightmares of that night.

After the last hoof beat faded, a general babble of voices broke out. The boys began talking at once. The girls came running to Sadie, asking a dozen questions. She sank weakly onto a bale of straw.

"Now I'm telling you, this is the real thing! No one can even pretend these wild horses aren't around!" Marvin Keim was yelling.

"Good thing we had this fire!"

"I mean, they were running!"

"Did you see that big, black one?"

A somber mood enveloped them. They knew they were extremely fortunate to have been by the blazing fire, all of them together. The sledding was over. No one felt like straying very far from the bonfire.

Mark reached out to Chester and said they'd better stay as a group and all return to the Detweiler farm together.

The walk back was quiet, the girls casting fearful glances in the direction of the trees.

Mark walked beside Sadie and held her gloved hand in his. She was grateful and let her hand rest inside his strong one.

"I'll see you next Saturday evening."

"Oh, yes," she breathed happily. "But try to get to my house fairly late."

"Why?"

"Well, Reuben is… He'll never go to bed if he knows you'll be there. He'll lie flat on the floor upstairs with his ear pressed against the floor and listen to every word we say."

Mark laughed his deep rolling laugh that Sadie loved to hear. It would be a very long time until Saturday evening.

Chapter 18

AFTER THE SLEDDING PARTY, THE AMISH community in Montana buzzed with the news of the wild horses. The women sat in their phone shanties and had long conversations about what had actually happened that evening. Mugs of coffee at the men's elbows turned cold as they talked, visualized, and tried to come up with a feasible plan.

Before church, when the men stood in the forebay of Jesse Troyer's barn, the topic was wild horses. And after services, around the long dinner table spread with traditional church food—pie, homemade bread, jam, pickles, red beets, homemade deer bologna, and slices of cheese, all washed down with cups of steaming coffee—the talk was wild horses.

Of course it was the Lord's day, and the sermon was not about wild horses, but instead a good, solid lecture on forgiveness and the wonders of allowing ourselves to be freed from any grudges or ill feeling toward others. Still, no one could keep their minds from the events of the youth bonfire.

Mothers shook their heads, children listened wide-eyed. It was not safe to be on the road after dark, especially alone with a horse and buggy.

There was an undercurrent of gossip about that Jacob Miller's Sadie as well. That girl had better slow down. What was she doing riding a horse with that stranger from Pennsylvania? Someone told Katie Schwartz that he had been raised Amish but that his parents were English. They clucked their tongues and shook their heads, saying nothing good could come of it, that Jacob and Annie better rein in their Sadie. She almost died in that accident. Her Ezra was gone, bless his soul, and here she was gallivanting about with this other man already.

That's what happens when someone is too pretty for her own good. Look at Aunt Lisbet. She ran off with the butcher from Clarksville, and if she hadn't been so pretty, it likely never would have happened. But then, her mother hadn't been very stable either so...

Mary Miller shrugged her shoulders and said Jacob Miller didn't look like himself these days. Someone mentioned Annie wasn't doing so well, but she looked all right to her.

They watched Annie as she brought more pies to the table, lowered them, then stooped to talk to little Clara Amstutz, patting her head and smiling so nicely. Nothing much wrong with her.

Sadie stood against the counter in the *kessle-haus* and listened halfheartedly as Lydiann and Leah talked endlessly about the wild horses. She was hungry, tired of the restless chatter, and wished those fussy older women would hurry up and eat so they could have their turn.

She skipped breakfast that morning, having overslept. She had tried to pull off looking tired and grouchy, although inside she was anything but that. She had lain awake, giddy with the thought of Mark Peight coming to see her. But her giddiness turned to concern when she thought of all the things that could go wrong between them.

What did he want to tell her? Was it something so terrible that there was no possible way they could begin dating, let alone get married?

She had slid out of bed, wrapped her warm robe around her, then stood at the window looking out over the snowy landscape with the stars scattered all over the night sky and prayed.

She always prayed at her window, standing. She knew the proper way was to kneel beside her bed and clasp her hands, but somehow she couldn't find God in the way she could when she stood by her window and saw the night sky, the stars, the whole wide world. She imagined God was just beyond those twinkling little lights, and he could see her from up there where he was. And so she prayed.

She asked God to direct her heart and to help her remain a sacrifice so she could discern his will for her life. She already knew without a doubt that she wanted Mark Peight for her husband someday. She wanted to be with him, listen to him talk, watch his deep, brown eyes crinkle at the corners when he laughed. She had been amazed at the depth of her own emotions the first time they met, but she had tried to hold him at a distance. She had felt good when she was in his presence. He had been so kind, so sincere, and that was something.

She would have married Ezra. She had planned on dating him. But God took him away. There was still a special part of her heart that was Ezra's, but there was another part—a bigger part—that belonged to Mark.

She ended her prayer.

Thank you, God, for Mark.

She had let the curtains fall, but caught them again when she saw a dark form moving slowly down the driveway. Surely it wasn't Mam on a frigid night like this?

The dark form continued forward, the head bent. Yes, it was Mam. Should she get dressed and go to her?

Sadie's heart beat rapidly as she struggled to suppress her fear of the unknown, wondering why Mam would roam the roads alone at night. Was she so troubled in her spirit that the freedom of the outdoors soothed her?

Sadie had remained by the window, watching until her mother returned, still plodding quietly, head still bent.

It was a pitiful sight. Love for her mother welled up in Sadie's heart like the fizz from a glass of soda. Dear Mam. She had always been the best Mam in the world. It was just now ... she was only a silent shadow. She went about doing mundane little tasks, but the bulk of the work fell on the girls' shoulders.

Sadie breathed a sigh of relief when the laundry room door creaked quietly, and she could be sure Mam had safely returned.

✿ ✪ ✿

At work on Monday morning, Sadie divulged her plans for Saturday evening. Dorothy's spirits soared.

"You got a honest-to-goodness date?" she yelled above the high, insistent whine of the hand-held mixer.

Sadie glanced at her happily. Dorothy clicked it off and tapped the beater against the bowl, streams of frothy egg running off.

"Well, do ya or don't cha?"

"Yes, I do. He's coming to our house," Sadie answered as she sliced oranges, popping a section into her mouth.

"Well, what are you gonna do? You don't have a television set to watch an' you can't go to the movies. So how are ya gonna entertain this young man?"

Sadie smiled.

"First, I have to think of some kind of brownies or bars or cookies to make. I have to have a snack, of course."

Dorothy's eyes lit up, her smile wide.

"I can sure help you out on that one!"

Dorothy turned to her eggs, poured them into a greased baking pan, and then got out the vicious looking chef's knife. She held it like a professor about to begin a lecture with his wooden pointer.

Sadie raised her eyebrows.

"We played Parcheesi!"

"What?"

"Parcheesi! It's the most fun game ya ever saw. I'll bring my game of Parcheesi, and you and yer feller can play. Aw, that's so sweet. Just like me and Jim. Now my Jim, he's different from other rough cowboys. He's a good man, my Jim. If he wasn't so stuck on riding those horses and working at this ranch, we'd have more money. But then, ya know, Sadie, he wouldn't be happy, an' what's money compared to being a purely contented soul? Huh? Tell me that. The whole world is moving faster and faster and faster tryin' to make more money, and it ain't bringin' nobody no happiness. Jes' look at my Jim settin' on the back of a horse, his chaw stuck in his cheek, and his old hat covering his bald head. Why he's happier 'n a coon in a fish pond. An' me? I like it right here in Richard Caldwell's kitchen cookin' up a storm."

She paused for breath, threw a handful of mushrooms

into the beaten eggs, and surveyed her breakfast casserole. Sadie looked over her shoulder.

"That's not very much food."

"This ain't for the cowhands. It's Barbara's. Richard Caldwell's taken to eatin' with her upstairs in her bedroom in the morning. He says she's feeling sickly. Well, it don't hurt that woman to lose a few pounds, let me tell you. You done with them oranges?"

Sadie nodded.

"You didn't tell me which recipe to make for Saturday night, yet."

"Give me time, give me time."

✢　✬　✢

After breakfast was over, Sadie and Dorothy sat down together at the great oak table with a stack of dog-eared, greasy cookbooks. Dorothy wet her thumb and began flipping pages.

"Okay, now. You gonna make these at home, or can I help you here?"

Sadie looked at Dorothy.

"Well, we're getting paid by the hour, so it wouldn't be very honest to bake something here and take it home. We'd be using their ingredients, and…

Dorothy snorted.

"So what? Richard Caldwell don't care."

"I know, but…"

"You Amish is strange ducks. Now whoever heard of being so painfully honest, you can't even bake a brownie or two with a wealthy guy's ingredients? Huh? Never heard such a thing in my life."

"But I'd feel guilty. Should I ask him first?"

"Naw. He don't care."

Sadie decided it would be condescending, perhaps even a bit self-righteous, to insist that such a minor thing be done her way. After all, Dorothy was the boss in the kitchen.

"Okay, Dottie, if you say so."

A profound whack on her backside with the large rubber spatula was her answer.

"Now, don't you go Dottie'n me again! It's just plain disrespectful."

"Okay, Dottie, if you say so."

They had a hearty laugh together, the kind of laugh that binds your heart to another person with pure good humor and friendship, the kind that keeps a smile on your face for a long time afterwards.

They flipped through the cookie and brownie sections, finally settling on a chocolate bar swirled with cream cheese. Dorothy assured Sadie they were so moist and delicious that you couldn't eat just one.

"What else are you servin' this guy?"

"Oh, coffee likely. And something salty. I thought of making those ham and cheese thingys that you roll up in a tortilla."

Dorothy wrinkled her nose.

"You Easterners don't know how to make a tortilla."

They flipped pages, searching for more recipes, and the subject of the wild horses came up. Dorothy shook her head wisely.

"They ain't no mystery. If any of these highfalutin men had a lick o' common sense, they'd know this band o' horses ain't wild. It's them stolen ones. Poor babies. They's runnin' so scared, it ain't even funny. Imagine now, Sadie. They lived in a warm barn, blanketed, fed, exercised, brushed, among trainers and people that treated 'em like kings and queens, and suddenly they're exposed to the wild world, and they can hardly survive. I told Jim they ain't gettin' them horses until they build a corral and round 'em up with them new-fangled helicopters. You know what he said? 'Pshaw!' But I don't care what my Jim says, they won't get 'em."

Sadie nodded.

"If Nevaeh had lived, he'd be a grand horse by now. He was no ordinary horse."

Dorothy nodded in agreement. "That he wasn't, that he wasn't."

There was a knock on the kitchen door, and Sadie hurried to open it, wiping her hands on her clean, white apron.

Dat!

Sadie blinked in surprise.

"Why, Dat! What brings you here?"

Dat's face was pale, his eyes somber.

"You need to come home, Sadie. Your mother is missing."

"Missing? You mean, you don't know where she is?"

Dat shook his head, searching Sadie's face.

What was it in Dat's eyes? Humiliation, pride, fear, self-loathing, shame? It was all there. She knew this would be very hard for him if the Amish community found out.

"But … she … she can't have gone far. She walks a lot. She's likely close by."

Turning, she told Dorothy she had to leave, getting her coat and scarf off the hook as she did so. Dorothy waved her hand, and Sadie followed Dat out to the car. He had hired a driver, so he must have been very concerned.

The ride home seemed like 30 miles instead of the usual eight. Dat said very little, and Sadie's heart pounded with fear as she thought of all the things that could have happened to Mam. She was so fragile, that was the thing. Her mind, her nerves—whatever they were—were like a banner in a stiff breeze attached to a solid anchor, but with a frayed rope. As long as Dat would not admit she needed help, who could keep the rope from snapping?

"Oh, dear God, please stay with her," Sadie prayed. "Wherever she is, just stay with her."

When they arrived home, Dat gathered his three daughters around him at the kitchen table. Anna and Reuben were still in school, but Leah and Rebekah had been summoned from their cleaning jobs.

Sadie looked at her sisters, their eyes welling with tears.

"Sadie, you know Mam better than any of us. Where could she have gone? And why?" Rebekah asked shakily.

Sadie took a deep breath, squared her shoulders, and looked directly into Dat's eyes. His fell beneath her gaze.

"Well, first, we need to have a long-overdue, honest, all-out talk about our mother. She is not well. She is having issues related to her mind. In plain words, she is mentally ill. And, Dat, you will not admit that. And as long as you don't, Mam cannot get better."

Dat shook his head back and forth, vehemently.

"No, she's not."

"Then what's wrong with her?" Sadie spoke quickly, forcefully.

"Don't speak to your father that way."

Sadie was on her feet, then, her hands palm down on the table. She leaned forward, her eyes boring into his.

"Dat! If it means putting some sense into your head,

I'm going to disobey you. Mam is more sick than any of us realize. She's living in an agony of depression and fear. She hears voices at night and sees things that aren't really there. She's hoarding stupid little things like hand-kerchiefs and barrettes. She's not working. She's much worse than any of us are even allowed to think she is. And it's all your fault, Dat! Your dumb pride!"

Leah and Rebekah looked on, horrified. No one talked to their father that way. Not ever.

"Sadie!" Dat spoke in a terrible voice, rising from his chair.

Sadie remained standing.

"I'm sorry, Dat," she said, her heart pounding. "I don't want to speak to you in this manner, but you are not God. You cannot make Mam better. We have to let our pride go, Dat!"

At this, she broke down, sobs engulfing her, racking her body.

"Mam is so sick, Dat! Please allow her to go to the hospital for help. I think she'd go!"

Rebekah and Leah were crying. Dat stood over them, his face grim, his eyes blazing. His daughters bent their heads.

"She's not as bad as you say, Sadie."

"Yes, she is! I will not back down. You need to let go of what people will say. Mental illness is no shame. She can't help it."

Dat sagged into his chair, his eyes weary.

"Well, what will they do at the hospital?" he asked.

"Evaluate her. Talk to her. Get her on the right medi-cation. They'll explain it to her. To you. Please, Dat."

"If you don't give up, I'm afraid Mam will do harm to herself—if she hasn't already," Rebekah said firmly.

Dat's head came up. His eyes opened wide with fear.
"No!"

"You're seeing in Mam what you want to see, Dat,
and not what's actually there. She's a courageous woman,
and she's doing her best to appear normal for your sake—
she is—but she's so pitiful," Leah wailed.

Sadie could see fear grasp her father. His breath came
in gasps, and he stood up.

"We need a plan to look for her now!" he ground out.

"We'll search our farm, first, the house, pasture, barn,
the woods. Everywhere," Sadie said.

"But what if she's not here?" Dat asked.

A great wave of pity rose in Sadie. He knew. He knew
it was true, the things they told him.

"Then we'll call the police."

"But…everyone will know."

"Exactly. And they'll help us look for her," Sadie said
firmly.

They got into their coats, boots, and scarves, their
faces pale, their hands shaking as they pulled on their
gloves. They opened the door and stepped out into the
brilliant sunshine. Somehow the sunlight was reassuring,
as if God was providing plenty of light for them to find
Mam. She couldn't have gone far, surely.

Dat searched the pasture, Leah went down the driveway calling Mam's name, Rebekah went to the buggy
shed, and Sadie walked off to begin searching the barn.

Charlie, the driving horse, nickered softly when she
opened the door. The barn cats came running to her,
wanting to be fed. She looked behind every bale of hay
and in Nevaeh's empty stall, calling Mam's name over
and over. She climbed the stairs to the hayloft, searching
it thoroughly.

Fear dried her mouth, made her breath come in gasps. Oh, Mam. We neglected you too long.

Remorse washed over her. They hadn't done enough soon enough. Where was she?

Sadie fought down the panic that threatened to engulf her, making her want to run and scream Mam's name. She had to remain calm, stay within reason. They would find her. Dat had probably found her already. He had to.

As the forenoon wore on and there was no sign of Mam, their fear and worry deepened. There was simply nowhere else to look, unless they walked the roads or called a driver to go looking for her. That was a bit uncommon and likely would not help at all.

"Before we call the police, we need to bring Anna and Reuben home from school. If they see policemen up here, they'll be beside themselves. Besides, they'll find out anyway," Sadie said.

The little parochial school was situated just below the Millers' driveway, nestled in a grove of pine and cedar trees, but in plain view of their house. The school was picturesque, covered in cedar shingles, stone laid carefully on the porch, two swinging doors and neat windows on either side, a split-rail fence surrounding it.

Rebekah offered to walk down and bring Anna and Reuben home. Dat took to wringing his hands, pacing, muttering to himself. Leah cried quietly.

Sadie stood on the porch not knowing what to do next. What did a person do when their mother was missing? She had prayed, was still praying.

Yet the sun shone on as brightly as ever, the snow sparkled, the branches waved in the midday breeze. The day went on as if all was as normal as ever. But a sense of unreality pervaded Sadie's senses. Suddenly it seemed as if this was not happening at all. Surely Mam would come walking out of the bedroom or up from the basement, bustling about like usual, her hair combed neatly, her white covering pinned to her graying hair, the pleats in her dress hanging just right the way they always did.

Mam, please, where are you? she cried, silently.

Rebekah came panting up the driveway, Anna and Reuben beside her, lunch buckets in tow. Anna was crying. Reuben was wide-eyed and grim, bravely battling his tears.

So she had told them.

They all went into the kitchen, trying to reason among themselves.

Now what?

Call the police?

Certainly.

Suddenly, Anna sat upright and, without a word, walked swiftly to her parent's bedroom. They heard the closet doors open, close quietly, then open again.

"Sadie, come here," she called.

Sadie looked questioningly at her sisters, then went to her parent's room. She found Anna standing, looking up at the top closet shelf.

"It's gone, Sadie!"

"What? What's gone?"

"Her suitcase. Their suitcase. The big one."

Sadie's heart sank as she joined Anna at the closet door.

"Oh, Anna. It is."

"Sadie, I heard her. I was working on my English at the kitchen table about a week ago, and she was puttering around the way she does and talking to herself. She kept saying over and over, *"Ya vell. Tzell home gay. Tzell."*

"Why didn't you tell us, Anna?"

"She often talks to herself and no one pays attention."

"Oh, I know. I know."

They hurried to the kitchen, telling the rest what Anna had said.

The news was Dat's undoing. He bent his head, shook it back and forth. No one spoke as Dat fought with his own thoughts. It seemed as if they could see his spirit breaking before them, a thin, glass vase shattering beneath the weight of a heavy object, ground to a thousand pieces, shattered with the knowledge of what he had always known. He had put his will before his wife's. He had loved his own life instead of giving it for her. He had not loved his wife as Christ loved the church.

He had wanted to move to Montana so badly. He had. And they had all honored his wishes as happily and contentedly as possible.

But was it right?

When he broke down in great, awful sobs, five pairs of arms encircled him, held him up. They were the arms of angels for Jacob Miller.

Chapter 19

It was an unusual thing, an Amish girl hugging her father. In an Amish home, love was an unspoken attitude, as common and as comfortable as the air you breathed or the clothes you wore. No one said "I love you" or hugged you, but there was no need. Home, church, school, it was all an atmosphere of safety. Because of this love and safety, everyone had a place and belonged. There was no need to find oneself. Your parents had already found you on the day you were born into the well-structured Amish heritage.

But seeing Dat's bent head and his heaving shoulders was more than any of them could bear, so surrounding him with their arms seemed the most natural thing in the world.

When they stepped back a bit self-consciously, Dat kept his head lowered. Digging into his worn, denim trouser pockets, he procured his wrinkled, red handkerchief, shook it, and blew his nose. Then he removed his glasses and wiped his eyes.

"Ach, my," he sighed.

The girls stood silently surrounding him, supporting him with their quiet presence. Reuben marched to the cupboard, swiping viciously at his eyes. The set of his shoulders said how shameful it was for a big guy like him to be crying. He opened the cupboard door, yanked at a glass, and went to the refrigerator to pour himself a glass of milk.

He sat down at the table, took a sip, then said angrily, "Well, I guess if Mam went so far as to take a suitcase, we better call the police."

Dat looked at Reuben, unseeing.

"Somebody better go out to the phone shanty and dial 911."

Did they actually have to?

Sadie took a deep breath to steady herself.

"Well?"

"If the police arrive, we all need to make sense. We have to tell the whole truth, Dat. She's mentally unstable and has been for…"

"Longer than any of you know," Dat groaned, holding his head in his hands.

Leah raised her eyebrows and looked at Rebekah.

"I…I persuaded her for much, much too long to carry on for her children's sake. I kept telling her there was nothing wrong—that it was all in her head. I told her to swallow all the pills she wanted, but to keep it from all of you, the church, and our community. No one needed to know."

He stopped, averted his eyes.

"This is my fault. She cried during the night. She cried a lot. She wanted to go back home to Ohio. I thought she'd get over it. It's worse in the wintertime."

Sadie was horrified.

"Dat! Why didn't you tell us? Why?"

He sighed. "Because I was afraid you would all want to return to Ohio with her."

"Well, we're here now," Sadie ground out. "I'm going to the phone."

She could never remember feeling such anger, such a gripping disgust that she actually felt like vomiting. What horrible pride controlled Dat? Why had Mam been so passive? What caused a person to slowly tilt outward and move toward the edge of reasoning? Was it all because, if it boiled right down to it, Mam refused to give up her own will and submit to Dat's will?

She yanked open the phone-shanty door, punched 911, and briskly told the dispatcher what she needed to know.

No sirens, please, she begged silently. The school children will go home and tell their parents there was a policeman at Jacob Millers' and tongues will wag. Well, it couldn't be helped. There was no time for her own foolish pride now.

The crunch of gravel heralded the policemen's arrival. Two of them stepped out of the unmarked vehicle. Sadie's heart beat loudly, and for a second she was glad it was a car that was not the usual kind the police drove with flashing blue lights and "Police" written across it in big letters.

The two men strode purposefully to the door, knocked, and stood aside politely when Dat opened it. They were kind but firm, writing on clipboards, searching the room with their eyes, speaking in short but professional tones.

The Millers answered truthfully. Dat spoke and the girls answered when they were asked. Reuben was white-faced, silent, frightened out of his wits. He slouched in his chair at the kitchen table, trying to appear brave, even nonchalant, but his huge blue eyes completely gave him away.

When Dat described Mam to the men, Anna stifled a sob, and Sadie's arms were instantly around her shoulders. She slid her face against Sadie, struggling to conceal her emotions.

The policemen's radios crackled, their badges and holsters gleamed. It all seemed like one big, awful dream that would come to a welcome halt the minute Sadie woke up.

One policeman went to the car while the remaining one told them he was alerting every radio station, television news channel, and airport.

"Why an airport?" Sadie blurted out. "She would never fly. We don't go... I mean, our beliefs forbid us to fly in an airplane. She wouldn't be in an airport. Perhaps a bus station? A train station? An Amish driver?"

"Amish driver? I thought you don't drive cars?" Mr. Connelly, the elder of the two, inquired.

"No, I mean, she would have called a person who provides transportation for us."

They made phone calls to every driver and neighbor on the list, but to absolutely no avail. Trucks and more troopers arrived, search parties sent to comb the entire region around the house and throughout the neighborhood.

Amish friends and relatives arrived, wide-eyed and in different stages of disbelief. Dat remained strong, his face a mixture of despair, agony, pride, shame, and finally, acceptance. There was nothing left to do as wailing sirens climbed the driveway, lights flashing, radios crackling messages.

Someone from the firehall set up a post inside the buggy shed with thermoses of hot coffee and sandwiches. Neighbors brought kettles of chili and vegetable soup, homemade rolls, smoked deer bologna, pies, and cookies. They comforted Dat, hugged the girls, whispered endearments.

Then darkness fell. With the darkness came a fresh despair, a sense of loss felt so deeply that Sadie thought she could not hold up against its crushing force. She cried with Anna. She went into the bathroom with Leah and sat on the edge of the bathtub and cried some more.

"Why? Why on earth did Dat let her go like this? How long has she been sick and we didn't know?"

Leah peered into the mirror and fixed a few stray blonde hairs. She shook her head in disgust at her swollen, red eyes.

"Well, I know one thing. Remember last year when we had church at our house? Sadie, I mean it, I honestly don't think we would have gotten ready without you. Mam got nothing accomplished all day. She just puttered around the way she does, you know.

Sadie sighed.

"There were lots of signs—if only we wouldn't have been so dense."

They sat for a few moments, Leah on the floor, Sadie on the edge of the bathtub.

"Do you think she became mentally ill from wanting to go back home?"

"Home?" Sadie's head jerked up in an angry motion. "Where is home?"

"For me, here. In Montana," Leah said flatly.

"Is it home to you?" Sadie asked.

"Of course."

Sadie said nothing.

There was a knock on the door. Richard Caldwell and his wife, Barbara, had come and wanted to speak to her. Surprised, Sadie went to the living room.

Sadie's boss and his wife sat uncomfortably, glancing at the softly hissing propane lamp. In spite of herself, Sadie hid a smile, knowing they had never set foot in an Amish home.

Despite their uneasiness, their concern was genuine, and their hugs bolstered Sadie's courage. Once again she was amazed at the change in Barbara, the tenderness in Richard Caldwell, and she was grateful.

"They'll find her, Sadie," Richard Caldwell boomed.

And then Dorothy came bustling into the living room, the soles of her inexpensive Dollar General shoes squeaking on the highly varnished hardwood, oak floor.

"Oh, my, oh, my!" she kept saying over and over as she gathered Sadie into her heavy arms. "You never let on! You never let on!" she kept saying.

Sadie knew that never again in their household would they take for granted the wonders of human sympathy. It was the genuine caring—that giving of oneself—that brought so much warmth to Sadie's heart. It was like an Olympic runner carrying the flaming torch, relaying hope from one person to the next.

How could one be crushed beneath despair when so many held them up? Rough cowhands, wealthy ranchers, plain Amish people, men of the law—they were all there, bound by the soft, gentle cord of caring. White-covered heads bobbed in conversation with permed and dyed heads, earrings twinkling beneath them, as tears flowed together.

Mam couldn't have gone far. She'd be okay.

Was there anything they could do?

Poor lady, she must have been in agony.

Sadie could almost see her father aging before her eyes. It was hard to look at him. Remorse is a terrible thing, she had read once. It's the hopelessness of wishing that you had not done things in the past, or that you could undo something you knew you couldn't.

That's where Jesus came in, Sadie thought. He died for pitiful creatures like us, people who make mistakes because of their human pride and wrongdoings.

Dear God, just stay with Dat. He didn't do it on purpose. He thought he was doing the right thing.

And then Mark came. Mark Peight. Would she ever tire of just thinking his name?

He was in the kitchen, taller than everyone else except Richard Caldwell. He was talking to Leroy Miller who was moving his hands to accompany his fiery red curls that flew about his head with every movement. His hair was plentiful, and it looked even more so the way he shook his head when he became agitated. His beard was as red as his curls, and it wagged up and down at an alarming rate.

Sadie wished they would all go home now and leave her with Mark. She knew that was quite selfish, but she wished it anyway. Finally she was able to catch his eye and almost swooned when he conveyed all his feelings in his direct look.

"Sadie, how are you?"

She turned into the waiting arms of Nancy Grayson, the taxi driver, as Leroy Miller broke into another passionate tirade, this time to Mark.

The clock's hands turned to ten o'clock, and still the Miller house was full of people who came to wish them well. Dat was becoming weary, his eyes drooping behind his glasses the way they did at the end of a long day. Reuben was curled up on the recliner covered with a blanket, his hands tucked beneath his cheek. He looked so young and so vulnerable, his usual tufts of hair on the back of his head sticking straight out, the way they always did when he hadn't brushed his hair completely.

Mark moved across the kitchen to stand by Sadie's side, being careful to keep an appropriate distance between them.

"Sadie, tell me what happened," he said quietly.

Tears immediately sprang to her eyes. It was the soft urging in his voice that showed how much he cared. She raised her eyes to his, then looked down as she saw Leroy Miller's flinty eyes watching their every move.

"Can you come upstairs with me?" she asked.

"You go first; I'll sneak away later," he said quietly.

Sadie went over to Reuben and took him upstairs to his bedroom, waiting outside his door until he had his pajamas on. Reuben would never change clothes in his sister's presence, properly locking the bathroom or bedroom door when any change of clothes or showering was necessary.

After the door was unlocked, she caught his shoulders and drew him against her. He did not pull back but laid his head against her shoulder as she held him, rocking him the way she did when he was two years old.

His hair smelled of shampoo and hay and little boy sweat and his hat. She could feel his thin shoulders shaking beneath his t-shirt as his breath caught in suppressed little sobs.

"Reuben. Listen. They'll find Mam. In this day and age, people don't disappear the way they used to. They have computers and video cameras and stuff we can't even imagine to track every traveler that moves through train or bus stations."

"But what if she's lying outside somewhere and she's cold?" Reuben asked, his breath catching on a sob of despair.

"Don't think that. Don't let yourself imagine such things. Remember to pray earnestly tonight, and God will watch over Mam and over you if you can't sleep, okay?"

Reuben nodded, crept into his bed, and pulled the covers up to his chin.

"You want the lamp on?" Sadie asked, brushing back a lock of hair.

"Nah."

Sadie blew out the steady, yellow flame that lit a room so cozily, then whispered, "Good-night."

She met Mark coming down the hallway uncertainly, never having been upstairs in the Miller household. It was not uncommon for a girl's friends to come upstairs to her bedroom on Sunday afternoons when church was over. All girls had chairs or loveseats in their bedrooms for that purpose.

Now, however, Sadie was uncertain. Should she ask Mark to come into her bedroom at a time like this? He might think her extremely bold, but where else could they go to talk about Mam?

"Is … is it all right to … go to my room?" she whispered.

"If you're okay with it."

She entered her room and lit the kerosene lamp with the lighter beside it, replaced the glass chimney, and turned it up to brighten the room.

Mark stood inside the door, waiting until Sadie asked him to sit down. His large frame seemed to fill the entire loveseat, so Sadie sat gingerly on the edge of the bed, her body tense, the pulse in her temples pounding. She pleated the fabric of her skirt over and over, her long, thin fingers never ceasing their movement. Her head bent, her voice barely audible, she related Mam's disappearance and the shameful, sad history of her parents' relationship.

"I think Mam is in a much more serious depression than any of us realized. The only person that had any idea was Dat, and he is much too stubborn or proud to admit anything is ever wrong in our family. As long as he can present a smiling group of good Christians to the Amish community, he thinks everything is just great."

Mark nodded. "Do all of you want to live here in Montana?" he asked after a respectful silence that was so typical of him.

"I have no choice, so this is home now. But if I was allowed to choose, I'd probably go back to Ohio."

"Why?"

"I miss family. I miss Eva most of all. We've been here for almost six years now, and I'm used to Montana. But…" she broke off, timidly.

"What?"

"Well, it's just that ever since the accident with Ezra and those wild horses, I sense a bad omen. It's as if fear is alive and haunting, and that black, devilish horse … and then Nevaeh...I don't know. Is there such a thing as an un-blessing? You know how the ministers say, an *unsayah*."

Mark was silent.

The small heart-shaped alarm clock ticked steadily. Only their breathing could be heard above it.

Then there was a great shout from the kitchen, followed by a hubbub of low voices, high ones, and everything in between.

Sadie jumped to her feet and dashed to the door. Mark following closely. As she pulled the door open, was it only her imagination, or did Mark place his hand on her waist, as if to steer her through the door like a gentleman?

Reuben's tousled head appeared.

And then Leah was pounding up the steps, calling her name, nearly colliding with all three of them.

"They found her! Oh, Sadie! She's been found!" Leah burst into sobs of relief.

"Where, Leah?"

"In an airport somewhere!" Leah said between her sobs.

"A what? Are you sure?"

They hurried down the stairs and into the crowd of people rejoicing and crying. So much relief. So much happiness. It was hard to grasp this joy when only moments before the despair had been so real.

Finally someone clapped their hands and the room grew silent. All heads turned to the aging, white-bearded gentleman who stood just inside the door. His eyes were kind but stern, and he was flanked by two policemen in heavy coats.

"Annie Miller has been found. She is extremely disoriented and her speech is totally incomprehensible. We need

Mr. Miller and any of the immediate family who wishes to accompany us."

Dat's sad eyes searched his daughters'.

"I'll go," Rebekah said immediately.

"I'll stay with Anna and Reuben," Leah volunteered.

"Come with us, Sadie," Dat said, a pleading note in his voice.

Sadie's heart melted. Forgiveness like a soothing balm ran joyously over her heart, coating it solidly with love for her father. He had only been doing what he felt was best for his family, regardless of how foolish it seemed now.

It was all surreal, the long ride through the night, the winding country roads turning onto the interstate highway, the kaleidoscope of bright lights, hissing tires, neon signs blinking. It seemed as if they had left the state of Montana.

Finally the car slowed onto an exit and circled the ramp to a red light. Turning left, they came onto a steady stream of vehicles and more red lights.

Sadie wondered what all these people were doing out in the middle of the night. She had no idea the world didn't sleep at night. How would they ever be able to get up and go to work the next morning? No wonder people were fired from their jobs. They should all be at home in bed getting their much needed eight hours of sleep.

The car slowed again and turned left into a huge parking area. The building ahead of them towered like the buildings in New York City. Well, almost.

Sadie counted eight stories.

Toshkoma Medical Center.

Mam was at a hospital!

Acceptance settled across Sadie's shoulders. It was a

yoke to bear—a heavy, sad feeling—but it was coupled with joy. There was finally help available for poor, dear Mam.

They found Mam sitting on a chair in a large, blue waiting room. Her cumbersome luggage was by her side. Her head was bent, her hands twisting and turning in her lap. She was wearing her black bonnet and her Sunday coat with the new buttons she had sewed on herself. Her woolen shawl was folded neatly on top of her big suitcase. She was mumbling to herself and didn't see them until Dat stood close to her, touched her shoulder, and said, "Annie."

At first, Sadie thought she would not recognize them. Her eyes were so clouded and she seemed a million miles away. She was talking in mumbles, laughing hoarsely, then crying.

Cold chills crept up Sadie's spine, the icy feelings of fear and dread.

Mam! Have we lost you completely through our neglect?

White-coated doctors joined them. Psychiatrists, nurses, men in authority, talking, talking. They could not admit Mam without her consent.

Mam sat so bent, so hysterical. Now she was saying, "Sadie, Sadie."

"Which one is Sadie?"

The little man with the bald head and black mustache reached for her, escorted her toward her mother.

Blindly, Mam reached for Sadie's hand.

Sadie fought back panic for a moment. This is your mother. Relax. She's just sick. She's not wild or dangerous. Just help her. Listen to her.

"Sadie, Sadie." It was all Mam could say, over and over.

Sadie bent her head to hear the garbled words. She tried to still her mother's restless hands, then bent closer. "What?"

Mam spoke in Pennsylvania Dutch.

"Halt aw. Halt aw. Halt um gaduld aw. Gaduld."

The voice went on, jumbled, begging for patience.

"Ich do, Mam, Ich do."

Then suddenly Mam lifted her head, looked at Sadie, and said in an articulate voice, "It was me that left Nevaeh out."

She began sobbing so heartbrokenly that Sadie was on her knees immediately, holding her mother as her shoulders heaved. Murmuring brokenly now, she told Sadie that she needed help.

Sadie stood up, nodded to the doctors, and told them Mam was willing to be admitted. Dat stood beside her uncomfortably, nodding his assent.

"Oh, yes. Yes. She most certainly will be admitted. Thank God. If that is what she wants."

Sadie nodded. Rebekah rushed to her mother. Together they guided her off the chair and into a waiting wheelchair. Dat grabbed the suitcase, and they all loaded into an elevator that clanged and pinged its way to the floor where Mam would be treated.

The doctors talked and asked so many questions that Sadie thought it must surely be morning when the last form was signed and completed. Dat turned hesitantly, not sure what he should do as they finally wheeled Mam to her room.

"Come, Dat. I think it's time you and Rebekah and I had the largest sized coffee this hospital's snack bar has to offer. Everything is going to be all right now. They'll adjust Mam's medication until they get it right, and she'll soon be okay."

Only now did Sadie have a chance to absorb what Mam had said about letting Nevaeh out of the barn. In this moment, Sadie felt that her beloved horse was a small price to pay for the stability of her mother's mental health.

Chapter 20

Spring came late that year. It was always later than Ohio springtime, but this time it was almost the end of May until the last chilly winds died away.

Sadie climbed one of the steep ridges surrounding her home. She was alone. The house was suffocating her, even with the windows open a bit at the top to allow the sweet smell of the earth to circulate about the rooms. So she decided to go for a walk.

Her breath came in short gasps, the calves of her legs ached, and she could feel the soft fabric of her robin's-egg blue dress attach itself to her perspiring body. The sun was warmer than she thought it would be, and she realized with great joy that they could be planting the garden soon.

Another spring, another garden, and here I am alone in Montana, she thought wryly.

It was when she was alone, and especially on days like today, that she thought of Mark Peight most.

Why had he done that? For the thousandth time she asked the wind, and, like always, there was no reply.

Even with Mam hospitalized, she had planned for that special date, that awaited Saturday evening when he would open his heart and tell her his life's story. Instead, a flat, white envelope had arrived in Friday's mail with small, neat handwriting addressing the letter to "Miss Sadie Miller."

Her life had not been the same since then. He had written on a yellow legal pad and minced no words in his flat, round script.

> *Dear Sadie,*
>
> *I'm going back to Pennsylvania. I can't write that I'm going home, because I don't necessarily have a home. I'm just going back.*
>
> *I simply can't be with you anymore without telling you the truth about myself. I apologize to you for being a coward. I'm not good enough for you and never will be.*
>
> *This is good-bye.*
>
> *Mark Peight*

That short letter literally rocked her world. It was as abrasive as steel wool on a smooth surface. It had hurt as badly as falling off a bike on a poorly paved road, tearing her skin into rough, raw patches. There was no way around the desolation of that letter. But she just had to give up and endure the pain without cringing or crying, which she did during the day. At night, she cried.

Who was he? Why did he run without leaving as much as an address or a phone number?

The wind had no answers. It caressed her warm face, played with the brown hair that straggled loose from her white covering, sighed in the branches of the pines, but had no answers for her as usual.

God was in nature, or so it seemed to Sadie. He spoke to her of his love when she saw twinkling stars, new wild-flowers, fresh-fallen snow. Sometimes his voice in nature was soft and warm like today's gentle breeze. Other times it was strong and powerful like in thunder and torrents of rain. But always, God was there.

She had much to be thankful for. She knew that sounded like an old cliché, an overused Amish phrase, but it was true.

She was thankful for her mother first. Dear, dear Mam. She had made an amazing comeback, but the struggle had been heartrending to watch.

After the doctors had observed, adjusted medications, and counseled, Mam finally underwent extensive thyroid surgery.

Her problems had been real, not imagined. A serious chemical imbalance, coupled with a diseased thyroid gland, had taken a horrible toll on Mam's mind, on her well-being. She had become so confused and was hallucinating and hearing voices which were very real to her.

The final straw, the one thing that had pushed her over the edge, was the cost of Sadie's hospital stay. Somehow, in her poor, twisted mind, she had linked this with the cost of keeping Nevaeh. That pressure troubled her so much that she released the horse, believing this was the only thing she could do to help pay the cost of Sadie's bill.

After her confession and complete breakdown, she

began to heal with Dat's support. He had long conversations with the physicians and therapists, nodding his head, listening, observing, and being completely supportive of Mam's care. It was wondrous to behold.

Mam smiled now. She ate healthy meals. She cooked and baked.

Dat offered to move back to Ohio. He told her it wasn't right that he had dragged her out to Montana against her wishes. Mam had a faraway look on her face—an unveiled glimpse of her homesickness. Then she had turned to Dat.

"But, Jacob, I don't think I could go back. I don't know if I could be at home there. This is home."

And Sadie knew she meant it.

She had laid a hand on Dat's arm, and her eyes were pure and clear and honest without a trace of malice or ill will.

"I love Montana now, Jacob. I haven't always. Sometimes I miss the folks in Ohio, but you know, whithersoever thou goest I will go."

She had smiled such a beautiful smile, her gray hair shining exactly like a halo about her head, that all the girls agreed she looked like a middle-aged angel.

Sadie still loved her job at the ranch. It was the one thing that kept her grounded, kept her sane. She could always stay busy cooking, cleaning, and doing laundry. Sometimes she rode the fine horses from Richard Caldwell's stables. But she never connected with another horse like Nevaeh or Paris. Horses, like life, were too unpredictable, so it was safer to stay away and not lose your head or your heart to a horse or, for that matter, to handsome Mark Peight either. You just got hurt or bruised.

Sadie flopped down in a meadow of wildflowers, wiping an arm across her forehead to dry it.

Puffy, white clouds trailed across the blue sky as Sadie lay on the soft carpet of flowers. An eagle soared across the treetops, riding the current with a natural ease. His head was white against the dark color of his outstretched wings.

She wondered what had happened with the herd of wild horses. There had been a great public outcry with posters tacked to the wall of the post office, the bank, and the local grocery. It was the main subject on Sundays after church and when visitors came to see Mam, but no one had a solution. Helicopters were never brought in because no one could prove the horses had ever damaged anything. As Dat said, it didn't amount to a hill of beans. And then the subject died off and everyone moved on to other topics.

The horses had been responsible for Nevaeh's death, Sadie felt sure, although she never spoke of it, not even to Leah or Rebekah.

She could feel her body relaxing with each intake of the sweet smell of wildflowers. Her eyelids felt heavy. God was, indeed, so good. How could anyone ever doubt his presence lying on a flower-strewn hillside in May?

She wasn't sure if she heard something first, or if she only felt it. She just knew the earth vibrated a bit, the way the hardwood floor in the living room did when Dat walked across it in his big boots.

She stayed still, every nerve tense, listening.

There. That sound.

It wasn't a rushing, scurrying sound. It was a stumbling, sliding sound.

Should she be afraid?

Strangely, she felt no fear. Surely the band of wild horses had gone. No one ever spoke of them anymore. Oh, the men snorted and said how incompetent the law was, unable to solve a mystery that was quite obviously under their nose. But who were they to say?

Amish people were a peaceable lot, driving their horses and buggies at a slow trot on the winding, country roads of Montana, taking care of family and friends, loving their neighbors—for the most part. If the law chose to ignore the obvious, they were in authority, and the Amish abided by their rules. No use fighting. It wasn't their way.

So Sadie listened, her pulse quickening, but not with dry-mouthed, raw fear. Instead she had an inquisitive feeling.

There now. It had stopped, so likely she had imagined it in the first place.

A jay called from the pines. Another one answered. They screamed the way blue jays do when they're disturbed. Then she heard a tearing sound like when a cow wraps its tongue around a tuft of grass and pulls or bites. The grass makes a soft, breaking sound. Perhaps someone's cows wandered up here.

Sadie sat up slowly so she wouldn't spook the cattle. They were amiable creatures for the most part, so she wasn't afraid, although she didn't want to start a stampede if she could help it.

She blinked.

She ran the back of her hand across her eyes and blinked again.

A horse!

Three!

Her hand went to the front of her dress to still her beating heart. The horses had not seen her. Slowly she turned her head just enough so that she could see them out of the corner of her eyes.

Her mind could not fathom the sight of the black horse. She knew he was there grazing, but it seemed like a dream. He was so gorgeous and much bigger than any driving horse or any horse in Richard Caldwell's stables, that was sure.

Was she in danger?

She shivered.

To get up and run would only show fear, and she desperately wanted to observe them, if even for a second.

Along with the black stallion, there was a brown mare. She was small and compact with a beautifully arched neck. Her mane and tail had been luxurious at one time but were unkempt now. They were matted with burrs, and the forelock needed a trim.

And then…

Sadie didn't remember opening her mouth, she just knew it had been open for some time because her tongue felt dry when she closed it again.

Paris!

It was Paris!

It couldn't be Paris.

The horse was exactly the color of Paris after she had lost her winter coat. Paris was honey-colored then, a rich, amber color that was complemented by the beige of her mane and tail.

This horse was that same color, and it, too, was a mare. She moved behind the black horse as he grazed slowly, clipping the grass with a crunching sound. There was only one thing better than hearing a horse eat grass and that was to hear him eat oats and corn from a wooden feed box. Horses bit deep into the oats, then lifted their nose a bit and chewed. Most of the oats fell out of the side of a horse's mouth when he did that, but he chewed them later until the feed box was completely clean.

Slowly Sadie got to her feet.

The black horse lifted his head, his ears pricked forward, and he wheeled immediately, lunging back the way he had come. The brown mare looked at Sadie, then ran off with the palomino following.

Sadie stayed rooted to the spot.

Involuntarily her arm reached out toward them.

"Paris!" she whispered.

The black horse disappeared, but Sadie had a feeling the mares' return to the woods was halfhearted. They hadn't made an all-out dash for the trees the way the big black had done.

Yes, they ran, but they were curious, too, Sadie thought.

Slowly, with her arm extended and hand reaching toward the mares, she walked through the wildflowers. She was talking, telling them the things she told horses, even if she couldn't see them through the forest.

"Come, Paris. Come on, you big baby. Don't be afraid. I'm not going to hurt you. It's about time you returned to the fold and started living a decent life after all the mischief you've been up to. Come on. Come on. Just let me look at you."

But she could not coax them out. The horses stayed in the safety of the trees.

"Well, okay, stay away then, Paris. But I'll be here tomorrow. I'll bring you some oats and corn and molasses and I'll leave a salt block. You'll love that."

She kept talking to the unseen horses, which may have been silly, but it may not have been either, she reasoned.

Those mares were not terrified. Sadie was certain about that.

Adrenaline surged through her veins as she turned. Yes!

But Dat would never let her come up here alone. Never. Especially if he knew there were any wild horses within a mile of her.

She could tell her parents she was going on a hike to get back in shape. But that wouldn't work. Her sisters would want to join her, and Leah, she knew, would catch on faster than anyone.

It would have to remain her secret. She'd bring a salt block by herself somehow.

She was running down the hill, her knees bearing the impact which she knew was no good for her newly healed bones.

When she got home, she tried to act as carefree as when she left the house, but she knew her cheeks were flushed. If her eyes showed any of the excitement she felt—which they probably did—she'd be a dead give-away. So she went to the barn to make plans.

Sadie stood back, surveying the interior of the barn. That Dat. He would never change. He hardly ever swept the forebay. Cobwebs hung from the floor joists above her head, and empty feed bags were strewn beside the wooden feed box. Dusty scooters and bikes and children's riding toys that should have been discarded a long time ago were all piled in one corner.

Bales of hay lay where they landed when Dat threw them down the hole from the second floor. He never carried the bales of hay over against the wall and stacked them neatly. He just broke them apart and fed the hay to Charlie from the area where they had landed, which

meant there was loose hay everywhere. It was embarrassing, the way this barn was always a mess.

Sadie sighed and got to work. At least this would keep
her out of the house so she could hide her excitement
about the horses and make her plans in secret.

✫ ✡ ✫

The following evening Sadie was in luck. She could
not believe her good fortune. The whole family went to
Dan Detweilers for the season's first cook-out, leaving
before Sadie got home from work.

Sadie was ecstatic. It was too perfect.

She immediately changed into her oldest clothes and
a pair of sturdy shoes. She grabbed Reuben's backpack,
the biggest one he owned, and hurried out to the barn.

Good! The feed bin was almost full so Dat wouldn't
notice if she took some of it up the mountain. He would
just think Charlie had gotten hungry.

There was no extra block of salt, but she remembered
to check Nevaeh's stall just in case.

Nostalgia enveloped her as she remembered that feeling of walking into the stall and being welcomed with
Nevaeh's funny blowing of breath from her nose. It
wasn't loud enough to be a nicker or whinny, just a soft
rustling of her nostrils instead.

There was still part of a salt block, and Sadie grabbed
it and put it in the bottom of her backpack. Opening a
white, plastic Wal-Mart bag, she carefully scooped some
of the sticky, pungent horse feed into it. She knotted the
bag securely and slipped it into the backpack with the
salt. She dashed back to the kitchen for a few apples and
stuck them into the pack with the rest of the things.

She slipped one shoulder into the strap. She had to bend over and struggle to get the other strap in place, but determination goaded her. She had to see what those horses would do when confronted with food they were unaccustomed to having. Surely they would remember it and long for it.

In Sadie's mind, the wild horses had to be connected with that wealthy person who lost his horses—the one she had seen on the news that Richard Caldwell had shown her. As long as the horses weren't found, there was no proof they had been stolen, so rumors swirled through the valley continuously. That's all the talk amounted to. Rumors.

Sadie had never entered the conversation at the ranch, but she had listened plenty and formed her own opinions.

Her opinion was confirmed, especially after seeing the horses up close. They weren't ordinary horses. Wild, yes, and definitely scruffy-looking, but not as small or as mangy as many western mustangs she had seen.

Sadie walked rapidly at first, then slowed. She knew climbing the ridge with 10 or 15 pounds on her back would be a daunting task, but she'd have to try.

She wished she would have taken time to eat. She felt her stomach rumble and hoped the adrenaline rush would propel her up the incline, because there wasn't much food in her body.

For one thing, it had been Dorothy's day to make chili, and she sure had been heavy-handed with the ground chilis. The dish was so hot, Sadie gasped and ran for the sink when she innocently put a large spoonful to her mouth.

"Dorothy!"

Dorothy chuckled.

"You're not good western stock, Sadie! You're just an Ohio Dutchman raised on milk pudding and chicken corn soup. You don't know what good chili is."

Sadie drank water, spluttering, her face turning red. "That stuff is on fire!"

Dorothy laughed and went about her duties, knowing the cowhands would not think the chili was too hot. So Sadie had made a cold bologna sandwich for herself and hadn't bothered to sit down long enough to eat all of it.

She could hardly keep her secret from Jim and Dorothy. She had even considered talking to Jim about it on the way to work but then decided against it. She didn't want anyone to know she thought the wild horses were still in the area, mostly for fear of a group of men following her up the ridge to round them up.

Turning off the road, Sadie started across the field on her way to the ridge where the trees met the open grass. She could feel her heartbeat increasing from exertion, but she could climb surprisingly well with the weight distributed evenly on her back. The wind caught her covering, and she grabbed it just before it tore off her head.

Oh, dear, she had forgotten to pin it.

If an Amish girl went outside for a hike on a windy day, she had to put in a few extra straight pins or her covering would not stay put.

Stopping, Sadie tied the strings loosely beneath her chin and decided to let it blow off if it wanted to—which is precisely what it did. She walked on, her brown hair in disarray now and her covering flapping about her backpack. The wind tore at her navy blue skirt, whirling it about her legs, but she pushed it down impatiently and kept walking.

Glancing at the sky, she noticed a bank of dark clouds

building in the west.

Hmm.

She hoped this was no spring thunderstorm. She knew how quickly storms could come up at this time of year, becoming quite violent.

The wind bent the grasses, tossing the purple and yellow flowers relentlessly. Dry leaves, leftover from the winter snow, skidded down the hill, and still Sadie climbed, her breath coming in gasps.

She stopped, turned to look back, and as always was awed at the sight before her.

She was glad they had decided to stay in Montana. It was home to them now, and she couldn't imagine moving back to Ohio where the landscape was flat, the homes too close to each other, and the roads crowded with traffic.

She still missed Eva though. Letters and phone calls were not the same as being with someone. Eva was getting married in the fall, and she still had Spirit, her horse. Sadie wished Eva could be here with her now. She'd have a fit. She would just have to write her a letter when she got back.

She watched the bank of dark clouds. They were farther away than they appeared to be, she knew, but the thought of being caught here in a thunderstorm did not appeal to her.

Finally, her breath tearing at her chest, she reached the spot close to where she had been when the horses first appeared. Carefully she tore the grass away and spread the feed in clumps with the salt on one side, the apples on the other. Then she sat down to catch her breath and wait.

The wind moaned in the trees, its intensity picking up as the pine branches bent to its power. The grasses whipped about now, and Sadie knew she could not stay or she'd be caught in a storm. She watched the clouds moving and expanding, and then she shouldered her empty backpack and started down.

"Okay, Paris and company, enjoy your dinner. I'll be back." She hoped the horses would find their feed before the deer or squirrels or birds did. Likely the wild creatures would get some of it.

Thin streaks of lightning flashed out of the dark clouds now, and Sadie hurried down the hill, the backpack flopping and her covering whipping around every which way.

She'd better hurry. How would she explain a soaking wet dress and a ruined covering if she got caught in the rain?

As it was, she had to run the last half mile as huge drops of cold rain began pelting down on her bare head.

Chapter 21

IT WAS SUNDAY. NOT JUST AN ORDINARY SUNDAY, but one of those rare days when the breeze is cool, the sun is pleasantly warm, and there are so many puffy, white clouds in the sky that you can lie on your back and find all sorts of shapes and animals and maybe even one that looks like a person you know.

Sadie sat on the glossy, oak bench at the Daniel Bontrager home and tried not to tap her fingers on the windowsill beside her. She also tried not to gaze out the window too much, but instead keep her focus on the visiting minister and the sermon he was preaching.

He was a portly, older gentleman from somewhere in Pennsylvania, and his voice had a thin, squeaky quality that was sort of endearing. His short beard wagged methodically as he expounded upon the Scriptures, telling the congregation about the seriousness of this life here on earth and encouraging them to shoulder the cross and follow the Lord Jesus, even in their younger years.

Sadie gazed unseeingly, knowing deep inside that her very own personal cross to bear was none other than

Mark Peight's disappearance. It would not become any easier just yet.

She had been so sure that God had plopped Mark Peight straight down from heaven. She had been so in love—was still so in love. She remembered the way he walked, the depth of his brown eyes, and his quiet ways. He never talked much at all, but when he did, the sound of his voice was like music. She loved to hear him talk, hanging onto every word and being warmed by the sound of his voice.

She sighed. Some things weren't meant to be.

She supposed if she could catch Paris—if that was possible—she'd be happy to have a horse of her own again, which was, after all, something.

Rebekah leaned over and whispered, "I need a tissue."

Sadie lifted her apron and dug into her pocket.

"Don't have one," she whispered back.

The minister droned on.

A fly buzzed by and settled on the windowsill. Sadie watched it and wondered how some people could catch houseflies in their hands the way they did. She had often tried but only hurt the palm of her hand, and the fly flew off unscathed.

She hoped her family would go somewhere this evening. She had been to the ridge only once all week and had not seen a trace of any of the horses. The feed, apples, and salt had all disappeared—every speck of them—but did the horses eat it? She could be feeding horses, deer, elk, even bears, although that was unlikely.

She did not want to go to the supper that would be held for the youth later in the day. She had to come up with a good excuse not to go, one that would be believable to her sisters.

There was always the flu bug going around, which was a good reason for staying in her room feigning serious stomach ailments, but that hardly ever worked with Leah. She could let Reuben in on her secret and then give her sister a whole sad row about Reuben needing to spend more time with her. No, that would be risky.

She looked for Reuben across the room where the men and boys sat facing the women. He was between two larger boys and looked small and innocent. He also looked very, very bored.

She caught his eye and gave him the slightest wink. He grinned and ducked his head, embarrassed at the boldness of his sister.

Sadie smiled, then felt a rush of excitement. She would let him in on her secret after all. He would love every minute of their excursions. He always loved even the thought of an adventure.

After the strains of the last hymn died away, Sadie filed out with the rest of the girls. They crowded together in a corner of the kitchen, waiting until the tables were set up.

Men turned the benches into tables by setting them on legs built for that purpose. The women brought armloads of clean, white tablecloths and spread them on top of the tables. The girls helped carry trays of peanut butter spread, cheese, ham, pickles, spiced red beets, butter, and huge platters of thickly sliced homemade bread, whole wheat on one side and white on the other. They placed a saucer, coffee cup, tumbler, knife, and fork at each setting along the lengthy tables.

Pitchers of water appeared like magic and glasses were filled. Pies—peach, blueberry, raspberry, custard, pumpkin, even a few mince pies—all found their way to the middle of the table.

The men were called in by the person who lived in the home where church was held, and they filed in by their age, the ministers going first. The women sat at a long table next to the men. The ministers' wives sat down first. The rest of the women sat in order by age.

They bowed their heads in silent prayer. Servers offered coffee to each individual, the only hot item for the traditional dinner at church. It was all very organized, although an English person wouldn't be able to tell upon observing. The women were constantly moving, the children dodged in and out, and the noise of conversation was amplified by the sheer number of people assembled in one large room.

Sadie ate hungrily, slathering the thick, gooey peanut butter spread on a heavy slice of whole wheat bread, deciding once again that it was truly the best thing ever. If you sat on a hard bench for three hours straight without any breakfast, the lunch at church was simply the most delicious food.

Sadie chewed the rich, nutty-tasting whole wheat bread accompanied by the sticky sweetness of peanut butter, marshmallow cream, and molasses. Spicy little red beets, pickles, and ham on another slice of white bread, washed down with the fragrant, hot coffee, rounded out the meal. Now she was ready for the grand finale, which was pie, of course.

Of all the pies at church, Sadie always watched for pumpkin. It was her all-time favorite. Pumpkin pie was sweet and custardy and shivery all at the same time, with a spicy flavor that perfectly complemented her cup of hot, black coffee. At home when Mam made pumpkin pie, Sadie spooned Cool Whip on top, but at church there was no extra Cool Whip so she ate it without.

She was finished eating and was piling some soiled dishes in a large bowl when someone tapped her elbow. Turning, she found herself face to face with the visiting minister. He smiled at her, and Sadie put down the bowl of soiled dishes to shake his proffered hand.

"Are you one of Jacob Miller's daughters?" he asked, his eyes alight with genuine curiosity.

"Yes. I am."

"Well, we're from Abbottstown, Pennsylvania. We had a young man come to our community not too long ago—four, five weeks, maybe. We, and the other two families we're traveling with, got to talking about our planned trip to Montana, and he said he was out here on vacation not too long ago. I don't remember his name. Melvin something, I think."

Sadie raised her eyebrows, "Melvin?"

"Yes. He talked of Jacob Millers. That's your dat, right?"

"Yes."

"Something about wild horses you had running around out here."

Sadie nodded.

"You can't think of Melvin's last name, can you?" he asked.

"No, I'm sorry. So many young men come and go that we often lose track of who they are and how long they stay," Sadie answered politely.

"Yes, it would appear so. Well, I sure wish I could think of this young man's name. It wasn't Peachy, but..."

He paused. "Anyway, it was nice talking to you."

He wandered off, and Sadie shook her head ruefully.

Whatever, she thought, a bit irritated. Everyone wanted to know who you were, especially people on vacation checking out these Montana-ians.

They all think we're a bit odd to live so far away from our home settlement, but they're much too polite to say so, she thought, then chided herself for thinking like an old hermit.

✧ ✬ ✧

The buggy ride home was a pure joy with the side windows flung open and the back canvas flap rolled up and secured with leather straps. Sadie hung her arm out the back, whistling lightly under her breath. Reuben was close beside her and Anna on his other side. Leah and Rebekah had gone home with Verna and Magdalena Amstutz, two of their favorite friends.

Reuben shifted his weight toward Sadie, folded his arms across his chest, and mumbled to himself.

"What?" Sadie asked, grabbing his ear and pulling him over.

He yanked his head away.

"I can't see why you couldn't have gone with Leah and Rebekah.

"Because..." Sadie said, pausing to purse her lips importantly, "I have better things to do."

"Like what? It's not like you have a boyfriend the way normal girls do."

"Normal? I'm normal," Sadie said, her eyes dancing.

"No, you're not. You're a queer duck!"

Sadie howled with laughter, an unladylike squawk of pure humor that made Dat turn around in his seat to see what was so funny. Mam chuckled, Anna grinned, and Reuben scowled, looking straight ahead.

The driving horse, good old dependable Charlie, plodded on through the lovely Montana landscape, the harness flapping rhythmically on his well-padded haunches. Some of the hair beneath the britching strap was darker in color, showing signs of moisture.

"Dat, Charlie's sweating already. He's getting fat. You feed him too much grain," Sadie said.

"Well, if Charlie's sweating, get out and walk!" Reuben said forcefully.

"All right, I will. It's a bee-you-tiful day. Walk with me, Reuben."

"No!"

"Yes! Come on. We only have two or three miles."

"Not me. No way!" Anna said, shaking her head.

"Dat, stop. Let me off. Come on, Reuben, you little chicken."

The buggy stopped, and Sadie looked back over the way they had come to make sure no one could see her less than modest exit out the back window of the buggy. She quickly scrambled out and over the springs along the back. When her foot hit the road, she pulled on Reuben's sleeve and begged him one more time to accompany her. To her great surprise, he piled out of the back and onto the road beside her.

Perfect!

With a crunch of steel wheels on gravel and Dat's "Hup!" the buggy moved off. Sadie wasted no time coming straight to the point. Breathlessly she told Reuben what she meant by saying she had better things to do.

"And, Reuben," she concluded, "I'm running out of excuses to go on walks by myself. I honestly think Mam is getting suspicious, or at least wonders what I'm up to. If Mam and Dat find out, they will not let me do this. And that horse! I can't tell you how beautiful she is! It's... She's exactly like...Paris!"

Reuben plodded on, his hands in his pockets, his hat shoved down so hard his ears looked painfully cramped. He looked less than thrilled and was still upset they had to walk so far.

"Paris? Who's Paris?"

"You know. Don't you remember Paris? That yellowish palomino I raced against Eva's Spirit?"

"Eva's spirit? That sounds spooky…like Eva had a ghost or something."

Sadie slapped Reuben's shoulder.

"You know which horse I mean."

Reuben stopped, squinted, then bent down to examine the remnant of a stone. He picked it up, held it to the sun, rubbed it, and announced, "Arrowhead!"

"Is it? Let me see."

Sadie turned it over in her hand but could certainly not distinguish any outstanding features that made it come close to looking even vaguely like an arrowhead. But she knew that to stay on good terms with Reuben, she would have to pronounce it one.

"Yup, Reuben, I think it was an arrowhead at one time."

"Do you?"

His troubles forgotten, especially the length of the walk home, he became wildly enthusiastic about looking for arrowheads.

"Yeah, I'll go with you this afternoon. But you can watch for horses, and I'll look for more of these."

He pocketed the very ordinary stone, his future vastly improved. Sadie cringed, despairing of her ability to break the news that he would have to lie quietly in the tall grass and wildflowers to watch for the horses.

"Don't you want to see the horses?" she began, tongue in cheek.

"Aah, I guess."

"Course you do. So we'll have to sit quietly. Sort of hide."

"I ain't walking all the way up there to sit there all that time. If I want to see a horse, I can go out to the barn and look at Charlie."

Sadie ground her teeth in frustration.

"Reuben! You are just like Dat!"

"Well."

Sadie realized her luck was running out. Self-righteous little man! Oh, he made her so angry.

"Okay, Reuben, I'll make a deal. Every time you go with me, and at least act as if you want to go, I'll give you five dollars."

"Five whole bucks?"

Even his hat came up off his ears at the mention of money. He clamped it back down then, lifted his shoulders, and started planning what he would do with such untold wealth.

"I need a scope for my pellet gun. How many times is this gonna take until you catch her?" he asked, watching her face with calculating eyes.

"Who knows? She may never come back. But if I don't try, I'll never be able to forgive myself," she said, her voice becoming thick with emotion.

Reuben looked at Sadie sideways and thought she was, indeed, the queerest duck he had ever met.

✿ ✡ ✿

And so they developed a pattern. Reuben filled the backpack and shouldered it until they were out of sight. Their parents thought they were hiking to get Sadie back into better health, especially to strengthen the muscles in her legs. They thought Reuben tagged along to look for arrowheads, explaining the backpack.

After two days of the feed disappearing and no sign of horses, Reuben demanded his $10. Sadie was in despair and, on top of that, had to cope with a rash that appeared on the calves of her legs. It was red, ugly, and so itchy she thought she would go crazy trying not to scratch.

Reuben said it was a sign from God that they shouldn't be up there against their parent's wishes, and Sadie asked him when he became so worried about being good. He told her if she didn't watch it, he wouldn't go with her anymore. Sadie scratched the rash on her legs, fought tears of sudden anger, and said, "Good, I'll go all by myself then. Stay home."

But he did go the next Friday afternoon, albeit reluctantly. It was achingly beautiful, one of those early summer days when everything seems tinged with a golden glow. Even the laundry on the line seemed whiter and the grass a vivid shade of lime green. Wildflowers grew in so much profusion, it seemed a bit surreal to be surrounded by so many different colors bobbing and waving around.

They walked and walked, then climbed up the ridge as usual. Reuben flopped into the grass, rolled on his back, and flung an arm across his eyes.

Sadie took the backpack, unzipped it, and heard them before she had a chance to scatter the oats.

She froze, her breath ragged from the climb.

There! A dark shadow. Another.

"Sadie!" Reuben called.

"Shhh!" she hissed.

He sat up, blinked.

She lifted a finger to her lips and drew her eyebrows down. It was then that she saw the raw fear in Reuben's eyes. He was afraid! Why, of course. That was why he was so reluctant to accompany her on her trips up here. Reuben had always been frightened of horses when he was small, and still was, only he tried not to let anyone know. All other Amish boys liked horses, drove them at a young age, and never showed any fear at all. But not every little boy had a father who didn't like horses and showed no interest in them the way Dat did.

"Come, Reuben."

Reuben came over to stand by her, and she put a protective arm around his thin shoulders. He did not pull away.

"Watch, Reuben. There at the tree line."

The wind blew softly as the trees whispered among themselves, the way trees do when the leaves are newly formed and velvety and rustling against each other. The grasses moved like waves of the ocean, restless, always moving in one direction or another, brushed by the ceaseless wind.

Sadie and Reuben stood together, her brown skirt blowing across his blue denim trousers. He wore no hat, leaving his hair free to blow in the wind in all its dark blonde glory. His brilliantly blue eyes were wide with fear now.

Sadie stood sturdily, unafraid. She did not believe for one minute that these horses would harm them, even the big black one. Perhaps if they were sitting on horses, the black stallion would become territorial and menacing, but it was unlikely with two human beings standing together.

These horses had been trained at one time, Sadie always felt sure. Why, she didn't know. She just sensed in her spirit that they were not totally wild and untrained. Frightened, alone, learning to fend for themselves, but not wild.

So she stood, her features relaxed.

"They won't hurt us, Reuben. Just stay calm."

"But...Sadie! That big black one chased Ezra's horse."

"Yes. But we're not horses. He won't hurt us. Just stay calm, Reuben."

"I want to go back."

"No. Just stay. Watch."

Bending, she scooped a handful of oats and corn into the palm of her hand. Holding it out, she advanced slowly toward the tree line.

"Come, Paris. Come on. Be a real good girl. You can have these oats if you want. Come here, you big, beautiful, gorgeous horse. I'm going to name you Paris, did you know that?"

Reuben clung to her, too afraid to stay by himself, terrified to go with her.

The sun was turning the lovely day into an evening of burnished copper with streaks of gold where the rays escaped the confines of a few scudding clouds.

At first Sadie thought Paris' face was a ray of sunlight dancing on the tree trunks. But when the horse flicked her ears, Sadie could see the perfect outline of her eyes all blended into the golden evening.

"Oh, Paris!" she whispered, completely at a loss for any other words.

"Sadie, I want to go home," Reuben said hoarsely.

"Reuben, trust me, okay? If I thought these horses would harm us, we wouldn't be here. They won't hurt us. Paris is the most curious of them all. Now watch."

She shook the oats in her hand and dribbled some of them on the ground, enticing the horse with the smell of the feed. The molasses made it sticky and gave off a pungent odor, one she never tired of smelling.

Sadie took another step, then stopped. She continued talking in soft, begging tones. She held her breath as Paris stepped out, a vision of beauty to Sadie.

"Come on, girl. Come get your feed."

She watched in disbelief as Paris lowered her head, snuffled at the blowing grasses, then lifted her head in a graceful motion. Her mane blew as if it was part of the earth itself.

Now she looked at Sadie, really looked at her. Sadie held her gaze steadily, talking in low tones. Reuben stood beside her.

"Sadie!" he whispered, pointing.

Paris snorted, retreated a few steps.

Sadie looked and saw the brown mare stealthily moving out from the trees, followed by the black stallion.

Her heart leaped.

Still she stood steadily.

She began calling to Paris in coaxing tones. The horse's ears flicked forward, then swiveled back. She threw her head up, only to lower it. She pawed the ground. The brown mare watched from the safety of the edge of the tree line.

Paris had burrs in her mane and forelock. Sadie's hands ached to feel the sturdy comb raking through that wonderful, thick mane. What would be better in all the world but to stand beside this horse with a bucket of warm water, fragrant with shampoo, and wash that honey-colored coat? To feed her carrots and apples and peppermint candy? Paris always ate peppermint patties. She loved dark chocolate.

Now Sadie was close enough to see the dark veins in the whites of her eyes. She saw the little whirl of lighter hair on the upper part of her chest.

"Paris, you are going to be my horse. You just don't know it yet. Come on, taste this. It's really good. It's corn and molasses. Can you smell it?"

The horse's hunger overcame her fear then, and she took another step forward. Sadie held out her arm, steadily talking.

When the moment came, it was beyond description. How could a nose feel so much like the nose of her past? It was heavy and soft and velvety all at the same time. It was lighter than the touch of a blue jay's feather. When Paris moved her mouth to gather up the feed, Sadie felt that funny little pressure horses make against the palm of your hand.

Sadie could not stop the tears of joy that welled up in her eyes.

She would not reach out with her other hand to stroke that wonderful mane. She just let Paris lip all the feed. Then Sadie slowly lifted her hand along the side of Paris' mouth to see if she would allow her nose to be touched.

The black whinnied a loud nicker, a call to retrieve her. Her ears went back. Then she lifted her head and wheeled, trotting back to the security she knew.

"Good-bye, Paris," Sadie called.

Then she turned, grabbed Reuben's hands, and shouted to the golden evening around them, "I have a horse! I have a horse!"

Sadie hugged Reuben and went running down the slope, leaving him to get the backpack, close it, and run down after her.

When she could talk, she solemnly told Reuben that he was the best brother in the whole wide world, and she would give him 10 whole dollars for this evening.

Immediately he calculated his wealth at $20. He was sorry he thought his sister was sort of strange, because she really wasn't. She was one of the best sisters in the world, which was allowing some, because sisters didn't rank very high according to Reuben.

Chapter 22

She told Richard Caldwell then. She told Dorothy and Jim and anyone who came into the kitchen after that. The ranch was abuzz with the news of these horses and Sadie's ability to touch one of them.

But she still did not tell her parents and, as far as she knew, none of her sisters suspected anything unusual. They seemed to accept Sadie's determination to strengthen the muscles in her leg by hiking and Reuben's sudden interest in accompanying her.

Dorothy had a fit. She waved her long-handled wooden spoon. She spluttered and talked "a blue streak" in Mam's words. She became so agitated one morning that Sadie watched her snapping little eyes and the heightened color in her cheeks with dismay.

Small, plump, and clearly disturbed, Dorothy stepped back from the stove and retied her apron. Retying her apron always meant a serious lecture, one that did not allow for any joking or smiling from Sadie.

"It'll be the death of you, Sadie Miller, you mark my words. That big black one will attack you. You think you know something about horses, young lady, but you don't.

They're unpredictable, same as all wild creatures."

"But…" Sadie started. She was promptly cut off.

Closing her eyes self-righteously and lifting herself to her full height—which was still not very tall—Dorothy put both fists to her soft, round hips and snorted.

"Don't even start, young lady. Your parents need to know about this. Yer puttin' that little Reuben in danger as well. You simply ought to be ashamed of yourself."

They were harsh words, coming from Dorothy.

Oh, shoot, Sadie thought.

"It ain't right, Sadie."

"But, Dorothy, please listen. You have no idea how much I loved my horse, Paris. We don't have the money to buy a horse like her now. And this palomino is even prettier, or she will be. She's so perfect, and surely if I can tame her, she'll be mine."

"That there thinkin' is gonna get you in serious trouble. You don't know whose horses they are. And if they're wild, you got the government or the state of Montana or whatever to wrestle with. An' you know how weird you Amish are about stuff like that. Nonresistant and all. You don't stand a chance."

Sadie let her shoulders slump dejectedly. Perhaps she should listen to Dorothy and at least let her parents know what she was up to.

Dorothy turned, brushing back a stray hair, and began scraping the biscuit pan. She nodded her head toward the stack of breakfast dishes.

"Best get to 'em."

Sadie swallowed her defeat, fighting back tears. Dorothy meant what she said, and going ahead with this adventure was just being openly rebellious and not very wise at all.

Halfheartedly, Sadie began scraping the bits of food clinging to the breakfast plates. What a mess! Whoever cleared the table could have put the scraps in one bowl and stacked these plates cleanly.

Suddenly she became so angry, she turned, faced Dorothy, and said, "You could have scraped these leftovers at least."

"Hmmm. A bit hoity-toity now, are we?"

"Yes, we are. I mean…yes, I am!"

She whirled and flounced away from the kitchen, pushing open the swinging oak doors with so much force that there was a resounding whack and an earsplitting yell that could only have come from the boss, Richard Caldwell.

Sadie was horrified to find him leaning heavily against the wall, holding his prominent nose while tears began forming in his eyes.

"Oh!" Sadie's hand went to her mouth, her eyes wide as she realized what she had done. She had lost her temper so that she swung those doors hard enough to smack them into Richard Caldwell who was just about to walk through to the kitchen.

His nose was clearly smarting, his expression boding no good for the person who had pushed the doors open. Blinking, he extracted a blue man's handkerchief from his pocket and began dabbing tenderly at his battered nose.

"You! Of all people," he muttered.

"I'm sorry," Sadie whispered.

"I'm okay. What got you so riled that you came charging through like that?"

"Oh, nothing. It was just…"

Sadie lifted miserable eyes to Richard Caldwell's face. "Well, Dorothy made me mad."

Richard Caldwell snorted, wiped his nose tentatively, then stared down at her. "You aren't going to cry, are you?"

"No. I mean..." She had never fought so hard in all her life to keep her composure. Reuben said if you thought of jelly bread, potato soup, a washcloth, or any object, you wouldn't cry or laugh, whichever one you didn't want to do. He assured her it really worked, but it certainly did not work now. Sadie even thought of white bread with a golden crust slathered with fresh, soft butter and homemade grape jelly, but it did absolutely no good. She simply stood in front of her big, intimidating boss and began crying like a little girl having a bad day at school.

She felt his big hand on her shoulder, steering her into his office.

"Sit down," he said, too suddenly and too gruffly to be very kind.

"Is it all Dorothy?" Richard Caldwell asked.

Sadie couldn't talk. She couldn't say one word with her mouth twisting the way it did when she cried and her nose and eyes both running.

Richard Caldwell handed her a box of tissues from the desk, and she grasped at them, a simple act of redeeming her broken pride.

"Well, it's not really Dorothy, or is it? I don't know. She's been going on and on about the danger of taking Reuben to feed the wild horses. She says my parents need to know. And...if they find out, it'll be the end of my dream to have that palomino horse...to have...Paris."

Richard Caldwell sat behind his desk, leaning on his elbows. He studied her intently, a mixture of emotions playing across his face. He cleared his throat a few times, as if that would delay having to say what he would eventually need to tell her.

Finally he said, "Why are you so sure that horse can be yours?"

"I can tame her. I can."

Sadie said this so emphatically, her voice became deeper, rich with an unnamed emotion.

Richard Caldwell said nothing. He could still remember her standing in that stall. He could still hear that broken Pennsylvania Dutch as she talked softly to that poor wreck of a horse. And then she lost that pet, likely because of the wild horses.

"Sadie, I want you to have that horse. But I think you're going about getting her the wrong way."

"No! I'm not. I know what I'm doing. She is already taking feed out of my hand."

"No, what I mean is, do you really think those horses are wild?"

She slowly shook her head.

"If they're not wild, then you'd be taking someone else's horse."

"No, no. I wouldn't. No one knows whose horses they are or has any idea where they came from."

Sadie was ripping a tissue into dozens of tiny pieces, her hands never ceasing their nervous movement.

"Now, Sadie," Richard Caldwell began.

"What?"

"You remember the story I showed you from the news? It wasn't too terribly long ago. Here at the ranch we all think that these horses are the stolen ones from... Ah, where was it? Hill County? Someplace south of here. As long as we let those horses run, it's okay, but if you'd tame that palomino and someone discovered her, how could you prove you weren't the horse thief?"

"Do I look like a horse thief?" Sadie said tersely.

Richard Caldwell's booming laugh filled the office. He shook his head.

"Well, then," Sadie said.

"We need to get to the bottom of this. If you tame that horse, then we'll have to try and locate the person who had those horses stolen. It can be done."

"You mean, I can go ahead and try?"

"Only if you tell your parents."

Sadie was already shaking her head back and forth.

"I can't."

"You have to."

Sadie remained silent, her thoughts racing.

"Did I ever tell you the story about the first dog I ever had?"

Sadie shook her head. A faraway look fell across Richard Caldwell's weather-worn face as he told Sadie about the time he found the dirty, near-dead dog. He hid nothing—sharing how his father shot the dog before he could get away, and how he snuck out in the middle of the night to bury the thin body. He told about the sorrow, anger, guilt, and even forgiveness that eventually followed.

"And I never had another dog until I left home. My father hated dogs, so…"

"Now you have seven or eight."

Richard Caldwell smiled, his eyes moist. He marveled at the onslaught of emotion she evoked in him. He could smell the wet grass, feel the smooth wooden handle of that shovel, and he knew exactly what this young woman was going through.

"So I need to wait to have a horse until I leave home, or what are you…?"

"No, no. I just want you to level with your parents."

"If I level with them, as you say, there will be nothing to worry about. It will be over. My father does not like horses. He doesn't understand that bond, that true... I don't know." Sadie hung her head miserably.

"I need to warn you, Sadie. You know if you tamed that mare and actually did take her home, the first problem is being caught and accused of being a horse thief. The second is that if the black stallion is as aggressive as you say, and if you have another horse with this palomino, he'll kill him or wreck your whole barn trying."

Sadie looked up.

Of course. She had not thought of that.

Defeat confronted her, raised its impossibly heavy head, and her spirit wavered within her. Like an accordion folding, the last notes dying away in a high, thin wail, she felt the piercing sadness of losing yet another horse.

Ach, Paris, I would have loved you so much.

Richard Caldwell watched the display of emotion on Sadie's beautiful face, the drooping of her big blue eyes, the loosening of her perfect mouth.

She sighed, ran her fingers along the crease of the leather chair. Then she stood up abruptly, unexpectedly. Her chin lifted, her eyes darkened, and she spoke quietly.

"All right then, Mr. Caldwell. I will take your advice. I know you're right. I've been blind, my own will leading Reuben and me into danger. I'll go home and speak to my father, and if it's over, it's over. Thank you."

Slowly she turned, her skirts swinging gracefully. She opened the door and was gone as quietly as a midsummer's breeze.

Richard Caldwell cleared his throat. He stared unseeingly at the opposite wall. Overwhelming pity knocked on his heart. He picked up a gold pen and scribbled on a notepad. He crossed his hands behind his head, put his boots on his desk, and stared at the ceiling.

That was one courageous young woman.

How could she? Just like that, she gave up. It was the way these odd Amish people raised their children. Once the parents said no, the no was accepted. Perhaps not immediately, but … it was something.

Suddenly he lowered his feet, swiveled the great, black, leather chair, and clicked on the computer, straightening his back as light danced across the screen.

✿ ✪ ✿

Sadie opened the door to the kitchen. Without speaking, she went to the supply closet and found the vacuum bags.

Dorothy peered over her glasses.

"Whatcha doin', honey?"

"I'll start the upstairs."

"Where've you been?"

"Talking to Richard Caldwell."

"About what?"

"Oh, I'm getting a raise—$20 an hour more."

"Pooh! Get along with you!"

As Sadie passed the downstairs office, she saw Richard Caldwell bent intently, his fingers working the keyboard of his computer.

✿ ✪ ✿

That evening, the Miller supper lasted much longer than usual. After everyone had eaten their fill of Mam's delicious fried chicken and baked potatoes, Sadie started the conversation.

Reuben looked up, wild-eyed.

"It's okay, Reuben. My boss told me a few things so I'm going to tell Dat and Mam."

With that, Sadie launched into a vivid account of her hikes, carefully watching Dat's expression. Mam's eyes were round with fright, then alarm, until finally, she burst out.

"Why, Sadie! I'm surprised at you. How could you do this?"

"Mam, it's the age-old thing! Same as it always was!"

"What do you mean?"

"You never understood my love of horses. Never."

Leah, Rebekah, and Anna all began talking at once. They scolded, asked questions, answered themselves, and just raised the most awful fuss Sadie had ever heard. She reached for the chicken platter. She knew the chicken was fattening and not very healthy, but it was the best fried chicken in all the world.

Mam rolled the chicken in flour, fried it in real butter, salted and peppered it generously, and when it was golden brown, laid it carefully on a baking sheet and finished it in the oven.

It was crispy and salty and buttery and fell off the bone in succulent mouthfuls. It was so good that you could eat a leg or thigh and not believe you had already eaten the whole thing. So you sort of went into denial about how much you were eating and reached for another piece. And it was perfectly all right because in the morning, you would have only an orange for breakfast. Not even a piece of toast. Certainly no butter or strawberry jelly.

Sadie put her fork into the perfectly done chicken thigh and pulled it away. She closed her eyes as she savored the rich flavor.

"Mmmm."

"How can you sit there and eat as if nothing in all the world is wrong and after you went and pulled off this horrendous deed?" Rebekah asked.

Sadie put down her fork, leaned forward, her eyes alight.

"You want to know why? Because I gave up. I won't go anymore. No one thinks it's safe. And Paris—I mean, the palomino—will no longer come to the field of wildflowers for food if I'm not there to give it, and now I'm trying to relax. And if I cry into my pillow tonight, Rebekah, you are going to be the last to know!"

Dat watched his daughters without comment. He could see the unshed tears in Sadie's eyes.

"Hey!" Reuben shouted above the din.

Everyone quieted, staring at normally disinterested Reuben.

"Rebekah, you know what? You should just hush up. You weren't up there on that ridge with Sadie. I was. It's something to see."

"I would like to see it," Dat said, quietly.

"You... What?"

All eyes turned to Dat who was sitting back in his chair, his eyes twinkling, running a hand casually through his thick, gray beard.

"Like I said, I would like to see where Sadie goes. I would like to see these horses. They're as mysterious as a phantom or a ghost, so I would like to see for myself what is happening up there and whether the horses really are dangerous. They may not be a threat at all. The stallion wouldn't be as long as there are no other horses around."

Mam nodded in agreement, watching Dat's face.

"But, you mean...? You mean I'm allowed to go again?"

"Yes. I'll go with you."

"Oh, Dat," Sadie breathed.

It was all she could say.

Reuben bounced up and down, knocked his water glass over, then ran for a tea towel as Anna yelled and jumped out of the way when water dribbled onto her lap.

"Hurry, Reuben," Leah said dryly.

The supper table was a bit chaotic after that. Sadie was so excited at the sudden and unexpected prospect of seeing Paris again that she ate another piece of fried chicken and a pumpkin whoopie pie and three slices of canned peaches. She was so full, even her ears felt warm to the touch.

"Are my ears red?" she asked, laughing.

"Magenta! Purple!" Anna shouted.

Mam told them all to quiet down, to get the dishes done and the kitchen swept. She still had some ironing to do. When Mam gave these barking orders and proceeded to do something she hadn't done in years, Sadie remembered to thank God for the gift of her mother's health and well-being. God had been good to all of them. It could have been so much worse and they all knew that. They would never again take Mam's health for granted.

✡ ✡ ✡

At Aspen East Ranch, the perfect moon rose and began its steady journey across the night sky into the starlit heavens. Gates creaked as gates do when the night air cools them, and horses moved slowly behind the fencing, their tails swishing as softly as the grasses surrounding them. A lone owl hooted down by the bunk house as a star fell, leaving a bright streak in the ever-enduring constellation of stars.

Most of the windows were dark, but the great window on the second story of the ranch house was a beacon of warm, yellow light.

Inside, Richard Caldwell sat at his desk. His wife, Barbara, was by his side. They were both leaning forward, staring intently at the bluish-white light from the computer. Half-eaten plates of food were on the desk, tall glasses of ice water forgotten, forming small rings of moisture on the glossy desktop.

"There!" Barbara said, pointing. "That email address might be it."

"But we don't know if it's from Hill Country."

"It could be."

The night wore on, and finally a victorious shout came from Richard Caldwell. Barbara was exultant, embracing her husband warmly.

"You did it!"

"Looks like it!"

Then he turned, dialed quite a few digits on his desk phone, winked at Barbara, and waited for someone at the other end to pick up the phone.

"Hello?" Richard Caldwell's voice boomed across the room. "Yes. Richard Caldwell here of Aspen East Ranch in Tacoma County."

"Yes."

There was a pause.

"I am looking for a Mr. Harold Ardwin."

"All right, yes, sir."

"I have a question to ask you. Are you the guy who had those horses stolen, oh, maybe about nine, 10 months ago?"

There was a long pause.

Richard Caldwell turned, raising his eyes to his wife who was leaning forward to hear the voice speaking to her husband. Her hands were clenched in anticipation, her eyes bright with interest.

"Well, is that right? Seriously? Mm-hmm."

Another long pause.

"Well, my wife and I would like to meet with you, if it's possible."

"Oh, oh, you are? Well, then we'll wait until you get back. Can you let us know what would be a good time?"

The two men exchanged a few pleasantries, they set a definite date, and Richard Caldwell carefully replaced the phone.

"They're leaving on vacation for three weeks."

"Awww."

Barbara was clearly disappointed.

"It's all right. We'll not breathe a word to Sadie."

"For sure."

"Or that Dorothy and her husband!"

They sat quietly, companionably, watching the silver moon in the night sky. Barbara slipped her hand beneath Richard Caldwell's elbow, laid her head on his massive shoulder, and sighed dreamily.

"Now we have two secrets: one to keep from Sadie and one to keep from everybody!"

"How long until we announce it?" Richard Caldwell asked, softly stroking his wife's abundant hair.

"I'm so excited. Oh, Richard, do you think everything will be okay? At our age and all?"

"It will be. Remember, if it's a girl, we're naming her Sadie."

"Of course."

"And would to God she'd be half the girl that Sadie Miller is. What touches my ... Well, I hate to sound like a softy, but she loves horses so much and has the most rotten luck I've ever seen. It's just not fair."

"But you know what they'd say, those Amish people: 'It's the will of God.'"

"Don't make fun of them, Barbara."

"Oh, Richard, I'm not. There was a time not long ago, I would have. But there has been such a great change in you that I have to believe she has brought goodness to the ranch. To us."

"She'll never know."

"That is God's way."

Chapter 23

AND SO BEGAN ONE OF THE BEST TIMES OF SADIE'S young life.

That first week the whole family joined her and Reuben on their hike up to the wildflowers at the edge of the surrounding forest. They took a bag of pungent horse feed, three apples, a bag of carrots, and a few slices of salt off the brick that was in Charlie's feed box.

It was a warm evening with a gentle, swirling breeze, the kind that whirls around you, going first one way and then another. It was a teasing sort of wind that pulls at your covering so that you have to adjust the straight pins at the side to keep it on.

Dat was puffing heartily by the time they were halfway up the ridge, but Mam was surprisingly agile. Her cheeks were flushed, her graying hair escaping her covering in the twirling wind, but her eyes sparkled with excitement at the prospect of actually seeing these fearful creatures.

Reuben behaved badly. He was clearly beside himself with anxiety. He stretched everything he told his parents about the palomino and especially about the black stallion. When Sadie gently corrected him, he became angry and pouted, falling back so far that they all had to wait for him to catch up. When Anna slowed down to walk with him, his wild stories started all over again—hands waving, eyebrows dancing at a fearful pace, blonde hair tossing in the breeze.

Dat laughed and shrugged his shoulders. "He's excited about showing us the horses. Let him go."

"How much farther?" asked Leah, her breath coming in gasps.

"Not far," Sadie assured them.

When they reached the field of wildflowers, Mam threw up her hands in amazement. "Ach, my goodness, Sadie! How could you keep all of this a secret? Why, it's absolutely *himmlisch* up here!"

"I know, Mam. It's lovely."

Reuben was telling everyone to hide, to either sit down or lie down and hold very, very still. Dat said he'd be glad to oblige, sinking wearily onto the carpet of grass and flowers.

"Do the horses always come when you're here?" Rebekah asked.

"Not always. But more and more it's a usual thing to see them."

Reuben distributed the feed. The wind sighed in the pines. The family whispered among themselves. Anna became extremely restless, making faces and gesticulating silently, asking Sadie, "How long?"

Sadie shrugged her shoulders, biting nervously on her lower lip.

Come on, Paris, she thought.

She watched the tree line carefully for the moving shadows that turned into real horses. This was the expectant moment when she always held her breath, unable to

grasp the fact that they had come one more time to eat
the feed she had brought. The miracle was new each time.

The horses did not disappoint her.

Sadie's body tensed as she heard them moving through
the trees. She held up one finger to quiet everyone, then
pointed.

Paris was first, as usual.

She stepped out, her ears pricked forward, and nickered softly. Sadie stood in a swift, quiet movement, then
proceeded forward, holding one hand out, palm upward.
She spoke softly in Pennsylvania Dutch, saying the same
words of endearment over and over.

Paris stretched her beautiful neck, her head lowered.
Sadie's hand touched her nose, a movement as natural as
the world around them. As sure as an apple falls from
the tree at harvesttime, Sadie's hand caressed first the
nose and then the neck of the honey-colored horse. She
combed the unruly mane with her fingertips and removed
burrs. She ran her hands along the rough coat where the
winter hair still clung, stubbornly refusing to allow the
honey color of the new, sleek growth to shine through.

"If only I had a comb and brush," she told Paris. "You
need a bath in the creek with my Pantene shampoo," she
chuckled.

She bent to lay her cheek against the horse's head, and
Paris stayed completely still. They stood together, a bright
picture against the backdrop of trees while Sadie's family
watched in amazement. There were tears in Mam's eyes
as she sought Dat's face. Dat looked at her, then smiled
and shook his head. Reuben saw the look pass between
them and was glad.

The brown mare stepped out then and walked easily
over to Sadie who began talking to her, caressing her face

and combing the mane with her fingertips, as she had done with Paris.

When the huge black walked hesitantly out behind the brown mare, Dat gasped. Mam looked at him questioningly. "Jacob, should we...?"

Dat shook his head.

Rebekah moved as if to stop Sadie, but Reuben held her back. "Let her go. She's okay. Watch."

Sadie appeared to ignore the black horse, but she kept him in her sight out of the corners of her eyes. He snorted, pawed the grass, tossed his head, and flicked his ears. He walked then, slowly and with a stiff gait, as if too proud to be beholden to anyone. He grabbed a mouthful of the feed hungrily. Then another.

The brown mare walked over, bent her head, and eagerly crunched an apple.

Slowly, Sadie reached out a hand to the black. He lifted his head, his nostrils flared, and his ears pricked steadily forward.

His coat was a mess, Sadie noted.

"Come here, boy. Come. Let me touch you. You were once used to it. *Sei brauf. Sei brauf.*"

Sadie kept one hand beneath Paris' chin, the other stretched out to the black. Talking quietly, she closed the gap between them until, like a feather drifting on a newly mowed field, she felt the soft dryness of the stallion's nose on her hand. He snorted and she removed her hand, but she did not move away.

Oh, the wonder of it!

The fearsome creature, the black phantom of the night that had created horrible dreams after Ezra's death, the snow, the pain—all of it gone. Here he was, standing in the golden light of the evening sun, and, in a different light, he was a different creature. There was nothing to be frightened about now.

Or was there?

She looked into the black's eyes so far above her head. He was huge. There were no whites of his eyes showing, but she could sense the wariness, the ability to whirl away and be gone in a few seconds.

Slowly she moved her hand up from his nose, stroking the long, broad face like a whisper. The hairs in his forelock were stuck together in a hopeless tangle of burrs, bits of leaves, and twigs, but they would have to remain there for now. No use pushing her luck. She had used up more than her fair share today.

When she turned to go, Paris followed her. Sadie's laughter rang out across the field, a sound of pure and unrestrained joy.

"Paris!"

The flowers nodded and sang "Paris!" with her. The clouds rolled and danced in jubilation. The trees joined in the symphony, bowed their heads for an encore, and sang "Paris!" in response. Sadie's heart overflowed with love, and she turned and threw her arms around Paris' neck, hugging her as tightly as possible.

"I have to let you go now. But I'm going to ride you yet. You watch, Paris. I will. Be good now until I come back."

When she joined her family on the trek down the hillside, she looked back and found Paris watching after her, her head lowered as if preparing to step down and follow her home if asked.

She asked Dat why she couldn't take Paris along home right then. Dat gave her the same wise answer Richard Caldwell had. Until they knew whose horses they were, it was best to let them roam wild.

✧ ✬ ✧

That evening when Sadie knelt by her bed, she thanked God for the wonderful way he had shown her family the horses. Her heart was full of gratitude, and she fell into bed tired, but so happy that she felt sure she would be smiling while she slept.

Despite her utter happiness, her mind turned to Mark Peight as it always did when she drifted off to sleep. The thought of him always brought a certain void, a question mark hanging in the air that never ceased to fill her with an unnamed longing, a particular kind of remorse.

Why? Why had he entered her life for so short a span? Why had he almost asked her for a date? But no. He had asked her, and she had said yes. Then Mam became ill, and he disappeared to Pennsylvania.

Was he still there? Would she ever see him again?

She truly did not know God's plan for her life as far as a husband was concerned. Ezra was taken from her, and she supposed Mark was very much a dream. Loving Mark had been much more than she had ever imagined, but he had also been taken.

Or…he just went.

It was maddening. It was also ridiculous. He was simply a great big chicken. Albeit, a good-looking chicken.

Sadie giggled, then buried her face in her pillow and cried great, fat tears of longing and frustration.

It would be different if she could do something about it, but she couldn't. Amish girls did not ask someone out or write a letter or try to find him or whatever a person could do. It was simply not done.

Girls were supposed to be shy and chaste, waiting

until someone asked them for a date, which happened for most of them. Sometimes a girl couldn't wait and went ahead and asked a guy out. But girls who did that were considered fast and didn't usually fare as well with guys, once they got serious about finding a wife.

Well, she wasn't going to hop on Amtrak or hire a driver or book a flight on an airliner to go traipsing off looking for Mark Peight.

She wondered who the Melvin Peachey was the visitng minister had talked about. He had known her family.

Melvin Peachy.

Mark Peight.

Suppose it had been him?

Sadie yawned, sleepiness settling over her like a warm blanket. She rolled onto her side, blinked at a twinkling star in the night sky, and thought drowsily, "I wish I may, I wish I might have Mark Peight here with me tonight."

It was a silly school-girl rhyme, but a sincere young girl's heart longing for the love of her life.

✿ ☼ ✿

Sadie made daily visits to the ridge now, sometimes accompanied by Reuben, sometimes by Anna, and sometimes by her other sisters. She much preferred Reuben's company, for the simple reason that he now shared her love of horses. He had learned to stroke the horses, and they followed him willingly wherever he went with the feed.

Sadie and Reuben studied an old Indian book explaining the method of handling horses with a rope. Dat had told them very firmly that they were not allowed to put a halter or a bridle on any of them, figuring that would put a stop to any thought of riding them.

Sadie felt a wee bit guilty for riding when Dat hoped she wouldn't, sort of like sneaking a cookie out of the Tupperware container in the pantry an hour before suppertime. But it wasn't as if they galloped dangerously around the field. It was more like giving pony rides at a kiddie petting zoo.

One thing led to another after they pored over the old Indian book. They simply put the rope around the horse's neck. Stopping, starting, and going left or right was much like neck reining, which Sadie was already used to. She accomplished that with a mere shifting of her body.

It had been a memorable evening when Reuben helped her climb onto Paris' back. She was unaccustomed to the feeling of riding bareback, especially without a bridle, so she felt a bit at odds. Her knees shook and her breath came in short gasps, making her mouth feel dry.

She laughed nervously when Reuben told her to calm down, that Paris wasn't going anywhere.

It was quite unlike anything she had ever experienced, the dizzying height of the horse, along with the feeling of riding a horse with no bridle, and then Reuben walking along, assuring her that Paris wasn't going anywhere.

It was exhilarating, a freedom Sadie reveled in, a butterfly emerging from the stuffiness of its larva.

In time, Reuben rode the brown mare and Sadie rode Paris. Sometimes they walked and sometimes they trotted until they perfected the rope technique. In a month, there was no holding back. They raced through the wildflowers, the black stallion watching or sometimes running along beside them.

The days were long, and their evenings together remained the joy of their lives. Their faces turned brown and their hair lightened in the summer sun. They formed

an unbreakable bond, their horses the tie that bound
them.

One evening as they sat side by side, their horses grazing quietly, Sadie voiced her longing to have Paris in the
barn.

Reuben wagged his head wisely.

"Can't do it, Sadie!"

"I know."

"It's too risky."

"Mm-hmm."

"One more ride?"

"Race ya!"

Sadie hopped up, ran over to Paris, grabbed a handful of her mane, and leaped up from the side, the way
they had practiced over and over. Reuben was more agile,
bounding up as if he had wings on his shoulder blades.

The horses lifted their heads, wheeled in the direction
the riders' knees prodded, and were off flying through the
long field of grass. Hooves pounded, and the grass made
a funny sort of rustling noise, an insistent whisper like a
weaving sound.

The wind rushed in Sadie's ears as she bent low over
Paris' neck, urging her on. Reuben looked back, laughing as they completed the long circle, coming back up the
slope as if their lives depended on being the first to arrive
at the starting point.

They slid to a stop, laughing breathlessly, their horses
panting.

"Forget it, Reuben. It was nose to nose."

"No way!"

"Yes, it was!"

"Paris isn't faster than mine, Sadie!"

"She beat her though."

"I don't think so."

"Give your horse a name, Reuben. You can't just call her 'the brown horse.'"

Reuben squared his shoulders and looked out across the valley, a serious expression stamped on his face.

"I can't."

"Why?"

"If I do, it'll be much harder to let go of her. You have to realize, Sadie, we can't always come up here on someone else's land and ride someone else's horses. I mean, come on. Duh!"

Sadie glanced sideways at him, shocked to find his eyes bright with unshed tears. He was very sure of himself in reprimanding her, but it was still hard for him to hide the feeling he had for the horse he had grown to love.

"I mean, what'll happen this winter? We can't come up here. You know that."

Sadie nodded.

"I guess you're right."

"Let's go home. Sun's sliding behind the mountain."

"Okay. See you, Paris."

Sadie turned, loosening the rope, stroking the honey-colored neck. The horses had been brushed over and over, their manes and forelocks trimmed, burrs removed from their tails. Still, they had never been bathed and shampooed the way Sadie would have liked. But it was something the way they were able to groom them at all, even the black.

Sadie stood by her horse's head murmuring, when she heard Reuben's short, "Shhh!"

She raised her head and froze when she saw two men standing close to the tree line watching them. Her hands dropped away and her arms went numb as she watched them approach. They were dressed in black, one much larger than the other.

"Sadie, let's run!" Reuben hissed.

Sadie shook her head. She blinked her eyes and squinted into the shadows.

Could it be?

Yes. It was.

Richard Caldwell.

She felt the tension leave her body, then smiled when he threw up a hand.

"Hey, Sadie."

Reuben came over to stand very close to her, and she welcomed his nearness.

"Richard Caldwell! This is a surprise! What brings you up here?"

Paris and the brown horse stood alert, their ears forward. The large black stallion was back farther, his head held high, his nostrils quivering, ready to bolt.

Richard Caldwell stopped, his hand indicating the smaller man at his side. Sadie watched warily as he stepped forward.

"I'm Harold Ardwin of Ardwin Stables."

"Yes?" Sadie was puzzled. She had never heard of this place, and why should she? What was he doing up here with Richard Caldwell? She thought she could trust Richard. Now he had blown her secret, and this would be the last evening of her life with Paris.

Richard Caldwell stepped forward.

"Harold Ardwin is the owner of the ranch where all the horses were stolen."

"Oh. So…"

"We've been watching you and your brother for close to an hour."

Sadie's face flushed, and she looked down at the toe of her boots, her long lashes sweeping her tanned cheeks.

Reuben coughed self-consciously.

No one spoke.

Harold Ardwin looked at the horses. He looked at Sadie and Reuben. He cleared his throat. "I believe I've found my horses."

Sadie kept her eyes on her boots and bit her lower lip. The bottoms of her denims were frayed and torn, her skirt dirty and dusty. She blinked hard. She swallowed. She tried to look up, but if she did, she knew the men would see her misery, so she kept her gaze on her boot tops.

She heard Harold move away, his highly polished boots with the intricate design moving through the grass with a soft rustle. His shoulders were powerful beneath the black shirt, his waist trim for a man she guessed to be close to 60 years old.

"This is Black Thunder of Ardwin Stables, the sire of our finest colts," he said firmly. The black stood as if carved in stone. He trembled, then turned and bolted, but only a short distance.

"Emma, can you get him back?" asked Richard Caldwell.

Reuben nodded, and Sadie walked after the black. She touched his nose with her outstretched hand, then cupped his chin, murmuring as she did so.

Harold Ardwin blinked and blinked again. He sniffed, then cleared his throat. He watched in disbelief as Sadie came back, the black following, a faithful pet who was as obedient and helpless as a kitten.

"Come here, boy! Don't you know who I am?" Harold Ardwin asked, his voice thick, his eyes misty.

Black Thunder whinnied. He had found his owner.

You just couldn't deny the recognition between a man and a horse.

This was a different kind of relationship than Sadie had with the big, black stallion. The black horse knew and respected Harold Ardwin, but Sadie had a hunch there was a stable boy at Ardwin Stables who spent more time with the horse than the wealthy owner did.

"After all this time. This is amazing," Harold kept repeating.

Finally he turned to the remaining two horses. "Butterfly and Sasha," he said, nodding toward them.

Sadie's heart sank. She had been foolish beyond belief. She had known this time would come. Paris was never hers. Never had been.

She felt old and weary then, and she wanted to run down the hillside without saying one more polite word to anyone. She wanted to get away where she could hold her sorrow and loss all by herself, stoic, accepting, and dry-eyed.

Reuben scuffed his foot against her boot.

"Answer, Sadie."

She raised her head.

"I'm sorry. What?"

"I asked, had you named the horses?"

"Only one. The … the palomino."

"Sasha?"

Sadie could only nod.

"Your riding is impeccable. I have never seen such a display of trust between a horse and a rider."

"Thank you."

Reuben grinned and grinned until Sadie elbowed his ribs slightly.

Richard Caldwell saw every emotion as it took control of Sadie's features—the horrible despair upon learning these were Harold's horses, the blaming of herself for getting too attached to Paris, the courage she had tried to muster when answering Harold, and how she failed miserably. It was every emotion he remembered feeling as he wrapped the body of his beloved dog in the pink towel and laid it gently in the cool, wet hole in the earth.

Courage was admirable, but sometimes your heart was so crumpled by pain that you couldn't really hold all the fragments together. Sometimes a broken heart couldn't be helped.

But not this time. Not if he could help it.

"We'll pay a visit to your house this evening, Sadie," he said, too tersely even to his own ears.

She nodded. There was nothing else to say, and besides, talking just didn't work around a lump in your throat. So she turned and walked down the hillside, Reuben at her heels.

Chapter 24

Sadie stormed into the kitchen perspiring, her hair a mess, her *dichly* falling off her head. She flung herself down on a kitchen chair, a layer of dust and bits of grass trailing after her. Reuben went to the laundry bathroom and stayed there.

Mam looked up from the bowl where she was sifting flour.

"My goodness, whatever happened to you?" she asked.

"Oh, Mam," Sadie wailed, then launched into the events of the afternoon, pouring out all the heartsickness that clogged every part of her being.

"And to make matters worse, they're coming here tonight. What for? Whatever in the world would they want here?"

Mam considered the situation for a moment, slowly wiping her hands over and over on the underside of her apron. "Well, whoever that Harold Arken..."

"Ardwin."

"...Ardwin is, he must be very wealthy. And now he is going to enter our humble dwelling. Richard Caldwell, too. If an important person arrives, we offer him the highest seat, and if a poor one enters, he always gets the lowest, but this is not good in Christ's eyes. So we'll not get flustered, and instead we'll light our propane lamp and serve them these apricot cookies and coffee, same as if Jack Entan arrived."

Sadie glanced at her mother, caught her glint of humor, and smiled wryly. Jack was the town's junk-hauler who lived in a less than appealing environment, in spite of everyone's best efforts to reform him.

"Mam!"

"I'm serious. They're only human beings, wealthy and important or not."

Sadie frowned. She straightened her legs, stared at her frayed denims and dusty boots, and stood up abruptly.

"I'm going to my room."

"Oh, there's a letter for you. It's on the hutch."

Mam returned to her baking, and Sadie went to the cupboard for the letter. She recognized the handwriting instantly.

Eva.

Oh good, she thought.

Sadie and Eva wrote constantly. Letters were their regular way of communicating. It was always a joyful day for Sadie when one of Eva's letters arrived.

Sometimes they would plan a time to be at their phone shanties and have a long conversation, but that had its drawbacks, especially in winter. Phone shanties were cold and uncomfortable, so telephone conversations were kept to a minimum. Sadie supposed the whole idea for having that church rule about phone shanties was because women were prone to gossip, and telephones were definitely an aid to that vice. Therefore, the less convenient a phone was, the less women would be gossiping on it.

Sadie ripped open the plain white envelope, unfolded the yellow legal pad paper, and eagerly devoured every word.

> *Dear Sadie,*
>
> *You will never guess what! My darling husband-to-be is allowing me to travel by train to spend a week with you. Are you sitting down? So I'm thinking of spending Christmas with you!!! Are there enough explanation points for that sentence?*
>
> *Our wedding is not until April, and he really wants me to do this before the wedding because he knows how close we are and that we haven't seen each other in years!*
>
> *Oh, Sadie! I am so excited. I won't be traveling alone because Dan Detweiler's parents are coming, too. Maybe if we can get enough people to come, we'll hire a van and won't need the train.*

Sadie chuckled at Eva's two sheets of questions about the trip. It was so typical of Eva and so dear. They shared everything, every little detail of their lives, including Mark Peight, the ranch, Dorothy, Richard Caldwell, Mam's mental illness. They held nothing back, which was why they had a continuing friendship that began when they were little first-graders in the one-room school they both attended.

Sadie sighed as she replaced the papers in the envelope. It was a long time to wait. Christmas seemed far away—another time, another world.

She heard Reuben unlock the bathroom door and walk into the kitchen to Mam.

"Why, Reuben, where were you? I had almost forgotten about you."

"In the bathroom," Reuben said in the gruffest, manliest voice he could possible muster.

"You've been in there awhile then."

"Yeah. You know we're getting company tonight?"

"Sadie told me."

"They shouldn't come here. All they want is our... those horses anyhow."

Mam nodded.

"We'll see, Reuben."

✿ ✡ ✿

Mam tidied the kitchen while Sadie and Reuben informed Dat about the company. Mam made a pot of coffee and arranged her famous apricot cookies on a plate. The cookies were not filled with apricots but with apricot jam mixed with other things. They were soft and sweet and crumbly and delicious, and no one made them the way Mam did.

Eventually a large silver SUV wound its way up their driveway. No one was very thrilled at the sound of its tires on crunching gravel, although no one said as much. It wouldn't be polite, and certainly not a Christian attitude to be inhospitable to company.

Dat greeted the two men at the door, invited them in, and introduced them to Mam. She shook hands with them, welcoming them into their home.

Richard Caldwell was even louder than usual, nervously talking nonstop, his face flushed, his eyes bearing a certain excitement. Harold Ardwin was very professional, smiling only enough to be polite. Mustaches did that to a person, though. A heavy mustache just sort of lifted up or settled back down, covering any smile that might be underneath it. An Amish man's beard wagged a lot when he talked, and his smile was bare and unhampered so you knew if he was sincere or not.

"Where are Sadie and Reuben?" Richard Caldwell thundered.

Sadie imagined Mam wincing, not being used to those decibels of sound.

Sadie moved out to the kitchen. She had showered, changed clothes, combed her hair neatly, and pinned her white covering perfectly in place. She had chosen a navy blue dress, which she fervently hoped would maker her seem older.

"Hello," she said quietly.

"You clean up well, Sadie," Richard Caldwell said, laughing.

Harold Ardwin said nothing.

They talked about the weather, the price of beef, the logging industry, the carpentry trade, anything but the horses.

Dusk was bringing shadows into the room, so Sadie got up and flicked a lighter beneath the mantle of the propane gas light. With a soft pop, it ignited, casting the room into a bright, yellow light.

Richard Caldwell was impressed, telling Dat so, but Harold Ardwin watched the soft hissing mantles carefully. He was clearly uncomfortable with his first encounter in an Amish home without electricity. Sadie stifled a giggle as he moved his chair farther away from the oak stand that contained the light.

After the light was lit, Mam and the girls served coffee. Both men drank their coffee hot and black and ate a countless amount of Mam's cookies. Richard Caldwell was profuse in his praise of her.

Then, as suddenly as the light popped on, Harold Ardwin said, "We watched your son and daughter this evening—late afternoon, really—riding the wild horses, which...are mine."

Dat blinked, listening carefully.

"I'm sure you know plenty of the local people have always felt these horses weren't mustangs."

Dat nodded.

"Horse thieves are notorious in our region. We still don't have all the pieces of this jigsaw puzzle, but I do know that Richard Caldwell here contacted me, told me the story of your daughter and her wild horses, and led me to her. It's impressive, what she's done."

There was a pause. No one breathed, it seemed.

"So, as a reward to her—to all of you—for finding Black Thunder, I give Butterfly and Sasha to you. One is for Sadie, and one for Reuben."

Sadie wanted to say something but couldn't. She tried. She even opened her mouth, but it sort of closed on its own and not one word escaped. She was shaken back to reality by Reuben's very loud and very sincere, "Thanks a lot. Thank you!"

He looked at Sadie as if to say, "Come on. Duh."

Sadie opened her mouth, and it instantly turned into a shaky mass like jello. Her nose burned and tears swam to the surface. She swallowed hard, tried to smile, but could only bite her lip as those despised tears slid down her cheeks.

Richard Caldwell knew Sadie and saw it all. Quickly

he was at her side, his arm around her shoulders.

"It's true, Sadie," he said gruffly, his voice thick with emotion.

Sadie nodded, swiped at the moisture on her cheeks, and whispered, "Thank you."

Harold Ardwin smiled then, a smile even the mustache could not diminish. He watched Sadie's face, and a softening came to his eyes.

"You love those horses, don't you?"

"Oh, my!"

It was all Sadie could say.

"And the sum still stands for finding my horses—$20,000."

Mam put up both hands and Dat protested.

"That is *unfadiened gelt*—unearned money—and we cannot accept it. It wouldn't be right."

"Well, then, let Reuben have it," Harold Ardwin said.

✿ ☆ ✿

When the headlights of the silver SUV found its way back down the drive, the Miller household was in an uproar. Everyone talked; no one listened. Reuben leaped onto the recliner and tipped the whole thing backward. Mam scolded and Dat said, "Wasn't that a fine kettle of fish, feeding three horses!"

Sadie said the reward money would pay their hospital bills so who cared if they needed to feed three horses, and Reuben said he wished Sadie would get married so her husband would have to buy horse feed and straw and hay and then there would be more room for the brown horse.

Sadie told him that if he didn't stop talking about "the brown horse" she'd lose it, and Reuben said whoever in all the world heard of a horse named Butterfly, especially if a guy owned her. Anna shrieked and teased him about being a guy if he had just turned 11, and Reuben's face turned red and he ate three cookies.

✿ ✡ ✿

Sadie and Reuben helped load Black Thunder, as he was known now, into the luxurious red and silver horse trailer. Sadie brought him down from the field by the tree line, followed by Paris and the brown horse.

It seemed as if the horses felt the homecoming and welcomed it. Paris stood by Sadie as Harold Ardwin led the black horse up the ramp. She was watching with her ears pricked forward, but she remained quietly by Sadie's side. Reuben sat on the brown horse, relaxed, his bare feet dangling out of his too-short denim trousers, his hair disheveled above his sun-browned face.

Black Thunder whinnied and rocked the trailer but, for the most part, settled back into his former way of traveling. It seemed as if he remembered everything and was ready to go.

Harold Ardwin thanked them both, shook hands, said he'd be back to visit his...their...two horses whenever he could, and was gone.

Sadie stood with her hand on Paris' neck. She stroked the horse absentmindedly, her thoughts completely at peace. Finally, she had a horse—a real, honest to goodness horse of her own, fair and square, and a beautiful one at that. The added bonus was getting to share everything with Reuben and his horse. The rides, the grooming, the companionship—it was all a gift, and God surely had something to do with it.

Thank you, God, for Paris.

It was that simple for her, but heartfelt in a way she had never experienced.

Turning, she smiled at Reuben.

"Ready?"

"Sure."

Sadie grabbed a handful of her horse's mane and leaped expertly onto her back, which was a signal for Reuben to turn the brown horse and start galloping home immediately.

✿　✡　✿

Mam was sitting at her sewing machine in front of the low double windows, working the treadle in a steady "thumpa, thumpa" sort of rhythm. It was the music of every Amish housewife's heart. It melded with the soul when accompanied by favorite hymns, which was "Amazing Grace" for her.

Mam steadily watched the presser foot as she hemmed a pair of blue denim work pants for Jacob. When she came to the end, she stopped, looked up, and reached for her scissors. Out of the corner of her eye she caught sight of a cloud of dust with two figures ahead of it.

The scissors clattered to the hardwood floor, her nervous hand knocking them off the sewing machine stand. The other hand wobbled to her chest and held her dress front in agitation.

"*Siss kenn Fashtant,*" she mouthed, "Sadie and Reuben!"

Oh, it wasn't safe. Their speed!

The horses were running neck and neck, coming up the winding drive faster than most cars. Reuben was bent low over the brown horse's neck. He was looking at Sadie and laughing, his blonde hair blowing across his face and mixing with the black hair from the horse's mane.

Sadie was bent double across the honey-colored horse, her blue dress tucked down in front but billowing out the side. Her *dichly* was attached only by one pin, dangerously close to disappearing, but it was the last thing on Sadie's mind.

The horses weren't really galloping. They were lunging great, long leaps, their feet hunched beneath their powerful bodies to propel them up the sloping driveway. As they flew past the house, Mam laid her head wearily on her arms and sighed deeply to catch her breath. It would take patience and strength to watch her son and daughter with their prize horses.

✵ ✡ ✵

Sadie sat up, slid off Paris' back, and ran to open the barn door. Reuben was at her heels, running across the gravel driveway as if he had shoes on.

"Beat you!" Sadie said as she turned, her face red with exertion, her eyes stinging from the dust particles, her chest heaving.

"You did not either. Not for one second did you beat me!" Reuben yelled.

"I did, Reuben."

"You did not. Paris did!"

With that, Reuben threw back his head and laughed just the way Dat did when something struck him as being really funny.

Charlie whinnied, then put on quite a show for his two new friends. He tossed his head and did a funny version of a graceful pirouette in the confines of his box stall, as if to impress them both with his ability.

Sadie and Reuben looked at each other and laughed in a shared comradeship none of them had ever felt for the other.

They groomed their horses, brushed them, cut their manes to perfection, and then at long last were able to shampoo, scrub, and rinse them with the water hose.

Sadie was in awe of Paris after she was finished. Her mane and tail were much lighter, her coat rich and velvety with an amber color that shone in the sun. Her small head and perfectly formed ears were the most beautiful things about her. Accompanied by the arch in her muscular neck, the horse was just too good to really be true.

"Just look at her," Sadie said in a voice of amazement.

Reuben stepped back, eyed Paris, and nodded.

"You know what?"

"Hmm?"

"If your horse is named Paris, would it be stupid if I named mine something like that?"

"You mean, like 'London'?"

"No," Reuben said snorting. "I mean, do you think 'Paris' is so … well, you know," Reuben said, clearly embarrassed.

"What?"

"Well, I think Cody would be a nice name for my horse. You know, Cody, Wyoming."

"But Cody is a boy's name."

"I don't care. I want to name my horse Cody, for Cody, Wyoming. Besides, you had a horse named Nevaeh, and he was a boy!"

It was all Sadie could do to keep from laughing. He certainly had a point.

She assured Reuben that Cody would be fine. In fact, Cody was a unique name, and she bet him anything his brown mare was the only one in Montana with the name Cody.

Reuben gave her a grin worth remembering.

✿ ✶ ✿

At work in the ranch kitchen, Sadie sang loudly and twirled around the kitchen holding a wooden spoon until Dorothy told her — quite sourly — that it was all right to be happy, but surely a horse wasn't worth all that adoration.

Sadie came to a stop beside her and announced, "I'll calm down now and get to work, but I can hardly contain so much joy! And then, to simply make my cup run over, Reuben rides with me," she chortled.

Dorothy shook her head.

"You know what? You don't really fit the mold of what I thought an Amish girl would be like at your age. Aren't you supposed to be gittin' married? An' here you are, as single as the day is long and don't give two hoots about it."

Sadie held up a large, shining kettle and scraped the inside with a rubber spatula. Slowly she set it down, turned, and said quietly and honestly, "Dorothy, you know I would love to be married. I'm just as unlucky in love as I am … was … with a horse."

"Luck has nothing to do with it," Dorothy shot back.

"Really?"

"Really."

Sadie put the leftover chili in a large Tupperware bowl and glanced sideways at Dorothy just to check her rate of approval or disapproval.

"Explain it to me," she ventured, carefully.

Dorothy sat down with a tired sigh, taking the toe of one shoe to dislodge the heel of the other. Then she kicked both her shoes under the table, stretched her short legs, flexed her toes inside the white, cotton Peds she wore, and wagged a short, square finger at Sadie.

"Mind you, they don't make these shoes the way they used to. I think the Dollar General is shifting too much of their work to China or Taiwan or Mexico or them other places. My feet hurt me awful. But they say they're puttin' in a new shoe store in town right next to the bank called 'Payless' or somethin'. Might try my next pair from there. Leastways if they have somethin' similar."

Sadie nodded sympathetically.

"Now, what was we talking about? Oh, luck or love."

Dorothy rubbed one knee.

"It's you pretty ones that have the biggest problems lots a' times. Too many fish in the sea, and you know you could snag every one of 'em if you wanted to. But yer too prissy. Too pertickler, so you are. Now me, I never had much in the way of looks and was right glad for Jim to come a' callin'. Told my Mom and Dad he ain't much to look at, but he's a decent, solid guy. Turned out I was right as rain, and he done me good for almost 50 years."

"That's all I want," Sadie nodded, soberly.

"Don't you have anyone at all?"

Sadie hesitated, then nodded.

"I do. His name is Mark."

"Well, are you dating him now? Is this the same one we looked up those recipes for?"

"Yes. But my mother was ill, and he went back to Pennsylvania. It was sudden … sort of mysterious."

"If it's meant to be, he'll be back."

Sadie nodded.

"Did I tell you Eva's coming for Christmas this year?"

"Naw! Go on!"

"Yes! She is!"

"Bless her heart."

"Time to start the laundry, Dottie, " Sadie said, glancing at the clock.

"Don't you 'Dottie' me!"

Chapter 25

Sᴀᴅɪᴇ ʙʀᴏᴜɢʜᴛ ᴛʜᴇ ᴄᴜʀʀʏ ᴄᴏᴍʙ ᴅᴏᴡɴ ᴀᴄʀᴏss the honey-colored neck, finishing with an elaborate flourish. It was mostly to impress Reuben who was working on a tangle in Cody's tail, his eyebrows drawn down as he concentrated.

"There!" Sadie said with a bright smile.

Reuben yanked on Cody's tail before looking up, his eyebrows rising with the movement of his head. He gave a low whistle in a very grown up way, or so he hoped.

"She's a picture!"

"Isn't she?"

Reuben nodded, then voiced his exasperation. "Sadie, what do you do if a tangle just won't come out?"

Sadie walked over, lifted Cody's tail, and told Reuben to go get a pair of scissors from Mam.

"Make sure the scissors are old, not the expensive ones she uses to cut fabric, if you know what's good for you."

"You mean, you're going to chop her tail right off— that far up?" he yelled as he dashed out the door.

Sadie answered but knew Reuben didn't hear anyway,

at the rate of speed in which he catapulted through the doorway.

When he returned, Sadie cut expertly through the coarse, black hair. The tail was shorter, but sleek and straight, and the stubborn tangle lay on the concrete floor of the forebay.

Stepping back, she surveyed the brown mare, then told Reuben to throw the cut hair into Paris' stall.

"Oh, no, I'm not going to. This bunch of horse hair would be any bird's dream come true—all this strong horse hair to build a good solid nest. Imagine the possibilities! Birds aren't picky, you know. They use almost anything to build a nest."

Sadie grinned, then told him to throw it out in the barnyard where the birds would find it.

They cleaned their saddles with an old piece of t-shirt and good saddle soap. Then they shook the saddle blankets over and over until the dirt and hair flew across the forebay. They wiped down the brown leather bridles, then began saddling up.

Reuben grunted as he swung his saddle up on Cody who lowered herself, bracing for the weight to land on her back. It was easier for Sadie who was taller and more experienced, but she nodded encouragement to Reuben.

"We wouldn't have to use saddles," he lamented.

"I know, Reuben, but it feels safer if we're going to ride along the highway. What if a large rig would come flying around a corner, blow its horn, and terrify the horses? They haven't been around much traffic lately."

"Cody!" Reuben yelled, then turned to Sadie.

"Why does she do that when I want to tighten the cinch?"

Sadie laughed.

"How would you like to run with a tight band around your stomach? She gets smart and puffs her stomach out while you're tightening it so that it's not too tight when you let go."

"Yeah, but then the saddle slips sideways. I'd rather ride bareback."

"Not this time."

Sadie swung herself up, adjusted her skirt, pinned her covering securely, then spoke softly to Paris. The horse stepped out eagerly, raising her head the minute she was out the door.

Reuben followed on Cody, still mumbling about using a saddle. His blonde hair lifted and separated in the never ceasing, restless Montana wind.

Paris stepped sideways, tossed her head, pranced forward and backward, dipped her head, then shook it from side to side as if to let Sadie know she was displeased about the saddle. It was an unnecessary evil that pinched her sides and was much too tight around her stomach.

"All right, Paris, now settle down. Be a good girl. Come on, come on. This saddle isn't going to hurt you."

"Cody likes hers," Reuben told her happily.

"Looks as if she does."

It was Saturday afternoon, and they were riding their horses a long way to see if they might possibly be able to purchase an old buggy. They had watched the ads in the local paper until they found one that sounded promising.

Buckboard. Good condition. $500.
Call 786-3142

Sadie and Reuben had huddled nervously in the phone shanty as Sadie dialed the number, then whacked their palms together in a resounding high-five when she hung up. They had raced across the driveway and into the house to tell Mam.

Mam smiled as her eyes crinkled and she told them she hoped it was as good as they thought. Then she shook her head after they raced back out the door, the wooden screen door slapping its usual annoyance.

How could you expect that Sadie to grow up as long as she loved horses so much? She couldn't care less about finding a husband as far as Mam could tell. It got discouraging at times, the way she just skipped over the part of life she should be concerned about most. After all, at 21 years old, her best chances were gone, and if she didn't soon worry about starting a relationship with a decent young man, she may not have any chances, in Mam's opinion.

Mam sighed as she watched Sadie and Reuben ride down the driveway. She hoped they wouldn't encounter too many Amish people. Riding a horse wasn't as ladylike as Mam thought it should be. A horse-drawn buggy was much more appropriate for getting around.

Then the thought hit her, and she sat down weakly and began fanning herself with the hem of her apron. Sadie and Reuben were thinking of breaking Paris and Cody so the horses would pull that rattling, derelict old buggy they were planning to purchase.

And that is exactly what they planned to do.

Reuben said the only harm the two horses could do would be to run and kick if they were both hitched to the same singletree. Sadie said the old buggy couldn't be in very good shape for only $500, but she would not want to see it fly into a thousand pieces. This caused Reuben to throw his head back and howl with glee at the sheer thought of so much excitement.

When had the change in Reuben started, and where would it stop? The small, thin body that had trembled beside her as they stood on the ridge waiting for the horses to appear had been transformed into an adventure-loving youth who seemed to find no reason to be careful. He rode Cody like the wind, having very little thought, if any, of the chance of a mishap.

Cody was chomping at the bit, tossing her head, waiting for the signal to run. Sadie told Reuben to hold her back. They had a long ride ahead of them, and there was no use working the horses into a lather so soon.

They turned right on to a county road, holding their horses at a brisk walk. The wind carried the same sighing note Sadie never tired of, and meadowlarks flew up and whirred away on busy, brown wings. The side of the road was dotted with small, pink bitterroot, which grew rampantly. It always added a touch of color, as if an artist had painted the deep pink when the picture was completed, simply to add interest.

Sadie's dress was a deep blue, though worn and a bit snug. She admitted this grudgingly. Too many days of healing that busted leg, she knew. Too many days sitting around the kitchen table with freshly baked cookies and cups of steaming coffee, laughing and talking and unaware of the amount of cookies she was consuming.

Her brown hair pulled loose from her covering and she tugged at it impatiently. She should have worn a *dichly*, but Mam would never allow it when she was in public and going to do business with a stranger.

They rounded a bend in the road, then began the climb up the lower hills of Sloam's Ridge. The pines sighed in the breeze, making Sadie's heart dip with the sadness of it.

Would the memories always raise their heads, crying for attention like a child craving to be remembered and noticed? It was never easy crossing this ridge in a buggy or a vehicle. Riding on horseback in the open air made it all even more memorable than before.

Even Reuben rode somberly, his head bent slightly, the back of his neck exposed between his hair and brown shirt collar. Cody swished her tail, flailing at unseen flies, walking steadily while Paris followed, their heads bobbing in unison.

Sadie tried not to look down the side of the steep embankment, turning her head to watch the pines on the opposite side of the road, following Reuben as Cody made her way carefully down the other side.

Sadie loved riding and being suspended above the ground, her feet solidly encased in stirrups. It was a support she could trust. She loved the creaking of the leather, the rocking gait of a horse moving along, the thick mane moving in that peculiar rhythm—hair so heavy it moved the skin beneath it. She loved the heavy, leather reins giving her the satisfaction of being in control of the beloved horse that carried her.

They came to a crossroad, and Reuben turned to look at Sadie. "Which way?"

Sadie pursed her lips. "Hmm. Right, I think."

"You wanna gallop?"

"We can."

Reuben leaned forward, making the squirrelly sound he always did, and Cody leaped ahead. Paris quickly followed, eager to run. They loped along easily, content to watch the surrounding countryside and for any passing vehicles.

Sadie caught sight of a lone person on the roof of the

old, weathered barn next to the Oxford place where Dat
had built one of his smallest log cabins.

Who in the world would even think of patching up
that old barn roof? The whole thing looked as if it could
go sailing into the wild blue yonder the minute a good
strong wind hit it broadside.

She watched, jumping as a piece of rusty metal went
sliding down along the rafters, falling to the ground
below. As they neared, she could see that the roof was
being dismantled, one piece of rusted steel at a time.

Reuben watched, then slowed Cody to a walk.

"Somebody's tearing down that barn."

"Wonder what for?" Sadie asked.

"Think the horses will get scared next time he tears a
piece of steel loose?"

"Let's wait here a moment."

They watched as the man on the roof pried off another
piece of steel before they urged the horses on. As they
passed, Sadie thought something seemed familiar. It was
the set of his shoulders or the way he raised his arms.

What was it? Why did the person on the roof seem so
familiar, as if she had seen him before?

He turned, noticing them, and stopped working.

Sadie recognized him at the same time he saw her, or
so it seemed. At first her mind grasped it, then her heart
engulfed it—this wonderful, all-consuming knowledge of
who was on the roof.

Then doubt and fear tore loose, a tornado so strong
she felt it suck her breath away along with her heart—
out and away, never to be recovered, torn away and
destroyed. She felt like a person drowning as she gasped
at the sight of the man on the roof.

It was Mark Peight.

His white teeth in that dark face! His smile! She had forgotten.

Her nerveless hands pulled on the reins, willing Paris to walk as slowly as she had ever walked before. He inclined his head in a sort of bow, an acknowledgment that he knew she was Sadie Miller, that he remembered her and was glad to see her.

Reuben looked up and then back at Sadie. His eyes showed the whites the whole way around, and he was completely at a loss for even one word for once in his young life.

He stopped Cody and Paris' nose bumped into Cody's rump.

"Is that...who I think it is? That Mark guy?" Reuben hissed.

Sadie didn't answer. She couldn't.

Her eyes were riveted on Mark's. He was so far away, but there was no space between them, no time, nothing but the great shower of light that appeared from somewhere to illuminate the distance between them.

Mark raised his hand, then called, "Hang on. I'll be down."

Sadie tried to fix the hair that had pulled loose from her covering, but it did no good so she let it go. Her fingers weren't working properly as it was, so she may as well not try.

Should she get down? Or stay up on Paris?

Better to dismount, fix her dress—her dress that was too old and too small. Why in the world hadn't she taken the time to change?

And then he stood before her, his hands reaching to her shoulders before looking at Reuben and dropping them to his sides.

"Sadie."

"Mark. Welcome back."

"Thank you. This is Reuben?"

Reuben nodded happily, his grin literally spreading from one side of his face to the other. All his teeth were shining visibly, his eyes crinkling to a thin line of pure delight.

"Why'd you come back to Montana? I thought you were going to stay in Pennsylvania," she asked slyly.

Mark laughed good-naturedly. It was a sound Sadie loved.

"Well, Pennsylvania is nice, but Montana is nicer."

Reuben smiled, and Sadie prayed he would keep his mouth closed.

He didn't, of course. "I bet! Sadie don't live in P.A.!"

Sadie cringed when he said "P.A." Oh, how common! How old-timer-like! He could have at least said "Pennsylvania."

Mark scuffed the toe of his work boot against a tuft of grass, averting his eyes. Those impossibly thick, black eyelashes swept his cheeks, and he didn't answer.

Sadie was humiliated to the point of tears. He probably hadn't come back for her at all, and here was Reuben blatantly throwing her at him, as if he was so sure of the fact that anyone would be glad to be dating his sister.

Mark raised his eyes which were crinkled at the corners, still good-natured, still kind.

"Well, now, Reuben, I don't know about that. Hey, you think the horses might be thirsty? It's a warm day. Come on down to the barn. Maybe you can give them a drink."

Reuben slid off his horse, bounding lightly on his feet, his thick hair lifting and falling.

"Where's your straw hat?" Mark asked, still grinning.

"Don't wear one. Can't. Blows off all the time."

"Fine by me. Can you take the horses, and I'll show your sister around my place?"

My place? My place. Oh, my. Mark Peight had bought this property?

Reuben grabbed the reins before Sadie could recover her senses and walked away jauntily, whistling under his breath.

They were alone.

Mark turned to her immediately. She couldn't breathe properly. It was this dress. It constricted her breathing. She was actually having irregular heartbeats, and there was a rushing sound in her ears.

"Hello."

That was all he said. She tried not to take a step forward, but she did. Her feet took steps of their own, and she closed the terrible distance between them.

He folded her soft form close to his heart and held her there for the space of a heartbeat, not nearly enough to assure her of his feelings for her.

Why did he pull away so quickly? He must not want her at all, or he would convey his love in the most natural way on earth, to have and to hold. Was she so repulsive to him that he could only hold her for the space of one heartbeat? The loss was too great to bear.

She steeled herself before meeting his brown eyes, willing herself to be strong even in his denial of her.

"You are still so beautiful—even more than I remember."

"Thank you," she whispered.

"I'm back. I bought this place, Sadie. I can't wait to get started remodeling and fixing it up."

He gestured toward the barn.

Sadie smiled then.

"It's actually yours?"

"Well, the bank's. I have a mortgage, of course. But, yes, it's mine. I will make my home here in Montana. I love it here, the wide open spaces, the clean air, but most of all, the work I do as a farrier. I get paid well for shoeing horses at these ranches. It's the opportunity of a lifetime. I do other things as well—trim hooves, float teeth... I'm sort of an overall horse guy who helps other people with their animals."

Sadie nodded, then looked around.

"Where is the house?"

Mark laughed.

"There isn't one."

"Where do you stay?"

"In the barn, but just for the summer. I'll probably have to winter over with my uncle."

"In... in the barn?"

"I fixed up a room. It's quite livable, actually."

There was a yell from the lower end of the barn, and Mark grinned down at Sadie.

"He found it."

He turned to her then and stepped very close, his hand touching her chin as light as a summer breeze.

"Sadie, before we go to be with Reuben, I have to talk to you. I'm back in Montana because of you. I can't be away from you—this much I know for sure. The rest... is painful. I need time. My life is a puzzle with most of the pieces lost. I never liked working on jigsaw puzzles with little ones around to lose all the pieces... but... Let's just say almost all my border pieces are lost. I'm not sure anything good can come of my determination to get you back, but if I don't try, my life stretches before me like a long, hard road without joy."

He paused, then gripped her shoulders.

"Please, Sadie."

What was that look in his brown eyes? So intense. So...

"Mark, I..."

"All I ask is your patience. I'll...I will learn to talk if you will listen. We can't date publicly for now. Can you agree to this for awhile, or am I asking too much?"

Sadie looked into his brown eyes, sure that she would follow him to the ends of the earth.

Whithersoever thou goest, I will go.

The words started as a high, keening note, a song that rolled down from the heavens on wings of angels. As clear as a windswept day after a storm, Sadie recognized her destiny and, smiling, took a step toward Mark, ready to at least begin on this path with him.

"Hey, guys! Where are you?"

Mark caught Sadie's hand, and they walked to the barn in the afternoon sunlight, the grasses and the bitterroot swaying by the driveway.

The End

The Glossary

Bisht—A Pennsylvania Dutch dialect word meaning, "Are you?"

Braufa gaul—A Pennsylvania Dutch dialect phrase meaning, "Good horse."

Broadfall pants—Pants worn by Amish men and fastened with buttons rather than a zipper.

Chrisht Kindly—A Pennsylvania Dutch dialect phrase meaning, "Christ Child."

Covering—A fine mesh headpiece worn by Amish females in an effort to follow the Amish interpretation of a New Testament teaching in 1 Corinthians 11.

Dat—A Pennsylvania Dutch dialect word used to address or to refer to one's father.

Denke—A Pennsylvania Dutch dialect word meaning, "Thank you."

Dichly—A Pennsylvania Dutch dialect word meaning, "head scarf" or "bandanna." A *dichly* is a triangle of cotton fabric, usually a men's handkerchief cut in half and hemmed, worn by Amish women and girls when they do yard work or anything strenuous.

Do net.—A Pennsylvania Dutch dialect phrase for "Do not."

Do net heila, Mam.—A sentence in Pennsylvania Dutch dialect meaning, "Don't cry, Mother."

Doo gehn myeh.—A sentence in Pennsylvania Dutch dialect meaning, "Here we go."

Doo kannsht. Komm on. Komm. Vidda. Vidda.—A sentence in Pennsylvania Dutch dialect meaning, "You can do it. Come on. Come. Again. Again."

Driver—When the Amish need to go somewhere, and it's too distant to travel by horse and buggy, they may hire someone to drive them in a car or van.

Eck—One corner of the room reserved for the wedding party during the wedding reception.

English—The Amish term for anyone who is not Amish.

Express wagon—Many Amish use express wagons to haul small loads around their farms or to neighboring farms and businesses. Pulled by a long tongue, an express wagon has removable sides and ends made of wooden slats, which steady and hold what it's carrying. Children also use it for play.

Freue Dich Velt—A Pennsylvania Dutch dialect phrase for the song "Joy to the World."

Grosfeelich—A Pennsylvania Dutch dialect word for "conceited."

Gut—A Pennsylvania Dutch dialect word for "good."

Halt aw. Halt aw. Halt um gaduld aw. Gaduld.—A sentence in Pennsylvania Dutch dialect meaning, "Have patience. Have patience. Have patience with me. Patience."

Himmlisch—A Pennsylvania Dutch dialect word meaning, "heavenly."

Himmlischer Vater, Ich danke dich.—A sentence in the Pennsylvania Dutch dialect meaning, "Heavenly Father, I thank you."

Himmlischer Vater im himmel—A phrase in the Pennsylvania Dutch dialect meaning, "Heavenly Father in heaven."

Hymn-Sing—Amish young people of dating age frequently gather in a home on a Sunday evening to sing hymns together. It is primarily a social event, including visiting and eating refreshments.

Ich do, Mam, Ich do.—A sentence in the Pennsylvania Dutch dialect meaning, "I do, Mom, I do."

In-between Sundays—Old Order Amish have church every other Sunday. This is an old custom that allows ministers to visit other church districts. An "in-between" Sunday is the day that a district does not hold church services.

Kessle-haus—The part of the house that Amish families use as a catch-all for coats, boots, umbrellas, laundry, and even for tasks such as mixing calf starter, warming baby chicks, and canning garden vegetables.

Mam—A Pennsylvania Dutch dialect word used to address or to refer to one's mother.

Mennonite—Another Anabaptist group which shares common beliefs with the Amish. The differences between the two groups lie in their practices. Mennonites tend to be more open to higher education and to mission activity and less distinctly different from the rest of the world in their dress, transportation, and use of technology.

Mommy—A Pennsylvania Dutch dialect word used to address or to refer to one's grandmother.

Ordnung—The Amish community's agreed-upon rules for living, based upon their understanding of the Bible, particularly the New Testament. The *Ordnung* varies some from community to community, often reflecting the leaders' preferences and the local traditions and historical practices.

Phone Shanty—Most Old Order Amish do not have telephone landlines in their homes so that incoming calls do not overtake their lives and so that they are not physically connected to the larger world. Many, however, build a small, fully enclosed structure, much like a commercial telephone booth, somewhere outside their house where they can make phone calls and retrieve phone messages.

Schecka hauslin—A Pennsylvania Dutch dialect phrase meaning, "snail house." Snail houses are little bits of pie dough rolled around brown sugar and butter, then popped in a hot oven for a few minutes.

Schpence—A Pennsylvania Dutch dialect word meaning, "ghost" or "spirit."

Schtup sell, Mam. Do net.—A sentence in Pennsylvania Dutch dialect meaning, "Stop it, Mother. Don't."

Sei brauf—A Pennsylvania Dutch dialect phrase meaning, "Be good."

Shtille Nacht, Heilige Nacht—A Pennsylvania Dutch dialect phrase for the song "Silent Night, Holy Night."

Siss kenn Fashtant—A very common phrase of exclamation in Pennsylvania Dutch—the phrase a woman says as she throws her hands in the air in astonishment. It means, "There is no sense."

Unfadiened gelt—A Pennsylvania Dutch dialect phrase for money that is not earned by working.

Unsayah—A Pennsylvania Dutch dialect word meaning, "curse" or "un-blessing."

Vee bisht doo?—A Pennsylvania Dutch dialect sentence meaning, "How are you?"

Ya vell. Tzell home gay. Tzell.—A sentence in Pennsylvania Dutch dialect meaning, "Yes, well. I'm going home. I am going."